PENGUIN  CLA

RIMBAUD

COLLECTED POEMS

Oliver Bernard has lived in Norfolk for the past twenty years. Translations apart, he has published two books and two pamphlets of verse. His Apollinaire selection originally published in Penguin is now published by Anvil Press Poetry in a revised and expanded edition. Also published are *Poems* (Samizdat, 1983) and *Five Peace Poems* (Five Seasons Press, Madley, Hereford HR2 9NZ, 1985).

RIMBAUD

COLLECTED POEMS

INTRODUCED AND EDITED BY
OLIVER BERNARD

*

WITH PLAIN
PROSE TRANSLATIONS
OF EACH POEM

PENGUIN BOOKS

PENGUIN BOOKS

Published by the Penguin Group
Penguin Books Ltd, 27 Wrights Lane, London W8 5TZ, England
Penguin Books USA Inc., 375 Hudson Street, New York, New York 10014, USA
Penguin Books Australia Ltd, Ringwood, Victoria, Australia
Penguin Books Canada Ltd, 10 Alcorn Avenue, Toronto, Ontario, Canada M4V 3B2
Penguin Books (NZ) Ltd, 182–190 Wairau Road, Auckland 10, New Zealand

Penguin Books Ltd, Registered Offices: Harmondsworth, Middlesex, England

First published 1962
Reprinted in Penguin Classics 1986
7 9 10 8

Copyright © Oliver Bernard, 1962
All rights reserved

Printed in England by Clays Ltd, St Ives plc
Set in Monotype Fournier

To Andrée and Suzanne and
Lucien and Rosette

CONTENTS

CONTENTS

CONTENTS

CONTENTS

LIFE OF RIMBAUD

1854

Jean-Nicolas-Arthur Rimbaud born (20 October) at Charleville, in his maternal grandfather's house. His father is Frédéric Rimbaud, Captain of Infantry, who has risen to this rank from that of a simple recruit. Much of his military career has been spent in Algeria. He is the author of certain unpublished military works and of a translation into French of the Koran, which his son will later use to learn Arabic. His mother's parents are agricultural proprietors in the district of Vouziers (Ardennes). Her severity probably owes much to the wild and dissolute character of her two brothers, as does her eventual ownership of her father's property. In any case it plays an important part in the break-up of her marriage with Captain Rimbaud, who leaves her for good when Rimbaud is six years old. Rimbaud never sees him again.

1862

Rimbaud goes as a day boy to the Rossat Institute in Charleville. Here, at the age of ten, he writes the story 'Le soleil était encore chaud ...' (p. 45).

1865

Enters the Collège de Charleville, aged ten.

1868

Rimbaud addresses 'under the strictest secrecy', sixty Latin hexameters to the Imperial Prince on the occasion of the latter's first Communion: his tutor asks Rimbaud's headmaster to thank him publicly. (But see also poem 'L'Enfant qui ramassa les balles', p. 198.)

1869

Rimbaud wins the Latin Poetry Prize at the Concours Académique (see Introduction, p. xxxii). In the same year his first

known French verse composition, 'Les Étrennes des orphe-
lins', is written. It appears in the *Revue pour tous* for 2
January 1870.

1870

Rimbaud moves up to the Class of Rhetoric, and becomes
friendly with Georges Izambard, a young teacher with revolu-
tionary tendencies, who encourages him, to the outrage of his
mother, to read Rabelais and Hugo. In his fifteenth year Rim-
baud is already a poet. He writes to Banville (see p. 3) too late
to have his 'Sensation', 'Ophélie', and 'Soleil et chair' pub-
lished in *Parnasse contemporain*; but his 'Première Soirée' ap-
pears, under the title 'Trois Baisers', in a satirical periodical
called *La Charge*. On 29 August Rimbaud sells his prize books
and takes the train to Paris, hoping to witness the fall of the
Imperial Government. He arrives owing the railway company
13 francs and is arrested and imprisoned. He writes to Izambard,
who rescues him and puts him up at Douai, where the Gindre
sisters, Izambard's adoptive 'aunts', take care of him. ('Les
Chercheuses de Poux', p. 142, written the following year, is
probably a description of their ministrations.) At his mother's
request, however, Izambard sends Rimbaud back to Charleville.
Ten days after his arrival there he runs away again, this time to
Belgium, hoping to find work on a newspaper in Charleroi.
During this journey he writes 'La Maline', 'Au Cabaret-Vert',
'Le Buffet', 'Rêvé pour l'hiver', and 'Ma Bohême'. He is un-
successful in his attempt to become a journalist, and goes to
Brussels, where he appears unannounced at the house of some
friends of Izambard's, who send him to Douai again, where the
'aunts' are delighted to see him. Here he writes 'Rages des
Césars', 'L'Éclatante Victoire de Sarrebrück', 'Le Dormeur du
val', and 'Le Mal'. His mother again has him sent back to Charle-
ville, where he witnesses the bombardments of Mézières and of
Charleville.

1871

He now spends his time in the library at Charleville, where his taste in reading scandalizes the librarians. They deliver, as unwillingly as possible, books on socialism, magic, and alchemy, and licentious novels to the precocious, scowling sixteen-year-old. His revenge on them is the poem 'Les Assis' (p. 113). In February he runs away for the third time, to Paris, where he spends a fortnight in extreme poverty. (See second paragraph under the title 'Adieu' in *Une Saison en enfer* (p. 344), the passage which begins '*L'automne. Notre barque élevée dans les brumes …*'). He returns to Charleville on foot, having passed through the lines of the Prussians who are soon to enter Paris (1 March), and then to abandon it to the Commune (3 March). On his return, he writes a Communist Constitution, which has not been found. On 13 May he writes a letter to Izambard in which he expounds his ideas about poetry; and on 15 May, to Demeny (another teacher, who, like Izambard, also wrote verses), the famous letter known as the Lettre du Voyant (p. 7). He is now violently anticlerical and antichristian: he chalks '*Merde à Dieu*' on public benches and stops priests in the street. When given four sous by a superior young shop assistant to get himself a haircut he shows the money to his friend Delahaye and says gleefully that it will do to pay for some tobacco for them. He and Delahaye are the Jean Baudry and Jean Balouche of the amusing second poem in *Bribes* (p. 175). In July, at the time of his sister Isabelle's first Communion, he writes 'Premières Communions'. In August he sends to Banville the poem called 'Ce qu'on dit au poëte à propos de fleurs'. He also sends poems, including 'Les Effarés' and 'Le Cœur volé', to Verlaine, who on reading them writes to their author: 'Come, beloved great soul, you are called, you are awaited.' Taking with him his poems, including 'Le Bateau ivre', and full of misgivings about literary society in Paris – though not about his own talent – Rimbaud arrives in the capital at the end of September, and stays with the Verlaines at the house of Verlaine's parents-in-law, shocking

them all, more or less, with his extreme youth, his personal
filthiness, his opinions, and his beloved clay pipe.

1872

Rimbaud and Verlaine spend their days, and part of their nights,
in the cafés of the Quartier Latin. There are scenes of violence
on this account between Verlaine and his long-suffering wife,
who has given birth to a son in October 1871, and is only
eighteen.

Not without justification, Verlaine's mother-in-law accuses
Rimbaud of corrupting Verlaine (who is ten years older). Rim-
baud quickly finds his feet in Paris, where he has learned to
drink absinthe ('Long live the Academy of Absomphe!' he says
in a letter to Delahaye), and to smoke hashish – an unpleasant
experience on the whole, at least the first time: 'What did you
see?' – 'White moons, black moons!' This is the reported con-
versation between him and Verlaine. By these and other means
he arrives indeed at the 'disordering of all the senses' mentioned
in the letters on pp. 5 and 7. On his return to Charleville in
March 1872, he writes the poems 'Mémoire', 'Michel et Chris-
tine', 'Larme', 'La Rivière de Cassis', 'Comédie de la soif'
(from which one may infer that, for him, drinking implied
suffering as well as pleasure), 'Bonne Pensée du matin', 'Fêtes
de la patience', and 'Chanson de la plus haute tour'. He has re-
turned home to give Verlaine a chance to be reconciled with his
wife – or at least for Verlaine's wife to be reconciled to their
friendship. Verlaine asks him to return to Paris at the end of
May, which he does. In June he writes his last poems in verse:
'Est-elle almée?', 'Âge d'or', 'Fêtes de la faim', 'Ô Saisons, ô
chateaux' – but this is also the beginning of the period of Les
Illuminations, among which 'Matinée d'ivresse' (p. 249) can be
taken for a description of his spiritual condition at a moment
when the 'disordering of all the senses' has been most completely
successful. At this time Les Illuminations are simply called
Poèmes en prose: it is only when Verlaine publishes them in 1886
that they receive their present title. In July 1872, Rimbaud and

Verlaine leave Paris for Belgium, and cross to England. They live at first in Howland Street, Tottenham Court Road, and become acquainted not only with Soho (which is full of left-wing political refugees from Paris and the Commune) but also with the Docks, the West End, and the London Sunday. They have very little money, and there is fierce competition for French pupils because there are so many Frenchmen in London at this time. Rimbaud's mother warns him that he may be implicated in the proceedings which Verlaine's wife's family are taking to separate Verlaine from their daughter, and on her advice he returns to Charleville for Christmas.

1873

Verlaine falls ill in London with influenza, writes to his own mother that he is dying, and implores her to come and see him and to send Rimbaud the fare to London too. Rimbaud arrives two days after Verlaine's mother, and when Verlaine has recovered, their life of pub-crawling and of walks in the city and suburbs begins again. Although Rimbaud said afterwards that Paris was just a 'pretty little provincial town', the *Illuminations* called 'Métropolitain' and 'Villes' seem to be very vivid and convincing descriptions of the horror of a large city such as London was at that time. The possibility that Rimbaud and Verlaine learned to smoke opium in Chinese dens near the Docks would help to explain the distortion of vision one encounters in these prose poems. Rimbaud returns to Roche, where his mother's farm is, in April. Rather than help on the farm, he shuts himself up to begin writing *Une Saison en enfer*. (For his feelings about manual work at this time, see the fourth paragraph under the title 'Mauvais Sang', p. 301.) In May, Verlaine again manages to persuade Rimbaud to go to England with him. Rimbaud consents but soon regrets having done so: the clinging nature of Verlaine's friendship disgusts him and provokes him to words and acts of cruelty. (See 'Vagabonds', p. 261, and 'Vierge Folle', p. 318.) It is also said that at this time Rimbaud fell in love with a girl he saw on the Under-

ground, whom he used to follow home but dared not speak to. (See 'Bottom', p. 283.) In any case, after a violent quarrel, Verlaine leaves Rimbaud (Letters pp. 17 and 20) and goes to Brussels, where Rimbaud follows him, and the shooting occurs: Verlaine fires two shots at Rimbaud, one of which hits him in the wrist. (See Rimbaud's Deposition, p. 22.) Rimbaud goes back to Roche with his arm in a sling and finishes writing *Une Saison en enfer*. Verlaine is sent to prison for two years for his part in the shooting incident.

1874

Having arranged to have *Une Saison en enfer* printed in Belgium, Rimbaud, who has renounced literature, speedily loses interest (the whole printing, except for half a dozen author's copies, remained at the printer's until 1914). Instead, with the intention of perfecting his English, Rimbaud goes to London with Germain Nouveau, a young poet he has met in Paris. He teaches in various establishments in England and Scotland. His mother and his sister Vitalie spend July with him in London. He and Nouveau both hold British Museum Library reader's tickets. Possibly he set up house with a girl. (See 'Ouvriers', p. 254.)

1875–80

Travel in Germany, Switzerland, Italy. Studies German, Spanish, Arabic, Italian, Dutch, and modern Greek. Joins the Dutch colonial army on a six-year engagement; deserts in Batavia after three weeks in the East Indies, and returns to France on an English sailing ship, walking home from Bordeaux. Visits Vienna, Holland, Germany, Sweden, Denmark. At the beginning of 1875, Rimbaud and Verlaine meet for the last time. Verlaine, now reconverted to Catholicism, begs Rimbaud to become so too. Verlaine arrived, says Rimbaud 'with a rosary in his claws', but (after some drinking in the old style, one assumes) 'made the 98 wounds of O.S. bleed again'. This was in Stuttgart. In 1877 he sails for Alexandria from Marseille but falls sick and is disembarked at Civita Vecchia,

visits Rome, and then goes home and spends the winter in Charleville. A second attempt to reach the East, from Hamburg, the following spring, also fails: but in October he crosses the mountains to Switzerland, then to Italy, and takes a boat for Alexandria. (See Letter, p. 30.) From there he obtains a job in Cyprus as a foreman of works, but catches typhoid and returns to Charleville in June 1879, where he spends the winter. In 1880 he is again in Cyprus, directing operations for the building of the Governor-General's residence. He cannot stand the climate, however, and leaves for Egypt. From Egypt he goes to Aden, arriving on 7 August 1880. There he finds employment with the firm of Viannay, Mazeran, Bardey et Cie, dealers in coffee and hides. They send him to their new trading post in Harar (Abyssinia). He arrives on 13 December 'after twenty days on horseback in the Somali desert'. (See Letter, p. 32.)

1881–91

Working as a buyer for Bardey, Rimbaud nevertheless dreams of exploration. He sends for technical books and photographic equipment to his mother, to whom he also sends money regularly. In 1882 and 1883 his employers ask him to investigate the territories of Somaliland and Galla. On his own initiative he also explores the entirely unknown region of Ogadine: he is the first European to cross this territory. On 10 December 1883, he sends a report to the Société de Géographie, who publish it. But although he sometimes talks to Alfred Bardey at length, it is not about literature; in fact he says that all that his stay in London brings to his mind is a 'period of drunkenness'. In 1885 he is living as husband and wife with a 'tall, slim' Abyssinian girl; but, because he wishes to become a gun-runner, he has her repatriated. His gun-running enterprise is not a success: Menelik, King of Choa, cheats him over the weapons. He returns to Harar and takes charge of a warehouse for one Tian, an exporter of hides, coffee, and musk. He obtains a licence to sell arms and ammunition and also helps in the slave traffic to Turkey and Arabia. Scraping and saving, he lives in the simplest

fashion; but his acts of charity to the negroes and his lack of business sense reduce his savings far below his expectations: in February 1891, when he is attacked by a tumour on the right knee (Letter, p. 37) he is worth about £2,000: on his arrival in France in May, where his right leg is amputated (Hôpital de la Conception, Marseille), about £1,500. This after eleven years in Africa. In August 1891, after a couple of months at home (Roche), his condition again worsens. He returns to Marseille. Dies on 10 December 1891, aged thirty-seven, in the Hôpital de la Conception.

INTRODUCTION

I N an age when criticism has never had it so good, a poet with
no claims to scholarship will think twice about writing an intro-
duction to Rimbaud's works. All the more so when he has pro-
vided a guide to their literal meaning. For (on the one hand)
what is there to be said of '*l'œuvre mince et fulgurante que, à la
fin du dix-neuvième siècle, Arthur Rimbaud nous abandonna avec
une sorte de dédain et sans avoir pris la peine d'en presque rien
publier*'[1] that has not already been said, and well said, by Dr
Enid Starkie, or Jean-Marie Carré, or the editors of the Pléiade
edition themselves? And (on the other hand) does not every
poem and prose poem and letter between these covers really
exist in its own right? The real presence of Rimbaud's poems,
and not their place in literature,[2] has so long been my concern
that instead of an introduction I feel like placing here the words
which Rimbaud said to his mother when, in 1873, just having
read it, she asked him what he meant by *Une Saison en enfer*: 'I
meant what it says: literally and in every sense.'

What Rimbaud himself would have thought of a conven-
tional critical introduction may be guessed from part of the
Lettre du Voyant (p. 9): 'Romanticism has never been pro-
perly judged. Who was there to judge it? The Critics!!' That
is the young poet speaking; as for the Abyssinian trader, Dr
Starkie tells us that at the age of thirty-three Rimbaud 'had *no
curiosity* about the fate and the success of his writings, which
were appearing in Paris as the work of "the late Arthur Rim-
baud" and out of which Verlaine alone was profiting'.[3] Again,

1. 'The slim and flashing work which, at the end of the nineteenth cen-
tury, Arthur Rimbaud left to us with a kind of disdain, and without having
taken the trouble to publish almost any of it.' Rolland de Renéville and
Jules Mouquet, editors of the Pléiade edition.

2. If 'place in literature' means anything. I suppose it is an academic
expression, and has to do with syllabuses.

3. Enid Starkie, *Arthur Rimbaud* (Faber, 1938; revised edition, Hamish
Hamilton, 1947).

there is the answer to his mother's question, quoted above, which is really a *refusal* to explain. As such, it is comparable with Dylan Thomas's statements: 'I made these poems for the love of man and in praise of God and I'd be a damned fool if I hadn't' – or: 'These poems *are* what they mean', a remark which might easily have been made by Rimbaud.

All I know, then, of Rimbaud's attitude to these matters supports me against taking the critical approach. For that reason, too, I have placed the bare facts of Rimbaud's life in front of this introductory note, so that people who want to know no more, before reading these poems, than who the man was who wrote them, can find out without having to absorb a whole body of critical opinions along with the facts. And for those in whom the poems awaken strong curiosity – it will not concern the others – the standard work on the subject in any language is Dr Starkie's remarkable book, from which I have already quoted; and very fortunate we are that it should have been written in English.

But – apart from the fact that not everyone has access to Dr Starkie's book – a literal translation like the one which follows cannot always succeed in conveying all literal meanings: some of Rimbaud's poems are obscure even in the original, even to educated French people, unless they have some knowledge of alchemy and magic. For Rimbaud's reading on these subjects was extensive, and he uses alchemical allusions freely and without bothering to give the reader any warning or indication that he is doing so, much as a 'Christian' poet may use words or phrases which have a religious connotation – even, perhaps, as I myself have done above, using a phrase which is associated with Communion: 'the real presence' of Rimbaud's poems. I think it is permissible to suggest a reason for this: Rimbaud, who had shown as a boy a religious nature, being possessed at the age of twelve of 'a burning faith, a passionate piety',[1] began to reject both God and the Church just as he was becoming a

---

1. Dr Starkie, op. cit.

poet. Whether the cause was aesthetic (see 'Les Pauvres à l'église'), or political (see 'Le Mal'), or psychological (his father had deserted his mother; his father was God; so was the Emperor, if it came to that), magic and alchemy were a substitute for religion. Better than that: they were the means of becoming god-like, and therefore 'better than' religion. That Rimbaud had this idea, and eventually renounced it, can be deduced partly from the last poems, partly from 'Délires II' in *Une Saison en enfer*, and perhaps most convincingly of all from Rimbaud's renunciation of literature itself. For if you begin, as a poet, by trying to become as a god, what will you do when your efforts fail? I think that Rimbaud realized that the '*magique étude*'[1] had failed; and I think his reaction was to reject everything he had done while pursuing it. His pride was monstrous. If all he had wanted to do had been to write poems – a mad enough ambition in itself – he would have had no reason either to stop trying to write them or to despise his whole work in later life. Yet he produced nothing after *Une Saison en enfer*; and when European traders, passing through Harar, mentioned the productions of his teens, ' "Absurd! Ridiculous! Disgusting!" was his invariable reply.'[2]

In any case, it is certain that among the books in the library at Charleville which the librarians – 'Les Assis' in the poem of that name – were so unwilling to deliver to the fifteen-year-old poet, there were works on alchemy and magic as well as books on socialism and eighteenth-century licentious novels. Michelet's *La Sorcière* (*The Witch*), and Éliphas Lévi's *Histoire de la Magie* (*History of Magic*) provide clues to many apparent obscurities in the later poems. For example, the '*saisons*' are also the 'seasons' of alchemy: the period needed to produce the 'philosophic gold'. The '*liqueur d'or*' of 'Larme' is the '*aurum potabile*' which, discouraged with the ill success of his 'magic pursuit of happiness' ('Ô saisons, ô châteaux'), the poet feels

1. See 'Ô Saisons, ô châteaux'.
2. Paterne Berrichon, preface to *Œuvres de J.-A. Rimbaud* (Mercure, 1898).

no thirst to drink. Here is the last of the 'Phrases' (p. 254), with Dr Starkie's commentary:

> *Avivant un agréable goût d'encre de Chine, une poudre noire pleut douce-*
> *ment sur ma veillée. – Je baisse les feux du lustre, je me jette sur le lit, et,*
> *tourné du côté de l'ombre, je vous vois, mes filles! mes reines!*

This passage has a beauty of image and harmony which does not depend on the meaning, yet this is further enhanced if the alchemical suggestion is perceived. The term '*encre*' is one used to symbolize blackness, the first stage, the stage of dissolution, which is a time of melancholy as well as of hope, for when the blackness appears it is a proof that the experiment is safely begun and there is the possibility of the gold, of complete success. Rimbaud uses the term 'Chinese ink', for Chinese ink is the blackest of all black inks. Then he turns down the light, throws himself on his couch and gives himself up to the vision. And out of the darkness come the '*filles*' and the '*reines*', the alchemical colours, in the progression towards the completion of the elixir, the full vision.

In another poem 'Enfance' (p. 235) there is the image '*Je vois long-temps la mélancolique lessive d'or du couchant*'. The word '*lessive*', 'wash-ing',[1] has no particular beauty in itself – though the whole line has harmony and evocative power and this evocative power is still further enhanced if we know that the term '*lessive*' is used for the secret substance of the hermetic philosopher, so called because it is used to purify or wash the metals. It is also called Azoth and that word is of great importance to alchemists, for it contains the first and last letters of the Hebrew, Greek, and Latin languages – the *aleph* and *thau* of Hebrew, the *alpha* and *omega* of Greek and the *a* and *z* of Latin. It serves also as the monogram of Hermetic Truth, the perfect sign of the absolute. This '*lessive*' joined with gold – fire – is all that the alchemist needs to begin the *Grande Œuvre*. All this adds an undertone of deeper meaning ...

This kind of scholarship is typical of Dr Starkie's book (and to my mind it is worth more than any amount of 'evaluation'). However there is one notoriously 'mystical' poem where I think scholarship – even Dr Starkie's – overreaches itself. This is the famous 'Voyelles' sonnet.

> *A noir, E blanc, I rouge, U vert, O bleu: voyelles,*
> *Je dirai quelque jour vos naissances latentes:*
> *A, noir corset velu des mouches éclatantes*
> *Qui bombinent autour des puanteurs cruelles,*

---

1. I make this word 'wash', i.e. that with which one washes; not the activity, and not what is washed – but that does not affect the argument.

Golfes d'ombre; E, candeurs des vapeurs et des tentes,
Lances des glaciers fiers, rois blancs, frissons d'ombelles;
I, pourpres, sang craché, rire des lèvres belles
Dans la colère ou les ivresses pénitentes;

U, cycles, vibrements divins des mers virides,
Paix de pâtis semés d'animaux, paix des rides
Que l'alchimie imprime aux grands fronts studieux;

O, suprême Clairon plein des strideurs étranges,
Silences traversés des Mondes et des Anges:
O l'Oméga, rayon violet de Ses Yeux!

A literary correspondent to *Le Temps* called Paul Bourde wrote to Rimbaud (whose request for a recommendation as a war correspondent Bourde had refused): 'Certain youths, whom I personally consider somewhat naïve, have tried to found a system on your "Sonnet des Voyelles". This little group calls you its master ...'[1] Indeed there is, perhaps, a temptation to speculate on the possibilities which the poem seems to suggest: that sounds and colours are mysteriously connected (for do not both travel by means of waves?). Was not the poet who discovered and set down what colours apply to what particular vowel-sounds indeed a seer, and possessed of some tremendous hidden knowledge? If vowels are colours, are not consonants perhaps *lines*? And so on. Dr Starkie explains it by alchemy: the colours follow the order of the colours obtained during an experiment. But if this is so, what is the purpose of mentioning the things which possess the colours chosen: flies, shadow, mists, kings, and so on? And what happens when you translate the poem? The sounds change. ... Luckily there is M. Lucien Sausy's interpretation,[2] which is a purely visual one.

1. 1887.
2. M. Sausy's interpretation first appeared in *Les Nouvelles littéraires* for 2 September 1933. It is quoted by the editors of the Pléiade edition under 'Notes et Variantes'. I have thought fit to simplify it somewhat.

What M. Sausy says amounts to this: the vowels *look like* the things Rimbaud mentions:

∀ A   (black) flies; gulfs of darkness

Ш   (white) tents; peaks, kings (' crowns); cow parsley

⊢   (red) spat blood; smiling lips

∪ ɯ ɯ   (green) waves – of seas and of meadows; the (?) greenish wrinkles on alchemists' brows

O   (blue) trumpet mouths; space; the blue or violet gaze of God's eyes, or of Rimbaud's mother's eyes, perhaps.

As the editors of the Pléiade edition observe, this interpretation has the merit of depending only on the text. At the risk of overreaching myself, I feel it is worth mentioning that one of Rimbaud's nicknames for his mother was '*la Bouche d'Ombre*', 'mouth of darkness' – after Hugo's poem – because of her way of pronouncing on matters connected with religion or morality. Rimbaud's mother, as Dr Starkie says, was certainly the alpha and omega of his life. In the sonnet above, the vowels are re-arranged so that O, omega, comes last. Against this letter, I have written 'or Rimbaud's mother's eyes perhaps'. Against A we find 'gulfs of darkness'. But these are speculations. What is true of this poem is true of 'Le Bateau ivre' and of all the others: no amount of research explains why they are poems.

Rimbaud's mother was, as I have suggested, a formidable lady of unimpeachable rectitude, whose importance in his life cannot be exaggerated. Faced with the task of bringing up, single-handed, Arthur, his elder brother, and his two sisters, she carried it out in what was, by her standards, an exemplary fashion. But she had, as far as can be discovered, no sense of

humour; and her severity was intensified by what had happened to her own brothers. When Rimbaud was eight, and his brother nine, 'Anxious that her boys should not waste the education so expensively provided for them ... she herself supervised their homework. ... Sometimes she would send them both supperless to bed because they had been unable to recite, without a slip, the hundreds of Latin verses she had set them to learn from memory, as a punishment ... and also to improve their facility in the language.'[1] (Rimbaud's feeling about study at this time is expressed with some force in *Le Soleil était encore chaud*.) But this is only part of the story. Even when Rimbaud was fifteen years old, Vitalie Rimbaud would wait for him and his brother every day at the gates of the Collège in order to make sure that they should form no undesirable acquaintances on the way home. No wonder that there seemed to be no escape from her supervision but the lavatory.[2] No wonder if she often received 'the blue gaze – which lies!' Arthur Rimbaud must have alternated from a very early age between 'sweating with obedience' and rejecting his obedience as a 'bitter hypocrisy' in his rebellion against everything which was alleged to be decent, respectable, and holy. In the absence of affection and of a father, he would naturally turn with love towards the men he saw returning from the fields in the evening;[3] but towards his father, too, his attitude would also suffer continual reversals. His father merited both love and hate: he had left his family when Rimbaud was six.

Freud, who occasionally rises to something like poetry, says somewhere that our first unhappy love-affair happens with our parents. In terms of Freudian psychology, Rimbaud's homosexual tendencies can, no doubt, be simply explained from his attitude towards his parents: fear of his mother (mixed with love); longing for his father (mixed with rejection). And just as he alternated between revolt and submission, so his flights from home were followed by his return; and his 'father-substitutes' –

1. Enid Starkie, op. cit.
2. For this and the three quotations which follow, see 'Les Poëtes de sept ans' (p. 124). 3. ibid.

whether it was God, or the Emperor, or Banville, or Verlaine, or the librarians at Charleville – were 'punished' in their turn.

Rimbaud denied his homosexuality several times, notably in the Deposition of 12 July 1873 on p. 28 in this volume. On the other hand, the *Stupra* could hardly have been written by someone unacquainted with homosexual practices. I myself am inclined to see 'Le Cœur volé' as a further suggestion, not that Rimbaud was by choice a homosexual, but that he was, shortly before he wrote it, forced into some homosexual act. On the other hand it may be that he was forced into some hetero-sexual act: the disgust is from the forcing. This disgust, digested, becomes the scatology of the *Stupra*, and, finally, the cruelty of the Infernal Bridegroom of *Une Saison en enfer*, the Bride, or 'Foolish Virgin', being Verlaine. Verlaine's friendship with Rim-baud is always made much of: people call it 'holy' or 'unholy', according to whether they are supposed to have had physi-cal relations or not. But although it seems clear that Rimbaud was homosexual (though not when he wrote 'À la musique' or 'Première Soirée', or 'Les Réparties de Nina', or 'Au Cabaret-Vert' – or when he lived with the tall, slim Abyssinian girl in Aden[1]), I do not think that his homosexuality matters nearly as much as what sort of person he was. I have a very vivid impression of Rimbaud from his verminous condition as he sat smoking his clay pipe at the Verlaines' family dinner-table on the first evening of their acquaintance, as well as from his gibe, re-ported by Verlaine, which began their final quarrel in London, and which led to the shooting incident three days later in Brus-sels: 'if you only knew how fucking silly you look with that herring in your hand!' I believe this is far more to the point, when one reads his poems, than the question of his homosex-uality. If this appears to need any underlining, one has only to glance at Jean-Marie Carré's appraisal of the situation between Rimbaud and Verlaine in the autumn of 1872, when Rimbaud was already becoming impatient with it. The question of homo-

1. 'Rimbaud in Abyssinia was never suspected of sodomy, but, on the contrary, he was known to associate with women' (Starkie, op. cit.).

sexual relations simply does not enter into it. At this time, says Carré,[1] 'everything separated them more and more. One of them could not manage to shake off an old love ... and in his moments of spleen he would steep himself in nostalgic regrets for his lost home life. The past clutched at him. ... The other, on the contrary, stretching out feverishly towards the future, felt himself changing, and turning into a "new man". His technique was changing too. He had already written some of the *Illuminations* ...'

His abandonment of literature after 1873 was definitive. His letters from Africa are hardly interesting. Even his geographical descriptions are of a strictly commercial nature. His conversation is reported to have been mordantly witty; but one of his most memorable remarks was made to his employer Bardey, in 1885: that he had known 'writers, artists and so on in the Latin Quarter' ('but no musicians', he added), and then, turning short, he concluded that he had '*seen enough of those birds*'.

Any reverence Rimbaud may have felt for the world of literature had already evaporated by the time he was of it. The letter to Banville (p. 3) was written when he was about fifteen and a half. At seventeen he would be parodying these same Parnassians. At eighteen he would carry out his 'Alchemy of the Word'. And at nineteen he would refer to this as 'one of my follies' – the other one being his pursuit of love. (See 'Délires II' in *Une Saison en enfer*.) What did he seek in Africa? – Gold. Not 'philosophic gold', but the real thing. Dr Johnson's saying, that a man can hardly be more innocently employed than when making money, seems true of Rimbaud at least. In Africa he was given the love and respect which he had given to no one, and got from no one, before. The regent of Abyssinia under Menelik, Ras Makonnen, in a message which Rimbaud received on his deathbed, voices the feelings of everyone who knew him in Africa.

This was in 1891 – and Rimbaud had spent the last half of his

---

1. Jean-Marie Carré, *La Vie aventureuse de Jean-Arthur Rimbaud* (Plon, Paris, 1926).

life without writing a single poem. His *Saison en enfer* is not the only work which gives off a smell of burning: it is only the one where he *describes* the hell with which he had become familiar. In his writings he is always, more or less, the child of the poem *Honte*, who can never cease to cheat and betray, and who stinks in the nostrils of the whole world: 'damned', as he says in the *Saison en enfer*, 'by the rainbow'. Here is a picture of him at the age of fourteen and a half – on the occasion of the Concours Académique at which he won the Latin Poetry prize:

The subject had upset the candidates: *Jugurtha* (king of Numidia, 111–106 B.C.). 'None of us expected *that*!' ... Tongues wagged, but pens hardly moved ... whispers of surprise and of dismay ... Rimbaud is silent as usual. Elbow on desk, chin in hand, deadpan: he has all the sulkiness of the Fantin-Latour canvas. He has written nothing and appears to be asleep. ... Arrival of the headmaster. ... 'What! You too? Well then, no brainier than the rest, after all?' 'I'm hungry!' growls the boy. After all, it's possible. The competition began at six in the morning, and now it's nine. Let him be brought some food! We must look after this young thoroughbred. ... The concierge, old Chocol, comes back with a covered basket from which he extracts huge slices of bread and butter. The others burst out laughing; but Rimbaud eats, snickering, his eye full of malice – and, having swallowed the last mouthful, leaps for his pen and writes his Latin verses at a single stroke:

Nascitur Arabiis ingens in collibus infans ...

... Long before the end of the examination he goes to the dais and hands in his paper with a sly look. Eighty lines of Latin, 'well-minted and ringing!' More than enough to save the honour of the Collège! The headmaster is delighted! But M. Perette, learning of this prowess, still shakes his head ... 'As intelligent as you like, but he will end badly!'[1]

1. Jean-Marie Carré, op. cit.

A handful of Rimbaud's 182 known letters are included in this selection – which includes all his known poems except for a few Latin poems written at school. The text is that of the Pléiade edition (Librairie Gallimard, 1954). I have tried to confine myself to the possible and give English equivalents for French words, occasionally for French phrases.

Acknowledgements are due to Mlle Andrée Grandperret of Morez, without whose help I should never have been able to do these translations; also to Enid Starkie for her book *Arthur Rimbaud*.

LETTERS AND OTHER
DOCUMENTS

À THÉODORE DE BANVILLE

Charleville (Ardennes), le 24 mai 1870

Cher Maître,

Nous sommes aux mois d'amour; j'ai dix-sept ans. L'âge des espérances et des chimères, comme on dit, – et voici que je me suis mis, enfant touché par le doigt de la Muse, – pardon si c'est banal, – à dire mes bonnes croyances, mes espérances, mes sensations, toutes ces choses des poëtes, – moi j'appelle cela du printemps.

Que si je vous envoie quelques-uns de ces vers, – et cela en passant par Alph. Lemerre, le bon éditeur, – c'est que j'aime tous les poëtes, tous les bons Parnassiens, – puisque le poëte est un Parnassien, – épris de la beauté idéale; c'est que j'aime en vous, bien naïvement, un

To Théodore de Banville

Charleville (Ardennes), 24 May 1870

Dear *Maître*,

We are now in the months of love; I am seventeen.[1] The hopeful, dreamy age, as they say – and I have begun, a child touched by the Muse – excuse this if it is a platitude – to express my beliefs, my hopes, my feelings, all those things proper to poets – this I call Spring.

And if I send you some of these verses – and this through Alph. Lemerre, the good publisher – it is because I love all poets, all good *Parnassiens* – since a poet *is* a *Parnassien* – in love with ideal beauty; it is because I admire in you, very naïvely (of course), a

---

1. In fact Rimbaud was fifteen years and seven months old when this letter was written. Banville was on the selection committee of *le Parnasse contemporain.*

descendant de Ronsard, un frère de nos maîtres de 1830, un vrai romantique, un vrai poëte. Voilà pourquoi. – C'est bête, n'est-ce pas, mais enfin? ...

Dans deux ans, dans un an peut-être, je serai à Paris.

– Anch'io, messieurs du journal, je serai Parnassien!

– Je ne sais ce que j'ai là ... qui veut monter ... – Je jure, cher maître, d'adorer toujours les deux déesses, Muse et Liberté.

Ne faites pas trop la moue en lisant ces vers: ... Vous me rendriez fou de joie et d'espérance, si vous vouliez, cher Maître, *faire faire* à la pièce *Credo in unam* une petite place entre les Parnassiens ... Je viendrais à la dernière série du *Parnasse*: cela ferait le Credo des poëtes! ... – Ambition! ô Folle!

ARTHUR RIMBAUD

. . . .

descendant of Ronsard, a brother of our masters of 1830, a real romantic, a real poet. That is why. – All this is foolish, I fear; but still? ...

In two years, in one year perhaps, I shall be in Paris.

– *Anch'io*, gentlemen of the Press, I too shall be a *Parnassien*.

– I do not know what it is inside me ... that wishes to come out ... – I swear, *cher maître*, that I shall always worship the two goddesses, the Muse and Freedom.

Do not frown too much when you read these verses: ... You would send me mad with joy and hope, *cher maître*, if you would *arrange to make room* for 'Credo in Unam'[1] among the *Parnassiens* ... I should be in the latest number of *Parnasse*: it would become the Credo of the poets! ... – O mad Ambition!

ARTHUR RIMBAUD

. . . .

---

[1] Given in this volume under the title 'Soleil et chair', p. 71.

À GEORGES IZAMBARD

Charleville, [*13*] *mai 1871*

Cher Monsieur!

VOUS revoilà professeur. On se doit à la Société, m'avez-vous dit; vous faites partie des corps enseignants: vous roulez dans la bonne ornière. – Moi aussi, je suis le principe: je me fais cyniquement *entretenir*; je déterre d'anciens imbéciles de collège: tout ce que je puis inventer de bête, de sale, de mauvais, en action et en paroles, je le leur livre: on me paie en bocks et en filles. *Stat mater dolorosa, dum pendet filius.* – Je me dois à la Société, c'est juste; – et j'ai raison. – Vous aussi, vous avez raison, pour aujourd'hui. Au fond, vous ne voyez en votre principe que poésie subjective: votre obstination à regagner le râtelier universitaire – pardon! – le prouve. Mais vous finirez toujours comme un satisfait qui n'a rien fait, n'ayant rien voulu faire. Sans compter que votre poésie subjective sera toujours horriblement fadasse. Un jour, j'espère, – bien d'autres espèrent la même chose, – je

To Georges Izambard

Charleville, [*13*] *May 1871*

My Dear Sir!

So you are a teacher again. One owes a duty to Society, you have told me; you belong to the teaching body: you are running along the right track – I too follow the principle: I am cynically getting myself *kept*. I dig up old imbeciles from our school: I serve up to them the stupidest, dirtiest, nastiest things I can think of in word and deed: I am paid for my trouble in beer and women. *Stat mater dolorosa, dum pendet filius* – My duty is to Society, quite true – and I'm right – You too are right, for the present. At bottom, all you see in your principle is subjective poetry: your obstinacy in going back to the pedagogical trough – excuse me – proves that. But you'll still end up self-satisfied, having done nothing, and never having wanted to do anything. Not to mention that your subjective poetry will always be disgustingly tepid. Some day I hope – many other

verrai dans votre principe la poésie objective, je la verrai plus sincèrement que vous ne le feriez! – Je serai un travailleur: c'est l'idée qui me retient quand les colères folles me poussent vers la bataille de Paris, – où tant de travailleurs meurent pourtant encore tandis que je vous écris! Travailler maintenant, jamais, jamais; je suis en grève.

Maintenant, je m'encrapule le plus possible. Pourquoi? Je veux être poëte, et je travaille à me rendre *voyant*: vous ne comprendrez pas du tout, et je ne saurais presque vous expliquer. Il s'agit d'arriver à l'inconnu par le dérègle-ment de *tous les sens*. Les souffrances sont énormes, mais il faut être fort, être né poëte, et je me suis reconnu poëte. Ce n'est pas du tout ma faute. C'est faux de dire: Je pense. On devrait dire: On me pense. Pardon du jeu de mots.

JE est un autre. Tant pis pour le bois qui se trouve violon, et nargue aux inconscients, qui ergotent sur ce qu'ils ignorent tout à fait!

---

people hope, too – that I shall see objective poetry in your principle. I shall see it more sincerely than you would! – I shall be a worker: that is the idea that holds me back when mad rage drives me towards the battle of Paris – where so many workers are still dying as I write to you! Work now? – never, never; I'm on strike.

I'm lousing myself up as much as I can these days. Why? I want to be a poet, and I am working to make myself a *seer*: you won't understand this at all, and I hardly know how to explain it to you. The point is, to arrive at the unknown by the disordering of *all the senses*. The sufferings are enormous, but one has to be strong, to be born a poet, and I have discovered I *am* a poet. It is not my fault at all. It is a mistake to say: I think. One ought to say: I am thought. Pardon the pun.[1]

I is someone else. So much the worse for the wood if it find itself a violin, and contempt to the heedless who argue about something they know nothing about!

---

[1] Louis XV is said to have asked Voltaire on his return from England: 'What did you learn there?' – 'To think' (*penser*). – 'Horses?' (*panser:* to groom).

Vous n'êtes pas *enseignant* pour moi. Je vous donne ceci: est-ce de la satire, comme vous diriez! Est-ce de la poésie? C'est de la fantaisie, toujours. – Mais, je vous en supplie, ne soulignez ni du crayon, ni trop de la pensée:

LE CŒUR SUPPLICIÉ

Mon triste cœur bave à la poupe

[. . . . .]

Ça ne veut pas rien dire.

RÉPONDEZ-MOI: chez M. Deverrière, pour A. R.

Bonjour de cœur,

ARTH. RIMBAUD

À PAUL DEMENY

Charleville, 15 mai 1871

J'AI résolu de vous donner une heure de littérature nouvelle. Je commence de suite par un psaume d'actualité:

You're not a *teacher* on my account. I give you the following: is it Satire, as you would say? Is it poetry? In any case it is fantasy. – But I beg you, please do not underscore it with your pencil, nor too much with your mind:

THE TORTURED HEART

My poor heart dribbles at the stern

[. . . . .]

This does not mean nothing.

ANSWER: c/o M. Deverrière, for A.R.

Hearty good wishes,

ARTH. RIMBAUD

To Paul Demeny

Charleville, 15 May 1871

I'VE decided to give you an hour of modern literature. I begin at once with a topical psalm:

7

CHANT DE GUERRE PARISIEN

Le printemps est évident, car ...

[. . . . .]

A. RIMBAUD

– Voici de la prose sur l'avenir de la poésie: –

Toute poésie antique aboutit à la poésie grecque, Vie harmonieuse. – De la Grèce au mouvement romantique, – moyen-âge, – il y a des lettrés, des versificateurs. D'Ennius à Theroldus, de Theroldus à Casimir Delavigne, tout est prose rimée, un jeu, avachissement et gloire d'innombrables générations idiotes: Racine est le pur, le fort, le grand. – On eût soufflé sur ses rimes, brouillé ses hémistiches, que le Divin Sot serait aujourd'hui aussi ignoré que le premier venu auteur d'*Origines*. – Après Racine, le jeu moisit. Il a duré deux mille ans!

Ni plaisanterie, ni paradoxe. La raison m'inspire plus de certitudes sur le sujet que n'aurait jamais eu de colères un Jeune-France. Du reste, libre aux *nouveaux* d'exécrer les ancêtres: on est chez soi et l'on a le temps.

PARISIAN WAR SONG

Spring is evidently here; for ...

[. . . . .]

A. RIMBAUD

– And now here is a discourse in prose on the future of poetry:

All ancient poetry culminated in Greek poetry, harmonious Life. – From Greece to the romantic movement – in the Middle Ages – there are men of letters, versifiers. From Ennius to Theroldus, from Theroldus to Casimir Delavigne, it's all rhymed prose, a game, the enfeeblement and glory of countless idiotic generations: Racine is the pure, strong, great man – If his rhymes had been effaced, and his hemistiches got mixed up, today the Divine Fool would be as unknown as any old author of *Origins*. After Racine the game gets crumby. It has been going on for two thousand years!

Neither joke nor paradox. My reason inspires me with more certitude on this subject than any *Young-France* was ever inspired with rage. Besides, *newcomers* are free to condemn their ancestors: one is at home, and there's plenty of time.

On n'a jamais bien jugé le romantisme. Qui l'aurait jugé? Les Critiques!! Les Romantiques? qui prouvent si bien que la chanson est si peu souvent l'œuvre, c'est-à-dire la pensée chantée et comprise du chanteur.

Car JE est un autre. Si le cuivre s'éveille clairon, il n'y a rien de sa faute. Cela m'est évident: j'assiste à l'éclosion de ma pensée: je la regarde, je l'écoute: je lance un coup d'archet: la symphonie fait son remuement dans les profondeurs, ou vient d'un bond sur la scène.

Si les vieux imbéciles n'avaient pas trouvé du Moi que la signification fausse, nous n'aurions pas à balayer ces millions de squelettes qui, depuis un temps infini, ont accumulé les produits de leur intelligence borgnesse, en s'en clamant les auteurs!

En Grèce, ai-je dit, vers et lyres rhythment l'Action. Après, musique et rimes sont jeux, délassements. L'étude de ce passé charme les curieux: plusieurs s'éjouissent à renouveler ces antiquités: – c'est pour eux. L'intelligence universelle a toujours jeté ses idées naturellement; les

Romanticism has never been properly judged. Who was there to judge it? The Critics!! The Romantics? who prove so clearly that the song is very seldom the work, that is to say, the idea sung and intended by the singer.

For *I* is someone else. If brass wakes up a trumpet, it is not its fault. To me this is obvious: I witness the unfolding of my own thought: I watch it, I listen to it: I make a stroke of the bow: the symphony begins to stir in the depths, or springs on to the stage.

If the old fools had not discovered only the *false* significance of the Ego, we should not now be having to sweep away those millions of skeletons which, since time immemorial, have been piling up the fruits of their one-eyed intellects, and claiming to be, themselves, the authors of them!

In Greece, I say, verses and lyres take their rhythm from Action. After that, music and rhymes are a game, a pastime. The curious are charmed with the study of this past: many of them delight in reviving these antiquities – that's their affair. Universal mind has

9

hommes ramassaient une partie de ces fruits du cerveau: on agissait par, on en écrivait des livres: telle allait la marche, l'homme ne se travaillant pas, n'étant pas encore éveillé, ou pas encore dans la plénitude du grand songe. Des fonctionnaires, des écrivains: auteur, créateur, poëte, cet homme n'a jamais existé!

La première étude de l'homme qui veut être poëte est sa propre connaissance, entière; il cherche son âme, il l'inspecte, il la tente, l'apprend. Dès qu'il la sait, il doit la cultiver! Cela semble simple: en tout cerveau s'accomplit un développement naturel; tant d'*égoïstes* se proclament auteurs; il en est bien d'autres qui s'attribuent leur progrès intellectuel! – Mais il s'agit de faire l'âme monstrueuse: à l'instar des comprachicos, quoi! Imaginez un homme s'implantant et se cultivant des verrues sur le visage.

Je dis qu'il faut être *voyant*, se faire *voyant*.

Le Poëte se fait *voyant* par un long, immense et raisonné *dérèglement* de *tous les sens*. Toutes les formes d'amour, de souffrance, de folie; il cherche lui-même, il

always thrown out its ideas naturally; men would pick up a part of these fruits of the brain: they acted through them, they wrote books through them: and so things went on, since man did not work on himself, either not yet being awake, or not yet in the fullness of the great dream. Writers, civil servants: author, creator, poet, *that* man never existed!

The first study for a man who wants to be a poet is the knowledge of himself, complete. He looks for his soul, inspects it, puts it to the test, learns it. As soon as he knows it, he must cultivate it! It seems simple: in every brain a natural development takes place; so many *egoists* proclaim themselves authors; there are plenty of others who attribute their intellectual progress to themselves! – But the soul has to be made monstrous, that's the point: after the fashion of the *comprachicos*, if you like! Imagine a man planting and cultivating warts on his face.

I say that one must be a *seer*, make onself a *seer*.

The poet makes himself a *seer* by a long, prodigious, and rational *disordering* of *all the senses*. Every form of love, of suffering, of

épuise en lui tous les poisons, pour n'en garder que les quintessences. Ineffable torture où il a besoin de toute la foi, de toute la force surhumaine, où il devient entre tous le grand malade, le grand criminel, le grand maudit, – et le suprême Savant! – Car il arrive à l'*inconnu*! Puisqu'il a cultivé son âme, déjà riche, plus qu'aucun! Il arrive à l'inconnu, et quand, affolé, il finirait par perdre l'intelligence de ses visions, il les a vues! Qu'il crève dans son bondissement par les choses inouïes et innommables: viendront d'autres horribles travailleurs; ils commenceront par les horizons où l'autre s'est affaissé!

– La suite à six minutes –

Ici j'intercale un second psaume *hors du texte*: veuillez tendre une oreille complaisante, – et tout le monde sera charmé. – J'ai l'archet en main, je commence:

madness; he searches himself, he consumes all the poisons in him, and keeps only their quintessences. This is an unspeakable torture during which he needs all his faith and superhuman strength, and during which he becomes the great patient, the great criminal, the great accursed – and the great learned one! – among men. – For he arrives at the *unknown*! Because he has cultivated his own soul – which was rich to begin with – more than any other man! He reaches the unknown; and even if, crazed, he ends up by losing the understanding of his visions, at least he has seen them! Let him die charging through those unutterable, unnameable things: other horrible workers will come; they will begin from the horizons where he has succumbed!

– Continued in six minutes –

Here I shall interpolate a second psalm to decorate the text: be so good as to lend a friendly ear, and everyone will be delighted. – I take the bow in my hand, and begin:

MES PETITES AMOUREUSES

Un hydrolat lacrymal lave ...

[. . . . .]

A. R.

Voilà. Et remarquez bien que, si je ne craignais de vous faire débourser plus de 60 c. de port, – moi pauvre effaré qui, depuis sept mois, n'ai pas tenu un seul rond de bronze! – je vous livrerais encore mes *Amants de Paris*, cent hexamètres, Monsieur, et ma *Mort de Paris*, deux cents hexamètres!

– Je reprends:

Donc le poëte est vraiment voleur de feu.

Il est chargé de l'humanité, des *animaux* même; il devra faire sentir, palper, écouter ses inventions; si ce qu'il rapporte de *là-bas* a forme, il donne forme; si c'est informe, il donne l'informe. Trouver une langue; – Du reste, toute parole étant idée, le temps d'un langage universel viendra! Il faut être académicien – plus mort qu'un fossile, – pour parfaire un dictionnaire, de quelque langue que ce soit.

MY LITTLE MISTRESSES

A tincture of tears washes...

[. . . . .]

A. R.

There. And take notice that if I were not afraid of making you spend more than sixty centimes on postage – I, poor urchin,[1] without a copper to my name for the last seven months! – I would also give you my *Lovers of Paris*, one hundred hexameters, Sir, and my *Death of Paris*, two hundred hexameters!

– To continue:

So, then, the poet really is the thief of fire.

He is responsible for humanity, even for the *animals*; he must see to it that his inventions can be smelt, felt, heard. If what he brings back from *down there* has form, he brings forth form; if it is formless, he brings forth formlessness. A language has to be found – for that matter, every word being an idea, the time of the universal language will come! One has to be an academician – deader than a fossil – to finish a dictionary of any language. Weak-minded people,

---

1. But see title of poem on p. 96.

Des faibles se mettraient *à penser* sur la première lettre de l'alphabet, qui pourraient vite ruer dans la folie!

Cette langue sera de l'âme pour l'âme, résumant tout, parfums, sons, couleurs, de la pensée accrochant la pensée et tirant. Le poëte définirait la quantité d'inconnu s'éveillant en son temps dans l'âme universelle: il donnerait plus – que la formule de sa pensée, que l'annotation *de sa marche au Progrès*! Énormité devenant norme, absorbée par tous, il serait vraiment *un multiplicateur de progrès*!

Cet avenir sera matérialiste, vous le voyez. – Toujours pleins du *Nombre* et de l'*Harmonie*, ces poèmes seront faits pour rester. – Au fond, ce serait encore un peu la Poésie grecque.

L'art éternel aurait ses fonctions, comme les poëtes sont citoyens. La Poésie ne rhythmera plus l'action; elle *sera en avant*.

Ces poëtes seront! Quand sera brisé l'infini servage de la femme, quand elle vivra pour elle et par elle, l'homme, – jusqu'ici abominable, – lui ayant donné son renvoi, elle

beginning by *thinking about* the first letter of the alphabet, would soon rush into madness!

This [new] language would be of the soul, for the soul, containing everything, smells, sounds, colours; thought latching on to thought and pulling. The poet would define the amount of the unknown awakening in the universal soul in his own time: he would produce more than the formulation of his thought or the measurement *of his march towards Progress*! An enormity who has become normal, absorbed by everyone, he would really be *a multiplier of progress*!

This future will, as you see, be materialistic. – Always filled with *Number* and *Harmony*, these poems will be made to endure. Essentially, it will be Greek poetry again, in a way.

Eternal art will have its function, since poets are citizens. Poetry will no longer take its rhythm from action; *it will be ahead of it*!

Poets like this will exist! When the unending servitude of women is broken, when she lives by and for herself, when man – hitherto abominable – has given her her freedom, she too will be a

sera poëte, elle aussi! La femme trouvera de l'inconnu!
Ses mondes d'idées différeront-ils des nôtres? – Elle
trouvera des choses étranges, insondables, repoussantes,
délicieuses; nous les prendrons, nous les comprendrons.

En attendant, demandons au *poëte* du *nouveau*, – idées
et formes. Tous les habiles croiraient bientôt avoir satis-
fait à cette demande: – ce n'est pas cela!

Les premiers romantiques on tété *voyants* sans trop bien
s'en rendre compte: la culture de leurs âmes s'est com-
mencée aux accidents: locomotives abandonnées, mais
brûlantes, que prennent quelque temps les rails. – Lamar-
tine est quelquefois voyant, mais étranglé par la forme
vieille. – Hugo, *trop cabochard*, a bien du VU dans les
derniers volumes: *Les Misérables* sont un vrai *poème*. J'ai
Les Châtiments sous main; *Stella* donne à peu près la
mesure de la *vue* de Hugo. Trop de Belmontet et de
Lamennais, de Jehovahs et de colonnes, vieilles énormités
crevées.

Musset est quatorze fois exécrable pour nous, généra-
tions douloureuses et prises de visions, – que sa paresse
d'ange a insultées! Ô! les contes et les proverbes fadasses!

poet! Woman will discover part of the unknown! Will her world of
ideas be different from ours? She will discover things strange and
unfathomable, repulsive and delicious. We shall take them unto
ourselves, we shall understand them.

Meanwhile let us ask the *poet* for the *new* – in ideas and in forms.
All the bright boys will imagine they can soon satisfy this demand: –
it is not so!

The first romantics were *seers* without quite realizing it: the
cultivation of their souls began accidentally: abandoned loco-
motives, but with their fires still alight, which the rails still carry
along for a while. – Sometimes Lamartine is a *seer*, but strangled by
the old form. Hugo, who is *too obstinate*, really has VISION in his
last works: *Les Misérables* is a real *poem*. I have *Les Châtiments*
with me; *Stella* shows the limit of Hugo's *vision*. Too many Bel-
montets and Lamennais, Jehovahs and columns, old cracked
enormities.

Musset is fourteen times execrable to us suffering generations
carried away by visions – to whom his angelic sloth is an insult! O!

ô les *Nuits*! ô *Rolla*, ô *Namouna*, ô *La Coupe*! tout est
français, c'est-à-dire haïssable au suprême degré; français,
pas parisien! Encore une œuvre de cet odieux génie qui
a inspiré Rabelais, Voltaire, Jean La Fontaine, commenté
par M. Taine! Printanier, l'esprit de Musset! Charmant,
son amour! En voilà, de la peinture à l'émail, de la poésie
solide! On savourera longtemps la poésie *française*, mais
en France. Tout garçon épicier est en mesure de débo-
biner une apostrophe Rollaque, tout séminariste emporte
les cinq cents rimes dans le secret d'un carnet. À quinze
ans, ces élans de passion mettent les jeunes en rut; à seize
ans, ils se contentent déjà de les réciter avec *cœur*; à dix-
huit ans, à dix-sept même, tout collégien qui a le moyen
fait le Rolla, écrit un Rolla! Quelques-uns en meurent
peut-être encore. Musset n'a rien su faire: il y avait des
visions derrière la gaze des rideaux: il a fermé les yeux.
Français, panadis, traîné de l'estaminet au pupitre de col-
lège, le beau mort est mort, et, désormais, ne nous don-
nons même plus la peine de le réveiller par nos abomina-
tions!

the insipid tales and proverbs! O the *Nuits*! O *Rolla*, O *Namouna*,
O *the Chalice*! it is all French, that is, detestable to the highest
degree; French, not Parisian! More work of the evil genius that in-
spired Rabelais, Voltaire, Jean La Fontaine, with M. Taine's com-
mentary! Springlike, the wit of Musset! Charming, his love!
There's enamel painting and solid poetry for you! *French* poetry
will be enjoyed for a long time – but in France. Every grocer's boy
can reel off a Rollaesque speech, every budding priest has the five
hundred rhymes hidden away in the secrecy of a notebook. At
fifteen, these outbursts of passion make boys lecherous, at sixteen
they are already content to recite them with *feeling*; at eighteen,
even at seventeen, every schoolboy who has the ability does a
Rolla, writes a Rolla! Perhaps some still die of it. Musset could
not do anything: there were visions behind the gauze of the
curtains: he closed his eyes. French, sloppy, dragged from bar-
room to schoolroom desk, the fine corpse is dead, and henceforth
let us not even bother to awaken it with our execrations!

Les seconds romantiques sont très *voyants*: Théophile Gautier, Leconte de Lisle, Théodore de Banville. Mais inspecter l'invisible et entendre l'inouï étant autre chose que reprendre l'esprit des choses mortes, Baudelaire est le premier voyant, roi des poëtes, *un vrai Dieu*. Encore a-t-il vécu dans un milieu trop artiste; et la forme si vantée en lui est mesquine. Les inventions d'inconnu réclament des formes nouvelles.

Rompue aux formes vieilles, – parmi les innocents, A. Renaud, – a fait son Rolla; – L. Grandet, – a fait son Rolla; – les gaulois et les Mussets, G. Lafenestre, Coran, Cl. Popelin, Soulary, L. Salles; les écoliers, Marc, Aicard, Theuriet; les morts et les imbéciles, Autran, Barbier, L. Pichat, Lemoyne, les Deschamps, les Des Essarts; les journalistes, L. Cladel, Robert Luzarches, X. de Ricard; les fantaisistes, C. Mendès; les bohèmes; les femmes; les talents, Léon Dierx et Sully-Prudhomme, Coppée; – la nouvelle école, dite parnassienne, a deux voyants, Albert Mérat et Paul Verlaine, un vrai poëte. – Voilà.

The second Romantics are very *seeing*: Théophile Gautier, Leconte de Lisle, Théodore de Banville. But because examining the invisible and hearing the unheard-of is quite different from recapturing the spirit of dead things, Baudelaire is the first *seer*, king of poets, *a real God*! Unluckily he lived in too artistic a circle; and the form which is so much praised in him is trivial. Inventions from the unknown demand new forms.

Broken-in to the old forms, among the simpletons, A. Renaud – has done his Rolla – L. Grandet – has done his Rolla; the Gauls and the Mussets, G. Lafenestre, Coran, Cl. Popelin, Soulary, L. Salles; the scholars, Marc, Aicard, Theuriet; the dead and the imbeciles, Autran, Barbier, L. Pichat, Lemoyne, the Deschamps, the Des Essarts; the journalists, L. Cladel, Robert Luzarches, X. de Ricard; the fantasists, C. Mendès; the bohemians; the women; the talents, Léon Dierx and Sully-Prudhomme, Coppée – the new school, called Parnassian, possesses two seers: Albert Mérat and Paul Verlaine, a real poet. – So there you are.

Ainsi je travaille à me rendre *voyant*. – Et finissons par un chant pieux.

ACCROUPISSEMENTS

Bien tard, quand il se sent l'estomac écœuré,
[. . . . .]

Vous seriez exécrable de ne pas répondre: vite, car dans huit jours, je serai à Paris, peut-être.

Au revoir,

A. RIMBAUD

À VERLAINE

Londres, vendredi après-midi
[4 juillet 1873]

REVIENS, reviens, cher ami, seul ami, reviens. Je te jure que je serai bon. Si j'étais maussade avec toi, c'est une plaisanterie où je me suis entêté, je m'en repens plus qu'on

So, then, I am working to make myself into a *seer* – And now let us close with a pious hymn.

SQUATTINGS

Very late, when he feels his stomach churn,
[. . . . .]

You will be damnable if you don't answer this: quickly, because in a week I shall be in Paris, perhaps.

Goodbye,

A. RIMBAUD

To Verlaine

London, Friday afternoon
(4 July 1873)

COME back, come back, my dear friend, my only friend, come back. I swear I shall be kind. If I was cross with you, it was a joke which I was obstinately determined to carry on; I repent of it more than

17

ne peut dire. Reviens, ce sera bien oublié. Quel malheur que tu aies cru à cette plaisanterie. Voilà deux jours que je ne cesse de pleurer. Reviens. Sois courageux, cher ami. Rien n'est perdu. Tu n'as qu'à refaire le voyage. Nous revivrons ici bien courageusement, patiemment. Ah! je t'en supplie. C'est ton bien d'ailleurs. Reviens, tu retrouveras toutes tes affaires. J'espère que tu sais bien à présent qu'il n'y avait rien de vrai dans notre discussion. L'affreux moment! Mais toi, quand je te faisais signe de quitter le fateau, pourquoi ne venais-tu pas? Nous avons vécu deux ans ensemble pour arriver à cette heure-là! Que vas-tu faire? Si tu ne veux pas revenir ici, veux-tu que j'aille te trouver où tu es?

Oui, c'est moi qui ai eu tort.

Oh! tu ne m'oublieras pas, dis?

Non, tu ne peux pas m'oublier.

Moi, je t'ai toujours là.

Dis, réponds à ton ami, est-ce que nous ne devons plus vivre ensemble?

Sois courageux. Réponds-moi vite.

can be said. Come back, it will be quite forgotten. How terrible that you should have taken that joke seriously. For two days I have not stopped crying. Come back. Be brave, dear friend. Nothing is lost. All you have to do is make another journey. We'll live here again, very bravely and patiently. Oh! I beg you! It's for your good, besides. Come back, you'll find all your things here. I hope you realize now that there was nothing real in our argument. That frightful moment! But you – when I signalled to you to get off the boat – why didn't you come? Have we lived together for two years to come to this? What are you going to do? If you won't come here, would you like me to come and meet you where you are?

Yes, *I* was in the wrong.

Oh! you won't forget me, will you?

No, you can't forget me.

As for me, I still have you, here.

Listen, answer your friend, must we not live together any more?

Be brave. Answer this quickly.

Je ne puis rester ici plus longtemps.
N'écoute que ton bon cœur.
Vite, dis si jè dois te rejoindre.
À toi toute la vie.

RIMBAUD

Vite, réponds: je ne puis rester ici plus tard que lundi
soir. Je n'ai pas encore un penny; je ne puis mettre ça à
la poste. J'ai confié à *Vermersch* tes livres et tes manu-
scrits.

Si je ne dois plus te revoir, je m'engagerai dans la
marine ou l'armée.

Ô reviens, à toutes les heures je repleure. Dis-moi de
te retrouver, j'irai. Dis-le-moi, télégraphie-moi. – Il faut
que je parte lundi soir. Où vas-tu? Que veux-tu faire?

I can't stay here much longer.
Do not read this except with goodwill.
Quick, tell me if I must come to you.
Yours, all my life.

RIMBAUD

Answer quickly: I can't stay here any later than Monday evening.
I haven't another penny; I can't post this. I have given *Vermersch*
your books and manuscripts to look after.

If I mustn't see you any more, I am going to enlist in the navy or
the army.

Oh come back, I keep weeping again all the time. Tell me to meet
you, I'll come. Tell me, send me a telegram. – I must leave on
Monday evening. Where will you go? What do you want to do?

À VERLAINE

[*Londres, 5 juillet 1873*]

Cher ami,

J'AI ta lettre datée *«En mer»*. Tu as tort, cette fois, et très tort. D'abord, rien de positif dans ta lettre. Ta femme ne viendra pas, ou viendra dans trois mois, trois ans, que sais-je? Quant à claquer, je te connais. Tu vas donc, en attendant ta femme et ta mort, te démener, errer, ennuyer des gens. Quoi? toi, tu n'as pas encore reconnu que les colères étaient aussi fausses d'un côté que de l'autre! Mais c'est toi qui aurais les derniers torts, puisque, même après que je t'ai rappelé, tu as persisté dans tes faux sentiments. Crois-tu que ta vie sera plus agréable avec d'autres que moi? *Réfléchis-y!* – Ah! certes non!

Avec moi seul tu peux être libre, et, puisque je te jure d'être très gentil à l'avenir, que je déplore toute ma part de torts, que j'ai enfin l'esprit net, que je t'aime bien, si tu ne veux pas revenir, ou que je te rejoigne, tu fais un

To Verlaine

[*London, 5 July 1873*]

My dear friend,

I HAVE your letter which is headed 'At sea'. You are wrong, this time, very wrong. To begin with, there is nothing positive in your letter. Your wife is not coming, or she is coming in three months, three years, or whatever. As for kicking the bucket, I know you too well. And so you are going – while you wait for your wife and for death – to struggle, to wander about, and to bore people. What! don't you realize yet that our anger was false, on both sides? But you will be in the wrong at the end, because, even after I called you back, you persisted in your unreal feelings. Do you think that your life will be happier with other people than it was with me? *Think about it*! Oh! surely not!

It is only with me that you can be free, and since I swear to be very nice to you in future, and deplore the whole of my part in the wrong, and since my head is clear, at last, and I like you very much, if you don't want to come back, or for me to join you, you

crime, et *tu t'en repentiras de* LONGUES ANNÉES *par la perte de toute liberté, et des ennuis plus atroces* peut-être que tous ceux que tu as éprouvés. Après ça, resonge à ce que tu étais avant de me connaître!

Quant à moi, je ne rentre pas chez ma mère. Je vais à Paris. Je tâcherai d'être parti lundi soir. Tu m'auras forcé à vendre tous tes habits, je ne puis faire autrement. Ils ne sont pas encore vendus: ce n'est que lundi matin qu'on me les emporterait. Si tu veux m'adresser des lettres à Paris, envoie à L. Forain, 289, rue Saint-Jacques (pour A. Rimbaud). Il saura mon adresse.

Certes, si ta femme revient, je ne te compromettrai pas en t'écrivant, – je n'écrirai jamais.

Le seul vrai mot, c'est: reviens. Je veux être avec toi, je t'aime. Si tu écoutes cela, tu montreras du courage et un esprit sincère.

are committing a crime, *and you will do penance for it for* LONG YEARS TO COME, *by losing all your freedom, and by sufferings more terrible* perhaps than any you have undergone. When you read this, think of what you were before you knew me!

For myself, I'm not going back to my mother's. I am going to Paris.

I shall try to be gone by Monday evening. You will have compelled me to sell all your suits, I can't do anything else. They aren't sold yet: they are not coming to get them from me until Monday evening. If you want to write to me in Paris, send letters to L. Forain, 289 rue Saint-Jacques (for A. Rimbaud). He will know my address.

One thing is certain: if your wife comes back, I shall never compromise you by writing to you – I shall never write.

One single true word: it is, come back. I want to be with you, I love you. If you listen to this, you will prove your courage and sincerity.

Autrement, je te plains.

Mais je t'aime, je t'embrasse et nous nous reverrons.

RIMBAUD

8 Great Colle, *etc* ... jusqu'à lundi soir, – ou mardi à midi, si tu m'appelles.

DÉPOSITION DE RIMBAUD DEVANT LE JUGE D'INSTRUCTION

12 juillet 1873

J'AI fait, il y a deux ans environ, la connaissance de Verlaine à Paris. L'année dernière, à la suite de dissentiments avec sa femme et la famille de celle-ci, il me proposa d'aller avec lui à l'étranger; nous devions gagner notre vie d'une manière ou d'une autre, car moi je n'ai aucune fortune personnelle, et Verlaine n'a que le produit de son travail

Otherwise, I'm sorry for you.

But I love you, I kiss you and we'll see each other again.

RIMBAUD

8 Great Colle, *etc*. ... until Monday evening – or Tuesday midday, if you send me word.

*Deposition by Rimbaud before the
Examining Magistrate*

12 July 1873

ABOUT two years ago I became acquainted with Verlaine in Paris. Last year, after some disagreements with his wife and with her family, he suggested that I should go abroad with him; we were going to have to make a living somehow or other, because I have no money of my own, and Verlaine only has what he can get from

et quelque argent que lui donne sa mère. Nous sommes venus ensemble à Bruxelles au mois de juillet de l'année dernière; nous y avons séjourné pendant deux mois environ; voyant qu'il n'y avait rien à faire pour nous dans cette ville, nous sommes allés à Londres. Nous y avons vécu ensemble jusque dans ces derniers temps, occupant le même logement et mettant tout en commun.

À la suite d'une discussion que nous avons eue au commencement de la semaine dernière, discussion née des reproches que je lui faisais sur son indolence et sa manière d'agir à l'égard des personnes de nos connaissances, Verlaine me quitta presque à l'improviste, sans même me faire connaître le lieu où il se rendait. Je supposai cependant qu'il se rendait à Bruxelles, ou qu'il y passerait, car il avait pris le bateau d'Anvers. Je reçus ensuite de lui une lettre datée «*En mer*», que je vous remettrai, dans laquelle il m'annonçait qu'il allait rappeler sa femme auprès de lui, et que si elle ne répondait pas à son appel dans trois jours, il se tuerait; il me disait aussi de lui écrire poste restante à Bruxelles. Je lui écrivis ensuite deux lettres dans lesquelles

his work and some money which his mother gives him. We came to Brussels together in the month of July last year; we stayed here for about two months; and seeing that there was nothing we could do in this town, we went to London. We lived there together until lately, sharing the same lodgings and using everything in common.

Following an argument which we had at the beginning of last week, arising from reproaches which I made to him about his indolence and his behaviour towards certain persons we knew, Verlaine left me practically without warning, without even telling me where he was going. However I supposed he was going to Brussels, or would pass through it, because he had taken the Antwerp boat. Then I received a letter from him headed 'At sea', which I shall hand to you, in which he told me that he was going to ask his wife to come to him where he was, and that if she had not answered his call within three days, he was going to kill himself; he also told me to write to him *poste restante* at Brussels. I immediately wrote him

je lui demandais de revenir à Londres ou de consentir à ce que j'allasse le rejoindre à Bruxelles. C'est alors qu'il m'envoya un télégramme pour venir ici, à Bruxelles. Je désirais nous réunir de nouveau, parce que nous n'avions aucun motif de nous séparer.

Je quittai donc Londres; j'arrivai à Bruxelles mardi matin, et je rejoignis Verlaine. Sa mère était avec lui. Il n'avait aucun projet déterminé: il ne voulait pas rester à Bruxelles, parce qu'il craignait qu'il n'y eût rien à faire dans cette ville; moi, de mon côté, je ne voulais pas consentir à retourner à Londres, comme il me le proposait, parce que notre départ devait avoir produit un trop fâcheux effet dans l'esprit de nos amis, et je résolus de retourner à Paris. Tantôt Verlaine manifestait l'intention de m'y accompagner, pour aller, comme il le disait, faire justice de sa femme et de ses beaux-parents; tantôt il refusait de m'accompagner, parce que Paris lui rappelait de trop tristes souvenirs. Il était dans un état d'exaltation très grande. Cependant il insistait beaucoup auprès de moi

two letters in which I asked him to come back to London or to consent to my rejoining him in Brussels. It was then that he sent me a telegram (telling me) to come here, to Brussels. I wanted us to be reunited again, because there was no reason why we should separate.

I left London, therefore; I arrived in Brussels on Tuesday morning, and went to meet Verlaine. His mother was with him. He had no fixed plan: he did not wish to stay in Brussels, because he feared that there would be nothing for him to do in this city; for my part, I did not wish to consent to return to London as he suggested, because our departure had caused too much bad feeling on the part of our friends, and I was determined to go back to Paris. Sometimes Verlaine gave me to understand that it was his intention to come with me, in justice, as he put it, to his wife and his wife's family; at other times he refused to come with me, because Paris brought back memories to him which were too painful. He was in a very excitable frame of mind. Nevertheless he was very insistent that I

24

pour que je restasse avec lui: tantôt il était désespéré, tantôt il entrait en fureur. Il n'y avait aucune suite dans ses idées. Mercredi soir, il but outre mesure et s'enivra. Jeudi matin, il sortit à six heures; il ne rentra que vers midi; il était de nouveau en état d'ivresse, il me montra un pistolet qu'il avait acheté, et quand je lui demandai ce qu'il comptait en faire, il répondit en plaisantant: «C'est pour vous, pour moi, pour tout le monde!» Il était fort surexcité.

Pendant que nous étions ensemble dans notre chambre, il descendit encore plusieurs fois pour boire des liqueurs; il voulait toujours m'empêcher d'exécuter mon projet de retourner à Paris. Je restai inébranlable. Je demandai même de l'argent à sa mère pour faire le voyage. Alors, à un moment donné, il ferma à clef la porte de la chambre donnant sur le palier et il s'assit sur une chaise contre cette porte. J'étais debout, adossé contre le mur d'en face. Il me dit alors: «Voilà pour toi, puisque tu pars!» ou quelque chose dans ce sens; il dirigea son pistolet sur moi et m'en lâcha un coup qui m'atteignit au poignet gauche;

should stay with him: he alternated between despair and rage. There was no coherence in his ideas. On Wednesday evening he had more than enough to drink and became drunk. On Thursday morning he went out at six o'clock and did not come back until nearly noon; he was again in a state of intoxication, he showed me a pistol which he had bought, and when I asked him what he intended to do with it, he replied in a joking manner: 'It's for you, for me, for everyone!' He was extremely overexcited.

While we were together in our bedroom, he went down several more times to drink liqueurs; he still wished to prevent me from carrying into execution my plan of going back to Paris. I remained resolute. I even asked his mother for some money for the journey. Then, at a given moment, he locked the door of the room which gave on to the staircase and sat on a chair against this door. I was standing, leaning my back on the wall facing it. He then said to me: 'This is for you, then, since you're going!' or words to this effect; he aimed his pistol at me and fired a shot at me which hit

le premier coup fut presque instantanément suivi d'un second, mais cette fois l'arme n'était plus dirigée vers moi, mais abaissée vers le plancher.

Verlaine exprima immédiatement le plus vif désespoir de ce qu'il avait fait; il se précipita dans la chambre contiguë occupée par sa mère, et se jeta sur le lit. Il était comme fou: il me mit son pistolet entre les mains et m'engagea à le lui décharger sur la tempe. Son attitude était celle d'un profond regret de ce qui lui était arrivé.

Vers cinq heures du soir, sa mère et lui me conduisirent ici pour me faire panser. Revenus à l'hôtel, Verlaine et sa mère me proposèrent de rester avec eux pour me soigner, ou de retourner à l'hôpital jusqu'à guérison complète. La blessure me paraissait peu grave, je manifestai l'intention de me rendre le soir même en France, à Charleville, auprès de ma mère. Cette nouvelle jeta Verlaine de nouveau dans le désespoir. Sa mère me remit vingt francs pour faire le voyage, et ils sortirent avec moi pour m'accompagner à la gare du Midi.

me in the left wrist; the first shot was almost immediately followed by a second, but this time the weapon was no longer pointing at me, but down at the floor.

Verlaine at once expressed the deepest regret for what he had done; he rushed into the adjoining room, which was occupied by his mother, and threw himself on the bed. He was like a madman: he put his pistol into my hands and pledged me to fire it at his temple. His attitude was of profound sorrow at what had happened to him.

About five o'clock in the afternoon, his mother and he brought me here to be treated. When we got back to the hotel, Verlaine and his mother made the suggestion that I should stay with them and be looked after, or go back to hospital until I was completely healed. The wound did not seem very serious to me, I told them I intended to return to France that very evening; to my mother's in Charleville. This news threw Verlaine into despair again. His mother gave me twenty francs for the journey, and they came out with me to accompany me to the Midi terminus.

Verlaine était comme fou. Il mit tout en œuvre pour me retenir; d'autre part, il avait constamment la main dans la poche de son habit où était son pistolet. Arrivés à la place Rouppe, il nous devança de quelques pas, et puis il revint sur moi. Son attitude me faisait craindre qu'il ne se livrât à de nouveaux excès. Je me retournai et je pris la fuite en courant. C'est alors que je priai un agent de police de l'arrêter.

La balle dont j'ai été atteint à la main n'est pas encore extraite: le docteur d'ici m'a dit qu'elle ne pourrait l'être que dans deux ou trois jours.

DEMANDE. – De quoi viviez-vous à Londres?

RÉPONSE. – Principalement de l'argent que Madame Verlaine envoyait à son fils. Nous avions aussi des leçons de français que nous donnions ensemble, mais ces leçons ne nous rapportaient pas grand'chose, une douzaine de francs par semaine, vers la fin.

D. – Connaissez-vous le motif des dissentiments de Verlaine et de sa femme?

Verlaine behaved as if he were mad. He did everything he could to stop me from going; besides which, he kept his hand all the time in the pocket of his jacket where his pistol was. When we arrived at the Place Rouppe, he went a few paces ahead of us, and then he came back towards me. His manner caused me to fear that he might give himself over to new excesses. I turned and ran away. It was then that I asked a police officer to arrest him.

The bullet in my hand has not yet been removed: the doctor here tells me that it will not be possible for two or three days.

QUESTION. What did you live on in London?

ANSWER. Mainly on the money which Madame Verlaine used to send to her son. We also had French lessons which we gave together, but these lessons did not earn us very much, about a dozen francs a week, towards the end.

Q. Do you know the reason for the disagreements between Verlaine and his wife?

R. – Verlaine ne voulait pas que sa femme continuât d'habiter chez son père.

D. – N'invoque-t-elle pas aussi comme grief votre intimité avec Verlaine?

R. – Oui, elle nous accuse même de relations immorales; mais je ne veux pas me donner la peine de démentir de pareilles calomnies.

Lecture faite, persiste et signe:

A. RIMBAUD, TH. T'SERSTEVENS, C. LIGOUR

ACTE DE RENONCIATION
DE RIMBAUD

Samedi 19 juillet 1873

JE soussigné Arthur Rimbaud, 19 ans, homme de lettres, demeurant ordinairement à Charleville (Ardennes, France), déclare, pour rendre hommage à la vérité, que le jeudi 10 courant, vers deux heures, au moment où M. Paul Verlaine, dans la chambre de sa mère, a tiré sur

A. Verlaine did not wish his wife to continue to live at her father's house.

Q. Does she not also name as a cause for complaint your intimacy with Verlaine?

A. Yes, she even accuses us of immoral relations; but I do not wish to trouble to give the lie to such calumnies.

Read, confirmed, and signed:

A. RIMBAUD, TH. T'SERSTEVENS, C. LIGOUR

Form of Renunciation by Rimbaud

Saturday 19 July 1873

I THE undersigned Arthur Rimbaud, 19 years of age, man of letters, residing normally in Charleville (Ardennes, France), declare, in order that the truth may be known, that on Thursday the 10th instant, about two o'clock, at the moment when M. Paul Verlaine, in

moi un coup de revolver qui m'a blessé légèrement au poignet gauche, M. Verlaine était dans un tel état d'ivresse qu'il n'avait point conscience de son action;

Que je suis intimement persuadé qu'en achetant cette arme, M. Verlaine n'avait aucune intention hostile contre moi, et qu'il n'y avait point de préméditation criminelle dans l'acte de fermer la porte à clef sur nous;

Que la cause de l'ivresse de M. Verlaine tenait simplement à l'idée de ses contrariétés avec Madame Verlaine, sa femme.

Je déclare, en outre, lui offrir volontiers et consentir à ma renonciation pure et simple à toute action criminelle, correctionnelle et civile, et me désiste dès aujourd'hui des bénéfices de toute poursuite qui serait ou pourrait être intentée par le Ministère public contre M. Verlaine, pour le fait dont il s'agit.

A. RIMBAUD

his mother's bedroom, fired a revolver shot at me which slightly wounded me in the left wrist, M. Verlaine was in a sufficient state of intoxication to render him quite unconscious of what he was doing;

That I am perfectly convinced that in buying this weapon M. Verlaine had no hostile intention towards me, and that there was no criminal premeditation in his action of locking the door of the room we were in;

That the only reason for M. Verlaine's state of intoxication was the thought of his disagreements with Madame Verlaine, his wife.

I further declare that I freely give and consent to my renunciation pure and simple to any action, criminal, correctional, or civil, and that I henceforth give up all rights to any benefit from any prosecution which may or might be instituted by the public Ministry against M. Verlaine for the actions herein specified.

A. RIMBAUD

AUX SIENS

Alexandrie, décembre 1878

Chers amis,

JE suis arrivé ici après une traversée d'une dizaine de jours, et, depuis une quinzaine que je me retourne ici, voici seulement que les choses commencent à mieux tourner! Je vais avoir un emploi prochainement; et je travaille déjà assez pour vivre, petitement il est vrai. Ou bien je serai occupé dans une grande exploitation agricole à quelque dix lieues d'ici (j'y suis déjà allé, mais il n'y aurait rien avant quelques semaines); – ou bien j'entrerai prochainement dans les douanes anglo-égyptiennes, avec bon traitement; – ou bien, je crois plutôt que je partirai prochainement pour Chypre, l'île anglaise, comme interprète d'un corps de travailleurs. En tous cas, on m'a promis quelque chose; et c'est avec un ingénieur français – homme obligeant et de talent – que j'ai affaire. Seulement voici ce qu'on demande de moi: un mot de toi, maman, avec légalisation de la mairie et portant ceci:

To His Family

Alexandria, December 1878

My dear friends,

I GOT here after about ten days' crossing, and it is only now that I have been here about a fortnight that things are taking a turn for the better! I shall soon have employment; though I already have work enough in order to live, though in a small way. Either I shall be engaged in a large-scale agricultural project about ten leagues from here (I've already been there, but there will be nothing for several weeks); – or I shall soon be joining the Anglo-Egyptian Customs, with a good salary; – or else, I think more likely, I shall be leaving soon for Cyprus, the English island, as an interpreter for a labour corps. In any case, I have been promised something; and I am dealing with a French engineer, an obliging and talented man. The only thing is, that they are asking me for something: a note from you, Mother, legalized by the *mairie*, saying this:

«Je soussignée, épouse Rimbaud, propriétaire à Roche, déclare que mon fils Arthur Rimbaud sort de travailler sur ma propriété, qu'il a quitté Roche de sa propre volonté, le 20 octobre 1878, et qu'il s'est conduit honorablement ici et ailleurs, et qu'il n'est pas actuellement sous le coup de la loi militaire.

Signé: Ep. R ...»

Et le cachet de la mairie qui est le plus nécessaire.

Sans cette pièce on ne me donnera pas un placement fixe, quoique je croie qu'on continuerait à m'occuper incidemment. Mais gardez-vous de dire que je ne suis resté que quelque temps à Roche, parce qu'on m'en demanderait plus long, et ça n'en finirait pas; ensuite ça fera croire aux gens de la compagnie agricole que je suis capable de diriger des travaux.

Je vous prie en grâce de m'envoyer ce mot le plus tôt possible: la chose est bien simple et aura de bons résultats, au moins celui de me donner un bon placement pour tout l'hiver.

'I the undersigned, wife of Rimbaud, property-owner, of Roche, declare that my son Arthur Rimbaud has until recently been working on my property; that he left Roche of his own free will on 20 October 1878, that he conducted himself honestly here and elsewhere, and that he is not at present liable to the action of military law.

Signed: Wife R...'

Plus the *mairie* stamp, which is the most important thing.

Without this form no one will give me a regular job, though I think they would employ me from time to time. But be careful not to say that I only stayed a little while at Roche, because then they would ask me about a far longer period, and there would be no end to it; besides, it will help to persuade the agricultural contractors that I am capable of taking charge of the work.

I beg you to be good enough to send me this note as soon as possible: it is a very simple affair and will have good results, the least of which will be to secure me a good job for the whole winter.

Je vous enverrai prochainement des détails et des descriptions d'Alexandrie et de la vie égyptienne. Aujourd'hui, pas le temps. Je vous dis au revoir. Bonjour à Frédéric, s'il est là. Ici il fait chaud comme l'été à Roche.

Des nouvelles.

A. RIMBAUD
poste française, Alexandrie,
Égypte

AUX SIENS

Harar, le 15 février 1881

Chers amis,

J'AI reçu votre lettre du 8 décembre, et je crois même vous avoir écrit une fois depuis. J'en ai, d'ailleurs, perdu la mémoire en campagne.

Je vous rappelle que je vous ai fait envoyer 300 francs: 1° d'Aden; 2° de Harar à la date du 10 décembre environ;

I shall soon be sending you details and descriptions of Alexandria and of Egyptian life. No time today. I'll say good-bye to you now. Hello to Frédéric, if he's there. It is as warm here as it is in summertime at Roche.

Send news.

A. RIMBAUD
French Post Office, Alexandria,
Egypt

To His Family

Harar, 15 February 1881

Dear friends,

I RECEIVED your letter of 8 December, and I think I even wrote to you once after that. But I've forgotten about it since I was in the country.

I should remind you that I have had 300 francs sent to you: 1st from Aden; 2ndly from Harar, about 10 December; 3rdly from

3° de Harar à la date du 10 janvier environ. Je compte qu'en ce moment vous avez déjà reçu ces trois envois de cent francs et mis en route ce que je vous ai demandé. Je vous remercie dès à présent de l'envoi que vous m'annoncez, mais que je ne recevrai pas avant deux mois d'ici, peut-être.

Envoyez-moi *Les Constructions métalliques*, par Monge, prix: 10 francs.

Je ne compte pas rester longtemps ici; je saurai bientôt quand je partirai. Je n'ai pas trouvé ce que je présumais; et je vis d'une façon fort ennuyeuse et sans profits. Dès que j'aurai 1.500 ou 2.000 francs, je partirai, et j'en serai bien aise. Je compte trouver mieux un peu plus loin. Écrivez-moi des nouvelles des travaux de Panama: aussitôt ouverts, j'irai. Je serai même heureux de partir d'ici, dès à présent. J'ai pincé une maladie, peu dangereuse par elle-même; mais ce climat-ci est traître pour toute espèce de maladie. On ne guérit jamais d'une blessure. Une coupure d'un millimètre à un doigt suppure pendant des mois et prend la gangrène très facilement. D'un autre

Harar, about 10 January. I trust that by now you have already received these three lots of a hundred francs and sent on the things I asked you for. I thank you now for the consignment which you tell me of, but which I shan't receive until about two months from now, perhaps.

Send me *Construction in Metal*, by Monge (price: 10 francs.)

I don't intend to stay here very long; I shall soon know when I am leaving. I haven't found what I thought I should find; and I am living in a very unpleasant and unprofitable way. As soon as I have 1,500 or 2,000 francs I shall leave, and I shall be very glad to. I expect to find something better a little farther on. Write and tell me some news about the Panama project: as soon as it is under way, I shall go. I shall even be glad to leave here, now. I caught an illness, not very dangerous in itself; but this climate is very treacherous for any kind of illness. Wounds don't heal. A cut on the finger a millimetre long suppurates for months, and can easily catch gangrene.

côté, l'administration égyptienne n'a que des médecins et des médicaments insuffisants. Le climat est très humide en été: c'est malsain; je m'y déplais au possible, c'est beaucoup trop froid pour moi.

En fait de livres, ne m'envoyez plus de ces manuels Roret.

Voici quatre mois que j'ai commandé des effets à Lyon, et je n'aurai encore rien avant deux mois.

Il ne faut pas croire que ce pays-ci soit entièrement sauvage. Nous avons l'armée, artillerie et cavalerie, égyptienne, et leur administration. Le tout est identique à ce qui existe en Europe; seulement, c'est un tas de chiens et de bandits. Les indigènes sont des Gallas, tous agriculteurs et pasteurs: gens tranquilles, quand on ne les attaque pas. Le pays est excellent, quoique relativement froid et humide; mais l'agriculture n'y est pas avancée. Le commerce ne comporte principalement que les peaux des bestiaux, qu'on trait pendant leur vie et qu'on écorche ensuite; puis du café, de l'ivoire, de l'or; des parfums,

Besides that, the Egyptian administration has only a very insufficient quantity of doctors and of medicines. The climate is very damp in summer: it's unhealthy; I find it unpleasant to a degree, it's far too cold for me.

About books: don't send me any more of those Roret handbooks.

Four months ago I asked for some things from Lyon, and I shall still get nothing for two months.

You mustn't think that this country is completely uncivilized. We have the Egyptian army, artillery and cavalry, and their administration. It is all identical with what exists in Europe; the only thing is, they're a lot of dogs and robbers. The natives are Gallas, all farmers and shepherds: peaceful people, when they're not attacked. The country is very good, although it is relatively cold and damp; but agriculture here is not advanced. Trade is carried on principally in hides of animals, which they milk while they are alive, and then flay; and then there is coffee, ivory, and gold; perfumes,

encens, musc, etc. Le mal est que l'on est à 60 lieues de la mer et que les transports coûtent trop.

Je suis heureux de voir que votre petit manège va aussi bien que possible. Je ne vous souhaite pas une réédition de l'hiver 1879–80, dont le me souviens assez pour éviter à jamais l'occasion d'en subir un semblable.

Si vous trouviez un exemplaire dépareillé du Bottin, Paris et Étranger (quand ce serait un ancien), pour quelques francs, envoyez-le-moi, en caisse: j'en ai spécialement besoin.

Fourrez-moi aussi une demi-livre de graines de betterave saccharifère dans un coin de l'envoi.

Demandez – si vous avez de l'argent de reste – chez Lacroix le *Dictionary of Engineering military and civil*, prix 15 francs. Ceci n'est pas fort pressé.

Soyez sûrs que j'aurai soin de mes livres.

Notre matériel de photographie et de préparation d'histoire naturelle n'est pas encore arrivé, et je crois que je serai parti avant qu'il n'arrive.

incense, musk, etc. The trouble is that one is 60 leagues from the sea and transport is too expensive.

I am glad to learn that your little riding-school is going as well as possible. I don't wish you any more editions of the winter of 1879–80, which I remember well enough to wish never to have to undergo its like again.

If you could find an odd copy of *Bottin, Paris et Étranger* (if it's an old one), for a few francs, send it to me, packed up: I particularly need one.

Stick half a pound of sugar-beet seed in a corner of the parcel, as well.

Go and get, if you have any money left over, from Lacroix, the *Dictionary of Engineering military and civil* (price 15 francs). This is not very urgent.

You may be sure that I shall take care of my books.

Our photographic and naturalist's materials have not arrived yet, and I think I shall be gone before they do come.

J'ai une foule de choses à demander; mais il faut que vous m'envoyiez le Bottin d'abord.

À propos, comment n'avez-vous pas retrouvé le dictionnaire arabe? Il doit être à la maison cependant.

Dites à Frédéric de chercher dans les papiers arabes un cahier intitulé: *Plaisanteries, jeux de mots*, etc., en arabe; et il doit y avoir aussi une collection de dialogues, de chansons ou je ne sais quoi, utile à ceux qui apprennent la langue. S'il y a un ouvrage en arabe, envoyez; mais tout ceci comme emballage seulement, car ça ne vaut pas le port.

Je vais vous faire envoyer une vingtaine de kilos café moka à mon compte, si ça ne coûte pas trop de douane.

Je vous dis: à bientôt! dans l'espoir d'un temps meilleur et d'un travail moins bête; car, si vous présupposez que je vis en prince, moi, je suis sûr que je vis d'une façon fort bête et fort embêtante.

I have a whole lot of things to ask you for; but you must send the *Bottin* first.

While I think of it, how was it that you couldn't find the Arabic dictionary? It must be in the house, all the same.

Tell Frédéric to try and find, among the Arabic papers, a notebook entitled: *Plaisanteries, jeux de mots*, etc., in Arabic; and there should also be a collection of conversations, songs, or I don't know what, useful for people who are learning the language. If there is a book in Arabic, send it; but all this only as packing; it's not worth the postage on its own account.

I am going to have twenty kilos or so of Moka coffee sent to you at my expense, if it doesn't cost too much in duty.

I shall say good-bye for now! in the hope of finding better weather and a less stupid kind of work; because if you think I live like a prince, I for my part am sure that I live in a very stupid and unpleasant way.

Ceci part avec une caravane, et ne vous parviendra pas avant fin mars. C'est un des agréments de la situation. C'est même le pire.

À vous,

RIMBAUD

AUX SIENS

Aden, le 30 avril 1891

Mes chers amis,

J'AI bien reçu votre lettre et vos deux bas; mais je les ai reçus dans de tristes circonstances.

Voyant toujours augmenter l'enflure de mon genou droit et la douleur dans l'articulation, sans pouvoir trouver aucun remède ni aucun avis, puisqu'au Harar nous sommes au milieu des négres et qu'il n'y a point là de médecins, je me décidai à descendre. Il fallait abandonner les affaires: ce qui n'était pas très facile, car j'avais

This is leaving with a caravan, and will not reach you before the end of March. That's one of the beauties of this situation. It's even the worst one of all.

Yours,

RIMBAUD

To His Family

Aden, 30 April 1891

My dear friends,

I GOT your letter and the two stockings all right, but I received them in sad circumstances.

Seeing that the swelling in my right knee and the pain in the joint still continued to get worse, and because I could get neither treatment nor advice, because at Harar we are in the midst of the negroes and there are no doctors here at all, I decided to come back. I had to leave the business: which was not very easy, because I had

de l'argent dispersé de tous les côtés; mais enfin je liquidai à peu près. Depuis une vingtaine de jours, j'étais couché au Harar et dans l'impossibilité de faire un seul mouvement, souffrant des douleurs atroces et ne dormant jamais. Je louai seize nègres porteurs, à raison de 15 thalaris l'un, du Harar à Zeilah; je fis fabriquer une civière recouverte d'une toile, et c'est là-dedans que je viens de faire, en douze jours, les 300 kilomètres de désert qui séparent les monts du Harar du port de Zeilah. Inutile de vous dire quelles souffrances j'ai subies en route. Je n'ai jamais pu faire un pas hors de ma civière; mon genou gonflait à vue d'œil, et la douleur augmentait continuellement.

Arrivé ici, je suis entré à l'hôpital européen. Il y a une seule chambre pour les malades payants: je l'occupe. Le docteur anglais, dès que je lui ai eu montré mon genou, a crié que c'est une tumeur synovite arrivée à un point très dangereux, par suite du manque de soins et des fatigues. Il parlait d'abord de couper la jambe; ensuite, il a décidé d'attendre quelques jours pour voir si le gonflement, avec les soins médicaux, diminuerait un peu. Il y a six jours de cela, et aucune amélioration, sinon que,

money out all over the place; but finally I wound it all up, just about. I had been lying in Harar for about three weeks, not being able to make a movement, suffering frightful pain, and never sleeping. I hired sixteen negro porters for 15 thalaris each, from Harar to Zeilah; I had a stretcher made, covered with canvas, and in it I have just made, in twelve days, the 300-kilometre journey across the desert which separates the Harar hills from the port of Zeilah. No point in telling you what I went through on the way. I was never able to take a step from my stretcher; my knee swelled visibly, and the pain increased all the time.

When I got here I went to the European Hospital. There is just one room for paying patients: I am in it. The English doctor, as soon as I showed him my knee, cried out that it was a synovial tumour which had arrived at a very dangerous stage, owing to lack of attention and fatigue. First of all he talked of cutting the leg off; then he decided to wait a few days to see if the swelling could be diminished with medical treatment. That was six days ago, and

comme je suis au repos, la douleur a beaucoup diminué.
Vous savez que la synovite est une maladie des liquides de
l'articulation du genou: cela peut provenir d'hérédité, ou
d'accidents, ou encore de bien des causes. Pour moi, cela
a été certainement causé par les fatigues des marches à pied
et à cheval au Harar. Enfin, au point où je suis arrivé, il
ne faut pas espérer que je guérisse avant au moins trois
mois, sous les circonstances les plus favorables. Et je suis
étendu, la jambe bandée, liée, reliée, enchaînée, de façon
à ne pouvoir la mouvoir. Je suis devenu un squelette: je
fais peur. Mon dos est tout écorché du lit; je ne dors pas
une minute. Et ici la chaleur est devenue très forte. La
nourriture de l'hôpital, que je paie pourtant assez cher, est
très mauvaise. Je ne sais quoi faire. D'un autre côté, je
n'ai pas encore terminé mes comptes avec mon associé,
monsieur Tian. Cela ne finira pas avant la huitaine. Je
sortirai de cette affaire avec 35 mille francs environ.
J'aurais eu plus; mais, à cause de mon malheureux départ,
je perds quelques milliers de francs. J'ai envie de me faire

there has been no improvement, except that, because I am resting,
the pain is much less. You know that synovitis is a disease of the
liquid of the knee joint: it can be due to heredity, or accidents, or a
lot of other causes. With me, it was certainly caused by the fatigue
of riding and walking in Harar. In any case, in the situation I am
in at the moment, there's no hope of my being better for at least
three months, at the best. And I am stretched out, with my leg
bandaged, wound round and round, and bound, so that I cannot
move it at all. I have become a skeleton: I frighten people. My
back is completely flayed, from the bed; I don't sleep a minute.
And the heat has become extreme here. The hospital food, which I
pay quite a lot for all the same, is very bad. I do not know what to
do. Besides all this, I haven't yet closed my accounts with my asso-
ciate, Monsieur Tian. It can't be done in less than another week. I
shall get out of this business with about 35 thousand francs. I
should have had more; but I am losing several thousand francs
owing to my unlucky departure. I should like to get myself taken

porter à un vapeur, et de venir me faire traiter en France. Le voyage me ferait encore passer le temps; et, en France, les soins médicaux et les remèdes sont bien meilleurs, et l'air bon. Il est fort probable que je vais venir. Les vapeurs pour la France sont malheureusement toujours combles, parce que tout le monde rentre des colonies à cette époque de l'année; et je suis un pauvre infirme qu'il faut transporter très doucement! Enfin, je vais prendre mon parti dans la huitaine.

Ne vous effrayez pas de tout cela, cependant. De meilleurs jours viendront. Mais, tout de même, c'est une triste récompense de tant de travail, de privations et de peines! Hélas! que notre vie est donc misérable!

Je vous salue de cœur.

RIMBAUD

P.S. – Quant aux bas, ils sont inutiles. Je les revendrai quelque part.

to a steamer, and come and get myself looked after in France. The journey would help to pass the time, at least; and in France both medical attention and medicines are much better, and the air is healthy. It is highly probable that I shall come. Unluckily the steamboats going to France are always packed, because everyone is coming back from the colonies at this time of year; and I am a poor sick man and need carrying very gently! Anyway, I'll make up my mind within a week.

Do not be too upset about all this, however. Better days will come. But all the same, it's a poor reward for so much work, and so many privations and troubles! Alas! How miserable life is, after all!

I greet you all fondly.

RIMBAUD

P.S. As for the stockings, they are useless. I shall sell them again somewhere.

SAVOURÉ À RIMBAUD

15 août 1891

Le ras Makonnen nous parle sans cesse de vous, disant que vous êtes le plus honnête des hommes et que vous avez souvent prouvé que vous étiez son véritable ami …

AU DIRECTEUR DES MESSAGERIES MARITIMES

[Dicté par Rimbaud à sa sœur, la veille de sa mort]

Marseille, 9 novembre 1891

UN LOT: UNE DENT SEULE
UN LOT: DEUX DENTS
UN LOT: TROIS DENTS
UN LOT: QUATRE DENTS
UN LOT: DEUX DENTS

Monsieur le Directeur,

JE viens vous demander si je n'ai rien laissé à votre compte. Je désire changer aujourd'hui de ce service-ci,

Savouré to Rimbaud

15 August 1891

Ras Makonnen is always talking to us about you, saying that you are the most honourable of men and that you have often proved that you were his true friend …

To the Director of Messageries Maritimes

[Dictated by Rimbaud to his sister, the day before his death]

Marseille, 9 November 1891

ITEM: ONE TUSK[1] ONLY
ITEM: TWO TUSKS
ITEM: THREE TUSKS
ITEM: FOUR TUSKS
ITEM: TWO TUSKS

---

1. Enid Starkie, who has seen the documents, says that ivory used to be listed in this way in Rimbaud's accounts. One assumes that, in his delirium, he imagined himself back in Africa again.

41

dont je ne connais même pas le nom, mais en tout cas
que ce soit le service d'Aphinar. Tous ces services sont
là partout, et moi, impotent, malheureux, je ne peux rien
trouver, le premier chien dans la rue vous dira cela.

Envoyez-moi donc le prix des services d'Aphinar à
Suez. Je suis complètement paralysé: donc je désire me
trouver de bonne heure à bord. Dites-moi à quelle heure
je dois être transporté à bord ...

Monsieur le Directeur,

I WISH to ask you if I still owe anything to your account. I wish
to change today from this [steamship] service, which I do not even
know the name of, but in any case let it be the Aphinar line. All
those lines are everywhere, here; and I, powerless, unhappy, can
find nothing; the first dog you meet in the street will be able to tell
you.

So send me the list of fares from Aphinar to Suez. I am com-
pletely paralysed: therefore I wish to be embarked early. Tell me at
what time I must be carried on board ...

«LE SOLEIL ÉTAIT ENCORE CHAUD...»

LE soleil était encore chaud; cependant il n'éclairait presque plus la terre; comme un flambeau placé devant les … ne les éclaire plus que par une faible lueur, ainsi le soleil, flambeau terrestre, s'éteignait en laissant échapper de son corps de feu une dernière et faible lueur, qui cependant laissait encore voir les feuilles vertes des arbres, les petites fleurs qui se flétrissaient, et le sommet gigantesque des pins, des peupliers et des chênes séculaires. Le vent rafraîchissant, c'est-à-dire une brise fraîche, agitait les feuilles des arbres avec un bruissement à peu près semblable à celui que faisaient les eaux argentées du ruisseau qui coulait à mes pieds. Les fougères courbaient leur front vert devant le vent. Je m'endormis, non sans m'être abreuvé de l'eau du ruisseau.

Je rêvai que …… j'étais né à Reims, l'an 1503.

Reims était alors une petite ville, ou pour mieux dire un bourg, cependant renommé à cause de sa belle cathédrale, témoin du sacre du roi Clovis.

THE sun was still warm; it hardly lit up the earth any more, however; just as a torch placed against the … only lights them up with a feeble light, so the sun, torch of the earth, was going out, letting a last feeble light escape from its body of fire, which nevertheless allowed the green leaves of the trees, the little fading flowers, and the enormous tops of the centuries-old pines, poplars, and oaks to be seen. The refreshing wind, that is to say a fresh breeze, moved the leaves of the trees with a rustling somewhat similar to that which the silvery waters of the brook made, flowing at my feet. The ferns bent their green heads before the wind. I fell asleep, not without refreshing myself with the water of the brook.

I dreamt that …… I was born in Rheims, in the year 1503.

At that time Rheims was a little town, or, to put it better, a borough, nevertheless famous for its beautiful cathedral, witness to the coronation of king Clovis.

Mes parents étaient peu riches, mais très honnêtes: ils n'avaient pour tout bien qu'une petite maison, qui leur avait toujours appartenu, et, en plus, quelques mille francs auxquels il faut encore ajouter les petits louis provenant des économies de ma mère.

Mon père était officier,* dans les armées du roi. C'était un homme grand, maigre, chevelure noire, barbe, yeux, peau de même couleur. Quoiqu'il n'eût guère, quand j'étais né, que 48 ou 50 ans, on lui en aurait certainement bien donné 60 ou 58. Il était d'un caractère vif, bouillant, souvent en colère, et ne voulant rien souffrir qui lui déplût.

Ma mère était bien différente: femme douce, calme, s'effrayant de peu de chose, et cependant tenant la maison dans un ordre parfait. Elle était si calme que mon père l'amusait comme une jeune demoiselle. J'étais le plus aimé. Mes frères étaient moins vaillants que moi et cependant plus grands. J'aimais peu l'étude, c'est-à-dire d'apprendre à lire, écrire et compter; mais si c'était pour arranger une

* Colonel des Cent-Gardes.

My parents were not very rich, but were very honest people: they possessed nothing in the world but a small house which had always belonged to them, and, besides that, a few thousand francs, to which must be added the few louis gained from small economies of my mother's.

My father was an officer,[1] in the King's armies. He was a tall thin man, with dark hair; and beard, eyes, and skin of the same hue. Although he was hardly 48 or 50 years old when I was born, he would certainly have been taken for 60 or 58. He was of a lively and ebullient nature, often angry, and unwilling to endure anything which displeased him.

My mother was very different: a sweet, calm woman, whom little upset, and who nevertheless kept the house in perfect order. She was of so calm a nature that my father amused her as if she had been a young girl. I was the best loved. My brothers were less valiant than I, and yet bigger. I had little love for study, that is to say learning to read, to write, and to count; but if it was a matter of arrang-

1. Colonel of the Household Cavalry.

maison, cultiver un jardin, faire des commissions, à la bonne heure! – je me plaisais à cela.

Je me rappelle qu'un jour mon père m'avait promis vingt sous si je lui faisais bien une division; je commençai, mais je ne pus finir. Ah! combien de fois ne m'a-t-il pas promis des sous, des jouets, des friandises, même une fois cinq francs, si je pouvais lui lire quelque chose.

Malgré cela, mon père me mit en classe dès que j'eus dix ans.

«Pourquoi, me disais-je, apprendre du grec, du latin? Je ne le sais. Enfin, on n'a pas besoin de cela! Que m'importe à moi que je sois reçu? À quoi cela sert-il d'être reçu? À rien, n'est-ce pas? Si, pourtant; on dit qu'on n'a une place que lorsqu'on est reçu. Moi, je ne veux pas de place; je serai rentier. Quand même on en voudrait une, pourquoi apprendre le latin? Personne ne parle cette langue. Quelquefois j'en vois, du latin, sur les journaux; mais, Dieu merci, je ne serai pas journaliste.

Pourquoi apprendre et de l'histoire et de la géographie? On a, il est vrai, besoin de savoir que Paris est en France,

ing a house, working in a garden, running errands, that was capital! – I enjoyed that.

I remember that one day my father had promised me twenty sous if I would do a division for him well; I began, but I could not finish. Oh! how often he promised me sous, toys, sweets, even, once, five francs, if I could read something to him.

In spite of this, my father sent me to school as soon as I was ten.

'Why', I would say to myself, 'learn Greek and Latin? I don't know. There's no need of it, anyway! What does it matter to me if I pass my exams? What is the use of passing one's exams? It is no use at all, is it? Yes it is, though: they say there is no employment without a pass. But I do not want any employment. I shall have a private income. Even if one did want to be employed, why learn Latin? No one speaks that language. Sometimes I see some Latin in the newspapers; but, thank God, I shall never be a journalist.

Why learn both history and geography? One has, it is true, to know that Paris is in France, but no one asks at what degree of

mais on ne demande pas à quel degré de latitude. De l'histoire: apprendre la vie de Chinaldon, de Nabopolassar, de Darius, de Cyrus, et d'Alexandre, et de leurs autres compères remarquables par leurs noms diaboliques, est un supplice. Que m'importe, à moi, qu'Alexandre ait été célèbre! Que m'importe? ... Que sait-on si les Latins ont existé? C'est peut-être, leur latin, quelque langue forgée; et, quand même ils auraient existé, qu'ils me laissent rentier, et conservent leur langue pour eux! Quel mal leur ai-je fait pour qu'ils me flanquent au supplice?

Passons au grec. Cette sale langue n'est parlée par personne, personne au monde! ... Ah! saperlipote de saperlipopette! sapristi! moi, je serai rentier; il ne fait pas si bon de s'user les culottes sur les bancs, saperlipopettouille!

latitude. Then take history: learning the lives of Chinaldon, of Nabopolassar, of Darius, of Cyrus, and of Alexander, and of their other cronies, outstanding for their diabolical names, is a torture. What does it matter to me that Alexander was famous? What does it *matter*? ... How does anyone know whether the Latins ever existed? Perhaps their Latin is some counterfeited language; and, even if they did exist, let them leave me to my private income, and keep their language for themselves! What evil have I done to them that they should put me to the torture?

Let us pass on to Greek. This rotten language is spoken by no one, no one in the world! ... Ah! 'sblood,[1] 'sbody! 'sdeath! *I* shall have an income; it's no fun wearing out one's breeches on benches, 'sbloodikins!

---

1. Rimbaud uses as oaths variations on the word '*sapristi*' which derives from *sacristi* and perhaps from *sacrée hostie*; I have substituted (God) 'sblood, etc., which has the same religious force.

Pour être décrotteur, gagner la place de décrotteur, il faut passer un examen; car les places qui vous sont accordées sont d'être ou décrotteur, ou porcher, ou bouvier. Dieu merci! je n'en veux pas, moi, saperli-pouille! Avec ça, des soufflets vous sont accordés pour récompense; on vous appelle animal, ce qui n'est pas vrai, bout d'homme, etc.

Ah! saperpouillotte! ...

(*La suite prochainement*)

ARTHUR

(*1864*)

In order to be a bootblack, to win employment as a bootblack, one must pass an examination; for the places one *can* obtain are, to be either a bootblack, or a swineherd, or a cowman. Thank God! *I* want none of it, 'sgibbet! And with that, boxes on the ears are given to you as rewards; you are called an animal (which is not true), 'piece of a man', etc.

Ah! 'steeth! 'sdeath! 'swounds!

(*To be continued soon*)

ARTHUR

(1864)

POEMS

LES ÉTRENNES DES ORPHELINS

I

L A chambre est pleine d'ombre; on entend vaguement
De deux enfants le triste et doux chuchotement.
Leur front se penche, encore alourdi par le rêve,
Sous le long rideau blanc qui tremble et se soulève ...
– Au dehors les oiseaux se rapprochent frileux;
Leur aile s'engourdit sous le ton gris des cieux;
Et la nouvelle Année, à la suite brumeuse,
Laissant traîner les plis de sa robe neigeuse,
Sourit avec des pleurs, et chante en grelottant ...

II

Or les petits enfants, sous le rideau flottant,
Parlent bas comme on fait dans une nuit obscure.
Ils écoutent, pensifs, comme un lointain murmure.

The Orphans' New-Year's Gift

I

THE room is full of shadow; you can hear, indistinctly, the sad soft whispering of two children. Their foreheads lean forward, still heavy with dreams, beneath the long white bed-curtain which shudders and rises ... Outside the birds crowd together, chilled; their wings are benumbed under the grey tints of the skies; and the New Year, with her train of mist, trailing the folds of her snowy garment, smiles through her tears, and, shivering, sings ...

II

But the little children, beneath the swaying curtain, talk in low voices as one does on a dark night. Thoughtfully they listen as to a

Ils tressaillent souvent à la claire voix d'or
Du timbre matinal, qui frappe et frappe encor
Son refrain métallique en son globe de verre ...
— Puis, la chambre est glacée ... on voit traîner à terre,
Épars autour des lits, des vêtements de deuil:
L'âpre bise d'hiver qui se lamente au seuil
Souffle dans le logis son haleine morose!
On sent, dans tout cela, qu'il manque quelque chose ...
— Il n'est donc point de mère à ces petits enfants,
De mère au frais sourire, aux regards triomphants?
Elle a donc oublié, le soir, seule et penchée,
D'exciter une flamme à la cendre arrachée,
D'amonceler sur eux la laine et l'édredon
Avant de les quitter en leur criant: pardon.
Elle n'a point prévu la froideur matinale,
Ni bien fermé le seuil à la bise hivernale? ...
— Le rêve maternel, c'est le tiède tapis,
C'est le nid cotonneux où les enfants tapis,
Comme de beaux oiseaux que balancent les branches,

far-off murmur ... They tremble often at the clear golden voice of the morning chime repeatedly striking its metallic refrain beneath its glass dome ... And then, the room is icy ... you can see, strewn here and there on the floor round the beds, mourning clothes: the bitter blast of winter which moans at the threshold blows its melancholy breath into the house! You can feel, in all this, that there is something missing ... Is there then no mother for these little children? No mother full of fresh smiles and looks of triumph? Did she forget, last night, stooping down by herself, to kindle a flame saved from the ashes, and to heap up the blankets and eiderdown on them before leaving them, calling out to them: forgive me! Did she not foresee the chill of the morning? Did she forget to close the door against the blast of winter? A mother's dream is the warm coverlet, the downy nest, where children, huddled like pretty birds rocked by the branches, sleep their sweet sleep full of white

Dorment leur doux sommeil plein de visions blanches! ...
– Et là, – c'est comme un nid sans plumes, sans chaleur,
Où les petits ont froid, ne dorment pas, ont peur,
Un nid que doit avoir glacé la bise amère ...

III

Votre cœur l'a compris: – ces enfants sont sans mère.
Plus de mère au logis! ... – et le père est bien loin! ...
– Une vieille servante, alors, en a pris soin.
Les petits sont tout seuls en la maison glacée;
Orphelins de quatre ans, voilà qu'en leur pensée
S'éveille, par degrés, un souvenir riant ...
C'est comme un chapelet qu'on égrène en priant:
– Ah! quel beau matin, que ce matin des étrennes!
Chacun, pendant la nuit, avait rêvé des siennes
Dans quelque songe étrange où l'on voyait joujoux,
Bonbons habillés d'or, étincelants bijoux,
Tourbillonner, danser une danse sonore,
Puis fuir sous les rideaux, puis reparaître encore!

dreams. – And here? – it is like a nest without feathers or warmth,
where the little ones are cold, do not sleep, are afraid; a nest that
the bitter blast must have frozen ...

III

Your heart has understood: – these children are motherless. No
mother in the place any more! ... and their father is far away! ...
– An old servant woman, then, has taken them under her care. The
little ones are alone in the icy house; four-year-old orphans, see
how in their thoughts, little by little, a smiling memory awakes ...
It's like a rosary which you tell, praying: – Ah what a beautiful
morning, that New Year's morning! Everyone had dreamt of his
dear ones that night, in some strange dream where you could see
toys, sweets covered with gold, sparkling jewels, all whirling and
dancing an echoing dance, and then disappearing beneath the cur-
tains, and then reappearing! You awoke in the morning and got up

On s'éveillait matin, on se levait joyeux,
La lèvre affriandée, en se frottant les yeux …
On allait, les cheveux emmêlés sur la tête,
Les yeux tout rayonnants, comme aux grands jours de
     fête,
Et les petits pieds nus effleurant le plancher,
Aux portes des parents tout doucement toucher …
On entrait! … Puis alors les souhaits … en chemise,
Les baisers répétés, et la gaîté permise!

IV

Ah! c'était si charmant, ces mots dits tant de fois!
– Mais comme il est changé, le logis d'autrefois:
Un grand feu pétillait, clair, dans la cheminée,
Toute la vieille chambre était illuminée;
Et les reflets vermeils, sortis du grand foyer,
Sur les meubles vernis aimaient à tournoyer …
– L'armoire était sans clefs! … sans clefs, la grande
     armoire!
On regardait souvent sa porte brune et noire …
Sans clefs! … c'était étrange! … on rêvait bien des fois

full of joy, with your mouth watering, rubbing your eyes … You
went with tangled hair and shining eyes, as on holiday mornings,
little bare feet brushing the floor, to tap softly on your parents'
door … You went in! … And then came the greetings … in your
nightshirt, kisses upon kisses, and fun all allowed!

IV

Ah how charming it was, those words so often spoken! – But how
the old home has changed! There used to be a big fire crackling
bright in the grate, so that the old bedroom was all lit up by it; and
the red reflection from the great hearth would play over the gleam-
ing furniture … – There was no key in the cupboard! … the big
cupboard with no key! … You kept looking at the dark brown
door … No key! … That was strange! … you kept wondering

Aux mystères dormant entre ses flancs de bois,
Et l'on croyait ouïr, au fond de la serrure
Béante, un bruit lointain, vague et joyeux murmure ...
— La chambre des parents est bien vide, aujourd'hui:
Aucun reflet vermeil sous la porte n'a lui;
Il n'est point de parents, de foyer, de clefs prises:
Partant, point de baisers, point de douces surprises!
Oh! que le jour de l'an sera triste pour eux!
— Et, tout pensifs, tandis que de leurs grands yeux bleus
Silencieusement tombe une larme amère,
Ils murmurent: «Quand donc reviendra notre mère?»

. . . .

V

Maintenant, les petits sommeillent tristement:
Vous diriez, à les voir, qu'ils pleurent en dormant,
Tant leurs yeux sont gonflés et leur souffle pénible!
Les tout petits enfants ont le cœur si sensible!
— Mais l'ange des berceaux vient essuyer leurs yeux,
Et dans ce lourd sommeil met un rêve joyeux,

about the mysteries sleeping within its wooden sides; and you seemed to hear, from the bottom of the huge keyhole, a far-off sound, an indistinct and joyful murmur ... — Their parents' bedroom is quite empty now: there is no red reflection shining under the door; there are no parents, no fire, no hidden keys; and so there are no kisses either, or pleasant surprises! Oh how sad their New Year's Day will be! — And sadly, while a bitter tear falls silently from their big blue eyes, they murmur: 'Oh when will our mother come back?'...

V

Now the little ones are dozing sadly: you would say, to see them, that they are crying in their sleep, their eyes are so swollen, their breathing so painful! Small children have such sensitive hearts! — But the guardian angel of the cradle comes and wipes their eyes and puts a happy dream into their heavy slumber, such a joyous dream

Un rêve si joyeux, que leur lèvre mi-close,
Souriante, semblait murmurer quelque chose …
– Ils rêvent que, penchés sur leur petit bras rond,
Doux geste du réveil, ils avancent le front,
Et leur vague regard tout autour d'eux se pose …
Ils se croient endormis dans un paradis rose …
Au foyer plein d'éclats chante gaîment le feu …
Par la fenêtre on voit là-bas un beau ciel bleu;
La nature s'éveille et de rayons s'enivre …
La terre, demi-nue, heureuse de revivre,
A des frissons de joie aux baisers du soleil …
Et dans le vieux logis tout est tiède et vermeil:
Les sombres vêtements ne jonchent plus la terre,
La bise sous le seuil a fini par se taire …
On dirait qu'une fée a passé dans cela! …
– Les enfants, tout joyeux, ont jeté deux cris … Là,
Près du lit maternel, sous un beau rayon rose,
Là, sur le grand tapis, resplendit quelque chose …

that their half-open lips seem, smiling, to murmur something. They
are dreaming that, leaning on their small round arms, in the sweet
gesture of awakening, they lift their heads and gaze mildly about
them … They seem to have fallen asleep in some rose-coloured
paradise … The fire crackles merrily in the bright hearth …
Through the window you can see a lovely blue sky over there;
nature is awakening and becoming drunk with sunlight … the earth,
half-bare, happy to be alive again, trembles with joy beneath the
sun's kisses. In the old home all is warm and flushed: no longer are
there mourning garments strewn on the floor, and the draught has
at last ceased to moan under the door … You would say that a fairy
had passed this way! … The children, full of happiness, give two
cries … Here, near their mother's bed, in a beautiful rose-coloured
ray of light, here on the big carpet, something shines … It is two

Ce sont des médaillons argentés, noirs et blancs,
De la nacre et du jais aux reflets scintillants;
Des petits cadres noirs, des couronnes de verre,
Ayant trois mots gravés en or: «À NOTRE MÈRE!»
. . . .

[Décembre 1869]

PREMIÈRE SOIRÉE

ELLE était fort déshabillée
Et de grands arbres indiscrets
Aux vitres jetaient leur feuillée
Malinement, tout près, tout près.

Assise sur ma grande chaise,
Mi-nue, elle joignait les mains.
Sur le plancher frissonnaient d'aise
Ses petits pieds si fins, si fins.

– Je regardai, couleur de cire,
Un petit rayon buissonnier
Papillonner dans son sourire
Et sur son sein, – mouche au rosier.

silvery plaques, black and white, glittering with mother-of-pearl
and jet; little black frames and wreaths of glass, with three words
engraved in gold: 'TO OUR MOTHER!'...

[December 1869]

The First Evening

SHE was very much half-dressed, and big indiscreet trees threw out
their leaves against the pane: cunningly, and close, quite close.

Sitting half naked in my big chair, she clasped her hands. Her
small and so delicate feet trembled with pleasure on the floor.

The colour of wax, I watched a little wild ray of light flutter on
her smiling lips and on her breast – an insect on the rose-bush.

– Je baisai ses fines chevilles.
Elle eut un doux rire brutal
Qui s'égrenait en claires trilles,
Un joli rire de cristal.

Les petits pieds sous la chemise
Se sauvèrent: «Veux-tu finir!»
– La première audace permise,
Le rire feignait de punir!

– Pauvrets palpitants sous ma lèvre,
Je baisai doucement ses yeux:
– Elle jeta sa tête mièvre
En arrière: «Oh! c'est encor mieux! ...

«Monsieur, j'ai deux mots à te dire ...»
– Je lui jetai le reste au sein
Dans un baiser, qui la fit rire
D'un bon rire qui voulait bien ...

– Elle était fort déshabillée
Et de grands arbres indiscrets
Aux vitres jetaient leur feuillée
Malinement, tout près, tout près.

1870

I kissed her delicate ankles. She laughed softly and suddenly, a string of clear trills, a lovely laugh of crystal.

The small feet fled beneath her petticoat: 'Stop it, do!' – The first act of daring permitted, her laugh pretended to punish me!

Softly I kissed her eyes – trembling beneath my lips, poor things – she threw back her fragile head: 'Oh come now! that's going too far!'

'Listen, sir, I have something to say to you ...' I transferred the rest to her breast in a kiss which made her laugh with a kind laugh that was willing ...

She was very much half-dressed, and big indiscreet trees threw out their leaves against the pane: cunningly, and close, quite close.

1870

SENSATION

PAR les soirs bleus d'été, j'irai dans les sentiers,
Picoté par les blés, fouler l'herbe menue:
Rêveur, j'en sentirai la fraîcheur à mes pieds.
Je laisserai le vent baigner ma tête nue.

Je ne parlerai pas, je ne penserai rien:
Mais l'amour infini me montera dans l'âme,
Et j'irai loin, bien loin, comme un bohémien,
Par la Nature, — heureux comme avec une femme.

Mars 1870

LE FORGERON

Palais des Tuileries, vers le 10 août 92

LE bras sur un marteau gigantesque, effrayant
D'ivresse et de grandeur, le front vaste, riant
Comme un clairon d'airain, avec toute sa bouche,
Et prenant ce gros-là dans son regard farouche,
Le Forgeron parlait à Louis Seize, un jour

Sensation

ON blue summer evenings I shall go down the paths, getting
pricked by the corn, crushing the short grass: in a dream I shall feel
its coolness on my feet. I shall let the wind bathe my bare head.

I shall not speak, I shall think about nothing: but endless love
will mount in my soul, and I shall travel far, very far, like a gipsy,
through the countryside — as happy as if I were with a woman.

March 1870

The Blacksmith

Palais des Tuileries, about 10 August 92

HIS arm resting on a huge hammer, terrible with drunkenness and
size, vast-browed, laughing like a bronze trumpet with his whole
mouth, and devouring that fat little man with his wild gaze, the
Blacksmith spoke to Louis the Sixteenth, one day when the People

Que le Peuple était là, se tordant tout autour,
Et sur les lambris d'or traînant sa veste sale.
Or le bon roi, debout sur son ventre, était pâle,
Pâle comme un vaincu qu'on prend pour le gibet,
Et, soumis comme un chien, jamais ne regimbait,
Car ce maraud de forge aux énormes épaules
Lui disait de vieux mots et des choses si drôles,
Que cela l'empoignait au front, comme cela!

«Or, tu sais bien, Monsieur, nous chantions tra la la
Et nous piquions les bœufs vers les sillons des autres:
Le Chanoine au soleil filait des patenôtres
Sur des chapelets clairs grenés de pièces d'or.
Le Seigneur, à cheval, passait, sonnant du cor,
Et l'un avec la hart, l'autre avec la cravache
Nous fouaillaient. – Hébétés comme des yeux de vache,
Nos yeux ne pleuraient plus; nous allions, nous allions,
Et quand nous avions mis le pays en sillons,
Quand nous avions laissé dans cette terre noire
Un peu de notre chair ... nous avions un pourboire:

was there, swirling all round and trailing its soiled coat across the
gilded panelling. But the dear king, upright on his belly, was pale,
pale as the victim you lead to the gallows; and cowed, like a dog,
made no resistance; for that huge-shouldered rascal from the forge
was telling him old-fashioned things; and such strange ones, it had
him by the short hair, just like that!

'Now, Sire, as you yourself know, we would sing tralala, and
drive the oxen in other people's furrows. Sitting in the sun, the
Canon would pour out Paternosters on limpid rosaries strung
with coins of gold. The Lord of the Manor would pass by on horse-
back, blowing his horn; and the one with the noose, and the other
with the riding-whip, lashed us on: bewildered, like cows' eyes,
our eyes no longer shed tears; we went on and on; and when we'd
ploughed the whole countryside, and left in the black soil some of
our own flesh ... we had our small reward: they set fire to our

On nous faisait flamber nos taudis dans la nuit;
Nos petits y faisaient un gâteau fort bien cuit.

... «Oh! je ne me plains pas. Je te dis mes bêtises,
C'est entre nous. J'admets que tu me contredises.
Or, n'est-ce pas joyeux de voir, au mois de juin,
Dans les granges entrer des voitures de foin
Énormes? De sentir l'odeur de ce qui pousse,
Des vergers quand il pleut un peu, de l'herbe rousse?
De voir des blés, des blés, des épis pleins de grain,
De penser que cela prépare bien du pain? ...
Oh! plus fort, on irait, au fourneau qui s'allume,
Chanter joyeusement en martelant l'enclume,
Si l'on était certain de pouvoir prendre un peu,
Étant homme, à la fin! de ce que donne Dieu!
– Mais voilà, c'est toujours la même vieille histoire! ...

«Mais je sais, maintenant! Moi, je ne peux plus croire,
Quand j'ai deux bonnes mains, mon front et mon marteau,
Qu'un homme vienne là, dague sur le manteau,
Et me dise: Mon gars, ensemence ma terre;

hovels in the middle of the night; our children made very well-done cakes inside.

... 'Oh, I'm not complaining. I'm just telling you my silly tales. It's between ourselves. I grant you may contradict me. But isn't it merry to see the big hay wagons in June coming into the barns? To smell the smell of things growing; or orchards when it rains a little, of hayfields? To see wheat, and still more wheat, with ears full of corn; to think that it promises plenty of bread? Ah! A man would go the more happily to the bright forge, to sing and ding at the anvil, if he were sure he'd be able to take a little – being, after all's said and done, a man! – of what God gives. But there you are, it's still the same old story! ...

'Only, now I know! I can't believe, any more, when I've two strong hands, a head between my shoulders, and my hammer, that a man who wears a dagger on his tunic can come up to me and say:

Que l'on arrive encor, quand ce serait la guerre,
Me prendre mon garçon comme cela, chez moi!
– Moi, je serais un homme, et toi, tu serais roi,
Tu me dirais: Je veux! ... – Tu vois bien, c'est stupide.
Tu crois que j'aime voir ta baraque splendide,
Tes officiers dorés, tes mille chenapans,
Tes palsembleu bâtards tournant comme des paons:
Ils ont rempli ton nid de l'odeur de nos filles
Et de petits billets pour nous mettre aux Bastilles,
Et nous dirons: C'est bien: les pauvres à genoux!
Nous dorerons ton Louvre en donnant nos gros sous!
Et tu te soûleras, tu feras belle fête,
– Et ces Messieurs riront, les reins sur notre tête!

«Non. Ces saletés-là datent de nos papas!
Oh! Le Peuple n'est plus une putain. Trois pas
Et tous, nous avons mis ta Bastille en poussière.
Cette bête suait du sang à chaque pierre

Go and sow my land, fellow; or that another can come, when there's a war, and take my own son away, just like that, in my own house! – Now suppose I were a man, and you were the king; you'd say to me: I require it! ... You can see, it's absurd. You imagine it gives me pleasure to see your splendid barn, your gilded officers, your thousand knaves, and your By-The-Grace-of-God bastards parading like peacocks: they have filled your nest with the perfume of our daughters, and with little warrants to put us all in Bastilles – and we're supposed to say: Very well: on your knees, the poor! We'll gild your Louvre with our pennies! And you'll get drunk and have a fine time: – and these gentlemen will laugh as they sit on our heads!

'No. That rubbish belongs to the time of our fathers! Oh, the People is no longer a whore! Three steps, and we razed all your Bastille to rubble. That beast sweated blood from every stone, the

Et c'était dégoûtant, la Bastille debout
Avec ses murs lépreux qui nous racontaient tout
Et, toujours, nous tenaient enfermés dans leur ombre!
– Citoyen! citoyen! c'était le passé sombre
Qui croulait, qui râlait, quand nous prîmes la tour!
Nous avions quelque chose au cœur comme l'amour.
Nous avions embrassé nos fils sur nos poitrines.
Et, comme des chevaux, en soufflant des narines
Nous allions, fiers et forts, et ça nous battait là ...
Nous marchions au soleil, front haut, – comme cela –
Dans Paris! On venait devant nos vestes sales.
Enfin! Nous nous sentions Hommes! Nous étions pâles,
Sire, nous étions soûls de terribles espoirs:
Et quand nous fûmes là, devant les donjons noirs,
Agitant nos clairons et nos feuilles de chêne,
Les piques à la main; nous n'eûmes pas de haine,
– Nous nous sentions si forts, nous voulions être doux!

. . . .

Bastille was an abomination while it stood, with its leprous walls
that told us the whole story, and yet still kept us within their
shadow! – Citizen! citizen! that was the murky past, which
crumbled and gave its death-rattle when we stormed the tower!
We had something in our hearts like being in love. We had kissed
our sons and held them to our breasts. And like horses, snorting
from the nostrils, we went forward, proud and strong, with *that*
beating in here ... We marched full in the sun, heads held high –
like this! – into Paris! They greeted us in our soiled clothes. At last!
We felt ourselves Men! We were pale, Sire, we were drunk with
terrifying hopes: and when we were there, in front of the black
dungeons, waving our bugles and our oakleaves, with pikes in our
fists – we had no hatred in us: we felt so strong that we wanted to
be gentle! ...

«Et depuis ce jour-là, nous sommes comme fous!
Le tas des ouvriers a monté dans la rue,
Et ces maudits s'en vont, foule toujours accrue
De sombres revenants, aux portes des richards.
Moi, je cours avec eux assommer les mouchards:
Et je vais dans Paris, noir, marteau sur l'épaule,
Farouche, à chaque coin balayant quèlque drôle,
Et, si tu me riais au nez, je te tuerais!
– Puis, tu peux y compter, tu te feras des frais
Avec tes hommes noirs, qui prennent nos requêtes
Pour se les renvoyer comme sur des raquettes
Et, tout bas, les malins! se disent: «Qu'ils sont sots!»
Pour mitonner des lois, coller de petits pots
Pleins de jolis décrets roses et de droguailles,
S'amuser à couper proprement quelques tailles,
Puis se boucher le nez quand nous marchons près d'eux,
– Nos doux représentants qui nous trouvent crasseux! –
Pour ne rien redouter, rien, que les baïonnettes ...

'And since that day, we have been like men possessed! The army of workers has risen in the street, and these accursed ones are off in a crowd always swelling with dark figures to haunt the doors of the rich. I go along with them to lay out the informers; I scour Paris, black-faced, hammer on shoulder, savage, sweeping something queer out of every corner, and if you were to laugh in my face I'd kill you! Well, you can count on this: it's going to cost you a lot: with your men in black who take our petitions only to bat them to and fro among themselves like tennis balls, and softly (the cunning ones!) say to each other: "How stupid they are!" – so that they may fake up laws, and stick little bills all over the place, full of pretty pink ordinances and sugar-coated pills; so that they may amuse themselves by shortening a few statures – and then hold their noses when we walk near them – our kind representatives who find us filthy! – and so that they may fear nothing, nothing whatever, except bayonets ... Very well! we've had

C'est très bien. Foin de leur tabatière à sornettes!
Nous en avons assez, là, de ces cerveaux plats
Et de ces ventres-dieux. Ah! ce sont là les plats
Que tu nous sers, bourgeois, quand nous sommes féroces,
Quand nous brisons déjà les sceptres et les crosses! ...»

. . . .

Il le prend par le bras, arrache le velours
Des rideaux, et lui montre en bas les larges cours
Où fourmille, où fourmille, où se lève la foule,
La foule épouvantable avec des bruits de houle,
Hurlant comme une chienne, hurlant comme une mer,
Avec ses bâtons forts et ses piques de fer,
Ses tambours, ses grands cris de halles et de bouges,
Tas sombre de haillons saignant de bonnets rouges:
L'Homme, par la fenêtre ouverte, montre tout
Au roi pâle et suant qui chancelle debout,
Malade à regarder cela!
     «C'est la Crapule,
Sire. Ça bave aux murs, ça monte, ça pullule:

enough of their pocketfuls of chaff! We've had enough, here, of
these flat-heads and god-bellies! Ah, that's the sort of dish you
offer us, you bourgeois, when we rage! when we are already break-
ing sceptres and croziers!'

. . . .

He takes him by the arm, tears back the velvet curtains, and
shows him the great courtyards below where the mob seethes and
seethes, and rises – the terrible mob with its sound of the tempest,
snarling like a bitch, yelling like a sea, with its stout sticks and iron
pikes, and its drums and its clamour of markets and slums; a dark
mass of rags flecked with blood-red caps: the Man, through the
open window, shows all this to the pale and sweating King, who
reels on his feet, sick at the sight!
 'That, Sire, is the Scum! It licks round the walls, it rises, it

– Puisqu'ils ne mangent pas, Sire, ce sont des gueux!
Je suis un forgeron: ma femme est avec eux,
Folle! Elle croit trouver du pain aux Tuileries!
– On ne veut pas de nous dans les boulangeries.
J'ai trois petits. Je suis crapule. – Je connais
Des vieilles qui s'en vont pleurant sous leurs bonnets
Parce qu'on leur a pris leur garçon ou leur fille:
C'est la crapule. – Un homme était à la Bastille,
Un autre était forçat: et tous deux, citoyens
Honnêtes. Libérés, ils sont comme des chiens:
On les insulte! Alors, ils ont là quelque chose
Qui leur fait mal, allez! C'est terrible, et c'est cause
Que se sentant brisés, que, se sentant damnés,
Ils sont là, maintenant, hurlant sous votre nez!
Crapule. – Là-dedans sont des filles, infâmes
Parce que, – vous saviez que c'est faible, les femmes –,
Messeigneurs de la cour, – que ça veut toujours bien –.
Vous [leur] avez craché sur l'âme, comme rien!
Vos belles, aujourd'hui, sont là. C'est la crapule.

. . . .

seethes: – because they don't eat, Sire, they're beggars! I am a blacksmith: my wife is with them, madwoman! She thinks she's going to find bread in the Tuileries! They don't want anything to do with us in the bakeries! I've got three little ones. I'm scum. – I know old women who go about weeping under their caps because someone has taken away their son or daughter: they're scum! – One man was in the Bastille, another was in the galleys, and both of them honest citizens. Let loose, they're like dogs: people insult them! So they have something here that hurts them, understand! It is terrible! And because of this, feeling themselves broken, feeling themselves accursed, they are there now, yelling under your nose! Scum. – Down there there are girls who are infamous because – you knew women were weak and complaisant, Gentlemen of the Court – you have spat on their souls as if it were nothing! And now your pretty ones are down there. They're scum.

. . . .

«Oh! tous les Malheureux, tous ceux dont le dos brûle
Sous le soleil féroce, et qui vont, et qui vont,
Qui dans ce travail-là sentent crever leur front,
Chapeau bas, mes bourgeois! Oh! ceux-là, sont les
    Hommes.

Nous sommes Ouvriers, Sire! Ouvriers! Nous sommes
Pour les grands temps nouveaux où l'on voudra savoir,
Où l'Homme forgera du matin jusqu'au soir,
Chasseur des grands effets, chasseur des grandes causes,
Où, lentement vainqueur, il domptera les choses
Et montera sur Tout, comme sur un cheval!
Oh! splendides lueurs des forges! Plus de mal,
Plus! — Ce qu'on ne sait pas, c'est peut-être terrible:
Nous saurons! — Nos marteaux en main, passons au crible
Tout ce que nous savons: puis, Frères, en avant!
Nous faisons quelquefois ce grand rêve émouvant
De vivre simplement, ardemment, sans rien dire
De mauvais, travaillant sous l'auguste sourire
D'une femme qu'on aime avec un noble amour:
Et l'on travaillerait fièrement tout le jour,

   'Oh, all the unfortunate people whose backs burn under the
fierce sun, and who go on and on with their heads fit to burst with
exertion – hats off, bourgeois! – those are Men! We are labourers,
Sire, labourers! We are for the great new times to come, when men
will wish an end to ignorance; when Man will forge from morning
till night, seeking great effects and great causes; when, gradually
victorious, he will tame all things and ride horseback upon them!
Oh splendid glare of the forges! And no more evil: none! What is
not known yet – and it may be terrible – we shall know, then! Let
us, hammer in hand, sort out all we know: and then, Brothers, for-
ward! Sometimes we dream that grand and stirring dream of the
simple, ardent life, where you speak no evil, but work beneath the
august smile of the woman you love with a noble love; and you
work all day, proudly, and you answer the call of duty as a

Écoutant le devoir comme un clairon qui sonne!
Et l'on se sentirait très heureux; et personne,
Oh! personne, surtout, ne vous ferait ployer!
On aurait un fusil au-dessus du foyer ...

. . . .

«Oh! mais l'air est tout plein d'une odeur de bataille.
Que te disais-je donc? Je suis de la canaille!
Il reste des mouchards et des accapareurs.
Nous sommes libres, nous! nous avons des terreurs
Où nous nous sentons grands, oh! si grands! Tout à
     l'heure
Je parlais de devoir calme, d'une demeure ...
Regarde donc le ciel! – C'est trop petit pour nous,
Nous crèverions de chaud, nous serions à genoux!
Regarde donc le ciel! – Je rentre dans la foule,
Dans la grande canaille effroyable, qui roule,
Sire, tes vieux canons sur les sales pavés;
– Oh! quand nous serons morts, nous les aurons lavés!
– Et si, devant nos cris, devant notre vengeance,
Les pattes des vieux rois mordorés, sur la France

trumpet-call. And you are very happy; and no one – above all! – no
one makes you bow the knee! You have a gun over the fireplace ...

. . . .

'Oh, but the air is full of the odour of battle! What was I telling
you? I belong to the mob! There remain informers and sharks. But
we are free! We have terrible moments, when we feel great! oh,
so great! Just now I was talking of peaceful work, and a home ...
But look at the sky! – It's too small for us! If we feared dying of heat,
we'd stay on our knees! – Look at the sky! – I'll go back to the
crowd, back to the huge and terrible mob that is rolling your can-
non, Sire, across the dirty cobbles: – oh, when we are dead, we shall
have washed them! – And if, against our cries and against our ven-
geance, the claws of old bedizened kings urge on their regiments in

Poussent leurs régiments en habits de gala,
Eh bien, n'est-ce pas, vous tous? Merde à ces chiens-là!»

. . . .

— Il reprit son marteau sur l'épaule.
                                        La foule
Près de cet homme-là se sentait l'âme soûle,
Et, dans la grande cour, dans les appartements,
Où Paris haletait avec des hurlements,
Un frisson secoua l'immense populace.
Alors, de sa main large et superbe de crasse,
Bien que le roi ventru suât, le Forgeron,
Terrible, lui jeta le bonnet rouge au front!

SOLEIL ET CHAIR

I

LE Soleil, le foyer de tendresse et de vie,
Verse l'amour brûlant à la terre ravie,
Et, quand on est couché sur la vallée, on sent

full dress uniforms across France — well, isn't it so, you lot? — Shit
to those dogs!'

. . . .

— He shouldered his hammer again. The crowd, with that man
near it, feels drunk to its soul, and in the great courtyard, and all
through those rooms, where Paris panted and yelled, a shudder
shook the huge populace. Then, with his broad hand, gilded with
dirt, although the potbellied king sweated, the Blacksmith, terrify-
ing, shoved the red cap on his head!

Sun and Flesh

I

THE Sun, the hearth of affection and life, pours burning love on
the delighted earth, and when you lie down in the valley you can

Que la terre est nubile et déborde de sang;
Que son immense sein, soulevé par une âme,
Est d'amour comme Dieu, de chair comme la femme,
Et qu'il renferme, gros de sève et de rayons,
Le grand fourmillement de tous les embryons!

Et tout croît, et tout monte!

                    – Ô Vénus, ô Déesse!

Je regrette les temps de l'antique jeunesse,
Des satyres lascifs, des faunes animaux,
Dieux qui mordaient d'amour l'écorce des rameaux
Et dans les nénufars baisaient la Nymphe blonde!
Je regrette les temps où la sève du monde,
L'eau du fleuve, le sang rose des arbres verts
Dans les veines de Pan mettaient un univers!
Où le sol palpitait, vert, sous ses pieds de chèvre;
Où, baisant mollement le clair syrinx, sa lèvre
Modulait sous le ciel le grand hymne d'amour;
Où, debout sur la plaine, il entendait autour
Répondre à son appel la Nature vivante;

smell how the earth is nubile and very full-blooded; how its huge breast, heaved up by a soul, is, like God, made of love, and, like woman, of flesh; and that it contains, big with sap and with sunlight, the vast pullulation of all embryos!

And everything grows, and everything rises!

– O Venus, O Goddess!

I long for the days of antique youth, of lascivious satyrs, and animal fauns, gods who bit, mad with love, the bark of the boughs, and among water-lilies kissed the Nymph with fair hair!

I long for the time when the sap of the world, river water, the rose-coloured blood of green trees, put into the veins of Pan a whole universe! When the earth trembled, green, beneath his goat-feet; when, softly kissing the fair Syrinx, his lips formed under heaven the great hymn of love; when, standing on the plain, he heard round about him living Nature answer his call; when the

Où les arbres muets, berçant l'oiseau qui chante,
La terre berçant l'homme, et tout l'Océan bleu
Et tous les animaux aimaient, aimaient en Dieu!

Je regrette les temps de la grande Cybèle
Qu'on disait parcourir, gigantesquement belle,
Sur un grand char d'airain, les splendides cités;
Son double sein versait dans les immensités
Le pur ruissellement de la vie infinie.
L'Homme suçait, heureux, sa mamelle bénie,
Comme un petit enfant, jouant sur ses genoux.
– Parce qu'il était fort, l'Homme était chaste et doux.

Misère! Maintenant il dit: Je sais les choses,
Et va, les yeux fermés et les oreilles closes.
– Et pourtant, plus de dieux! plus de dieux! l'Homme est
      Roi,
L'Homme est Dieu! Mais l'Amour, voilà la grande Foi!
Oh! si l'homme puisait encore à ta mamelle,
Grande mère des dieux et des hommes, Cybèle;
S'il n'avait pas laissé l'immortelle Astarté

silent trees cradling the singing bird, earth cradling mankind, and
the whole blue Ocean, and all living creatures loved, loved in God!

I long for the time of great Cybele who was said to travel, gigan-
tically lovely, in a great bronze chariot, through splendid cities; her
twin breasts poured, through the vast deeps, the pure streams of
infinite life. Mankind sucked joyfully at her blessed nipple, like a
small child playing on her knees. – Because he was strong, Man was
gentle and chaste.

Misfortune! Now he says: I understand things; and goes about
with eyes shut and ears closed. – And again: No more gods! no
more gods! Man is King, Man is God! – But the great Faith is
Love! Oh if only man still drew sustenance from your nipple, great
mother of gods and of men, Cybele! If only he had not forsaken
immortal Astarte, who long ago, rising in the tremendous bright-

Qui jadis, émergeant dans l'immense clarté
Des flots bleus, fleur de chair que la vague parfume,
Montra son nombril rose où vint neiger l'écume,
Et fit chanter, Déesse aux grands yeux noirs vainqueurs,
Le rossignol aux bois et l'amour dans les cœurs!

II

Je crois en toi! je crois en toi! Divine mère,
Aphrodité marine! – Oh! la route est amère
Depuis que l'autre Dieu nous attelle à sa croix;
Chair, Marbre, Fleur, Vénus, c'est en toi que je crois!
– Oui, l'Homme est triste et laid, triste sous le ciel vaste,
Il a des vêtements, parce qu'il n'est plus chaste,
Parce qu'il a sali son fier buste de dieu,
Et qu'il a rabougri, comme une idole au feu,
Son corps Olympien aux servitudes sales!
Oui, même après la mort, dans les squelettes pâles
Il veut vivre, insultant la première beauté!
– Et l'Idole où tu mis tant de virginité,
Où tu divinisas notre argile, la Femme,

ness of blue waters – flower-flesh perfumed by the wave – showed her rosy navel, towards which the foam came snowing, and – being a goddess with great conquering black eyes – made the nightingale sing in the woods and love in men's hearts!

II

I believe! I believe in you! divine mother, sea-borne Aphrodite! – oh, the path is bitter, since the other God harnessed us to his cross! Flesh, marble, flower, Venus: in you I believe! – Yes: Man is sad and ugly; sad under the vast sky; he possesses clothes because he is no longer chaste, because he has defiled his proud, godlike head, and because he has bent, like an idol in the furnace, his Olympian form towards base slaveries! Yes: even after death, in the form of pale skeletons, he wishes to live and insult the original beauty! – And the Idol in whom you placed such maidenhood, Woman, in whom you rendered our clay divine, so that Man might

Afin que l'Homme pût éclairer sa pauvre âme
Et monter lentement, dans un immense amour,
De la prison terrestre à la beauté du jour,
La Femme ne sait plus même être courtisane!
— C'est une bonne farce! et le monde ricane
Au nom doux et sacré de la grande Vénus!

III

Si les temps revenaient, les temps qui sont venus!
— Car l'Homme a fini! l'Homme a joué tous les rôles!
Au grand jour, fatigué de briser des idoles
Il ressuscitera, libre de tous ses Dieux,
Et comme il est du ciel, il scrutera les cieux!
L'Idéal, la pensée invincible, éternelle,
Tout; le dieu qui vit, sous son argile charnelle,
Montera, montera, brûlera sous son front!
Et quand tu le verras sonder tout l'horizon,
Contempteur des vieux jougs, libre de toute crainte,
Tu viendras lui donner la Rédemption sainte!
— Splendide, radieuse, au sein des grandes mers

bring light into his poor soul, and slowly ascend, in unbounded love, from the earthly prison to the beauty of day — Woman no longer knows even how to be a courtesan! — It's a fine farce! and the world snickers at the sweet and sacred name of great Venus!

III

If only the times which have come and gone might come again! — For Man is finished! Man has played all the parts! In the broad daylight, wearied with breaking idols, he will revive, free of all his gods; and since he is of heaven, he will scan the heavens! The Ideal, that eternal, invincible thought, which is all — the living god within his fleshly clay — will rise, mount, burn beneath his brow! And when you see him plumbing the whole horizon, despising old yokes, and free from all fear, you will come and give him holy Redemption! Resplendent, radiant, from the bosom of the huge seas, you

Tu surgiras, jetant sur le vaste Univers
L'Amour infini dans son infini sourire!
Le Monde vibrera comme une immense lyre
Dans le frémissement d'un immense baiser!

– Le Monde a soif d'amour: tu viendras l'apaiser.
· ·

[Ô! L'Homme a relevé sa tête libre et fière!
Et le rayon soudain de la beauté première
Fait palpiter le dieu dans l'autel de la chair!
Heureux du bien présent, pâle du mal souffert,
L'Homme veut tout sonder, – et savoir! La Pensée,
La cavale longtemps, si longtemps oppressée,
S'élance de son front! Elle saura Pourquoi! …
Qu'elle bondisse libre, et l'Homme aura la Foi!
– Pourquoi l'azur muet et l'espace insondable?
Pourquoi les astres d'or fourmillant comme un sable?
Si l'on montait toujours, que verrait-on là-haut?
Un Pasteur mène-t-il cet immense troupeau
De mondes cheminant dans l'horreur de l'espace?

will rise up and give to the vast Universe infinite Love with its eternal smile! The World will vibrate like an immense lyre in the trembling of an infinite kiss!

– The World thirsts for love: you will come and slake its thirst.
· ·

(Oh! Man has raised his free, proud head! And the sudden blaze of primordial beauty makes the god quiver in the altar of the flesh! Happy in the present good, pale from the ill suffered, Man wishes to plumb all depths – and know all things! Thought, so long a jade, and for so long oppressed, springs from his forehead! She will know Why! Let her but gallop free, and Man will find Faith! – Why the blue silence, unfathomable space? Why the golden stars, teeming like sands? If one ascended forever, what would one see up there? Does a shepherd drive this enormous flock of worlds on a journey through this horror of space? And do all these worlds,

Et tous ces mondes-là, que l'éther vaste embrasse,
Vibrent-ils aux accents d'une éternelle voix?
– Et l'Homme, peut-il voir? peut-il dire: Je crois?
La voix de la pensée est-elle plus qu'un rêve?
Si, l'homme naît si tôt, si la vie est si brève,
D'où vient-il? Sombre-t-il dans l'Océan profond
Des germes, des Fœtus, des Embryons, au fond
De l'immense Creuset d'où la Mère-Nature
Le ressuscitera, vivante créature,
Pour aimer dans la rose, et croître dans les blés? ...

Nous ne pouvons savoir! – Nous sommes accablés
D'un manteau d'ignorance et d'étroites chimères!
Singes d'hommes tombés de la vulve des mères,
Notre pâle raison nous cache l'infini!
Nous voulons regarder: – le Doute nous punit!
Le doute, morne oiseau, nous frappe de son aile ...
– Et l'horizon s'enfuit d'une fuite éternelle! ...

. . . .

contained in the vast ether, tremble at the tones of an eternal voice?
– And Man, can he see? can he say: I believe? Is the language of
thought any more than a dream? If man is born so quickly, if life is
so short, whence does he come? Does he sink into the deep Ocean
of germs, of Foetuses, of Embryos, to the bottom of the huge
Crucible where Nature the Mother will resuscitate him, a living
creature, to love in the rose and to grow in the corn? ...

We cannot know! We are weighed down with a cloak of ignor-
ance, hemmed in by chimaeras! Men like apes, dropped from our
mothers' wombs, our feeble reason hides the infinite from us! We
wish to perceive: – and Doubt punishes us! Doubt, dismal bird,
beats us down with its wing ... and the horizon rushes away in end-
less flight! ...

. . . .

Le grand ciel est ouvert! les mystères sont morts
Devant l'Homme, debout, qui croise ses bras forts
Dans l'immense splendeur de la riche nature!
Il chante ... et le bois chante, et le fleuve murmure
Un chant plein de bonheur qui monte vers le jour! ...
– C'est la Rédemption! c'est l'amour! c'est l'amour! ...]

. . . .

IV

Ô splendeur de la chair! ô splendeur idéale!
Ô renouveau d'amour, aurore triomphale
Où, courbant à leurs pieds les Dieux et les Héros,
Kallipyge la blanche et le petit Éros
Effleureront, couverts de la neige des roses,
Les femmes et les fleurs sous leurs beaux pieds écloses!
– Ô grande Ariadné, qui jettes tes sanglots
Sur la rive, en voyant fuir là-bas sur les flots,
Blanche sous le soleil, la voile de Thésée,
Ô douce vierge enfant qu'une nuit a brisée,

The vast heaven is open! the mysteries lie dead before erect Man who folds his strong arms among the vast splendour of abundant Nature! He sings ... and the woods sing: the river murmurs a song full of happiness which rises towards the light! ... – It is Redemption! It is love! It is love! ...) [1]

. . . .

IV

O splendour of flesh! O ideal splendour! O renewal of love, triumphal dawn when, prostrating the Gods and the Heroes before their feet, white Callipyge and little Eros, covered with the snow of rose petals, will caress women and flowers beneath their lovely outstretched feet! – O great Ariadne who pour out your tears on the shore, as you see, out there on the waves, the sail of Theseus flying white under the sun; O sweet virgin child whom a night has

---

1. These thirty-six lines are omitted in Rimbaud's latest known MS.

Tais-toi! Sur son char d'or brodé de noirs raisins,
Lysios, promené dans les champs Phrygiens
Par les tigres lascifs et les panthères rousses,
Le long des fleuves bleus rougit les sombres mousses.
– Zeus, Taureau, sur son cou berce comme une enfant
Le corps nu d'Europé, qui jette son bras blanc
Au cou nerveux du Dieu frissonnant dans la vague ...
Il tourne lentement vers elle son œil vague;
Elle laisse traîner sa pâle joue en fleur
Au front de Zeus; ses yeux sont fermés; elle meurt
Dans un divin baiser, et le flot qui murmure
De son écume d'or fleurit sa chevelure.
– Entre le laurier-rose et le lotus jaseur
Glisse amoureusement le grand Cygne rêveur
Embrassant la Léda des blancheurs de son aile;
– Et tandis que Cypris passe, étrangement belle,
Et, cambrant les rondeurs splendides de ses reins,
Étale fièrement l'or de ses larges seins
Et son ventre neigeux brodé de mousse noire,
– Héraclès, le Dompteur, qui, comme d'une gloire,

broken, be silent! On his golden chariot studded with black grapes
Lysios, who has been drawn through Phrygian fields by lascivious
tigers and russet panthers, reddens the dark mosses along the blue
rivers. – Zeus, the Bull, cradles on his neck like a child the nude body
of Europa who throws her white arm round the God's muscular
neck which shivers in the wave ... Slowly he turns his dreamy eye
towards her; she droops her pale flowerlike cheek on the brow of
Zeus; her eyes are closed; she is dying in a divine kiss; and the mur-
muring waters strew the flowers of their golden foam on her hair. –
Between the oleander and the gaudy lotus tree slips amorously the
great dreaming Swan, enfolding Leda in the whiteness of his wing;
– And while Cypris goes by, strangely beautiful, and, arching the
marvellous curves of her back, proudly displays the golden vision
of her big breasts and snowy belly embroidered with black moss –
Hercules, Tamer of beasts, in his strength, robes his huge

Fort, ceint son vaste corps de la peau du lion,
S'avance, front terrible et doux, à l'horizon!

Par la lune d'été vaguement éclairée,
Debout, nue, et rêvant dans sa pâleur dorée
Que tache le flot lourd de ses longs cheveux bleus,
Dans la clairière sombre où la mousse s'étoile,
La Dryade regarde au ciel silencieux ...
– La blanche Séléné laisse flotter son voile,
Craintive, sur les pieds du bel Endymion,
Et lui jette un baiser dans un pâle rayon ...
– La Source pleure au loin dans une longue extase ...
C'est la nymphe qui rêve, un coude sur son vase,
Au beau jeune homme blanc que son onde a pressé.
– Une brise d'amour dans la nuit a passé,
Et, dans les bois sacrés, dans l'horreur des grands arbres,
Majestueusement debout, les sombres Marbres,
Les Dieux, au front desquels le Bouvreuil fait son nid,
– Les Dieux écoutent l'Homme et le Monde infini!

Mai 70

body with the lion's skin as with a glory, and faces the horizon, his
brow terrible and sweet!

Vaguely lit by the summer moon, erect, naked, dreaming in her
pallor of gold, streaked by the heavy wave of her long blue hair,
in the shadowy glade where stars spring in the moss, the Dryad
gazes up at the silent sky ... – White Selene, timidly, lets her veil
float over the feet of beautiful Endymion, and throws him a kiss in a
pale beam ... The Spring sobs far off in a long ecstasy ... It is the
nymph who dreams, with one elbow on her urn, of the handsome
white stripling her wave has pressed against. – A soft wind of love
has passed in the night, and in the sacred woods, amid the standing
hair of the great trees, erect in majesty, the shadowy Marbles, the
Gods on whose brows the Bullfinch has his nest – the Gods listen
to Men, and to the infinite World.

May 70

OPHÉLIE

I

Sur l'onde calme et noire où dorment les étoiles
La blanche Ophélia flotte comme un grand lys,
Flotte très lentement, couchée en ses longs voiles ...
– On entend dans les bois lointains des hallalis.

Voici plus de mille ans que la triste Ophélie
Passe, fantôme blanc, sur le long fleuve noir.
Voici plus de mille ans que sa douce folie
Murmure sa romance à la brise du soir.

Le vent baise ses seins et déploie en corolle
Ses grands voiles bercés mollement par les eaux;
Les saules frissonnants pleurent sur son épaule,
Sur son grand front rêveur s'inclinent les roseaux.

Les nénuphars froissés soupirent autour d'elle;
Elle éveille parfois, dans un aune qui dort,
Quelque nid, d'où s'échappe un petit frisson d'aile;
– Un chant mystérieux tombe des astres d'or.

Ophelia

I

On the calm black water where the stars are sleeping, white Ophelia floats like a great lily; floats very slowly, lying in her long veils ... – In the far-off woods you can hear them sound the mort.

For more than a thousand years sad Ophelia has passed, a white ghost, down the long black river. For more than a thousand years her sweet madness has murmured its ballad to the evening breeze.

The wind kisses her breasts and unfolds in a wreath her great veils rocked gently by the waters; the shivering willows weep on her shoulder, the rushes lean over her wide, dreaming brow.

The ruffled water-lilies are sighing about her; at times she rouses, in a slumbering alder, some nest from which escapes the small rustle of wings; – A mysterious anthem falls from the golden stars.

II

Ô pâle Ophélia! belle comme la neige!
Oui, tu mourus, enfant, par un fleuve emporté!
— C'est que les vents tombant des grands monts de
    Norwège
T'avaient parlé tout bas de l'âpre liberté;

C'est qu'un souffle, tordant ta grande chevelure,
À ton esprit rêveur portait d'étranges bruits;
Que ton cœur écoutait le chant de la Nature
Dans les plaintes de l'arbre et les soupirs des nuits;

C'est que la voix des mers folles, immense râle,
Brisait ton sein d'enfant, trop humain et trop doux;
C'est qu'un matin d'avril, un beau cavalier pâle,
Un pauvre fou, s'assit muet à tes genoux!

Ciel! Amour! Liberté! Quel rêve, ô pauvre Folle!
Tu te fondais à lui comme une neige au feu;
Tes grandes visions étranglaient ta parole
— Et l'Infini terrible effara ton œil bleu!

II

O pale Ophelia! beautiful as snow! Yes, child, you died, carried off by a river! — It was the winds falling from the great mountains of Norway that spoke to you in low voices of bitter freedom;

It was a breath of wind, that, twisting your great tresses, brought strange rumours to your dreaming mind; it was your heart, listening to the song of Nature, in the groans of the trees and the sighs of the nights;

It was the voice of mad seas, the great roar, that shattered your child's heart, too human, too soft; it was the fair pale nobleman, one morning in April, the poor madman who sat dumb at your knees!

Heaven! Love! Freedom! What a dream, oh poor crazed Girl! You melted to him as snow does to a fire; your marvellous visions choked your words — and fearful Infinity dazzled your blue eye!

III

— Et le Poëte dit qu'aux rayons des étoiles
Tu viens chercher, la nuit, les fleurs que tu cueillis,
Et qu'il a vu sur l'eau, couchée en ses longs voiles,
La blanche Ophélia flotter, comme un grand lys.

BAL DES PENDUS

Au gibet noir, manchot aimable,
Dansent, dansent les paladins,
Les maigres paladins du diable,
Les squelettes de Saladins.

Messire Belzébuth tire par la cravate
Ses petits pantins noirs grimaçant sur le ciel,
Et, leur claquant au front un revers de savate,
Les fait danser, danser aux sons d'un vieux Noël!

III

— And the Poet says that by starlight you come seeking, in the
night, the flowers that you gathered; and that he has seen on the
water, lying in her long veils, white Ophelia floating, like a great
lily.

Dance of the Hanged Men

On the black gallows, one-armed friend, the paladins are dancing,
dancing; the lean, the devil's, paladins; the skeletons of Saladins.

Sir Beelzebub pulls by the scruff his little black puppets who grin
at the sky, and with a backhander in the head like a kick, makes
them dance, dance, to an old carol-tune!

Et les pantins choqués enlacent leurs bras grêles:
Comme des orgues noirs, les poitrines à jour
Que serraient autrefois les gentes damoiselles,
Se heurtent longuement dans un hideux amour.

Hurrah! les gais danseurs, qui n'avez plus de panse!
On peut cabrioler, les tréteaux sont si longs!
Hop! qu'on ne sache plus si c'est bataille ou danse!
Belzébuth enragé racle ses violons!

Ô durs talons, jamais on n'use sa sandale!
Presque tous ont quitté la chemise de peau;
Le reste est peu gênant et se voit sans scandale.
Sur les crânes, la neige applique un blanc chapeau:

Le corbeau fait panache à ces têtes fêlées,
Un morceau de chair tremble à leur maigre menton:
On dirait, tournoyant dans les sombres mêlées,
Des preux, raides, heurtant armures de carton.

And the puppets, shaken about, entwine their thin arms; their breasts pierced with light, like black organ-pipes – which once gentle ladies pressed to their own – jostle together protractedly in hideous love-making.

Hurray! the gay dancers, you whose bellies are gone! You can cut capers on such a long stage! Hop! never mind whether it's fighting or dancing! – Beelzebub, maddened, saws on his fiddles!

Oh the hard heels! no one's pumps are wearing out! And nearly all have taken off their shirts of skin; the rest is not embarrassing and can be seen without shame. On each skull the snow places a white hat:

the crow acts as a plume for these cracked brains; a scrap of flesh clings to each lean chin: you would say, to see them turning in their dark combats, they were stiff knights clashing pasteboard armour.

Hurrah! la bise siffle au grand bal des squelettes!
Le gibet noir mugit comme un orgue de fer!
Les loups vont répondant des forêts violettes:
À l'horizon, le ciel est d'un rouge d'enfer ...

Holà, secouez-moi ces capitans funèbres
Qui défilent, sournois, de leurs gros doigts cassés
Un chapelet d'amour sur leurs pâles vertèbres:
Ce n'est pas un moustier ici, les trépassés!

Oh! voilà qu'au milieu de la danse macabre
Bondit dans le ciel rouge un grand squelette fou
Emporté par l'élan, comme un cheval se cabre:
Et, se sentant encor la corde raide au cou,

Crispe ses petits doigts sur son fémur qui craque
Avec des cris pareils à des ricanements,
Et, comme un baladin rentre dans la baraque,
Rebondit dans le bal au chant des ossements.

Hurrah! the wind whistles at the skeletons' grand ball! The black
gallows moans like an organ of iron! The wolves howl back from
the violet forests: and on the horizon the sky is hell-red ...

Ho there, shake up those funereal braggarts, craftily telling
with their great broken fingers the beads of their loves on their pale
vertebrae: hey! the departed! this is no monastery here!

Oh but see how from the middle of this Dance of Death springs
into the red sky a great skeleton, mad, carried away by his own
impetus, like a rearing horse: and, feeling the rope tight again
round his neck,

clenches his knuckles on his thighbone with a crack, uttering
cries like mocking laughter, and then like a mountebank into his
booth, skips back into the dance to the music of the bones!

Au gibet noir, manchot aimable,
Dansent, dansent les paladins,
Les maigres paladins du diable,
Les squelettes de Saladins.

LE CHÂTIMENT DE TARTUFE

TISONNANT, tisonnant son cœur amoureux sous
Sa chaste robe noire, heureux, la main gantée,
Un jour qu'il s'en allait, effroyablement doux,
Jaune, bavant la foi de sa bouche édentée,

Un jour qu'il s'en allait, «Oremus», – un Méchant
Le prit rudement par son oreille benoîte
Et lui jeta des mots affreux, en arrachant
Sa chaste robe noire autour de sa peau moite.

Châtiment! ... Ses habits étaient déboutonnés,
Et le long chapelet des péchés pardonnés
S'égrenant dans son cœur, Saint Tartufe était pâle! ..

On the black gallows, one-armed friend, the paladins are dancing, dancing; the lean, the devil's, paladins; the skeletons of Saladins.

Tartufe's Punishment

RAKING, raking, his amorous thoughts underneath his chaste robe of black, happy, his hand gloved, one day as he went along, fearsomely sweet, yellow, dribbling piety from his toothless mouth,

One day as he went along, 'Let us Pray', – a Wicked One seized him roughly by his saintly ear and snapped frightful words at him, tearing off the chaste robe of black wrapped about his moist skin.

Punishment! – His clothes were unbuttoned; and, the long chaplet of pardoned sins being told in his heart, St Tartufe was so pale! ...

86

Donc, il se confessait, priait, avec un râle!
L'homme se contenta d'emporter ses rabats ...
– Peuh! Tartufe était nu du haut jusques en bas!

VÉNUS ANADYOMÈNE

COMME d'un cercueil vert en fer blanc, une tête
De femme à cheveux bruns fortement pommadés
D'une vieille baignoire émerge, lente et bête,
Avec des déficits assez mal ravaudés;

Puis le col gras et gris, les larges omoplates
Qui saillent; le dos court qui rentre et qui ressort;
Puis les rondeurs des reins semblent prendre l'essor;
La graisse sous la peau paraît en feuilles plates;

L'échine est un peu rouge; et le tout sent un goût
Horrible étrangement; on remarque surtout
Des singularités qu'il faut voir à la loupe ...

So he confessed and prayed, with a death rattle! The man
contented himself with carrying off his clerical bands ... – Faugh!
Tartufe was naked from his top to his toe!

Venus Anadyomene

As from a green zinc coffin, a woman's head with brown hair
heavily pomaded rises out of an old bath, slowly and stupidly, with
its bald patches pretty clumsily hidden;

then the fat greyish neck, and the broad and protuberant
shoulder-blades; the short back with its hollows and bulges; then
the curves of the buttocks seem to soar; the lard beneath the skin
appears as flat flakes;

the spine's rather red; and the whole thing has a smell which is
strangely disgusting; one notices especially oddities which should
be studied with a lens ...

Les reins portent deux mots gravés: CLARA VENUS;
— Et tout ce corps remue et tend sa large croupe
Belle hideusement d'un ulcère à l'anus.

LES RÉPARTIES DE NINA

. . . .

LUI: Ta poitrine sur ma poitrine,
   Hein? nous irions,
  Ayant de l'air plein la narine,
   Aux frais rayons

  Du bon matin bleu, qui vous baigne
   Du vin de jour? ...
  Quand tout le bois frissonnant saigne
   Muet d'amour

  De chaque branche, gouttes vertes,
   Des bourgeons clairs,
  On sent dans les choses ouvertes
   Frémir des chairs:

The buttocks bear two engraved words: CLARA VENUS; and this whole body moves and then sticks out its broad rump – hideously bejewelled with an anal ulcer.

Nina's Replies

. . . .

HE: Your breast on my breast, eh? we could go, with our nostrils full of air, into the cool light

 of the blue good morning that bathes you in the wine of daylight? ... When the whole shivering wood bleeds, dumb with love,

 from every branch green drops, pale buds, you can feel in things unclosing the quivering flesh:

Tu plongerais dans la luzerne
  Ton blanc peignoir,
Rosant à l'air ce bleu qui cerne
  Ton grand œil noir,

Amoureuse de la campagne,
  Semant partout,
Comme une mousse de champagne,
  Ton rire fou:

Riant à moi, brutal d'ivrèsse,
  Qui te prendrais
Comme cela, – la belle tresse,
  Oh! – qui boirais

Ton goût de framboise et de fraise,
  Ô chair de fleur!
Riant au vent vif qui te baise
  Comme un voleur,

Au rose églantier qui t'embête
  Aimablement:
Riant surtout, ô folle tête,
  À ton amant! ...

you would bury in the lucerne your white gown, changing to
rose-colour in the fresh air the blue tint which encircles your great
black eyes,
  in love with the country, scattering everywhere, like champagne
bubbles, your crazy laughter:
  laughing at me, suddenly, drunkenly – I should catch you like
this – lovely hair, ah! – I should drink in
  your taste of raspberry and strawberry, oh flower-flesh! Laugh-
ing at the fresh wind kissing you like a thief,
  at the wild rose teasing you pleasantly: laughing more than
anything, oh madcap, at your lover! ...

[Dix-sept ans! Tu seras heureuse!
        Oh! les grands prés,
La grande campagne amoureuse!
        – Dis, viens plus près! ...]

– Ta poitrine sur ma poitrine,
        Mêlant nos voix,
Lents, nous gagnerions la ravine,
        Puis les grands bois! ...

Puis, comme une petite morte,
        Le cœur pâmé,
Tu me dirais que je te porte,
        L'œil mi-fermé ...

Je te porterais, palpitante,
        Dans le sentier:
L'oiseau filerait son andante:
        Au Noisetier ...

Je te parlerais dans ta bouche;
        J'irais, pressant
Ton corps, comme une enfant qu'on couche,
        Ivre du sang

(Seventeen! You'll be so happy! Oh the big meadows! the wide
loving countryside! – Listen, come closer! ...)

Your breast on my breast, mingling our voices, slowly we'd
reach the stream; then the great woods! ...

Then, like a little ghost, your heart fainting, you'd tell me to
carry you, your eyes half closed ...

I'd carry your quivering body along the path: the bird would
spin out his andante: *Hard by the hazel tree* ...

I'd speak into your mouth; and go on, pressing your body like a
little girl's I was putting to bed, drunk with the blood

Qui coule, bleu, sous ta peau blanche
    Aux tons rosés:
Et te parlant la langue franche ...
    Tiens! ... – que tu sais ...

Nos grands bois sentiraient la sève,
    Et le soleil
Sablerait d'or fin leur grand rêve
    Vert et vermeil.

. . . .

Le soir? ... Nous reprendrons la route
    Blanche qui court,
Flânant, comme un troupeau qui broute,
    Tout à l'entour. ...

Les bons vergers à l'herbe bleue,
    Aux pommiers tors!
Comme on les sent toute une lieue
    Leurs parfums forts!

Nous regagnerons le village
    Au ciel mi-noir;
Et ça sentira le laitage
    Dans l'air du soir;

that runs blue under your white skin with its tints of rose: and
speaking to you in that frank tongue ... There! ... that you under-
stand. ...

Our great woods would smell of sap, and the sunlight would
dust with fine gold their great green and bronze dream.

. . . .

In the evening? ... We'd take the white road which meanders,
like a grazing herd, all over the place ...

Oh the pleasant orchards with blue grass and twisted apple trees!
How you can smell a whole league off their strong perfume!

We'd get back to the village when the sky was half dark; and
there'd be a smell of milking in the evening air;

Ça sentira l'étable, pleine
De fumiers chauds,
Pleine d'un lent rhythme d'haleine,
Et de grands dos

Blanchissant sous quelque lumière;
Et, tout là-bas,
Une vache fientera, fière,
À chaque pas ...

– Les lunettes de la grand'mère
Et son nez long
Dans son missel; le pot de bière
Cerclé de plomb,

Moussant entre les larges pipes
Qui crânement,
Fument: les effroyables lippes
Qui, tout fumant,

Happent le jambon aux fourchettes
Tant, tant et plus:
Le feu qui claire les couchettes
Et les bahuts.

it would smell of the cowshed full of warm manure, filled with
the slow rhythm of breathing, and with great backs
    gleaming under some light or other; and right down at the far
end there'd be a cow dunging proudly at every step ...
    – Grandmother's spectacles and her long nose deep in her missal;
the jug of beer circled with pewter
    foaming among the big-bowled pipes gallantly smoking: and
the frightful blubber lips which, still puffing,
    snatch ham from forks: so much, and more: the fire lighting up
the bunks and the cupboards.

Les fesses luisantes et grasses
    Du gros enfant
Qui fourre, à genoux, dans les tasses,
    Son museau blanc

Frôlé par un mufle qui gronde
    D'un ton gentil,
Et pourlèche la face ronde
    Du cher petit ...

[Noire, rogue au bord de sa chaise,
    Affreux profil,
Une vieille devant la braise
    Qui fait du fil;]

Que de choses verrons-nous, chère,
    Dans ces taudis,
Quand la flamme illumine, claire,
    Les carreaux gris! ...

– Puis, petite et toute nichée
    Dans les lilas
Noirs et frais: la vitre cachée,
    Qui rit là-bas ...

The shining fat buttocks of the fat baby on his hands and knees
who nuzzles into the cups; his white snout
    tickled by a gently growling muzzle that licks all over the round
face of the little darling ...
    (Black and haughty on her chair's edge, a terrifying profile, an
old woman in front of the embers, spinning)
    What sights we shall see, dearest, in those hovels, when the
bright fire lights up the grey window panes! ...
    – And then, small and nestling right inside the cool dark lilacs:
the hidden window smiling in there ...

Tu viendras, tu viendras, je t'aime!
   Ce sera beau.
Tu viendras, n'est-ce pas? et même ...

ELLE: — *Et mon bureau?*

[*15 août 1870*]

À LA MUSIQUE

Place de la Gare, à Charleville

SUR la place taillée en mesquines pelouses,
Square où tout est correct, les arbres et les fleurs,
Tous les bourgeois poussifs qu'étranglent les chaleurs
Portent, les jeudis soirs, leurs bêtises jalouses.

— L'orchestre militaire, au milieu du jardin,
Balance ses schakos dans la *Valse des fifres:*
— Autour, aux premiers rangs, parade le gandin;
Le notaire pend à ses breloques à chiffres.

You'll come! you will come! I love you so! It will be lovely. You
will come, won't you? and even ...
SHE: – *And what about my office?*

[*August 15 1870*]

Scene Set to Music

Place de la Gare, Charleville

ON the square which is chopped into mean little plots of grass,
the square where all is just so, both the trees and the flowers, all
the wheezy townsfolk whom the heat chokes bring, each Thursday
evening, their envious silliness.

The military band, in the middle of the gardens, swing their
shakos in the *Waltz of the Fifes*: round about, near the front rows,
the town dandy struts, the notary, hanging like a charm from his
own watch chain.

Des rentiers à lorgnons soulignent tous les couacs:
Les gros bureaux bouffis traînent leurs grosses dames
Auprès desquelles vont, officieux cornacs,
Celles dont les volants ont des airs de réclames;

Sur les bancs verts, des clubs d'épiciers retraités
Qui tisonnent le sable avec leur canne à pomme,
Fort sérieusement discutent les traités,
Puis prisent en argent, et reprennent: «En somme! ...»

Épatant sur son banc les rondeurs de ses reins,
Un bourgeois à boutons clairs, bedaine flamande,
Savoure son onnaing d'où le tabac par brins
Déborde – vous savez, c'est de la contrebande; –

Le long des gazons verts ricanent les voyous;
Et, rendus amoureux par le chant des trombones,
Très naïfs, et fumant des roses, les pioupious
Caressent les bébés pour enjôler les bonnes ...

Private incomes in pince-nez point out all the false notes: great counting-house desks, bloated, drag their stout spouses – close by whom, like bustling elephant keepers, walk females whose flounces remind you of sales.

On the green benches, retired grocers' clubs, poking the sand with their knobbed walking canes, gravely discuss trade agreements and then take snuff from silver boxes, and resume: 'In short! ...'

Spreading over his bench all the fat of his rump, a pale-buttoned burgher, a Flemish corporation, savours his Onnaing, whence shreds of tobacco hang loose – You realize, it's smuggled, of course ...

Along the grass borders yobs laugh in derision; and, melting to love at the sound of trombones, very simple, and sucking at roses, the little foot-soldiers fondle the babies to get round their nurses...

– Moi, je suis, débraillé comme un étudiant,
Sous les marronniers verts les alertes fillettes:
Elles le savent bien; et tournent en riant,
Vers moi, leurs yeux tout pleins de choses indiscrètes.

Je ne dis pas un mot: je regarde toujours
La chair de leurs cous blancs brodés de mèches folles:
Je suis, sous le corsage et les frêles atours,
Le dos divin après la courbe des épaules.

J'ai bientôt déniché la bottine, le bas ...
– Je reconstruis les corps, brûlé de belles fièvres.
Elles me trouvent drôle et se parlent tout bas ...
– Et mes désirs brutaux s'accrochent à leurs lèvres ...

LES EFFARÉS

Noirs dans la neige et dans la brume,
Au grand soupirail qui s'allume,
Leurs culs en rond,

As for me, I follow, dishevelled like a student, under the green chestnuts, the lively young girls – which they know very well, and they turn to me, laughing, eyes which are full of indiscreet things.

I don't say a word: I just keep on looking at the skin of their white necks embroidered with stray locks: I go hunting, beneath bodices and thin attire, the divine back below the curve of the shoulders.

Soon I've discovered the boot and the stocking ... – I re-create their bodies, burning with fine fevers. They find me absurd, and talk together in low voices ... – And my savage desires fasten on to their lips ...

The Transfixed

BLACK in the snow and fog, at the great lighted airshaft, their bums rounded,

À genoux, cinq petits – misère! –
Regardent le Boulanger faire
    Le lourd pain blond.

Ils voient le fort bras blanc qui tourne
La pâte grise et qui l'enfourne
    Dans un trou clair.

Ils écoutent le bon pain cuire.
Le Boulanger au gras sourire
    Grogne un vieil air.

Ils sont blottis, pas un ne bouge,
Au souffle du soupirail rouge
    Chaud comme un sein.

Quand pour quelque médianoche,
Façonné comme une brioche
    On sort le pain,

Quand, sous les poutres enfumées,
Chantent les croûtes parfumées,
    Et les grillons,

on their knees, five little ones – what anguish! – watch the baker
making the heavy white bread.

They see the strong white arm that shapes the grey dough and
sets it to bake in a bright hole.

They listen to the good bread cooking. The Baker with his fat
smile hums an old tune.

They are huddled together, not one of them moves, in the waft
of air from the red vent, warm as a breast.

And when, for some midnight breakfast, plaited like a brioche,
the bread is taken out;

when, under the smoky beams, the fragrant crusts hiss, and
the crickets sing;

97

Que ce trou chaud souffle la vie,
Ils ont leur âme si ravie
    Sous leurs haillons,

Ils se ressentent si bien vivre,
Les pauvres Jésus pleins de givre,
    Qu'ils sont là tous,

Collant leurs petits museaux roses
Au treillage, grognant des choses
    Entre les trous,

Tout bêtes, faisant leurs prières
Et repliés vers ces lumières
    Du ciel rouvert,

Si fort, qu'ils crèvent leur culotte
Et que leur chemise tremblote
    Au vent d'hiver.

[*20 sept. 70*]

how this warm hole breathes life! Their souls are so ravished
under their rags,
    they feel life so strong in them, poor frozen Jesuses, that they
all stay,
    sticking their little pink snouts against the wire netting, grunting
things through the holes,
    quite stupid, saying their prayers, and bending down towards
those lights of opened heaven
    so hard, they split their trousers, and their shirt tails flutter in the
winter wind.

[*20 September 70*]

ROMAN

I

On n'est pas sérieux, quand on a dix-sept ans.
– Un beau soir, foin des bocks et de la limonade,
Des cafés tapageurs aux lustres éclatants!
– On va sous les tilleuls verts de la promenade.

Les tilleuls sentent bon dans les bons soirs de juin!
L'air est parfois si doux, qu'on ferme la paupière;
Le vent chargé de bruits, – la ville n'est pas loin, –
A des parfums de vigne et des parfums de bière ...

II

– Voilà qu'on aperçoit un tout petit chiffon
D'azur sombre, encadré d'une petite branche,
Piqué d'une mauvaise étoile, qui se fond
Avec de doux frissons, petite et toute blanche ...

Romance

I

When you are seventeen you aren't really serious. – One fine evening, you've had enough of beer and lemonade! – and the rowdy cafés with their dazzling lights! – You go walking beneath the green lime trees of the promenade.

The lime trees smell good on fine evenings in June! The air is so soft sometimes, you close your eyelids; the wind, full of sounds – the town's not far away – carries odours of vines, and odours of beer ...

II

– Then you see a very tiny rag of dark blue, framed by a small branch, pierced by an unlucky star which is melting away with soft little shivers, small, perfectly white ...

Nuit de juin! Dix-sept ans! – On se laisse griser.
La sève est du champagne et vous monte à la tête ...
On divague; on se sent aux lèvres un baiser
Qui palpite là, comme une petite bête ...

III

Le cœur fou Robinsonne à travers les romans,
– Lorsque, dans la clarté d'un pâle réverbère,
Passe une demoiselle aux petits airs charmants,
Sous l'ombre du faux-col effrayant de son père ...

Et, comme elle vous trouve immensément naïf
Tout en faisant trotter ses petites bottines,
Elle se tourne, alerte et d'un mouvement vif ...
– Sur vos lèvres alors meurent les cavatines ...

IV

Vous êtes amoureux. Loué jusqu'au mois d'août.
Vous êtes amoureux. – Vos sonnets La font rire.
Tous vos amis s'en vont, vous êtes mauvais goût.
– Puis l'adorée, un soir, a daigné vous écrire! ...

June night! Seventeen! – You let yourself get drunk. The sap
is champagne and goes straight to your head ... You are wan-
dering; you feel a kiss on your lips which quivers there like some-
thing small and alive ...

III

Your mad heart goes Crusoeing through all the romances – when,
under the light of a pale street lamp passes a young girl with charm-
ing little airs, in the shadow of her father's terrifying stiff collar ...
   And because you strike her as absurdly naïf, as she trots along in
her little ankle boots, she turns, wide awake, with a brisk move-
ment ... And then *cavatinas* die on your lips ...

IV

You're in love. Taken until the month of August. You're in love. –
Your sonnets make Her laugh, all your friends disappear, you are
not quite the thing. – Then your adored one, one evening, conde-
scends to write to you! ...

– Ce soir-là, ... – vous rentrez aux cafés éclatants,
Vous demandez des bocks ou de la limonade ...
– On n'est pas sérieux, quand on a dix-sept ans
Et qu'on a des tilleuls verts sur la promenade.

23 septembre 70

«... Français de soixante-dix,
bonapartistes, républicains, souve-
nez-vous de vos pères en 92, etc.»

PAUL DE CASSAGNAC (*Le Pays*)

Morts de Quatre-vingt-douze et de Quatre-vingt-
treize,
Qui, pâles du baiser fort de la liberté,
Calmes, sous vos sabots, brisiez le joug qui pèse
Sur l'âme et sur le front de toute humanité;

Hommes extasiés et grands dans la tourmente,
Vous dont les cœurs sautaient d'amour sous les haillons,
Ô soldats que la Mort a semés, noble Amante,
Pour les régénérer, dans tous les vieux sillons;

That evening ... – you go back again to the dazzling cafés, you
ask for beer, or for lemonade ... You are not really serious when
you are seventeen, and there are lime trees in leaf on the pro-
menade.

23 September 70

'... *Frenchmen of '70! Bona-
partists! Republicans! Remember your
forefathers of '92 ...*', etc.

PAUL DE CASSAGNAC (*Le Pays*)

Dead men of '92 and of '93, who, pale from the hard kiss of free-
dom and calm, trampled under your clogs the yoke which weighs
on the soul and the brow of all humanity;
    men exalted and grown great in tempest, you whose hearts leapt
with love under your rags, O soldiers whom Death, noble Mistress,
has sown in all the old furrows, so that they may be regenerated;

Vous dont le sang lavait toute grandeur salie,
Morts de Valmy, Morts de Fleurus, Morts d'Italie,
Ô million de Christs aux yeux sombres et doux;

Nous vous laissions dormir avec la République,
Nous, courbés sous les rois comme sous une trique.
– Messieurs de Cassagnac nous reparlent de vous!

Fait à Maζas, 3 septembre 1870

LE MAL

Tandis que les crachats rouges de la mitraille
Sifflent tout le jour par l'infini du ciel bleu;
Qu'écarlates ou verts, près du Roi qui les raille,
Croulent les bataillons en masse dans le feu;

Tandis qu'une folie épouvantable broie
Et fait de cent milliers d'hommes un tas fumant;
– Pauvres morts! dans l'été, dans l'herbe, dans ta joie,
Nature! ô toi qui fis ces hommes saintement! ...

you whose blood washed clean every defiled greatness, dead men of Valmy, of Fleurus, of Italy, O million Christs with your soft dark eyes;

we were leaving you to sleep alongside the Republic; we, cowering under monarchs as if under cudgels. – Messrs de Cassagnac are talking to us about you again!

Done at Maζas, 3 September 1870

Evil

While the red gobs of spit of the grape-shot whistle all day through the infinitude of blue sky; while scarlet or green, close by the King who jeers at them, whole battalions fall crumbling into the fire;

while a terrible madness grinds down and makes of a hundred thousand men a smoking heap; – Poor dead men! – O Nature! in summer, in the grass, in your joy, you who fashioned these men in holiness! ...

– Il est un Dieu, qui rit aux nappes damassées
Des autels, à l'encens, aux grands calices d'or;
Qui dans le bercement des hosannah s'endort,

Et se réveille, quand des mères, ramassées
Dans l'angoisse, et pleurant sous leur vieux bonnet noir,
Lui donnent un gros sou lié dans leur mouchoir!

RAGES DES CÉSARS

L'HOMME pâle, le long des pelouses fleuries,
Chemine, en habit noir, et le cigare aux dents:
L'Homme pâle repense aux fleurs des Tuileries
– Et parfois son œil terne a des regards ardents ...

– All this while, there is a God who laughs at damask altar-
cloths and incense, and at the great golden chalices; who dozes to
the lullaby of Hosannas,
    and who wakes up when mothers, drawn together in suffering,
and weeping under their old black bonnets, give him the penny
which they have tied up in their handkerchiefs!

Paroxysms of Caesars

THE pale Man[1] trudges along by the flowery lawns dressed in
mourning, a cigar between his teeth: the pale Man recalls the flowers
of the Tuileries – and sometimes his lustreless eye becomes keen ...

---

1. This is Napoleon III in 1870, ill and in prison at Wilhelms-
hoehe, Prussia. The 'Accomplice' is Émile Ollivier, Minister at the
outbreak of the Franco-Prussian war. Ollivier did not oppose
Napoleon's III's declaration of war in 1870.

Car l'Empereur est soûl de ses vingt ans d'orgie!
Il s'était dit: «Je vais souffler la Liberté
Bien délicatement, ainsi qu'une bougie!»
La Liberté revit! Il se sent éreinté!

Il est pris. – Oh! quel nom sur ses lèvres muettes
Tressaille? Quel regret implacable le mord?
On ne le saura pas. L'Empereur a l'œil mort.

Il repense peut-être au Compère en lunettes ...
– Et regarde filer de son cigare en feu,
Comme aux soirs de Saint-Cloud, un fin nuage bleu.

RÊVÉ POUR L'HIVER

A ... Elle

L'HIVER, nous irons dans un petit wagon rose
　　　Avec des coussins bleus.
Nous serons bien. Un nid de baisers fous repose
　　　Dans chaque coin moelleux.

For the Emperor is drunk with his twenty years' orgy! He said to himself: 'I shall blow Liberty out very neatly, as if it were a candle!' Liberty lives again! His back feels broken!

He has been taken prisoner. Ah! what name trembles on his silent lips? What relentless remorse does he feel? We shall never know. The Emperor's eye is dead.

He is thinking, perhaps, of his old Accomplice in spectacles ... – And watching, rising from his burning cigar, as he used to on evenings in St Cloud, a thin wreath of smoke.

A Dream for Winter

To ... Her

IN the winter we shall travel in a little pink railway carriage with blue cushions. We shall be comfortable. A nest of mad kisses lies in wait in each soft corner.

Tu fermeras l'œil, pour ne point voir, par la glace,
　　　　Grimacer les ombres des soirs,
Ces monstruosités hargneuses, populace
　　　　De démons noirs et de loups noirs.

Puis tu te sentiras la joue égratignée ...
Un petit baiser, comme une folle araignée,
　　　　Te courra par le cou ...

Et tu me diras: «Cherche!» en inclinant la tête,
—Et nous prendrons du temps à trouver cette bête
　　　　– Qui voyage beaucoup ...
　　　　　　　　　En wagon, le 7 octobre 70

LE DORMEUR DU VAL

C'EST un trou de verdure où chante une rivière
Accrochant follement aux herbes des haillons
D'argent; où le soleil, de la montagne fière,
Luit: c'est un petit val qui mousse de rayons.

You will close your eyes, so as not to see, through the glass, the evening shadows pulling faces, those snarling monsters, a population of black devils and black wolves.

Then you'll feel something tickle your cheek ... A little kiss like a crazy spider will run round your neck ...

And you'll say to me 'Find it!' bending your head – And we'll take a long time to find that creature – which is a great traveller. ..
　　　　　　　　In a railway carriage, 7 October 70

The Sleeper in the Valley

IT is a green hollow where a stream gurgles, crazily catching silver rags of itself on the grasses; where the sun shines from the proud mountain: it is a little valley bubbling over with light.

Un soldat jeune, bouche ouverte, tête nue,
Et la nuque baignant dans le frais cresson bleu,
Dort; il est étendu dans l'herbe, sous la nue,
Pâle dans son lit vert où la lumière pleut.

Les pieds dans les glaïeuls, il dort. Souriant comme
Sourirait un enfant malade, il fait un somme:
Nature, berce-le chaudement: il a froid.

Les parfums ne font pas frissonner sa narine;
Il dort dans le soleil, la main sur sa poitrine
Tranquille. Il a deux trous rouges au côté droit.

Octobre 70

AU CABARET-VERT

Cinq heures du soir

DEPUIS huit jours, j'avais déchiré mes bottines
Aux cailloux des chemins. J'entrais à Charleroi.
– Au Cabaret-Vert: je demandai des tartines
De beurre et du jambon qui fût à moitié froid.

A young soldier, open-mouthed, bare-headed, with the nape of
his neck bathed in cool blue cresses, sleeps; he is stretched out on
the grass, under the sky, pale on his green bed where the light falls
like rain.

His feet in the yellow flags, he lies sleeping. Smiling as a sick
child might smile, he is having a nap. Cradle him warmly, Nature;
he is cold.

No odour makes his nostril quiver; he sleeps in the sun, his hand
on his breast, at peace. There are two red holes in his right side.

October 70

At the Green Inn
Five in the evening

FOR a whole week I had ripped up my boots on the stones of the
roads. I walked into Charleroi. – Into the Green Inn: I asked for
some slices of bread and butter, and some half-cooled ham.

Bienheureux, j'allongeai les jambes sous la table
Verte: je contemplai les sujets très naïfs
De la tapisserie. – Et ce fut adorable,
Quand la fille aux tétons énormes, aux yeux vifs,

– Celle-là, ce n'est pas un baiser qui l'épeure! –
Rieuse, m'apporta des tartines de beurre,
Du jambon tiède, dans un plat colorié,

Du jambon rose et blanc parfumé d'une gousse
D'ail, – et m'emplit la chope immense, avec sa mousse
Que dorait un rayon de soleil arriéré.

Octobre 70

LA MALINE

Dans la salle à manger brune, que parfumait
Une odeur de vernis et de fruits, à mon aise
Je ramassais un plat de je ne sais quel met
Belge, et je m'épatais dans mon immense chaise.

Happy, I stuck out my legs under the green table: I studied the artless patterns of the wallpaper – and it was charming when the girl with the huge breasts and lively eyes,
– a kiss wouldn't scare that one! – smilingly brought me some bread and butter and lukewarm ham, on a coloured plate; –
pink and white ham, scented with a clove of garlic – and filled my huge beer mug, whose froth was turned into gold by a ray of late sunshine.

October 70

The Sly One

In the brown dining-room, which was perfumed with the scent of polish and fruit, I was shovelling up at my ease a plateful of some Belgian dish or other, and sprawling in my enormous chair.

En mangeant, j'écoutais l'horloge, – heureux et coi.
La cuisine s'ouvrit avec une bouffée,
– Et la servante vint, je ne sais pas pourquoi,
Fichu moitié défait, malinement coiffée.

Et, tout en promenant son petit doigt tremblant
Sur sa joue, un velours de pêche rose et blanc,
En faisant, de sa lèvre enfantine, une moue,

Elle arrangeait les plats, près de moi, pour m'aiser;
– Puis, comme ça, – bien sûr, pour avoir un baiser, –
Tout bas: «Sens donc: j'ai pris *une* froid sur la joue …»
Charleroi, octobre 70

While I ate, I listened, happy and silent, to the clock. The kitchen door opened with a gust, and the servant girl came in, I don't know what for, neckerchief loose, hair dressed impishly.

And, passing her little finger tremblingly across her cheek, a pink and white peach-bloom, pouting with her childish mouth,

she tidied the plates standing close to me, to make me feel comfortable; – and then, just like that, – to get a kiss of course – said **very** softly: 'Feel, then, I' got a cold in the cheek …'
Charleroi, October 70

L'ÉCLATANTE VICTOIRE DE SARREBRÜCK

remportée aux cris de Vive l' Empereur!

(Gravure belge brillamment coloriée,
se vend à Charleroi, 35 centimes)

Au milieu, l'Empereur, dans une apothéose
Bleue et jaune, s'en va, raide, sur son dada
Flamboyant; très heureux, – car il voit tout en rose,
Féroce comme Zeus et doux comme un papa;

En bas, les bons Pioupious qui faisaient la sieste
Près des tambours dorés et des rouges canons,
Se lèvent gentiment. Pitou remet sa veste,
Et, tourné vers le Chef, s'étourdit de grands noms!

À droite, Dumanet, appuyé sur la crosse
De son chassepot, sent frémir sa nuque en brosse,
Et: «Vive l'Empereur!!» – Son voisin reste coi ...

The Famous Victory of Sarrebrück
won to shouts of Long Live the Emperor!

(Belgian print, brilliantly coloured,
on sale at Charleroi, 35 centimes)

In the centre the Emperor, in a blue and yellow apotheosis, gallops
away sitting stiff on his flamboyant gee-gee; very happy – because
he sees everything rose-tinted – fierce as Zeus, and kind as Papa;

below, the good little infantrymen who were having a nap by the
gilded drums and vermilion cannon, get up politely. Pitou puts his
tunic back on, and, facing the C. in C., drowns his sorrows in
thoughts of great names!

On the right Dumanet, leaning on the stock of his Chassepot
rifle, feels the hair rising on the back of his neck and shouts 'Long
Live the Emperor!' His neighbour stays silent ...

Un schako surgit, comme un soleil noir ... – Au centre,
Boquillon rouge et bleu, très naïf, sur son ventre
Se dresse, et, – présentant ses derrières –: «De quoi? ...»

Octobre 70

LE BUFFET

C'EST un large buffet sculpté; le chêne sombre,
Très vieux, a pris cet air si bon des vieilles gens;
Le buffet est ouvert, et verse dans son ombre
Comme un flot de vin vieux, des parfums engageants;

Tout plein, c'est un fouillis de vieilles vieilleries,
De linges odorants et jaunes, de chiffons
De femmes ou d'enfants, de dentelles flétries,
De fichus de grand'mère où sont peints des griffons;

–C'est là qu'on trouverait les médaillons, les mèches
De cheveux blancs ou blonds, les portraits, les fleurs
    sèches
Dont le parfum se mêle à des parfums de fruits.

A shako rises up, like a black sun ... In the middle, Boquillon,
red and blue, very simple-minded, lying on his stomach, gets up
and – presenting his posterior – asks: 'What on? ...'

October 70

The Cupboard

IT's a broad carved wooden cupboard; the ancient dark-coloured
oak has taken on that pleasant air that old people have; the cup-
board is open, and gives off from its kindly shadows inviting
aromas like a breath of old wine;

full to overflowing, it's a jumble of quaint old things: fragrant
yellowed linen, rags of women's or children's clothes, faded laces,
grandmothers' kerchiefs embroidered with griffins;

– here you could find lockets, and locks of white or blonde hair,
portraits and dried flowers whose smell mingles with the smell of
fruit.

— Ô buffet du vieux temps, tu sais bien des histoires,
Et tu voudrais conter tes contes, et tu bruis
Quand s'ouvrent lentement tes grandes portes noires.

Octobre 70

MA BOHÈME

(*Fantaisie*)

JE m'en allais, les poings dans mes poches crevées;
Mon paletot aussi devenait idéal;
J'allais sous le ciel, Muse! et j'étais ton féal;
Oh! là là! que d'amours splendides j'ai rêvées!

Mon unique culotte avait un large trou.
— Petit Poucet rêveur, j'égrenais dans ma course
Des rimes. Mon auberge était à la Grande-Ourse.
— Mes étoiles au ciel avaient un doux frou-frou.

Et je les écoutais, assis au bord des routes,
Ces bons soirs de septembre où je sentais des gouttes
De rosée à mon front, comme un vin de vigueur;

— O cupboard of olden times, you know plenty of stories; and you'd like to tell them; and you clear your throat every time your great dark doors slowly open.

October 70

My Bohemian Existence

(*A Fantasy*)

I WENT off with my hands in my torn coat pockets; my overcoat too was becoming ideal; I travelled beneath the sky, Muse! and I was your vassal; oh dear me! what marvellous loves I dreamed of!

My only pair of breeches had a big hole in them. — Stargazing Tom Thumb, I sowed rhymes along the way. My tavern was at the Sign of the Great Bear. — My stars in the sky rustled softly.

And I listened to them, sitting on the road-sides on those pleasant September evenings while I felt drops of dew on my forehead like vigorous wine;

Où, rimant au milieu des ombres fantastiques,
Comme des lyres, je tirais les élastiques
De mes souliers blessés, un pied près de mon cœur!

TÊTE DE FAUNE

DANS la feuillée, écrin vert taché d'or,
Dans la feuillée incertaine et fleurie
De fleurs splendides où le baiser dort,
Vif et crevant l'exquise broderie,

Un faune effaré montre ses deux yeux
Et mord les fleurs rouges de ses dents blanches.
Brunie et sanglante ainsi qu'un vin vieux,
Sa lèvre éclate en rires sous les branches.

Et quand il a fui – tel qu'un écureuil –
Son rire tremble encore à chaque feuille,
Et l'on voit épeuré par un bouvreuil
Le Baiser d'or du Bois, qui se recueille.

1871

and while, rhyming among the fantastical shadows, I plucked
like the strings of a lyre the elastics of my tattered boots, one foot
close to my heart!

Faun's Head

AMONG the foliage, green casket flecked with gold; in the uncer-
tain foliage that blossoms with gorgeous flowers where sleeps the
kiss, vivid, and bursting through the sumptuous tapestry,
a startled faun shows his two eyes and bites the crimson flowers
with his white teeth. Stained and ensanguined like mellow wine, his
mouth bursts out in laughter beneath the branches.
And when he has fled – like a squirrel – his laughter still vibrates
on every leaf, and you can see, startled by a bullfinch, the Golden
Kiss of the Wood, gathering itself together again.

1871

LES ASSIS

Noirs de loupes, grêlés, les yeux cerclés de bagues
Vertes, leurs doigts boulus crispés à leurs fémurs,
Le sinciput plaqué de hargnosités vagues
Comme les floraisons lépreuses des vieux murs;

Ils ont greffé dans des amours épileptiques
Leur fantasque ossature aux grands squelettes noirs
De leurs chaises; leurs pieds aux barreaux rachitiques
S'entrelacent pour les matins et pour les soirs!

Ces vieillards ont toujours fait tresse avec leurs sièges,
Sentant les soleils vifs percaliser leur peau,
Ou, les yeux à la vitre où se fanent les neiges,
Tremblant du tremblement douloureux du crapaud.

Et les Sièges leur ont des bontés: culottée
De brun, la paille cède aux angles de leurs reins;
L'âme des vieux soleils s'allume emmaillottée
Dans ces tresses d'épis où fermentaient les grains.

Those Who Sit

Dark with knobbed growths, peppered with pock-marks like
hail, their eyes ringed with green, their swollen fingers clenched on
their thigh-bones, their skulls caked with indeterminate crusts like
the leprous growths on old walls;

in amorous seizures they have grafted their weird bone struc-
tures to the great dark skeletons of their chairs; their feet are en-
twined, morning and evening, on the rickety rails!

These old men have always been one flesh with their seats, feel-
ing bright suns drying their skins to the texture of calico, or else,
looking at the window-panes where the snow is turning grey,
shivering with the painful shiver of the toad.

And their Seats are kind to them; coloured brown with age, the
straw yields to the angularities of their buttocks; the spirit of an-
cient suns lights up, bound in these braids of ears in which the corn
fermented.

Et les Assis, genoux aux dents, verts pianistes,
Les dix doigts sous leur siège aux rumeurs de tambour,
S'écoutent clapoter des barcarolles tristes,
Et leurs caboches vont dans des roulis d'amour.

– Oh! ne les faites pas lever! C'est le naufrage …
Ils surgissent, grondant comme des chats giflés,
Ouvrant lentement leurs omoplates, ô rage!
Tout leur pantalon bouffe à leurs reins boursouflés.

Et vous les écoutez, cognant leurs têtes chauves
Aux murs sombres, plaquant et plaquant leurs pieds tors,
Et leurs boutons d'habit sont des prunelles fauves
Qui vous accrochent l'œil du fond des corridors!

Puis ils ont une main invisible qui tue:
Au retour, leur regard filtre ce venin noir
Qui charge l'œil souffrant de la chienne battue,
Et vous suez, pris dans un atroce entonnoir.

And the Seated Ones, knees drawn up to their teeth, green
pianists whose ten fingers keep drumming under their seats, listen
to the tapping of each other's melancholy barcarolles; and their
heads nod back and forth as in the act of love.

– Oh don't make them get up! It's a catastrophe! They rear up
growling like tom-cats when struck, slowly spreading their shoul-
ders … What rage! Their trousers puff out at their swelling back-
sides.

And you listen to them as they bump their bald heads against the
dark walls, stamping and stamping with their crooked feet; and
their coat-buttons are the eyes of wild beasts which fix yours from
the end of the corridors!

And then they have an invisible weapon which can kill: return-
ing, their eyes seep the black poison with which the beaten bitch's
eye is charged, and you sweat, trapped in a horrible funnel.

Rassis, les poings noyés dans des manchettes sales,
Ils songent à ceux-là qui les ont fait lever
Et, de l'aurore au soir, des grappes d'amygdales
Sous leurs mentons chétifs s'agitent à crever.

Quand l'austère sommeil a baissé leurs visières,
Ils rêvent sur leur bras de sièges fécondés,
De vrais petits amours de chaises en lisière
Par lesquelles de fiers bureaux seront bordés.

Des fleurs d'encre crachant des pollens en virgule
Les bercent, le long des calices accroupis
Tels qu'au fil des glaïeuls le vol des libellules
– Et leur membre s'agace à des barbes d'épis.

LES DOUANIERS

Ceux qui disent: Cré Nom, ceux qui disent: Macache,
Soldats, marins, débris d'Empire, retraités,
Sont nuls, très nuls, devant les Soldats des Traités
Qui tailladent l'azur frontière à grands coups d'hache.

Reseated, their fists retreating into soiled cuffs, they think about those who have made them get up and, from dawn until dusk, their tonsils in bunches tremble under their meagre chins, fit to burst.

When austere slumbers have lowered their lids they dream on their arms of seats become fertile; of perfect little loves of openwork chairs surrounding dignified desks.

Flowers of ink dropping pollen like commas lull them asleep in their rows of squat flower-cups like dragonflies threading their flight along the flags – and their *membra virilia* are aroused by barbed ears of wheat.

The Customs Men

Those who say Gord Struth; those who say Swelp Me – pensioned soldiers and sailors, the wreckage of Empire – are nothing, nothing at all, compared with the Warriors of Excise who slash the blue frontiers with their great axe-blows.

Pipe aux dents, lame en main, profonds, pas embêtés,
Quand l'ombre bave aux bois comme un mufle de vache,
Ils s'en vont, amenant leurs dogues à l'attache,
Exercer nuitamment leurs terribles gaîtés!

Ils signalent aux lois modernes les faunesses.
Ils empoignent les Fausts et les Diavolos.
«Pas de ça, les anciens! Déposez les ballots!»

Quand sa sérénité s'approche des jeunesses,
Le Douanier se tient aux appas contrôlés!
Enfer aux Délinquants que sa paume a frôlés!

ORAISON DU SOIR

Je vis assis, tel qu'un ange aux mains d'un barbier,
Empoignant une chope à fortes cannelures,
L'hypogastre et le col cambrés, une Gambier
Aux dents, sous l'air gonflé d'impalpables voilures.

Pipes in their teeth, blades in their hands, deep, unruffled, when
darkness noses at the woods like a cow's muzzle, off they go, lead-
ing their dogs, to hold their nocturnal and terrible revels!

They report the bacchantes to the laws of today. They clap hands
on the shoulders of Fausts and of Devils: 'Now then, none of that,
you old-fashioned creatures! Put those bundles down!'

And, when his serene highness accosts the young, the Customs
Man holds fast to all contraband charms! The Inferno for Offenders
whom his hand has frisked!

Evening Prayer

I spend my life sitting – like an angel in the hands of a barber – a
deeply fluted beer mug in my fist, belly and neck curved, a Gambier
pipe in my teeth, under the air swelling with impalpable veils of
smoke.

Tels que les excréments chauds d'un vieux colombier,
Mille Rêves en moi font de douces brûlures:
Puis par instants mon cœur triste est comme un aubier
Qu'ensanglante l'or jeune et sombre des coulures.

Puis, quand j'ai ravalé mes Rêves avec soin,
Je me tourne, ayant bu trente ou quarante chopes,
Et me recueille, pour lâcher l'âcre besoin:

Doux comme le Seigneur du cèdre et des hysopes,
Je pisse vers les cieux bruns, très haut et très loin,
Avec l'assentiment des grands héliotropes.

CHANT DE GUERRE PARISIEN

> LE printemps est évident, car
> Du cœur des Propriétés vertes,
> Le vol de Thiers et de Picard
> Tient ses splendeurs grandes ouvertes!

Like the warm excrements in an old dovecote, a thousand dreams burn softly inside me, and at times my sad heart is like sap-wood bled on by the dark yellow gold of its sweats.

Then, when I have carefully swallowed my dreams, I turn, having drunk thirty or forty tankards, and gather myself together to relieve bitter need:

as sweetly as the Saviour of Hyssops and of Cedar I piss towards dark skies, very high and very far; and receive the approval of the great heliotropes.

Parisian War Song

SPRING is evidently here; for the ascent of Thiers and Picard from the green Estates lays its splendours wide open!

117

Ô Mai! Quels délirants culs nus!
Sèvres, Meudon, Bagneux, Asnières,
Écoutez donc les bienvenus
Semer les choses printanières!

Ils ont schako, sabre et tam-tam,
Non la vieille boîte à bougies;
Et des yoles qui n'ont jam ... jam ...
Fendent le lac aux eaux rougies!

Plus que jamais nous bambochons
Quand viennent sur nos fourmilières
Crouler les jaunes cabochons
Dans des aubes particulières:

Thiers et Picard sont des Éros,
Des enleveurs d'héliotropes,
Au pétrole ils font des Corots:
Voici hannetonner leurs tropes ...

Ils sont familiers du Grand Truc! ...
Et couché dans les glaïeuls, Favre
Fait son cillement aqueduc,
Et ses reniflements à poivre!

O May! What delirious bare bums! O Sèvres, Meudon, Bagneux,
Asnières, listen now to the welcome arrivals scattering springtime
joys!

They have shakos, and sabres, and tom-toms, and none of the old
candleboxes; and skiffs which have nev ... nev ... are cutting the
lake of bloodstained waters.

More than ever before, we roister, as on to our ant-heaps come
tumbling the yellow heads, on these extraordinary dawns:

Thiers and Picard are Cupids; and beheaders of sunflowers too;
they paint peaceful landscapes (Corots) with insecticide (paraffin):
look how their tropes de-cockchafer the trees ...

'They're familiars of the Great What's-his-name! ....' – And
Favre, lying among the irisis, blinks and weeps crocodile tears, and
sniffs his peppery sniff!

La Grand'ville a le pavé chaud
Malgré vos douches de pétrole,
Et décidément, il nous faut
Vous secouer dans votre rôle ...

Et les Ruraux qui se prélassent
Dans de longs accroupissements,
Entendront des rameaux qui cassent
Parmi les rouges froissements.

MES PETITES AMOUREUSES

Un hydrolat lacrymal lave
     Les cieux vert-chou:
Sous l'arbre tendronnier qui bave ...,
     Vos caoutchoucs

Blancs de lunes particulières
     Aux pialats ronds,
Entrechoquez vos genouillères
     Mes laiderons!

The Big City has hot cobblestones, in spite of your showers of paraffin; and decidedly we shall have to liven you up in your parts ...

And the Rustics who take their ease in long squattings will hear boughs breaking among the red rustlings.

My Little Mistresses

A TINCTURE of tears washes the cabbage-green skies: under the dripping tree with tender shoots ..., your waterproofs

whitened by peculiar moons with round staring eyes, knock your kneecaps together, my ugly ones!

Nous nous aimions à cette époque,
    Bleu laideron!
On mangeait des œufs à la coque
    Et du mouron!

Un soir, tu me sacras poëte,
    Blond laideron:
Descends ici, que je te fouette
    En mon giron;

J'ai dégueulé ta bandoline,
    Noir laideron;
Tu couperais ma mandoline
    Au fil du front.

Pouah! mes salives desséchées,
    Roux laideron;
Infectent encor les tranchées
    De ton sein rond!

Ô mes petites amoureuses,
    Que je vous hais!
Plaquez de fouffes douloureuses
    Vos tétons laids!

We loved each other in those days, blue ugly one! We used to eat boiled eggs and chickweed!

One evening you anointed me poet, blonde ugly one: come down here and let me smack you across my knee;

I have puked up your brilliantine, dark ugly one; you would stop the sound of my mandolin before it was out of my head.

Ugh! my dried spittle, red-headed ugly one, still infects the wrinkles of your round breast!

Oh my little mistresses, how I hate you! Plaster with painful blisters your ugly bosoms!

Piétinez mes vieilles terrines
    De sentiment;
– Hop donc! soyez-moi ballerines
    Pour un moment! ...

Vos omoplates se déboîtent,
    Ô mes amours!
Une étoile à vos reins qui boitent,
    Tournez vos tours.

Et c'est pourtant pour ces éclanches
    Que j'ai rimé!
Je voudrais vous casser les hanches
    D'avoir aimé!

Fade amas d'étoiles ratées,
    Comblez les coins!
– Vous crèverez en Dieu, bâtées
    D'ignobles soins!

Sous les lunes particulières
    Aux pialats ronds,
Entrechoquez vos genouillères,
    Mes laiderons!

Trample upon my little pots of feeling; – now then jump! be ballerinas for me, just for a moment! ...

Your shoulder-blades are out of joint, O my loves! with a star on your hobbling backs, turn in your turns.

And yet after all, it's for these shoulders of mutton that I've made rhymes! I'd like to break your hips for having loved!

Insipid heap of fallen stars, pile up in the corners! – You'll be extinguished in God, saddled with ignoble cares!

Under peculiar moons with round staring eyes, knock your kneecaps together, my ugly ones!

ACCROUPISSEMENTS

BIEN tard, quand il se sent l'estomac écœuré,
Le frère Milotus, un œil à la lucarne
D'où le soleil, clair comme un chaudron récuré,
Lui darde une migraine et fait son regard darne,
Déplace dans les draps son ventre de curé.

Il se démène sous sa couverture grise
Et descend, ses genoux à son ventre tremblant,
Effaré comme un vieux qui mangerait sa prise,
Car il lui faut, le poing à l'anse d'un pot blanc,
À ses reins largement retrousser sa chemise!

Or, il s'est accroupi, frileux, les doigts de pied
Repliés, grelottant au clair soleil qui plaque
Des jaunes de brioche aux vitres de papier;
Et le nez du bonhomme où s'allume la laque
Renifle aux rayons, tel qu'un charnel polypier.

. . . .

Squattings

VERY late, when he feels his stomach churn, Brother Milotus, one eye on the skylight whence the sun, bright as a scoured stewpan, darts a megrim at him and dizzies his sight, moves his priest's belly under the sheets.

He struggles beneath the grey blanket and gets out, his knees to his trembling belly, flustered like an old man who has swallowed a pinch of snuff, because he has to tuck up his nightshirt in armfuls round his waist with one hand grasping the handle of a white chamberpot!

Now he is squatting, chilly, his toes curled up, his teeth chattering in the bright sunshine which daubs the yellow of cake upon the paper panes; and the old fellow's nose, its crimson catching fire, snuffles in the rays like a polypary of flesh.

. . . .

Le bonhomme mijote au feu, bras tordus, lippe
Au ventre: il sent glisser ses cuisses dans le feu,
Et ses chausses roussir, et s'éteindre sa pipe;
Quelque chose comme un oiseau remue un peu
À son ventre serein comme un monceau de tripe!

Autour, dort un fouillis de meubles abrutis
Dans des haillons de crasse et sur de sales ventres;
Des escabeaux, crapauds étranges, sont blottis
Aux coins noirs: des buffets ont des gueules de chantres:
Qu'entr'ouvre un sommeil plein d'horribles appétits.

L'écœurante chaleur gorge la chambre étroite;
Le cerveau du bonhomme est bourré de chiffons:
Il écoute les poils pousser dans sa peau moite,
Et, parfois, en hoquets fort gravement bouffons
S'échappe, secouant son escabeau qui boite …

. . . .

Et le soir, aux rayons de lune, qui lui font
Aux contours du cul des bavures de lumière,
Une ombre avec détails s'accroupit, sur un fond
De neige rose, ainsi qu'une rose trémière …
Fantasque, un nez poursuit Vénus au ciel profond.

The old fellow simmers at the fire, his arms twisted, his blubber
lip on his belly: he feels his thighs slipping into the fire, and his
breeches scorching, and his pipe going out; something resembling a
bird stirs a little in his serene belly which is like a mountain of tripe!

Round about him sleeps a jumble of stunned furniture among
tatters of filth, lying on soiled bellies; stools cower like weird toads
in dark corners: cupboards have maws like choirmasters, yawning
with a sleepiness which is full of revolting appetites.

The sickening heat stuffs the narrow room; the old fellow's head
is crammed with rags: he listens to the hairs growing in his moist
skin, and sometimes, with deep and clownish hiccoughs, moves
away, shaking his rickety stool …

. . . .

And in the evening, in rays of moonlight which leaves dribbles
of light on the contours of his buttocks, a shadow with details
squats against a background of snow-coloured pink like a holly-
hock … Fantastic, a nose follows Venus in the deep sky.

LES POËTES DE SEPT ANS

À M. P. Demeny

Et la Mère, fermant le livre du devoir,
S'en allait satisfaite et très fière, sans voir,
Dans les yeux bleus et sous le front plein d'éminences
L'âme de son enfant livrée aux répugnances.

Tout le jour il suait d'obéissance; très
Intelligent; pourtant des tics noirs, quelques traits
Semblaient prouver en lui d'âcres hypocrisies!
Dans l'ombre des couloirs aux tentures moisies,
En passant il tirait la langue, les deux poings
À l'aine, et dans ses yeux fermés voyait des points.
Une porte s'ouvrait sur le soir: à la lampe
On le voyait, là-haut, qui râlait sur la rampe,
Sous un golfe de jour pendant du toit. L'été
Surtout, vaincu, stupide, il était entêté
À se renfermer dans la fraîcheur des latrines:
Il pensait là, tranquille et livrant ses narines.

The Seven-year-old Poets

To M. P. Demeny

And the Mother, closing the exercise book, went away satisfied and very proud, without seeing in the blue eyes, under the forehead full of 'bumps', the soul of her child given over to loathings.

All day long he sweated with obedience; very intelligent; and yet certain unpleasant habits, characteristics, seemed to betray bitter hypocrisies in him! Passing along in the darkness of corridors with mildewed wallpaper, he would stick out his tongue, his two fists in his groin; and he would see specks on his closed eyelids. A door opened on to the evening: by lamplight you could see him up there, gasping on the stairway, under a gulf of light hanging from the roof. In summer especially, defeated and stupefied, he would obstinately shut himself up in the coolness of the latrines: here he would think in peace, surrendering his nostrils.

Quand, lavé des odeurs du jour, le jardinet
Derrière la maison, en hiver, s'illunait,
Gisant au pied d'un mur, enterré dans la marne
Et pour des visions écrasant son œil darne,
Il écoutait grouiller les galeux espaliers.
Pitié! Ces enfants seuls étaient ses familiers
Qui, chétifs, fronts nus, œil déteignant sur la joue,
Cachant de maigres doigts jaunes et noirs de boue
Sous des habits puant la foire et tout vieillots,
Conversaient avec la douceur des idiots!

Et si, l'ayant surpris à des pitiés immondes,
Sa mère s'effrayait; les tendresses, profondes,
De l'enfant se jetaient sur cet étonnement.
C'était bon. Elle avait le bleu regard, – qui ment!

À sept ans, il faisait des romans sur la vie
Du grand désert, où luit la Liberté ravie,
Forêts, soleils, rives, savanes! – Il s'aidait
De journaux illustrés où, rouge, il regardait
Des Espagnoles rire et des Italiennes.

When, washed clean of the smells of daytime, the little garden behind the house, in winter, filled with moonlight – lying at the foot of a wall, buried in marl, and, for visions, rubbing hard at his dazzled eyes, he would listen to the scabby wall-trees creaking. Pity! Only those children were his familiars who, stunted and bareheaded, their eyes fading on their cheeks, hiding lean fingers yellow and black with mud under clothes stinking of excrement, all old-fashioned, conversed with the gentleness of idiots!

And if, having surprised him at unclean compassions, his mother took fright, the deep signs of the child's affection would throw themselves, in defence, upon her astonishment. Everything was all right. She had received that blue gaze – which lies!

At the age of seven he made up romances about life in the great desert, where Freedom shines in joy: forests, suns, shores, savannahs! – He helped himself with illustrated papers, in which, reddening, he stared at smiling Spanish and Italian women. [But] when,

Quand venait, l'œil brun, folle, en robes d'indiennes,
— Huit ans, — la fille des ouvriers d'à côté,
La petite brutale, et qu'elle avait sauté,
Dans un coin, sur son dos, en secouant ses tresses,
Et qu'il était sous elle, il lui mordait les fesses,
Car elle ne portait jamais de pantalons;
— Et, par elle meurtri des poings et des talons,
Remportait les saveurs de sa peau dans sa chambre.

Il craignait les blafards dimanches de décembre,
Où, pommadé, sur un guéridon d'acajou,
Il lisait une Bible à la tranche vert-chou;
Des rêves l'oppressaient chaque nuit dans l'alcôve.
Il n'aimait pas Dieu; mais les hommes, qu'au soir fauve,
Noirs, en blouse, il voyait rentrer dans le faubourg
Où les crieurs, en trois roulements de tambour,
Font autour des édits rire et gronder les foules.
— Il rêvait la prairie amoureuse, où des houles
Lumineuses, parfums sains, pubescences d'or,
Font leur remuement calme et prennent leur essor!

brown-eyed and flighty, dressed in cotton print, the eight-year-old
daughter of the working people nearby came — the little savage —
and jumped on him from behind in a corner, shaking her locks, and
he was underneath her, he bit her arse, for she never wore knickers—
and black and blue from her fists and her heels, he took back to his
bedroom the taste of her skin.

He feared the wan December Sundays when, brilliantined, at a
mahogany pedestal table, he would read a Bible with cabbage-
green edges; every night dreams oppressed him in the alcove. He
loved not God, but the men he saw in the lurid evenings, coming
back dark, in smocks, to the outskirts of the town, where the town
criers, with three rolls on the drum, make crowds laugh and
grumble around the edicts. — He dreamed of the meadow full of
love, where waves of light, wholesome odours, and golden downi-
nesses calmly stir and take their flight!

Et comme il savourait surtout les sombres choses,
Quand, dans la chambre nue aux persiennes closes,
Haute et bleue, âcrement prise d'humidité,
Il lisait son roman sans cesse médité,
Plein de lourds ciels ocreux et de forêts noyées,
De fleurs de chair aux bois sidérals déployées,
Vertige, écroulements, déroutes et pitié!
– Tandis que se faisait la rumeur du quartier,
En bas, – seul, et couché sur des pièces de toile
Écrue, et pressentant violemment la voile!

26 mai 1871

LES PAUVRES À L'ÉGLISE

PARQUÉS entre des bancs de chêne, aux coins d'église
Qu'attiédit puamment leur souffle, tous leurs yeux
Vers le chœur ruisselant d'orrie et la maîtrise
Aux vingt gueules gueulant les cantiques pieux;

And how, above all things, he relished what is dark: as in his bare
room, with the shutters closed, high-ceilinged, blue, and pierced
with bitter damp, he would read his novel, studied without cease,
full of leaden, ochrish skies and drowned forests, flowers of flesh
unfolding in starry woods, vertigo, collapses, retreats in disorder,
and pity! – while, below, the street-noises continued – alone,
lying on unbleached linen, and with violent presentiments of sails!

26 May 1871

Poor People in Church

PENNED between oaken pews, in corners of the church which their
breath stinkingly warms, all their eyes on the chancel dripping with
gold, and the choir with its twenty pairs of jaws bawling pious
hymns;

Comme un parfum de pain humant l'odeur de cire,
Heureux, humiliés comme des chiens battus,
Les Pauvres au bon Dieu, le patron et le sire,
Tendent leurs oremus risibles et têtus.

Aux femmes, c'est bien bon de faire des bancs lisses,
Après les six jours noirs où Dieu les fait souffrir!
Elles bercent, tordus dans d'étranges pelisses,
Des espèces d'enfants qui pleurent à mourir.

Leurs seins crasseux dehors, ces mangeuses de soupe,
Une prière aux yeux et ne priant jamais,
Regardent parader mauvaisement un groupe
De gamines avec leurs chapeaux déformés.

Dehors, le froid, la faim, [et puis] l'homme en ribote.
C'est bon. Encore une heure; après, les maux sans nom!
– Cependant, alentour, geint, nasille, chuchote
Une collection de vieilles à fanons:

sniffing the odour of wax as if it were the odour of bread, happy,
and humbled like beaten dogs, the Poor offer up to God, the Lord
and Master, their ridiculous stubborn *oremuses*.

For the women it is very pleasant to wear the benches smooth;
after the six black days on which God has made them suffer. They
nurse, swaddled in strange-looking shawls, creatures like children
who weep as if they would die.

Their unwashed breasts hanging out, these eaters of soup, with a
prayer in their eyes, but never praying, watch a group of hoydens
wickedly showing off with hats all out of shape.

Outside is the cold, and hunger – and a man on the booze. All
right. There's another hour to go; afterwards, nameless ills! –
Meanwhile all around an assortment of old dewlapped women
whimpers, snuffles, and whispers:

Ces effarés y sont et ces épileptiques
Dont on se détournait hier aux carrefours;
Et, fringalant du nez dans des missels antiques,
Ces aveugles qu'un chien introduit dans les cours.

Et tous, bavant la foi mendiante et stupide,
Récitent la complainte infinie à Jésus
Qui rêve en haut, jauni par le vitrail livide,
Loin des maigres mauvais et des méchants pansus,

Loin des senteurs de viande et d'étoffes moisies,
Farce prostrée et sombre aux gestes repoussants;
– Et l'oraison fleurit d'expressions choisies,
Et les mysticités prennent des tons pressants,

Quand, des nefs où périt le soleil, plis de soie
Banals, sourires verts, les Dames de quartiers
Distingués, – ô Jésus! – les malades du foie
Font baiser leurs longs doigts jaunes aux bénitiers.

1871

These are the distracted persons and the epileptics from whom, yesterday, you turned away at street crossings; there too are the blind who are led by a dog into courtyards, poking their noses into old-fashioned missals.

– And all of them, dribbling a stupid grovelling faith, recite their unending complaint to Jesus who is dreaming up there, yellow from the livid stained glass window, far above evil thin men and wicked pot-bellied ones,

far from the smell of meat and mouldy fabric, and the exhausted sombre farce of repulsive gestures – and as the prayer flowers in choice expressions, and the mysteries take on more emphatic tones,

from the aisles, where the sun is dying, trite folds of silk and green smiles, the ladies of the better quarters of the town – oh Jesus! – the sufferers from complaints of the liver, make their long yellow fingers kiss the holy water in the stoups.

1871

LE CŒUR VOLÉ

MON triste cœur bave à la poupe,
Mon cœur couvert de caporal:
Ils y lancent des jets de soupe,
Mon triste cœur bave à la poupe:
Sous les quolibets de la troupe
Qui pousse un rire général,
Mon triste cœur bave à la poupe,
Mon cœur couvert de caporal!

Ithyphalliques et pioupiesques,
Leurs quolibets l'ont dépravé!
Au gouvernail on voit des fresques
Ithyphalliques et pioupiesques.
Ô flots abracadabrantesques,
Prenez mon cœur, qu'il soit lavé!
Ithyphalliques et pioupiesques,
Leurs quolibets l'ont dépravé!

Quand ils auront tari leurs chiques,
Comment agir, ô cœur volé?
Ce seront des hoquets bachiques:
Quand ils auront tari leurs chiques:

The Cheated Heart

MY poor heart dribbles at the stern, my heart covered with *caporal*: they squirt upon it jets of soup, my poor heart dribbles at the stern: under the gibes of the whole crew which bursts out in a single laugh, my poor heart dribbles at the stern, my heart covered with *caporal*!

Ithyphallic, erkish, lewd, their gibes have corrupted it! In the wheelhouse you can see *graffiti*, ithyphallic, erkish, lewd. O abracadantic waves, take my heart that it may be cleansed! Ithyphallic, erkish, lewd, their gibes have corrupted it!

When they have finished chewing their quids, what shall we do, o cheated heart? It will be bacchic hiccups then: when they have

J'aurai des sursauts stomachiques,
Moi, si mon cœur est ravalé:
Quand ils auront tari leurs chiques
Comment agir, ô cœur volé?

[*Mai 1871*]

L'ORGIE PARISIENNE

OU

PARIS SE REPEUPLE

Ô LÂCHES, la voilà! Dégorgez dans les gares!
Le soleil essuya de ses poumons ardents
Les boulevards qu'un soir comblèrent les Barbares.
Voilà la Cité sainte, assise à l'occident!

Allez! on préviendra les reflux d'incendie,
Voilà les quais, voilà les boulevards, voilà
Les maisons sur l'azur léger qui s'irradie
Et qu'un soir la rougeur des bombes étoila!

finished chewing their quids: I shall have stomach heavings then, if
I can swallow down my heart: when they have finished chewing
their quids what shall we do, o cheated heart?

[*May 1871*]

The Parisian Orgy or *Paris is Repeopled*

O COWARDS! There she is! Pile out into the stations! The sun with
its fiery lungs blew clear the boulevards that, one evening, the Bar-
barians filled. Here is the holy City, seated in the West!

Come! we'll stave off the return of the fires; here are the quays,
here are the boulevards, here are the houses against the pale, radiant
blue – starred, one evening, by the red flashes of bombs!

Cachez les palais morts dans des niches de planches!
L'ancient jour effaré rafraîchit vos regards.
Voici le troupeau roux des tordeuses de hanches:
Soyez fous, vous serez drôles, étant hagards!

Tas de chiennes en rut mangeant des cataplasmes,
Le cri des maisons d'or vous réclame. Volez!
Mangez! Voici la nuit de joie aux profonds spasmes
Qui descend dans la rue. Ô buveurs désolés,

Buvez! Quand la lumière arrive intense et folle,
Fouillant à vos côtés les luxes ruisselants,
Vous n'allez pas baver, sans geste, sans parole,
Dans vos verres, les yeux perdus aux lointains blancs?

Avalez, pour la Reine aux fesses cascadantes!
Écoutez l'action des stupides hoquets
Déchirants! Écoutez sauter aux nuits ardentes
Les idiots râleux, vieillards, pantins, laquais!

Hide the dead palaces with forests of planks! Affrighted, the
dying daylight freshens your looks. Look at the red-headed troop
of the wrigglers of hips: be mad, you'll be comical, being haggard!

Pack of bitches on heat, eating poultices: the cry from the houses
of gold calls you! Plunder! Eat! See the night of joy and deep
twitchings coming down on the street. O desolate drinkers,

Drink! When the light comes, intense and crazed, to ransack
round you the rustling luxuries, you're not going to dribble into
your glasses without motion or sound, with your eyes lost in white
distances?

Knock it back: to the Queen whose buttocks cascade in folds!
Listen to the working of stupid tearing hiccups! Listen to them
leaping in the fiery night: the panting idiots, the aged, the nonen-
tities, the lackeys!

Ô cœurs de saleté, bouches épouvantables,
Fonctionnez plus fort, bouches de puanteurs!
Un vin pour ces torpeurs ignobles, sur ces tables ...
Vos ventres sont fondus de hontes, ô Vainqueurs!

Ouvrez votre narine aux superbes nausées!
Trempez de poisons forts les cordes de vos cous!
Sur vos nuques d'enfants baissant ses mains croisées
Le Poëte vous dit: «Ô lâches, soyez fous!

Parce que vous fouillez le ventre de la Femme,
Vous craignez d'elle encore une convulsion
Qui crie, asphyxiant votre nichée infâme
Sur sa poitrine, en une horrible pression.

Syphilitiques, fous, rois, pantins, ventriloques,
Qu'est-ce que ça peut faire à la putain Paris,
Vos âmes et vos corps, vos poisons et vos loques?
Elle se secouera de vous, hargneux pourris!

O hearts of filth, appalling mouths; work harder, mouths of foul stenches! Wine for these ignoble torpors, at these tables ... Your bellies are melting with shame, O Conquerors!

Open your nostrils to these superb nauseas! Steep the tendons of your necks in strong poisons! Laying his crossed hands on the napes of your childish necks, the Poet says to you: 'O cowards! be mad!

Because you are ransacking the guts of Woman, you fear another convulsion from her, crying out, and stifling your infamous perching on her breast with a horrible pressure.

Syphilitics, madmen, kings, puppets, ventriloquists! what can you matter to Paris the whore? your souls or your bodies, your poisons or your rags? She'll shake you off, you pox-rotten snarlers!

Et quand vous serez bas, geignant sur vos entrailles,
Les flancs morts, réclamant votre argent, éperdus,
La rouge courtisane aux seins gros de batailles
Loin de votre stupeur tordra ses poings ardus!»

Quand tes pieds ont dansé si fort dans les colères,
Paris! quand tu reçus tant de coups de couteau,
Quand tu gis, retenant dans tes prunelles claires
Un peu de la bonté du fauve renouveau,

Ô cité douloureuse, ô cité quasi morte,
La tête et les deux seins jetés vers l'Avenir
Ouvrant sur ta pâleur ses milliards de portes,
Cité que le Passé sombre pourrait bénir:

Corps remagnétisé pour les énormes peines,
Tu rebois donc la vie effroyable! tu sens
Sourdre le flux des vers livides en tes veines,
Et sur ton clair amour rôder les doigts glaçants!

And when you are down, whimpering on your bellies, your sides wrung, clamouring for your money back, distracted, the red harlot with her breasts swelling with battles will clench her hard fists, far removed from your stupor!'

When your feet, Paris, danced so hard in anger! when you had so many knife wounds; when you lay helpless, still retaining in your clear eyes a little of the goodness of the tawny spring;

O city in pain; O city almost dead, with your face and your two breasts pointing towards the Future which opens to your pallor its thousand million gates; city whom the dark Past could bless:

body galvanized back to life to suffer tremendous pains, you are drinking in dreadful life once more! You feel the ghastly pale worms flooding back in your veins, and the icy fingers prowling on your unclouded love!

Et ce n'est pas mauvais. Les vers, les vers livides
Ne gêneront pas plus ton souffle de Progrès
Que les Stryx n'éteignaient l'œil des Cariatides
Où des pleurs d'or astral tombaient des bleus degrés.

Quoique ce soit affreux de te revoir couverte
Ainsi; quoiqu'on n'ait fait jamais d'une cité
Ulcère plus puant à la Nature verte,
Le Poëte te dit: «Splendide est ta Beauté!»

L'orage te sacra suprême poésie;
L'immense remuement des forces te secourt;
Ton œuvre bout, la mort gronde, Cité choisie!
Amasse les strideurs au cœur du clairon lourd.

Le Poëte prendra le sanglot des Infâmes,
La haine des Forçats, la clameur des Maudits;
Et ses rayons d'amour flagelleront les Femmes.
Ses strophes bondiront: Voilà! voilà! bandits!

And it does you no harm. The worms, the pale worms, will obstruct your breath of Progress no more than the Stryx could extinguish the eyes of the Caryatides, from whose blue sills fell tears of sidereal gold.

Although it is frightful to see you again covered in this fashion; although no city was ever made into a more foul-smelling ulcer on the face of green Nature, the Poet says to you: 'Your Beauty is Marvellous!'

The tempest sealed you in supreme poetry; the huge stirring of strength comes to your aid; your work comes to the boil, death groans, O chosen City! Hoard in your heart the stridors of the ominous trumpet.

The Poet will take the sobs of the Infamous, the hate of the Galley-slaves, the clamour of the Damned; and the beams of his love will scourge Womankind. His verses will leap out: There's for you! There! Villains!

– Société, tout est rétabli: – les orgies
Pleurent leur ancien râle aux anciens lupanars:
Et les gaz en délire, aux murailles rougies,
Flambent sinistrement vers les azurs blafards!

Mai 1871

LES MAINS DE JEANNE-MARIE

JEANNE-MARIE a des mains fortes,
Mains sombres que l'été tanna,
Mains pâles comme des mains mortes.
– Sont-ce des mains de Juana?

Ont-elles pris les crèmes brunes
Sur les mares de voluptés?
Ont-elles trempé dans des lunes
Aux étangs de sérénités?

Ont-elles bu des cieux barbares,
Calmes sur les genoux charmants?
Ont-elles roulé des cigares
Ou trafiqué des diamants?

– Society, and everything, is restored: – the orgies are weeping with dry sobs in the old brothels: and on the reddened walls the gaslights in frenzy flare balefully upwards to the wan blue skies!

May 1871

Jeanne-Marie's Hands

JEANNE-MARIE has strong hands; dark hands tanned by the summer; pale hands like dead hands. – Are they the hands of Donna Juana?

Did they get their dusky cream colour sailing on pools of sensual pleasure? Have they dipped into moons, in ponds of serenity?

Have they drunk [heat] from barbarous skies, calm upon enchanting knees? Have they rolled cigars, or traded in diamonds?

136

Sur les pieds ardents des Madones
Ont-elles fané des fleurs d'or?
C'est le sang noir des belladones
Qui dans leur paume éclate et dort.

Mains chasseresses des diptères
Dont bombinent les bleuisons
Aurorales, vers les nectaires?
Mains décanteuses de poisons?

Oh! quel Rêve les a saisies
Dans les pandiculations?
Un rêve inouï des Asies,
Des Khenghavars ou des Sions?

— Ces mains n'ont pas vendu d'oranges,
Ni bruni sur les pieds des dieux:
Ces mains n'ont pas lavé les langes
Des lourds petits enfants sans yeux.

Ce ne sont pas mains de cousine
Ni d'ouvrières aux gros fronts
Que brûle, aux bois puant l'usine,
Un soleil ivre de goudrons.

On the burning feet of Madonnas have they tossed golden flowers? It is the black blood of belladonnas that blazes and sleeps in their palms.

Hands which drive the diptera with which the auroral bluenesses buzz, towards the nectars? Hands which measure out poisons?

Oh what Dream has stiffened them in pandiculations? Some extraordinary dream of the Asias, of Khenghavars or Zions?

These hands have neither sold oranges nor become sunburnt at the feet of the gods: these hands have never washed the napkins of heavy babies without eyes.

These are not the hands of a cousin, nor of working women with round foreheads burnt by a sun which is drunk with the smell of tar in woods that stink of factories.

Ce sont des ployeuses d'échines,
Des mains qui ne font jamais mal,
Plus fatales que des machines,
Plus fortes que tout un cheval!

Remuant comme des fournaises,
Et secouant tous ses frissons,
Leur chair chante des Marseillaises
Et jamais des Eleisons!

Ça serrerait vous cous, ô femmes
Mauvaises, ça broierait vos mains,
Femmes nobles, vos mains infâmes
Pleines de blancs et de carmins.

L'éclat de ces mains amoureuses
Tourne le crâne des brebis!
Dans leurs phalanges savoureuses
Le grand soleil met un rubis!

Une tache de populace
Les brunit comme un sein d'hier;
Le dos de ces Mains est la place
Qu'en baisa tout Révolté fier!

These are benders of backbones; hands that never work harm; more inevitable than machines, stronger than carthorses!

Stirring like furnaces, shaking off all their chills of fear, their flesh sings Marseillaises, and never Eleisons!

They will grasp your necks, O evil women; they will pulverize your hands, noblewomen; your infamous hands full of white and of carmine.

The splendour of these hands of love turns the heads of the lambs! On their spicy fingers the great sun sets a ruby!

A stain of the populace makes them brown like the breasts of women of antiquity; and the backs of these Hands are the place where every proud Rebel has kissed them!

Elles ont pâli, merveilleuses,
Au grand soleil d'amour chargé,
Sur le bronze des mitrailleuses
À travers Paris insurgé!

Ah! quelquefois, ô Mains sacrées,
À vos poings, Mains où tremblent nos
Lèvres jamais désenivrées,
Crie une chaîne aux clairs anneaux!

Et c'est un Soubresaut étrange
Dans nos êtres, quand, quelquefois,
On veut vous déhâler, Mains d'ange,
En vous faisant saigner les doigts!

LES SŒURS DE CHARITÉ

Le jeune homme dont l'œil est brillant, la peau brune,
Le beau corps de vingt ans qui devrait aller nu,
Et qu'eût, le front cerclé de cuivre, sous la lune
Adoré, dans la Perse, un Génie inconnu,

Marvellous, they have paled in the great sunshine full of love [of the cause] on the bronze casing of machine-guns throughout insurgent Paris!

Ah, sometimes, O blessed Hands, at your wrists, Hands where our never-sobered lips tremble, cries out a chain of bright links!

And there's a strange and sudden Start in our beings when, sometimes, they try, angelic Hands, to make your sunburn disappear, by making your fingers bleed!

The Sisters of Charity

The young man whose eye is bright, whose skin is brown; the handsome twenty-year-old body which should go naked, and which, its brow circled with copper, under the moon, would have been worshipped in Persia by an unknown Genie;

Impétueux avec des douceurs virginales
Et noires, fier de ses premiers entêtements,
Pareil aux jeunes mers, pleurs de nuits estivales,
Qui se retournent sur des lits de diamants;

Le jeune homme, devant les laideurs de ce monde,
Tressaille dans son cœur largement irrité,
Et, plein de la blessure éternelle et profonde,
Se prend à désirer sa sœur de charité.

Mais, ô Femme, monceau d'entrailles, pitié douce,
Tu n'es jamais la Sœur de charité, jamais,
Ni regard noir, ni ventre où dort une ombre rousse,
Ni doigts légers, ni seins splendidement formés.

Aveugle irréveillée aux immenses prunelles,
Tout notre embrassement n'est qu'une question:
C'est toi qui pends à nous, porteuse de mamelles,
Nous te berçons, charmante et grave Passion.

impetuous, with a softness both virginal and dark, proud of his
first obstinacies, like the young seas, tears of summer nights,
turning on beds of diamonds;

the young man face to face with the ugliness of this world, shud-
ders in his heart, generously provoked; and, filled with the deep
unhealing wound, begin to desire his sister of charity.

But O Woman, heap of bowels, sweet compassion, you never
are the Sister of charity, never: neither your dark look, nor your
belly where sleeps a russet shadow, nor your light fingers, nor
splendidly shaped breasts.

Blind one, unawakened, with enormous irises, the whole of our
union is only a questioning; it is you who hang on us, O bearer of
breasts; it is we who nurse you, charming, grave Passion.

Tes haines, tes torpeurs fixes, tes défaillances,
Et tes brutalités souffertes autrefois,
Tu nous rends tout, ô Nuit pourtant sans malveillances,
Comme un excès de sang épanché tous les mois.

— Quand la femme, portée un instant, l'épouvante,
Amour, appel de vie et chanson d'action,
Viennent la Muse verte et la Justice ardente
Le déchirer de leur auguste obsession.

Ah! sans cesse altéré des splendeurs et des calmes,
Délaissé des deux Sœurs implacables, geignant
Avec tendresse après la science aux bras almes,
Il porte à la nature en fleur son front saignant.

Mais la noire alchimie et les saintes études
Répugnent au blessé, sombre savant d'orgueil;
Il sent marcher sur lui d'atroces solitudes.
Alors, et toujours beau, sans dégoût du cercueil,

Your hatreds, your unmoving torpors, your failings, and your brutalizations suffered long ago, you give everything back to us, O Night still without malevolence, like an excess of blood which is shed every month.

— When Woman, taken on for an instant, terrifies him; love, the call of life and song of action; they come: the green Muse and burning Justice, to tear him to pieces with their august obsessions.

Ah! thirsting without cease for splendours and calms, forsaken by the two implacable Sisters, whimpering fondly after knowledge whose arms are full of nourishment, he brings to nature in flower his forehead covered with blood.

But dark alchemy and sacred study are repugnant to the wounded one, the sombre scholar of pride; he feels marching towards him atrocious solitudes. Then, and still handsome, without disgust of the coffin,

Qu'il croie aux vastes fins, Rêves ou Promenades
Immenses, à travers les nuits de Vérité,
Et t'appelle en son âme et ses membres malades,
Ô Mort mystérieuse, ô sœur de charité!

Juin 1871

LES CHERCHEUSES DE POUX

QUAND le front de l'enfant, plein de rouges tourmentes,
Implore l'essaim blanc des rêves indistincts,
Il vient près de son lit deux grandes sœurs charmantes
Avec de frêles doigts aux ongles argentins.

Elles assoient l'enfant devant une croisée
Grande ouverte où l'air bleu baigne un fouillis de fleurs,
Et dans ses lourds cheveux où tombe la rosée
Promènent leurs doigts fins, terribles et charmeurs.

Il écoute chanter leurs haleines craintives
Qui fleurent de longs miels végétaux et rosés,
Et qu'interrompt parfois un sifflement, salives
Reprises sur la lèvre ou désirs de baisers.

he must believe in vast purposes, in immense Dreams or Journeys across the night of Truth, and he must call you in his soul and sick limbs, O mysterious Death, O sister of charity!

June 1871

The Seekers of Lice

WHEN the child's head, full of red torments, implores the white swarm of indistinct dreams, there come near his bed two charming grownup sisters with slim fingers and silvery nails.

They sit the child down in front of a casement, wide open to where the blue air bathes a tangle of flowers, and in his heavy hair on which the dew falls, their fine, fearful, magical fingers go moving.

He listens to the sigh of their apprehensive breath which smells of long roseate honeys of plants, and is interrupted now and then by a hiss: spittle caught on the lip or wishes for kisses.

Il entend leurs cils noirs battant sous les silences
Parfumés; et leurs doigts électriques et doux
Font crépiter parmi ses grises indolences
Sous leurs ongles royaux la mort des petits poux.

Voilà que monte en lui le vin de la Paresse,
Soupir d'harmonica qui pourrait délirer;
L'enfant se sent, selon la lenteur des caresses,
Sourdre et mourir sans cesse un désir de pleurer.

LES PREMIÈRES COMMUNIONS

I

VRAIMENT, c'est bête, ces églises des villages
Où quinze laids marmots encrassant les piliers
Écoutent, grasseyant les divins babillages,
Un noir grotesque dont fermentent les souliers:
Mais le soleil éveille, à travers des feuillages,
Les vieilles couleurs des vitraux irréguliers.

He hears their dark eyelashes beating in the odorous silence; and their fingers, electrical, sweet, among his grey indolences make the deaths of the little lice crackle under their sovereign nails.

It is then that there rises in him the wine of Sloth; a harmonica sigh which could induce delirium; the child feels, according to the slowness of their caresses, surging and dying away continually a desire to cry.

First Communion

I

REALLY, it's stupid, these village churches where fifteen ugly ducklings, soiling the pillars, listen, gargling responses to the divine prattle, to a black freak whose boots are fermenting: but the sun awakens, shining through the leaves, the ancient colours in irregular stained glass.

La pierre sent toujours la terre maternelle.
Vous verrez des monceaux de ces cailloux terreux
Dans la campagne en rut qui frémit solennelle,
Portant près des blés lourds, dans les sentiers ocreux,
Ces arbrisseaux brûlés où bleuit la prunelle,
Des nœuds de mûriers noirs et de rosiers fuireux.

Tous les cent ans, on rend ces granges respectables
Par un badigeon d'eau bleue et de lait caillé:
Si des mysticités grotesques sont notables
Près de la Notre-Dame ou du Saint empaillé,
Des mouches sentant bon l'auberge et les étables
Se gorgent de cire au plancher ensoleillé.

L'enfant se doit surtout à la maison, famille
Des soins naïfs, des bons travaux abrutissants;
Ils sortent, oubliant que la peau leur fourmille
Où le Prêtre du Christ plaqua ses doigts puissants.
On paie au Prêtre un toit ombré d'une charmille
Pour qu'il laisse au soleil tous ces fronts brunissants.

The stone always smells of its mother earth. You will see piles of earthy boulders like these in the rutting countryside solemnly quivering, bearing, close by the heavy corn, those hard-bitten shrubs where the sloe is turning blue, and tangles of brambles and rambling rose-bushes.

They make these barns look respectable once every hundred years with a colour-wash of blue water and curdled milk: and if more grotesque mysteries are worth noting, close by the stuffed Madonna or Saint, flies smelling of inns and cowsheds gorge themselves on wax on the sunlit floor.

The child's duty is above all to his home, to a family whose cares are simple and whose work stupefying and honest; they leave, then, forgetting how their skin crawls where the Priest of Christ has laid his powerful fingers. There is a house shaded with hornbeams that is paid for for the Priest, so that he may release all these foreheads which are getting sun-tanned into the sunshine.

Le premier habit noir, le plus beau jour de tartes,
Sous le Napoléon ou le petit Tambour
Quelque enluminure où les Josephs et les Marthes
Tirent la langue avec un excessif amour
Et que joindront, au jour de science, deux cartes,
Ces seuls doux souvenirs lui restent du grand Jour.

Les filles vont toujours à l'église, contentes
De s'entendre appeler garces par les garçons
Qui font du genre après Messe ou vêpres chantantes.
Eux qui sont destinés au chic des garnisons,
Ils narguent au café les maisons importantes,
Blousés neuf, et gueulant d'effroyables chansons.

Cependant le Curé choisit pour les enfances
Des dessins; dans son clos, les vêpres dites, quand
L'air s'emplit du lointain nasillement des danses,
Il se sent, en dépit des célestes défenses,
Les doigts de pied ravis et le mollet marquant;
– La Nuit vient, noir pirate aux cieux d'or débarquant.

The first black suit; the best pastry day; beneath Napoleon or
The Little Drummer Boy, some coloured plate where Josephs and
Marthas stick out their tongues with excess of love – which will be
joined on the day of knowledge by two maps – only these sweet
mementoes of the great Day will remain.

The girls always go to church and are pleased to hear themselves
called little bitches by the boys who put on airs after Mass or
Sung Vespers. These, who are destined for the manners of garrisons,
snap their fingers in the café at the important families, dressed in
new jackets and yelling frightful songs.

Meanwhile the Curé chooses pictures for the children; in his gar-
den, after vespers, when the air fills with the distant twanging of the
dancing; and in spite of divine prohibitions, he feels his toes enrap-
tured and his calves beating time; – Night comes, dark pirate
disembarking on to golden skies.

II

Le Prêtre a distingué parmi les catéchistes,
Congrégés des Faubourgs ou des Riches Quartiers,
Cette petite fille inconnue, aux yeux tristes,
Front jaune. Les parents semblent de doux portiers.
«Au grand Jour, le marquant parmi les Catéchistes,
Dieu fera sur ce front neiger ses bénitiers.»

III

La veille du grand Jour, l'enfant se fait malade.
Mieux qu'à l'Église haute aux funèbres rumeurs,
D'abord le frisson vient, — le lit n'étant pas fade —
Un frisson surhumain qui retourne: «Je meurs …»

Et, comme un vol d'amour fait à ses sœurs stupides,
Elle compte, abattue et les mains sur son cœur,
Les Anges, les Jésus et ses Vierges nitides
Et, calmement, son âme a bu tout son vainqueur.

II

The Priest has noticed among the catechists congregated from the
Suburbs or from Well-off Neighbourhoods, this little unknown girl
with sad eyes and a sallow forehead. Her parents seem to be humble
caretakers. 'On the great Day, singling it out among the catechists,
God will cause His blessings to snow down on this head.'

III

On the eve of the great Day, the child becomes ill. Even better than
in the tall church with its dismal murmurs comes, first, the shivering
fit – bed is not insipid – a superhuman shudder which returns: 'I am
dying …'

   And, like a theft of love committed at the expense of her stupid
sisters, she counts, exhausted, her hands on her heart, Angels,
Jesuses, and glimmering Virgins; and calmly her soul has swal-
lowed her conqueror whole.

Adonaï! ... – Dans les terminaisons latines,
Des cieux moirés de vert baignent les Fronts vermeils,
Et, tachés du sang pur des célestes poitrines,
De grands linges neigeux tombent sur les soleils!

– Pour ses virginités présentes et futures
Elle mord aux fraîcheurs de ta Rémission,
Mais plus que les lys d'eau, plus que les confitures,
Tes pardons sont glacés, ô Reine de Sion!

IV

Puis la Vierge n'est plus que la vierge du livre.
Les mystiques élans se cassent quelquefois ...
Et vient la pauvreté des images, que cuivre
L'ennui, l'enluminure atroce et les vieux bois;

Des curiosités vaguement impudiques
Epouvantent le rêve aux chastes bleuités
Qui s'est surpris autour des célestes tuniques,
Du linge dont Jésus voile ses nudités.

Adonaï! ... in Latin endings, skies shot with green bathe crimson brows, and great snowy linens, spotted with the pure blood from heavenly breasts, fall across suns!
– For her virginities, present and future, she bites on the refreshment of thy Remission, but more than water-lilies, more than sweetmeats, thy forgivenesses are like ice [to the tooth] O Queen of Zion!

IV

Then the Virgin is no longer anything more than the virgin of the book. Mystical impulses are sometimes shattered ... And the poverty of images comes, and is sheathed with bronze by boredom, the hideous colour print and the old woodcut.
Vaguely indecent curiosities startle the dream about chaste bluenesses which suddenly finds itself among the heavenly tunics and the linen with which Christ veils his nakedness.

Elle veut, elle veut, pourtant, l'âme en détresse,
Le front dans l'oreiller creusé par les cris sourds,
Prolonger les éclairs suprêmes de tendresse,
Et bave ... – L'ombre emplit les maisons et les cours.

Et l'enfant ne peut plus. Elle s'agite, cambre
Les reins et d'une main ouvre le rideau bleu
Pour amener un peu la fraîcheur de la chambre
Sous le drap, vers son ventre et sa poitrine en feu ...

V

À son réveil, – minuit, – la fenêtre était blanche.
Devant le sommeil bleu des rideaux illunés,
La vision la prit des candeurs du dimanche;
Elle avait rêvé rouge. Elle saigna du nez,

Et, se sentant bien chaste et pleine de faiblesse,
Pour savourer en Dieu son amour revenant
Elle eut soif de la nuit où s'exalte et s'abaisse
Le cœur, sous l'œil des cieux doux, en les devinant;

She yearns, she yearns, even so, her soul in distress, her head in
the pillow pierced with muffled outcries, to prolong the supreme
flashes of tenderness; and she dribbles ... Darkness fills the houses
and the courtyards.

And the child can bear it no longer. She rouses herself, arches her
back, and opens the blue bed-curtain with one hand to bring, a little,
the coolness of the room under the sheet to her burning belly and
breast ...

V

When she awoke – at midnight – the window was white. Beyond
the bluish slumber of the moonlit curtains the vision took hold of
her of the whiteness of Sunday; she had dreamed of red. Her nose
was bleeding,

and, feeling all chaste and full of weakness, in order to taste her
love returning to God, she thirsted for night, where, guessing at
the imminence of the soft skies, the heart exalts itself and bows
down beneath them;

De la nuit, Vierge-Mère impalpable, qui baigne
Tous les jeunes émois de ses silences gris;
Elle eut soif de la nuit forte où le cœur qui saigne
Écoule sans témoin sa révolte sans cris.

Et faisant la Victime et la petite épouse,
Son étoile la vit, une chandelle aux doigts,
Descendre dans la cour où séchait une blouse,
Spectre blanc, et lever les spectres noirs des toits.

VI

Elle passa sa nuit sainte dans des latrines.
Vers la chandelle, aux trous du toit coulait l'air blanc,
Et quelque vigne folle aux noirceurs purpurines,
En deçà d'une cour voisine s'écroulant.

La lucarne faisait un cœur de lueur vive
Dans la cour où les cieux bas plaquaient d'ors vermeils
Les vitres; les pavés puant l'eau de lessive
Soufraient l'ombre des murs bondés de noirs sommeils.

. . . .

for night, the impalpable Virgin Mother, who bathes all young
emotions in her grey silences; she thirsted for unflinching night
where the bleeding heart pours out with no witness its rebellion
with no outcry.

And, acting the part of the Victim and of the little bride, her star
saw her with a candle in her hand go down to the courtyard
where a jacket was drying: a white ghost raising the black ghosts
of the roofs.

VI

She spent her holy night in the lavatories. Towards the candle,
through the holes in the roof, flowed the white air and some wild
vine with purplish blacknesses tumbling down, on the near side of a
neighbouring courtyard.

The light above made a heart of living brightness in the court-
yard where low skies plated the window-panes with rosy gold;
the cobblestones, stinking of dirty washing water, dusted the
shadows of the slumber-crammed dark walls with sulphur ...

VII

Qui dira ces langueurs et ces pitiés immondes,
Et ce qu'il lui viendra de haine, ô sales fous
Dont le travail divin déforme encor les mondes,
Quand la lèpre à la fin mangera ce corps doux?

. . . .

VIII

Et quand, ayant rentré tous ses nœuds d'hystéries,
Elle verra, sous les tristesses du bonheur,
L'amant rêver au blanc million des Maries,
Au matin de la nuit d'amour, avec douleur:

«Sais-tu que je t'ai fait mourir? J'ai pris ta bouche,
Ton cœur, tout ce qu'on a, tout ce que vous avez;
Et moi, je suis malade: Oh! je veux qu'on me couche
Parmi les Morts des eaux nocturnes abreuvés!

VII

Who will utter these languors and unclean compassions, and how much hatred will come to her, O filthy lunatics whose holy work still warps the worlds, when leprosy at last devours this sweet body?

. . . .

VIII

And when, having swallowed down all her hysterias, she sees, in the melancholy begotten of happiness, her lover dreaming of the white million Marys on the morning after the night of love, [she will cry] painfully:

'Do you know that I have done you to death? I have taken your mouth, your heart, all a man has, all you have; and I myself sicken: Oh! how I wish I were laid among the Dead who are drenched in the waters of night!

«J'étais bien jeune, et Christ a souillé mes haleines.
Il me bonda jusqu'à la gorge de dégoûts!
Tu baisais mes cheveux profonds comme les laines,
Et je me laissais faire ... Ah! va, c'est bon pour vous,

«Hommes! qui songez peu que la plus amoureuse
Est, sous sa conscience aux ignobles terreurs,
La plus prostituée et la plus douloureuse,
Et que tous nos élans vers Vous sont des erreurs!

«Car ma Communion première est bien passée.
Tes baisers, je ne puis jamais les avoir sus:
Et mon cœur et ma chair par ta chair embrassée
Fourmillent du baiser putride de Jésus!»

IX

Alors l'âme pourrie et l'âme désolée
Sentiront ruisseler tes malédictions.
— Ils auront couché sur ta Haine inviolée,
Échappés, pour la mort, des justes passions,

'I was full young, and Christ tainted my breath. He crammed me to the throat with loathings! You kissed my hair thick as a fleece, and I offered no resistance ... Ah! there, it is all very well for you,

'Men! who little dream that the most loving woman is, beneath her conscience with its ignoble fears, the most strumpeted and the most full of pain, and that all our impulses towards You are follies!

'For my first Communion is long past. Your kisses I shall never be able to know: and my heart and my flesh which your flesh has embraced seethe with the rotten kisses of Jesus!'

IX

So then the putrid soul and the desolate soul will feel Thy malediction streaming down. — They will have lain down upon Thy inviolate Hatred, having escaped legitimate passions in favour of death,

Christ! ô Christ, éternel voleur des énergies,
Dieu qui pour deux mille ans vouas à ta pâleur,
Cloués au sol, de honte et de céphalalgies,
Ou renversés, les fronts des femmes de douleur.

Juillet 1871

L'HOMME JUSTE

(*Fragments*)

. . . .

Ah! qu'il s'en aille, lui, la gorge cravatée
De honte, ruminant toujours mon ennui, doux
Comme le sucre sur la denture gâtée,
— Tel que la chienne après l'assaut des fiers toutous
Léchant son flanc d'où part une entraille emportée.

Christ! O Christ! eternal thief of vigour! God who for two thousand years hast dedicated to Thy pallor the brows of sorrowful women, nailed to the earth in shame and in headaches — or overthrown completely.

July 1871

The Just Man
(*Fragments*)

. . . .

Ah! away with him, that one, with his throat that wears the necktie of shame, ruminating always on my boredom, as sweet as sugar on a bad tooth — like the bitch after the assault of the fine bow-wows, licking her flank from which the torn gut hangs.

. . . .
. . . .
. . . .
. . . .

Ô justes, nous chierons dans vos ventres de grès!

. . . .

Le Juste restait droit sur ses hanches solides:
Un rayon lui dorait l'épaule; des sueurs
Me prirent: «Tu veux voir rutiler les bolides?
Et, debout, écouter bourdonner les flueurs
D'astres lactés, et les essaims d'astéroïdes?

«Par des farces de nuit ton front est épié,
Ô Juste! Il faut gagner un toit. Dis ta prière,
La bouche dans ton drap doucement expié;
Et si quelque égaré choque ton ostiaire,
Dis: Frère, va plus loin, je suis estropié!»

. . . .
. . . .
. . . .
. . . .

O just men, we'll shit in your stone[-jug] stomachs!

. . . .

The Just Man sat straight on his solid buttocks: a ray of light
gilded his shoulder; sweats took hold of me: 'Do you want to see
the meteors glowing red? To stand and hear the hum of the influence
of the milky stars and the swarms of asteroids?

'Nocturnal pranks have ruffled your head, O Just Man! A roof
must be found. Say your prayer with your mouth in your sheet,
having undergone easy atonement; and if some lost wanderer
knocks against your ossuary, say: "Brother, try elsewhere, I am
crippled!"'

Et le Juste restait debout, dans l'épouvante
Bleuâtre des gazons après le soleil mort:
«Alors, mettrais-tu tes genouillères en vente,
Ô Vieillard? Pèlerin sacré! barde d'Armor!
Pleureur des Oliviers! main que la pitié gante!

«Barbe de la famille et poing de la cité,
Croyant très doux: ô cœur tombé dans les calices,
Majestés et vertus, amour et cécité,
Juste! plus bête et plus dégoûtant que les lices!
Je suis celui qui souffre et qui s'est révolté!

«Et ça me fait pleurer sur mon ventre, ô stupide,
Et bien rire, l'espoir fameux de ton pardon!
Je suis maudit, tu sais! je suis soûl, fou, livide,
Ce que tu veux! Mais va te coucher, voyons donc,
Juste! Je ne veux rien à ton cerveau torpide.

«C'est toi le Juste, enfin, le Juste! C'est assez!
C'est vrai que ta tendresse et ta raison sereines
Reniflent dans la nuit comme des cétacés,
Que tu te fais proscrire et dégoises des thrènes
Sur d'effroyables becs-de-cane fracassés!

And the Just Man stood still, in the bluish terror of lawns after
the sun is dead: 'Well then! would you put up your kneecaps for
sale, O Aged One? Holy Pilgrim! bard of Armorica! weeper of the
Olives! hand gloved with pity!

'Beard of the family and fist of the city, very gentle believer: O
heart fallen among the chalices, majesties and virtues, love and
blindness, Just Man! stupider and more disgusting than hound
bitches! I am he who suffers and who has risen up in revolt!

'And it makes me weep on my belly, oh fool, and laugh loudly,
the famous hope of your pardon! I am accursed, you know! I am
drunk, mad, livid, whatever you like! But go and lie down; go on,
Just Man! I want nothing from your sluggish brain.

'It's you who are the Just One, after all! The Just Man! It's
enough! It's true that your serene tender feelings and reason blow
like whales in the night; that you get yourself ostracized and spout
funeral laments on frightful old smashed up flat-noses!

154

«Et c'est toi l'œil de Dieu! le lâche! Quand les plantes
Froides des pieds divins passeraient sur mon cou,
Tu es lâche! Ô ton front qui fourmille de lentes!
Socrates et Jésus, saints et justes, dégoût!
Respectez le Maudit suprême aux nuits sanglantes.»

J'avais crié cela sur la terre, et la nuit
Calme et blanche occupait les cieux pendant ma fièvre.
Je relevai mon front: le fantôme avait fui,
Emportant l'ironie atroce de ma lèvre ...
– Vents nocturnes, venez au maudit! Parlez-lui,

Cependant que silencieux sous les pilastres
D'azur, allongeant les comètes et les nœuds
D'univers, remuement énorme sans désastres,
L'Ordre, éternel veilleur, rame aux cieux lumineux
Et de sa drague en feu laisse filer les astres!

[*Juillet 1871*]

'And it's you who are the eye of God! a coward! Though the
cold soles of the divine feet were treading on my neck, you're a
coward! Oh! your head seething with nits! Socrates and Jesus, holy
and just, what disgust! Have some respect for the supreme Accursed
One of the bloodstained nights!'

Thus I cried on earth, and the calm white night filled the skies
during my fever. I raised my head: the phantom had fled, taking
with him the terrible irony of my tongue ... – O winds of night,
come to the accursed one! Speak to him,

while silently under the pillars of blue, past comets and the inter-
stices of the universe, enormous stirring without disasters, Order,
the eternal watchman, rows through the luminous heavens and
from his flaming dragnet lets fall the shooting stars!

[*July 1871*]

CE QU'ON DIT AU POËTE
À PROPOS DE FLEURS

A Monsieur Théodore de Banville

I

AINSI, toujours, vers l'azur noir
Où tremble la mer des topazes,
Fonctionneront dans ton soir
Les Lys, ces clystères d'extases!

À notre époque de sagous,
Quand les Plantes sont travailleuses,
Le Lys boira les bleus dégoûts
Dans tes Proses religieuses!

– Le lys de monsieur de Kerdrel,
Le Sonnet de mil huit cent trente,
Le Lys qu'on donne au Ménestrel
Avec l'œillet et l'amarante!

Des lys! Des lys! On n'en voit pas!
Et dans ton Vers, tel que les manches
Des Pécheresses aux doux pas,
Toujours frissonnent ces fleurs blanches!

To the Poet on the Subject of Flowers

To Monsieur Théodore de Banville

I

THUS continually towards the dark azure, where the sea of topazes shimmers, will function in your evening the Lilies, those pessaries of ecstasy!

In our own age of sago, when Plants work for their living, the lily will drink blue [virginal] loathings from your religious Prose!

—Monsieur de Kerdrel's lily, the Sonnet of eighteen-thirty, the Lily they bestow on the Bard [at Toulouse] together with the pink and the amaranth!

Lilies! lilies! none to be seen! yet in your Verse, like the sleeves of the soft-footed Women of Sin, always these white flowers shiver!

Toujours, Cher, quand tu prends un bain,
Ta Chemise aux aisselles blondes
Se gonfle aux brises du matin
Sur les myosotis immondes!

L'amour ne passe à tes octrois
Que les Lilas, – ô balançoires!
Et les Violettes du Bois,
Crachats sucrés des Nymphes noires! ...

II

Ô Poëtes, quand vous auriez
Les Roses, les Roses soufflées,
Rouges sur tiges de lauriers,
Et de mille octaves enflées!

Quand BANVILLE en ferait neiger,
Sanguinolentes, tournoyantes,
Pochant l'œil fou de l'étranger
Aux lectures mal bienveillantes!

Always, Dear Man, when you bathe, your Shirt with yellow oxters swells in the morning breezes above the muddy forget-me-nots!
Love gets through your Customs only Lilacs – O eye-wash! – and the Wild Violets, sugary spittle of the dark Nymphs! ...

II

O Poets, if you had Roses, blown Roses, red upon laurel stems and swollen with a thousand octaves!
If BANVILLE would make them snow down, blood-tinged, whirling, blacking the wild eye of the stranger with his ill-disposed interpretations!

De vos forêts et de vos prés,
O très paisibles photographes!
La Flore est diverse à peu près
Comme des bouchons de carafes!

Toujours les végétaux Français,
Hargneux, phtisiques, ridicules,
Où le ventre des chiens bassets
Navigue en paix, aux crépuscules;

Toujours, après d'affreux dessins
De Lotos bleus ou d'Hélianthes,
Estampes roses, sujets saints
Pour de jeunes communiantes!

L'Ode Açoka cadre avec la
Strophe en fenêtre de lorette;
Et de lourds papillons d'éclat
Fientent sur la Pâquerette.

Vieilles verdures, vieux galons!
Ô croquignolés végétales!
Fleurs fantasques des vieux Salons!
– Aux hannetons, pas aux crotales,

In your forests and in your meadows, O very peaceful photographers! the Flora is more or less diverse, like the stoppers on decanters!

Always those French vegetables, cross-grained, phthisical, absurd, navigated by the peaceful bellies of basset-hounds in twilight;

always, after frightful drawings of blue Lotuses or Sunflowers, pink prints, holy pictures for young girls making their communion!

The Asoka Ode agrees with the loretto window stanza form; and heavy, vivid butterflies are dunging on the Daisy.

Old greenery, and old galloons! O vegetable fancy biscuits! Fancy-flowers of old drawing-rooms! – For cockchafers, not rattlesnakes,

Ces poupards végétaux en pleurs
Que Grandville eût mis aux lisières,
Et qu'allaitèrent de couleurs
De méchants astres à visières!

Oui, vos bavures de pipeaux
Font de précieuses glucoses!
– Tas d'œufs frits dans de vieux chapeaux,
Lys, Açokas, Lilas et Roses! ...

III

Ô blanc Chasseur, qui cours sans bas
À travers le Pâtis panique,
Ne peux-tu pas, ne dois-tu pas
Connaître un peu ta botanique?

Tu ferais succéder, je crains,
Aux Grillons roux les Cantharides,
L'or des Rios au bleu des Rhins, –
Bref, aux Norwèges les Florides:

these puling vegetable baby dolls which Grandville would have put round the margins [of a drawing], and which sucked in their colours from ill-natured stars with eyeshades!

Yes! the droolings from your shepherds' pipes make some priceless glucoses! – Pile of fried eggs in old hats: Lilies, Asokas, Lilacs, Roses!

III

O white Hunter, running stockingless across the Panic pastures, can you not, ought you not to know your botany a little?

I'm afraid you'd make succeed to russet Crickets, Cantharides; and Rio golds to blues of Rhine – in short, to Norways, Floridas:

Mais, Cher, l'Art n'est plus, maintenant,
– C'est la vérité, – de permettre
À l'Eucalyptus étonnant
Des constrictors d'un hexamètre;

Là ...! Comme si les Acajous
Ne servaient, même en nos Guyanes,
Qu'aux cascades des sapajous,
Au lourd délire des lianes!

– En somme, une Fleur, Romarin
Ou Lys, vive ou morte, vaut-elle
Un excrément d'oiseau marin?
Vaut-elle un seul pleur de chandelle?

– Et j'ai dit ce que je voulais!
Toi, même assis là-bas, dans une
Cabane de bambous, – volets
Clos, tentures de perse brune, –

Tu torcherais des floraisons
Dignes d'Oises extravagantes! ...
– Poëte! ce sont des raisons
Non moins risibles qu'arrogantes! ...

But, my dear Chap, Art does not consist, now – it's the truth –
in allowing the astonishing Eucalyptus boa-constrictors a hexa-
meter long;
    there now! As if Mahogany served only – even in our Guianas –
as helter-skelters for monkeys among the heavy vertigo of the
lianas!
    In short, is a flower, Rosemary or Lily, dead or alive, worth the
excrement of one sea-bird? is it worth a solitary candle-drip?
    – And I mean what I say! You, even sitting over there in a
bamboo hut – with the shutters closed, and brown Persian rugs for
hangings –
    you would scrawl [about] blossoms worthy of extravagant Oise
departments! ... – Poet! these are reasonings no less absurd than
arrogant!

IV

Dis, non les pampas printaniers
Noirs d'épouvantables révoltes,
Mais les tabacs, les cotonniers!
Dis les exotiques récoltes!

Dis, front blanc que Phébus tanna,
De combien de dollars se rente
Pedro Velasquez, Habana;
Incague la mer de Sorrente

Où vont les Cygnes par milliers;
Que tes Strophes soient des réclames
Pour l'abatis des mangliers
Fouillés des hydres et des lames!

Ton quatrain plonge aux bois sanglants
Et revient proposer aux Hommes
Divers sujets de sucres blancs,
De pectoraires et de gommes!

IV

Speak, not of pampas in the spring, black with terrible revolts, but of tobacco and cotton-trees! Speak of exotic harvests!

Say, white face which Phoebus has tanned, how many dollars Pedro Velasquez of Havana makes a year; cover with excrement the sea of Sorrento

where the Swans go in thousands; let your lines campaign for the clearing of the mangrove swamps riddled with pools and water-snakes!

Your quatrain plunges into the bloody thickets and comes back to offer to Humanity various subjects: white sugar, bronchial lozenges, and rubbers!

Sachons par Toi si les blondeurs
Des Pics neigeux, vers les Tropiques,
Sont ou des insectes pondeurs
Ou des lichens microscopiques!

Trouve, ô Chasseur, nous le voulons,
Quelques garances parfumées
Que la Nature en pantalons
Fasse éclore! – pour nos Armées!

Trouve, aux abords du Bois qui dort,
Les fleurs, pareilles à des mufles,
D'où bavent des pommades d'or
Sur les cheveux sombres des Buffles!

Trouve, aux prés fous, où sur le Bleu
Tremble l'argent des pubescences,
Des Calices pleins d'Œufs de feu
Qui cuisent parmi les essences!

Trouve des Chardons cotonneux
Dont dix ânes aux yeux de braises
Travaillent à filer les nœuds!
Trouve des Fleurs qui soient des chaises!

Let us know, through You, whether the yellownesses of snow
Peaks near the Tropics are insects which lay many eggs, or micro-
scopic lichens!

Find, O Hunter, we desire it, one or two scented madder plants
which Nature may cause to bloom in trousers – for our Armies!

Find, on the outskirts of the Sleeping Wood, flowers which look
like snouts, out of which drip golden pomades on to the dark hair of
buffaloes!

Find, in wild meadows, where on the Blue Grass shivers the
silver of downy growths, Calyxes full of fiery Eggs cooking
among the essential oils!

Find downy Thistles whose wool ten asses with glaring eyes
labour to spin! Find Flowers which are chairs!

Oui, trouve au cœur des noirs filons
Des fleurs presque pierres, – fameuses! –
Qui vers leurs durs ovaires blonds
Aient des amygdales gemmeuses!

Sers-nous, ô Farceur, tu le peux,
Sur un plat de vermeil splendide
Des ragoûts de Lys sirupeux
Mordant nos cuillers Alfénide!

V

Quelqu'un dira le grand Amour,
Voleur des sombres Indulgences:
Mais ni Renan, ni le chat Murr
N'ont vu les Bleus Thyrses immenses!

Toi, fais jouer dans nos torpeurs,
Par les parfums les hystéries;
Exalte-nous vers des candeurs
Plus candides que les Maries ...

Yes: find in the heart of coal-black seams flowers that are almost
stones – marvellous ones! – which, close to their hard pale ovaries,
bear gemlike tonsils!

Serve us, O Stuffer – this you can do – on a splendid vermilion
plate, stews of syrupy Lilies [strong enough] to corrode our
German-silver spoons!

V

Someone will speak about great Love, the thief of black Indul-
gences: but neither Renan nor Murr the cat have seen the immense
Blue Thyrsuses!

You, quicken in our sluggishness, by means of scents, hysteria!
Exalt us towards purities whiter than the Marys ...

Commerçant! colon! médium!
Ta Rime sourdra, rose ou blanche,
Comme un rayon de sodium,
Comme un caoutchouc qui s'épanche!

De tes noirs Poèmes, – Jongleur!
Blancs, verts, et rouges dioptriques,
Que s'évadent d'étranges fleurs
Et des papillons électriques!

Voilà! c'est le Siècle d'enfer!
Et les poteaux télégraphiques
Vont orner, – lyre aux chants de fer,
Tes omoplates magnifiques!

Surtout, rime une version
Sur le mal des pommes de terre!
– Et, pour la composition
De Poèmes pleins de mystère

Tradesman! Colonial! Medium! Your rhyme will well up, pink or white, like a blaze of sodium, like a bleeding rubber-tree!

But from your dark poems – Juggler! – dioptric white and green and red, let strange flowers burst out, and electric butterflies!

See! it's the Century of hell! and the telegraph poles, the iron-voiced lyre, are going to adorn your magnificent shoulders!

Above all, though, give us a rhymed account of the potato blight! – and, in order to compose Poems full of mystery – intended

Qu'on doive lire de Tréguier
A Paramaribo, rachète
Des Tomes de Monsieur Figuier,
– Illustrés! – chez Monsieur Hachette!

Alcide Bava
A. R.
14 juillet 1871

LE BATEAU IVRE

Comme je descendais des Fleuves impassibles,
Je ne me sentis plus guidé par les haleurs:
Des Peaux-Rouges criards les avaient pris pour cibles,
Les ayant cloués nus aux poteaux de couleurs.

J'étais insoucieux de tous les équipages,
Porteur de blés flamands ou de cotons anglais.
Quand avec mes haleurs ont fini ces tapages,
Les Fleuves m'ont laissé descendre où je voulais.

to be read from Tréguier[1] to Paramaribo, go and buy a few
Volumes by Monsieur Figuier – illustrated! – at Hachette's!

Alcide Bava
A. R.
14 July 1871

The Drunken Boat

As I was floating down unconcerned Rivers, I no longer felt
myself steered by the haulers: gaudy Redskins had taken them for
targets, nailing them naked to coloured stakes.

I cared nothing for all my crews, carrying Flemish wheat or
English cottons. When, along with my haulers, those uproars were
done with, the Rivers let me sail downstream where I pleased.

---

1. In northern France.

Dans les clapotements furieux des marées,
Moi, l'autre hiver, plus sourd que les cerveaux d'enfants,
Je courus! Et les Péninsules démarrées
N'ont pas subi tohu-bohus plus triomphants.

Le tempête a béni mes éveils maritimes.
Plus léger qu'un bouchon j'ai dansé sur les flots
Qu'on appelle rouleurs éternels de victimes,
Dix nuits, sans regretter l'œil niais des falots!

Plus douce qu'aux enfants la chair des pommes sures,
L'eau verte pénétra ma coque de sapin
Et des taches de vins bleus et des vomissures
Me lava, dispersant gouvernail et grappin.

Et dès lors, je me suis baigné dans le Poème
De la Mer, infusé d'astres, et lactescent,
Dévorant les azurs verts; où, flottaison blême
Et ravie, un noyé pensif parfois descend;

Into the ferocious tide-rips, last winter, more absorbed than the minds of children, I ran! And the unmoored Peninsulas never endured more triumphant clamourings.

The storm made bliss of my sea-borne awakenings. Lighter than a cork, I danced on the waves which men call eternal rollers of victims, for ten nights, without once missing the foolish eye of the harbour lights!

Sweeter than the flesh of sour apples to children, the green water penetrated my pinewood hull and washed me clean of the bluish wine-stains and the splashes of vomit, carrying away both rudder and anchor.

And from that time on I bathed in the Poem of the Sea, star-infused and churned into milk, devouring the green azures; where, entranced and pallid flotsam, a dreaming drowned man sometimes goes down;

Où, teignant tout à coup les bleuités, délires
Et rhythmes lents sous les rutilements du jour,
Plus fortes que l'alcool, plus vastes que nos lyres,
Fermentent les rousseurs amères de l'amour!

Je sais les cieux crevant en éclairs, et les trombes
Et les ressacs et les courants: je sais le soir,
L'Aube exaltée ainsi qu'un peuple de colombes,
Et j'ai vu quelquefois ce que l'homme a cru voir!

J'ai vu le soleil bas, taché d'horreurs mystiques,
Illuminant de longs figements violets,
Pareils à des acteurs de drames très-antiques
Les flots roulant au loin leurs frissons de volets!

J'ai rêvé la nuit verte aux neiges éblouies,
Baiser montant aux yeux des mers avec lenteurs,
La circulation des sèves inouïes,
Et l'éveil jaune et bleu des phosphores chanteurs!

where, suddenly dyeing the bluenesses – deliriums and slow rhythms under the gleams of the daylight, stronger than alcohol, vaster than music – ferment the bitter rednesses of love!

I have come to know the skies splitting with lightnings, and the waterspouts, and the breakers and currents; I know the evening, and Dawn rising up like a flock of doves, and sometimes I have seen what men have imagined they saw!

I have seen the low-hanging sun speckled with mystic horrors lighting up long violet coagulations like the performers in antique dramas; waves rolling back into the distances their shiverings of venetian blinds!

I have dreamed of the green night of the dazzled snows, the kiss rising slowly to the eyes of the seas, the circulation of undreamed-of saps, and the yellow-blue awakening of singing phosphorus!

J'ai suivi, des mois pleins, pareille aux vacheries
Hystériques, la houle à l'assaut des récifs,
Sans songer que les pieds lumineux des Maries
Pussent forcer le mufle aux Océans poussifs!

J'ai heurté, savez-vous, d'incroyables Florides
Mêlant aux fleurs des yeux de panthères à peaux
D'hommes! Des arcs-en-ciel tendus comme des brides
Sous l'horizon des mers, à de glauques troupeaux!

J'ai vu fermenter les marais énormes, nasses
Où pourrit dans les joncs tout un Léviathan!
Des écroulements d'eaux au milieu des bonaces,
Et les lointains vers les gouffres cataractant!

Glaciers, soleils d'argent, flots nacreux, cieux de braises!
Échouages hideux au fond des golfes bruns
Où les serpents géants dévorés des punaises
Choient, des arbres tordus, avec de noirs parfums!

I have followed, for whole months on end, the swells battering the reefs like hysterical herds of cows, – never dreaming that the luminous feet of the Marys could muzzle by force the snorting Oceans!

I have struck, do you realize, incredible Floridas, where mingle with flowers the eyes of panthers in human skins! Rainbows stretched like bridles under the seas' horizon to glaucous herds!

I have seen the enormous swamps seething, traps where a whole leviathan rots in the reeds! Downfalls of waters in the midst of the calm, and distances cataracting down into abysses!

Glaciers, suns of silver, waves of pearl, skies of red-hot coals! Hideous wrecks at the bottom of brown gulfs where the giant snakes, devoured by vermin, fall from the twisted trees with black odours!

J'aurais voulu montrer aux enfants ces dorades
Du flot bleu, ces poissons d'or, ces poissons chantants.
– Des écumes de fleurs ont bercé mes dérades
Et d'ineffables vents m'ont ailé par instants.

Parfois, martyr lassé des pôles et des zones,
La mer dont le sanglot faisait mon roulis doux
Montait vers moi ses fleurs d'ombre aux ventouses jaunes
Et je restais, ainsi qu'une femme à genoux ...

Presque île, ballottant sur mes bords les querelles
Et les fientes d'oiseaux clabaudeurs aux yeux blonds.
Et je voguais, lorsqu'à travers mes liens frêles
Des noyés descendaient dormir, à reculons! ...

Or moi, bateau perdu sous les cheveux des anses,
Jeté par l'ouragan dans l'éther sans oiseau,
Moi dont les Monitors et les voiliers des Hanses
N'auraient pas repêché la carcasse ivre d'eau;

I should have liked to show to children those dolphins of the blue wave, those golden, those singing fishes. – Foam of flowers rocked my driftings, and at times ineffable winds would lend me wings.

Sometimes, a martyr weary of poles and zones, the sea whose sobs sweetened my rollings lifted its shadow-flowers with their yellow sucking disks towards me, and I hung there like a kneeling woman ...

[I was] almost an island, tossing on my beaches the brawls and droppings of pale-eyed, clamouring birds. And I was scudding along when across my frayed cordage drowned men sank backwards into sleep! ...

But now I, a boat lost under the hair of coves, hurled by the hurricane into the birdless ether; I, whose wreck, dead-drunk and sodden with water, neither Monitor nor Hanse ships would have fished up;

Libre, fumant, monté de brumes violettes,
Moi qui trouais le ciel rougeoyant comme un mur
Qui porte, confiture exquise aux bons poëtes,
Des lichens de soleil et des morves d'azur;

Qui courais, taché de lunules électriques,
Planche folle, escorté des hippocampes noirs,
Quand les juillets faisaient crouler à coups de triques
Les cieux ultramarins aux ardents entonnoirs;

Mois qui tremblais, sentant geindre à cinquante lieues
Le rut des Béhémots et les Maelstroms épais,
Fileur éternel des immobilités bleues,
Je regrette l'Europe aux anciens parapets!

J'ai vu des archipels sidéraux! et des îles
Dont les cieux délirants sont ouverts au vogueur:
— Est-ce en ces nuits sans fonds que tu dors et t'exiles,
Million d'oiseaux d'or, ô future Vigueur? —

free, smoking, risen from violet fogs, I who bored through the wall of the reddening sky which bears a sweetmeat good poets find delicious: lichens of sunlight [mixed] with azure snot;

who ran, speckled with lunula of electricity, a crazy plank with black sea-horses for escort, when Julys were crushing with cudgel blows skies of ultramarine into burning funnels;

I who trembled to feel at fifty leagues' distance the groans of Behemoth's rutting, and of the dense Maelstroms; eternal spinner of blue immobilities, I long for Europe with its age-old parapets!

I have seen archipelagos of stars! and islands whose delirious skies are open to sailors: — Do you sleep, are you exiled in those bottomless nights, O million golden birds, Life Force of the future?

Mais, vrai, j'ai trop pleuré! Les Aubes sont navrantes.
Toute lune est atroce et tout soleil amer:
L'âcre amour m'a gonflé de torpeurs enivrantes.
Ô que ma quille éclate! Ô que j'aille à la mer!

Si je désire une eau d'Europe, c'est la flache
Noire et froide où vers le crépuscule embaumé
Un enfant accroupi plein de tristesses, lâche
Un bateau frêle comme un papillon de mai.

Je ne puis plus, baigné de vos langueurs, ô lames,
Enlever leur sillage aux porteurs de cotons,
Ni traverser l'orgueil des drapeaux et des flammes,
Ni nager sous les yeux horribles des pontons.

VOYELLES [1]

A NOIR, E blanc, I rouge, U vert, O bleu: voyelles,
Je dirai quelque jour vos naissances latentes:
A, noir corset velu des mouches éclatantes
Qui bombinent autour des puanteurs cruelles,

But, truly, I have wept too much! The Dawns are heartbreaking. Every moon is atrocious and every sun bitter: sharp love has swollen me up with heady languors. O let my keel split! O let me sink to the bottom!

If there is one water in Europe I want, it is the black cold pool where into the scented twilight a child squatting full of sadness launches a boat as fragile as a butterfly in May.

I can no more, bathed in your languors, O waves, sail in the wake of the carriers of cottons; nor undergo the pride of the flags and pennants; nor pull past the horrible eyes of the hulks.

Vowels [1]

A black, E white, I red, U green, O blue: vowels, I shall tell, one day, of your mysterious origins: A, black velvety jacket of brilliant flies which buzz around cruel smells,

1. See Introduction, pp. xxiv–xxvi.

Golfes d'ombre; E, candeurs des vapeurs et des tentes,
Lances des glaciers fiers, rois blancs, frissons d'ombelles;
I, pourpres, sang craché, rire des lèvres belles
Dans la colère ou les ivresses pénitentes;

U, cycles, vibrements divins des mers virides,
Paix des pâtis semés d'animaux, paix des rides
Que l'alchimie imprime aux grands fronts studieux;

O, suprême Clairon plein des strideurs étranges,
Silences traversés des Mondes et des Anges:
– O l'Oméga, rayon violet de Ses Yeux!

———

L'ÉTOILE a pleuré rose au cœur de tes oreilles,
L'infini roulé blanc de ta nuque à tes reins;
La mer a perlé rousse à tes mammes vermeilles,
Et l'Homme saigné noir à ton flanc souverain.

gulfs of shadow; E, whiteness of vapours and of tents, lances of proud glaciers, white kings, shivers of cow-parsley; I, purples, spat blood, smile of beautiful lips in anger or in the raptures of penitence;

U, waves, divine shudderings of viridian seas, the peace of pastures dotted with animals, the peace of the furrows which alchemy prints on broad studious foreheads;

O, sublime Trumpet full of strange piercing sounds, silences crossed by Angels and by Worlds – O the Omega! the violet ray of Her Eyes!

———

THE star has wept rose-colour in the heart of your ears, the infinite rolled white from your nape to the small of your back; the sea has broken russet at your vermilion nipples, and Man bled black at your royal side.

LES CORBEAUX

Seigneur, quand froide est la prairie,
Quand, dans les hameaux abattus,
Les longs angélus se sont tus ...
Sur la nature défleurie
Faites s'abattre des grands cieux
Les chers corbeaux délicieux.

Armée étrange aux cris sévères,
Les vents froids attaquent vos nids!
Vous, le long des fleuves jaunis,
Sur les routes aux vieux calvaires,
Sur les fossés et sur les trous
Dispersez-vous, ralliez-vous!

Par milliers, sur les champs de France,
Où dorment des morts d'avant-hier,
Tournoyez, n'est-ce pas, l'hiver,
Pour que chaque passant repense!
Sois donc le crieur du devoir,
Ô notre funèbre oiseau noir!

The Rooks

Lord, when the meadowland is cold, and when in the downcast hamlets the long Angeluses are silent ... down on Nature barren of flowers let them sweep from the wide skies, the dear delightful rooks.

Strange army with your stern cries, the cold winds are assaulting your nests! You – along yellowed rivers, over the roads with their old Calvarys, over ditches, over holes – disperse! and rally!

In your thousands, over the fields of France where the day before yesterday's dead are sleeping, wheel in the wintertime, won't you, so that each traveller may remember! Be, then, the one who calls men to duty, O funereal black bird of ours!

Mais, saints du ciel, en haut du chêne,
Mât perdu dans le soir charmé,
Laissez les fauvettes de mai
Pour ceux qu'au fond du bois enchaîne,
Dans l'herbe d'où l'on ne peut fuir,
La défaite sans avenir.

But, ye saints of the sky, at the oak tree top, the masthead lost in the enchanted twilight, leave alone the warblers of May, for the sake of those whom, in the depths of the wood, in the undergrowth from which there is no escaping, defeat without a future has enslaved.

BRIBES[1]

I

Au pied des sombres murs, battant les maigres chiens,

II

Oh! si les cloches sont de bronze,
Nos cœurs sont pleins de désespoir!
En juin mil huit cent soixante-onze,
Trucidés par un être noir,
Nous Jean Baudry, nous Jean Balouche,
Ayant accompli nos souhaits,
Mourûmes en ce clocher louche
En abominant Desdouets!

FRAGMENTS[1]

I

At the foot of dark walls, beating the skinny dogs,

II

Oh, as true as the bells are bronze, our hearts are full of despair! In June, eighteen seventy-one, massacred by a black being, we Jean Baudry, we Jean Balouche, having accomplished our wishes, died in this ambiguous belfry, [firm in our] loathing [of] Desdouets![2]

---

1. The name given by the editors of the Pléiade edition to this collection of fragments and isolated verses.

2. Desdouets was Rimbaud's headmaster. The belfry was ambiguous because Rimbaud found a chamber-pot in it – which he hurled down on to the square.

III

Derrière tressautait en des hoquets grotesques
Une rose avalée au ventre du portier.

IV

Brune, elle avait seize ans quand on la maria.
. . . .

Car elle aime d'amour son fils de dix-sept ans.

V

[LA PLAINTE DU VIEILLARD
MONARCHISTE À. M. HENRI PERRIN,
JOURNALISTE RÉPUBLICAIN]

. . . .
. . . . .Vous avez
Menti, sur mon fémur! vous avez menti, fauve
Apôtre! Vous voulez faire des décavés
De nous? Vous voudriez peler notre front chauve?
Mais moi, j'ai deux fémurs bistournés et gravés!

III

Behind [his waistcoat] jumped up and down in grotesque hiccups
a swallowed rose in the porter's belly.

IV

Dark-haired, she was sixteen when they married her.
. . . .

For she is in love with her seventeen-year-old son.

V

[*The Complaint of the Old Monarchist to M. Henri Perrin, a
Republican Journalist*]

. . . . You have lied, on my thigh-
bone! you have lied, tawny apostle! You want to turn us into ruined
men? You'd like to skin our bald heads? But I have two thighbones,
twisted and embossed!

Parce que vous suintez tous les jours au collège
Sur vos collets d'habit de quoi faire un beignet,
Que vous êtes un masque à dentiste, au manège
Un cheval épilé qui bave en un cornet,
Vous croyez effacer mes quarante ans de siège!

J'ai mon fémur! j'ai mon fémur! j'ai mon fémur!
C'est cela que depuis quarante ans je bistourne
Sur le bord de ma chaise aimée en noyer dur;
L'impression du bois pour toujours y séjourne;
Et quand j'apercevrai, moi, ton organe impur,

À tous tes abonnés, pître, à tes abonnées,
Pertractant cet organe avachi dans leurs mains,
. . . .
Je ferai retoucher, pour tous les lendemains,
Ce fémur travaillé depuis quarante années!

Because every day at school you sweat enough on your suit col-
lars to fry a fritter; because you're [as false as] a dentist's disguise,[1]
a bald riding-school horse frothing at the mouth and long in the
tooth as well, you think to wipe out my forty years of office!
I have my thighbone! I have my thighbone! I have my thigh-
bone! That's what I have been twisting for forty years on the edge
of my well-loved hard walnut chair; the imprint of the wood stays
always on it; and I, when I behold your impure organ,
all your subscribers, buffoon, all your subscribers, handling that
sloppy organ in their hands, ... I shall
touch them, for all tomorrows to come, with this thighbone which
has been worked on forty years!

_____

1. There is a French expression, 'to lie like a puller of teeth'.

VI

[LA PLAINTE DES ÉPICIERS]

Qu'il entre au magasin quand la lune miroite
À ses vitrages bleus,
Qu'il empoigne à nos yeux la chicorée en boîte

VII

. . . . Sont-ce
. . . . . . [des tonneaux?] . . . . qu'on défonce?
. . . . Non!
C'est un chef cuisinier ronflant comme un basson.

VIII

. . . . Parmi les ors, les quartz, les porcelaines,
. . . . un pot de nuit banal,
Reliquaire indécent des vieilles châtelaines,
Courbe ses flancs honteux sur l'acajou royal.

VI

[*The Complaint of the Grocers*]

Let him enter the shop when the moon is reflected in its blue panes;
let him seize under our noses tins of chicory

VII

. . . . . Is it . . . [casks?] . . . . . being staved in? . . . .
. . No! It is a cook-chef snoring like a bassoon.

VIII

. . . . . Among the gold and quartz and porcelain objects . . .
. . . a common chamber-pot, unseemly reliquary of old Ladies of
the Manor, rounds its shameful sides on the royal mahogany.

IX

Oh! les vignettes pérennelles!

X

Et le poëte soûl engueulait l'Univers.

XI

VERS POUR LES LIEUX

De ce siège si mal tourné
Qu'il fait s'embrouiller nos entrailles,
Le trou dut être maçonné
Par de véritables canailles.

Quand le fameux Tropmann détruisit Henri Kink
Cet assassin avait dû s'asseoir sur ce siège
Car le con de Badingue et le con d'Henri V
Sont bien dignes vraiment de cet état de siège.

IX

Oh! the eternal vignettes!

X

And the poet, drunk, stormed at the Universe.[1]

XI

Lines for Places

Of this seat, so badly shaped that it ties our bowels in knots, the hole must have been botched by some genuine blackguards.

When the famous Tropmann destroyed Henri Kink,[2] the murderer must have sat upon this seat; for Badingue and Henry V, the cunts, are truly very worthy of a seat in this state [or, this state of siège].

---

1. There was a café at Charleville called L'Univers.
2. In 1869, Tropmann killed the whole Kink family for their money.

XII

Il pleut doucement sur la ville.

XIII

Prends-y garde, ô ma vie absente!

XIV

Le clair de lune, quand le clocher sonnait douze ...

XII

It is raining softly on the town.

XIII

See to it, O my absent life!

XIV

The moonlight, as the church clock was striking twelve ...

LES STUPRA

Les anciens animaux saillissaient, même en course,
Avec des glands bardés de sang et d'excrément.
Nos pères étalaient leur membre fièrement
Par le pli de la gaine et le grain de la bourse.

Au moyen âge pour la femelle, ange ou pource,
Il fallait un gaillard de solide grément;
Même un Kléber, d'après la culotte qui ment
Peut-être un peu, n'a pas dû manquer de ressource.

D'ailleurs l'homme au plus fier mammifère est égal;
L'énormité de leur membre à tort nous étonne;
Mais une heure stérile a sonné: le cheval

Et le bœuf ont bridé leurs ardeurs, et personne
N'osera plus dresser son orgueil génital
Dans les bosquets où grouille une enfance bouffonne.

THE STUPRA[1]

The ancient beasts bred even on the run, their glans encrusted with blood and excrement. Our forefathers displayed their members proudly by the fold of the sheath and the grain of the scrotum.

In the middle ages, for a female, angel or sow, a fellow whose gear was substantial was needed; [and] even a Kléber, judging by his breeches – which exaggerate, perhaps, a little – can't have lacked resources.

Besides, man is equal to the proudest mammal; we are wrong to be surprised at the hugeness of their members; but a sterile hour has struck: the gelding

and the ox have bridled their ardours, and no one will dare again to raise his genital pride in the copses teeming with comical children.

1. Latin: defilements, pollutions by lust.

Nos fesses ne sont pas les leurs. Souvent j'ai vu
Des gens déboutonnés derrière quelque haie,
Et, dans ces bains sans gêne où l'enfance s'égaie,
J'observais le plan et l'effet de notre cul.

Plus ferme, blême en bien des cas, il est pourvu
De méplats évidents que tapisse la claie
Des poils; pour elles, c'est seulement dans la raie
Charmante que fleurit le long satin touffu.

Une ingéniosité touchante et merveilleuse
Comme l'on ne voit qu'aux anges des saints tableaux
Imite la joue où le sourire se creuse.

Oh! de même être nus, chercher joie et repos,
Le front tourné vers sa portion glorieuse,
Et libres tous les deux murmurer des sanglots?

Our buttocks are not theirs. I have often seen people unbuttoned
behind some hedge; and, in those shameless bathings where chil-
dren are gay, I used to observe the form and performance of our
arse.

Firmer, in many cases pale, it possesses striking forms which
the screen of hairs covers; for women, it is only in the charming
parting that the long tufted silk flowers.

A touching and marvellous ingenuity such as you see only in
[the faces of] angels in holy pictures imitates the cheek where the
smile makes a hollow.

Oh! for us to be naked like that, seeking joy and repose, facing
one's companion's glorious part, both of us free, and murmuring
sobs?

Obscur et froncé comme un œillet violet,
Il respire, humblement tapi parmi la mousse
Humide encor d'amour qui suit la rampe douce
Des fesses blanches jusqu'au bord de son ourlet.

Des filaments pareils à des larmes de lait
Ont pleuré sous l'autan cruel qui les repousse
À travers de petits caillots de marne rousse,
Pour s'aller perdre où la pente les appelait.

Mon rêve s'aboucha souvent à sa ventouse;
Mon âme, du coït matériel jalouse,
En fit son larmier fauve et son nid de sanglots.

C'est l'olive pâmée et la flûte câline,
Le tube d'où descend la céleste praline,
Chanaan féminin dans les moiteurs enclos.

Dark and wrinkled like a purple pink, it breathes, nestling
humbly among the moss still damp with love that follows the
gentle slope of the white buttocks to its crater's edge.

Filaments like tears of milk have wept in the cruel South wind
which pushes them back across little clots of reddish marl to lose
themselves where the slope called them.

My dream has often kissed its opening; my soul, jealous of
physical coitus, has made this its fawn-coloured tear-bottle, its nest
of sobs.

It is the rapturous olive and the wheedling flute, the tube from
which the heavenly burnt almond falls, feminine Canaan enclosed
with moistures.

ALBUM DIT «ZUTIQUE»

Conneries

COCHER IVRE

Pouacre
Boit:
Nacre
Voit:

Acre
Loi,
Fiacre
Choit!

Femme
Tombe,
Lombe

Saigne:
Geigne.
Clame!

A. R.

ALBUM CALLED 'ZUTIQUE'[1]

Conneries.[2]

Drunken Coachman

UNWASHED drinks: mother-of-pearl sees: bitter law [of gravity?],
carriage falls! Woman tumbles, loin bleeds: whimpers. Outcry!

A. R.

---

1. *Zut:* to hell with you!
2. *Con:* cunt.

JEUNE GOINFRE

Casquette
De moire,
Quéquette
D'ivoire,

Toilette
Très noire,
Paul guette
L'armoire,

Projette
Languette
Sur poire,

S'apprête,
Baguette,
Et foire.

A. R.

Young Greedyguts

Cap of silk moiré, little wand[1] of ivory, clothes very dark. Paul watches the cupboard, sticks out little tongue at pear, prepares, gives a poke, and squitters.

A. R.

---

1. *Quéquette* is slang for penis. The whole poem can be read as having an indecent meaning, presumably.

PARIS

Aʟ. Godillot, Gambier,
Galopeau, Wolf-Pleyel,
– O Robinets! – Menier,
– O Christs! – Leperdriel!

Kinck, Jacob, Bonbonnel!
Veuillot, Tropmann, Augier!
Gill, Mendès, Manuel,
Guido Gonin! – Panier

Des Grâces! L'Hérissé!
Cirages onctueux!
Pains vieux, spiritueux!

Aveugles! – puis, qui sait? –
Sergents de ville, Enghiens
Chez soi! – Soyons chrétiens!

A. R.

Paris

Aʟ[phonse] Godillot, Gambier, Galopeau, Wolf[f]-Pleyel, – O
Robinets! – Menier, – O Christs! – Leperdriel! [1]

Kinck, Jacob, Bonbonnel! Veuillot, Tropmann, Augier! Gill,
Mendès, Manuel, Guido Gonin! – Basket
of the Graces! L'Hérissé! Unctuous waxes! Old loaves, spirits!

Blind men! – but then who knows? – Beadles, [Dukes of]
Enghien. – In one's own home! – [For God's sake] let's be christ-
ian! [2]

A. R.

---

1. Taken from contemporary shopfronts, the names represent
sellers of shoes, clay pipes, frock-coats, pianos, (uncertain), choco-
late, (—), and surgical appliances and medicine.

2. In the second half of the octave of this sonnet, and in the sestet,
one notices the names of the murderer and his victim – cf. 'Lines for
Places' – and of the hatter L'Hérissé. 'Enghien-les-Bains in your
own home' was a claim made by a pharmacist of the time for his
Enghien Mineral Water Tablets. The Duke of Enghien (1772–
1804) was a royal pretender whom Bonaparte caused to be shot at
Vincennes.

VIEUX DE LA VIEILLE

Aux paysans de l'empereur!
À l'empereur des paysans!
Au fils de Mars,
Au glorieux 18 mars!
Où le ciel d'Eugénie a béni les entrailles!

LES LÈVRES CLOSES
Vu à Rome

Il est à Rome, à la Sixtine,
Couverte d'emblèmes chrétiens,
Une cassette écarlatine
Où sèchent des nez fort anciens:

Nez d'ascètes de Thébaïde,
Nez de chanoines du Saint-Graal
Où se figea la nuit livide,
Et l'ancien plain-chant sépulcral.

The Old Guard

To the emperor's peasants! To the peasants' emperor! To the sons of Mars, to the glorious 18 March![1] When heaven blessed the guts of Eugénie!

Lips Sealed
(Seen in Rome)

There is in Rome at the Sistine, covered with Christian emblems, a little scarlet skullcap in which ancient noses lie drying:

noses of Thebaid ascetics, noses of canons of the Holy Grail, in which leaden-hued night coagulated, and the old sepulchral plain-chant.

---

1. On this day the Empress gave birth to a son.

Dans leur sécheresse mystique,
Tous les matins, on introduit
De l'immondice schismatique
Qu'en poudre fine on a réduit.

Léon Dierx
A. R.

FÊTE GALANTE

RÊVEUR, Scapin
Gratte un lapin
Sous sa capote.

Colombina
– Que l'on pina! –
– Do, mi, – tapote

L'œil du lapin
Qui tôt, tapin
Est en ribote.

Paul Verlaine
A. R.

Into their mystic desiccation every morning there is poured schismatic filth reduced to a fine powder.

Léon Dierx
A. R.

Love-Feast [1]

DREAMY, Scapin tickles a rabbit under his coat.
Columbine – who got fucked – Do, mi – strums
on the rabbit's eye which soon, losing control, gets tipsy.

Paul Verlaine
A. R.

---

1. Parody on a poem by Verlaine.

L'ANGELOT MAUDIT

Toits bleuâtres et portes blanches
Comme en de nocturnes dimanches

Au bout de la ville, sans bruit
La rue est blanche, et c'est la nuit.

La rue a des maisons étranges
Avec des persiennes d'anges.

Mais, vers une borne, voici
Accourir, mauvais et transi,

Un noir angelot qui titube,
Ayant trop mangé de jujube.

Il fait caca: puis disparaît:
Mais son caca maudit paraît,

Sous la lune sainte qui vaque,
De sang sale un léger cloaque.

Louis Ratisbonne
A. RIMBAUD

The Accursed Cherub

Bluish roofs and white doors as on nocturnal Sundays,
at the town's end, the road without sound is white, and it is
night.
The street has strange houses with shutters [made] of angels
[' wings].
But look how he runs towards a boundary-stone, evil and shiver-
ing,
A dark cherub who staggers, having eaten too many jujubes.
He does a cack: then disappears: but his cursed cack appears
Under the holy empty moon, a slight cesspool of dirty blood.

Louis Ratisbonne
A. RIMBAUD

189

LYS

Ô BALANÇOIRE! Ô lys, Clysopompes d'argent!
Dédaigneux des travaux, dédaigneux des famines!
L'aurore vous emplit d'un amour détergent!
Une douceur de ciel beurre vos étamines!

Armand Silvestre

A. R.

L'HUMANITÉ chaussait le vaste enfant Progrès

Louis-Xavier de Ricard

ARTHUR RIMBAUD

REMEMBRANCES DU VIEILLARD IDIOT

PARDON, mon père!

Jeune, aux foires de campagne,
Je cherchais, non le tir banal où tout coup gagne,
Mais l'endroit plein de cris où les ânes, le flanc
Fatigué, déployaient ce long tube sanglant
Que je ne comprends pas encore! ...

Lily

O SWING! O Lily! Enema of silver! Disdainful of labours, disdainful of famines! Dawn fills you with a detergent love! A heavenly sweetness butters your stamens!

Armand Silvestre

A. R.

HUMANITY was lacing the shoes of the vast infant Progress.

Louis-Xavier de Ricard

ARTHUR RIMBAUD

Memories of the Feeble-minded Old Man

FORGIVENESS, Father! When I was young, at country fairs, I sought, not the dull shooting gallery where every shot wins, but the place full of shouts where donkeys, with weary flanks, display that long bloody tube which I still do not understand! ...

Et puis ma mère,
Dont la chemise avait une senteur amère
Quoique fripée au bas et jaune comme un fruit,
Ma mère qui montait au lit avec un bruit
– Fils du travail pourtant, – ma mère, avec sa cuisse
De femme mûre, avec ses reins très gros où plisse
Le linge, me donna ces chaleurs que l'on tait.

Une honte plus crue et plus calme, c'était
Quand ma petite sœur, au retour de la classe,
Ayant usé longtemps ses sabots sur la glace,
Pissait, et regardait s'échapper de sa lèvre
D'en bas, serrée et rose, un fil d'urine mièvre …!

Ô pardon!
Je songeais à mon père parfois:
Le soir, le jeu de cartes et les mots plus grivois,
Le voisin, et moi qu'on écartait, choses vues …
– Car un père est troublant! – et les choses conçues! …

And then my mother … whose shift had a bitter odour although it was ragged at the hem and yellow as a fruit; my mother, who climbed into bed with a noise – which was, all the same, a son of toil – my mother with her ripe woman's thigh, with her very fat rump where the linen makes a fold – gave me heats of the kind one does not talk about.

A cruder and calmer shame was when my little sister, coming back from school, having worn her clogs down for a long time on the ice, would piss, and watch escaping from her nether lip, tight and pink, a fragile thread of urine …!

O forgiveness! … I used to think of my father sometimes: in the evening, the card game, and the bawdiest words; our neighbour, and myself whom they thrust aside; things seen … – for a father is disturbing! – and things imagined! … His knee,

Son genou, câlineur parfois; son pantalon
Dont mon doigt désirait ouvrir la fente ... – oh! non! –
Pour avoir le bout gros, noir et dur de mon père,
Dont la pileuse main me berçait! ...

                               Je veux taire
Le pot, l'assiette à manche, entrevue au grenier,
Les almanachs couverts en rouge, et le panier
De charpie, et la Bible, et les lieux, et la bonne,
La Sainte-Vierge et le crucifix ...

                               Oh! personne
Ne fut si fréquemment troublé, comme étonné!
Et maintenant que le pardon me soit donné:
Puisque les sens infects m'ont mis de leurs victimes,
Je me confesse de l'aveu des jeunes crimes! ...

. . . .

sometimes apt to fondle; his trousers whose fly my finger wanted to open ... – Oh! no! – To have the thick dark hard bit of my father, whose hairy hand rocked me! ...

I don't want to speak of the pot, the dish with the handle, glimpsed in the attic; the almanacs covered with red, and the basket of lint, and the Bible, and the latrines, and the servant girl; the Holy Virgin and the crucifix ...

Oh! no one was so often disturbed, as if astounded! And now, so that forgiveness may be granted me: since the infected senses have made me their victims, I make my confession of the crimes of my youth! ...

. . . .

Puis! – qu'il me soit permis de parler au Seigneur! –
Pourquoi la puberté tardive et le malheur
Du gland tenace et trop consulté? Pourquoi l'ombre
Si lente au bas du ventre? et ces terreurs sans nombre
Comblant toujours la joie ainsi qu'un gravier noir?

Moi, j'ai toujours été stupéfait! Quoi savoir?
. . . .
Pardonné? ...
            Reprenez la chancelière bleue,
Mon père.
        Ô cette enfance! . . . .
. . . .
. . . . – et tirons-nous la queue!
François Coppée
A. R.

And besides! – may I be permitted to speak to the Lord! – why
puberty tardily come, and why the pain of the obstinate and too-
much-consulted glans? Why the shadow so slow at the base of the
belly? and these numberless terrors which bury joy as if under
black gravel?

Myself, I have always been stupefied! What is there to know?
. . . .

Forgiven? ... take back the blue hassock, Father. O that child-
hood! . . . . – and let us jerk our tails off!
François Coppée
A. R.

Vieux Coppées

Les soirs d'été, sous l'œil ardent des devantures,
Quand la sève frémit sous les grilles obscures
Irradiant au pied des grêles marronniers,
Hors de ces groupes noirs, joyeux ou casaniers,
Suceurs de brûle-gueule où baiseurs du cigare,
Dans le kiosque mi-pierre étroit où je m'égare,
– Tandis qu'en haut rougeoie une annonce d'*Ibled*, –
Je songe que l'hiver figera le Tibet
D'eau propre qui bruit, apaisant l'onde humaine,
– Et que l'âpre aquilon n'épargne aucune veine.

François Coppée
A. RIMBAUD

Aux livres de chevet, livres de l'art serein,
Obermann et Genlis, *Vert-vert* et le *Lutrin*,
Blasé de nouveauté grisâtre et saugrenue,
J'espère, la vieillesse étant enfin venue,
Ajouter le traité du Docteur Venetti.

Old 'Coppées'

On summer evenings, under the burning eye of the shopfronts, when the sap simmers under the dark gratings which radiate from the foot of the slender chestnut trees; outside those dark groups of joyful or home-loving people, suckers of cutty pipes or kissers of cigars, in the narrow kiosk half of stone into which I stray – while above me glows an *Ibled* advertisement – I muse how winter will congeal Tibet with sounding clean water, lulling the human swell – and how the bitter north wind spares not one vein.

François Coppée
A. RIMBAUD

To the bedside books, books of serene art; Obermann and Genlis, *Vert-vert* and the *Lectern*, I hope, when old age at last has come, and I am indifferent to boring preposterous novelties, to add the treatise of Doctor Venetti. Disillusioned [, then,] with the stupefied

Je saurai, revenu du public abêti,
Goûter le charme ancien des dessins nécessaires.
Écrivain et graveur ont doré les misères
Sexuelles, et c'est, n'est-ce pas, cordial:
DR VENETTI, *Traité de l'Amour conjugal.*

F. Coppée
A. R.

J'OCCUPAIS un wagon de troisième: un vieux prêtre
Sortit un brûle-gueule et mit à la fenêtre,
Vers les brises, son front très calme aux poils pâlis.
Puis ce chrétien, bravant les brocarts impolis,
S'étant tourné, me fit la demande énergique
Et triste en même temps d'une petite chique
De caporal, – ayant été l'aumônier-chef
D'un rejeton royal condamné derechef –
Pour malaxer l'ennui d'un tunnel, sombre veine
Qui s'offre aux voyageurs, pré-Soissons, ville d'Aisne.

public, I shall be able to appreciate the old-fashioned charm of the
illustrations. Writer and engravers have gilded the sexual miseries,
and it is stimulating, is it not: DR VENETTI, *Treatise on Conjugal
Love.*

F. Coppée
A. R.

I WAS occupying a third-class carriage: an old priest took out a
cutty pipe and put his very calm forehead with faded hairs out of
the window, towards the breezes. Then this Christian, braving im-
polite jests, turning, made the energetic and at the same time sad
request to me of a little pinch of *caporal* – having once been
chaplain-in-chief to a royal scion condemned for the second time –
in order to ease the boredom of a tunnel, dark vein which opens
to travellers at pré-Soissons, a town in Aisne.

JE préfère sans doute, au printemps, la guinguette
Où des marronniers nains bourgeonne la baguette,
Vers la prairie étroite et communale, au mois
De mai. Des jeunes chiens rabroués bien des fois
Viennent près des Buveurs triturer des jacinthes
De plate bande. Et c'est, jusqu'aux soirs d'hyacinthe,
Sur la table d'ardoise où, l'an dix-sept cent vingt,
Un diacre grava son sobriquet latin
Maigre comme une prose à des vitraux d'église,
La toux des flacons noirs qui jamais ne les grise.

François Coppée

A. R.

ÉTAT DE SIÈGE?

LE pauvre postillon, sous le dais de fer blanc,
Chauffant une engelure énorme sous son gant,
Suit son lourd omnibus parmi la rive gauche,
Et de son aine en flamme écarte la sacoche.
Et, tandis que, douce ombre où des gendarmes sont,

I PREFER without a doubt in the spring the suburban café, where the branches of the dwarf chestnut trees break into leaf towards the narrow common, in the month of May. Young dogs, often scolded, come near the Drinkers to trample down the hyacinths of the flower-bed. And until the hyacinth evenings, on the slate table where in the year 1720 a deacon engraved his Latin nickname, thin as an inscription on a church window, there's the splutter of the black bottles that never makes them drunk.

François Coppée

A. R.

State of Siege? [1]

THE poor omnibus driver under the tin canopy, warming a huge chilblain inside his glove, follows his heavy omnibus along the left bank, and from his inflamed groin thrusts away the moneybag. And while [in the] soft shadow where there are policemen, the re-

---

1. See 'Bribes', XI, p. 179, for another instance of the phrase: 'state of siege'.

L'honnête intérieur regarde au ciel profond
La lune se bercer parmi sa verte ouate,
Malgré l'édit et l'heure encore délicate,
Et que l'omnibus rentre à l'Odéon, impur
Le débauché glapit au carrefour obscur!

François Coppée

A. R.

RESSOUVENIR

Cette année où naquit le Prince impérial
Me laisse un souvenir largement cordial
D'un Paris limpide où des N d'or et de neige
Aux grilles du palais, aux gradins du manège,
Éclatent, tricolorement enrubannés.

Dans le remous public des grands chapeaux fanés,
Des chauds gilets à fleurs, des vieilles redingotes,
Et des chants d'ouvriers anciens dans les gargotes,
Sur de châles jonchés l'Empereur marche, noir
Et propre, avec la Sainte Espagnole, le soir.

François Coppée

spectable interior of the bus looks at the moon in the deep sky rock-
ing among its green cotton wool, in spite of the Edict and the still
delicate hour, and the fact that the bus is returning to the Odeon,
the lewd wanton utters piercing cries at the darkened square!

François Coppée

A. R.

Remembrance

The year when the imperial Prince was born has left me a gener-
ously comforting memory of a limpid Paris where N's of gold and
snow at the palace gates and on the mounting-blocks burst out, be-
ribboned in tricolour. In the swirl of crowds, great faded hats,
warm flowered waistcoats, old frock-coats, and the songs of old
workmen in the dining-rooms; on the strewn shawls the Emperor
walks, neat and black, with the Sanctified Spanish-woman, in the
evening.

François Coppée

197

L'ENFANT qui ramassa les balles, le Pubère
Où circule le sang de l'exil et d'un Père
Illustre entend germer sa vie avec l'espoir
De sa figure et de sa stature et veut voir
Des rideaux autres que ceux du Trône et des Crèches,
Aussi son buste exquis n'aspire pas aux brèches
De l'Avenir! – Il a laissé l'ancien jouet. –
Ô son doux rêve! O son bel Enghien!* Son œil est
Approfondi par quelque immense solitude;
«Pauvre jeune homme, il a sans doute l'Habitude!»

                                    François Coppée

* *Parce que «Enghien chez soi».*

THE child who collected balls, the Pubescent, in whom flows the
blood of exile and of an illustrious Father, feels his life springing up
with the hope of his face and his figure, and wishes to see different
curtains from those of the Throne and the Crib; besides, his ex-
quisite head and shoulders do not aspire to storm the breaches of
the Future! – He has left the old plaything – O his sweet dream! O
his fine Enghien!* His eye is deepened by some enormous solitude:
'Poor young man, he has no doubt acquired the Habit of it!'[1]

                                    François Coppée

* *Because 'Enghien in your own home'.* [The footnote is Rim-
baud's. We might say: 'a do-it-yourself Enghien'.]

---

1. An insinuation that the imperial Prince masturbates. For
Enghien, see 'Paris', p. 186.

DERNIERS VERS
(1872)

MÉMOIRE

I

L'EAU claire; comme le sel des larmes d'enfance,
L'assaut au soleil des blancheurs des corps de femme;
la soie, en foule et de lys pur, des oriflammes
sous les murs dont quelque pucelle eut la défense;

l'ébat des anges; – Non ... le courant d'or en marche,
meut ses bras, noirs et lourds, et frais surtout, d'herbe. Elle
sombre, ayant le Ciel bleu pour ciel-de-lit, appelle
pour rideaux l'ombre de la colline et de l'arche.

II

Eh l'humide carreau tend ses bouillons limpides!
L'eau meuble d'or pâle et sans fond les couches prêtes;

LAST LINES (1872)
Memory
I

CLEAR water; [stinging] like the salt of a child's tears, the white-
ness of women's bodies attacking the sun; silken, in masses and
of pure lily, banners under the walls a maiden defended;
the frolic of angels – No ... the current of gold in motion moves
its arms, dark and tired and above all cool, of green. She [the weed]
sinks, and having the blue Heaven for a canopy, takes for curtains
the shade of the hill and of the arch.

II

Oh! the wet surface stretches out its clear bubbles! The water
covers the made beds with pale and bottomless gold; [it is as if] the

Les robes vertes et déteintes des fillettes
font les saules, d'où sautent les oiseaux sans brides.

Plus pure qu'un louis, jaune et chaude paupière
le souci d'eau – ta foi conjugale, ô l'Épouse! –
au midi prompt, de son terne miroir, jalouse
au ciel gris de chaleur la Sphère rose et chère.

III

Madame se tient trop debout dans la prairie
prochaine où neigent les fils du travail; l'ombrelle
aux doigts; foulant l'ombelle; trop fière pour elle;
des enfants lisant dans la verdure fleurie

leur livre de maroquin rouge! Hélas, Lui, comme
mille anges blancs qui se séparent sur la route,
s'éloigne par delà la montagne! Elle, toute
froide, et noire, court! après le départ de l'homme!

faded green dresses of little girls [were] play[ing] at willows, out of
which leap the unbridled birds.

Purer than a gold louis, yellow warm eyelid, the marsh marigold
– thy conjugal faith O Spouse! – at noon sharp, from its dull
mirror, envies the rosy beloved Sphere in the sky wan with heat.

III

Madame holds herself too erect in the neighbouring meadow where
the threads of [the spider's] toil are snowing down; parasol in her
fingers; crushing the cow-parsley; too proud for her; children
reading in the flowery greenness

their red morocco book! Alas, He, like a thousand white angels
parting on the roadway, makes off beyond the mountain! She,
quite cold, and dark, runs! after the flight of the man!

IV

Regret des bras épais et jeunes d'herbe pure!
Or des lunes d'avril au cœur du saint lit! Joie
des chantiers riverains à l'abandon, en proie
aux soirs d'août qui faisaient germer ces pourritures!

Qu'elle pleure à présent sous les remparts! l'haleine
des peupliers d'en haut est pour la seule brise.
Puis, c'est la nappe, sans reflets, sans source, grise:
un vieux, dragueur, dans sa barque immobile, peine.

V

Jouet de cet œil d'eau morne, je n'y puis prendre,
ô canot immobile! oh! bras trop courts! ni l'une
ni l'autre fleur: ni la jaune qui m'importune,
là; ni la bleue, amie à l'eau couleur de cendre.

IV

Nostalgia for the thick young arms of pure green! Gold of the
April moons in the heart of the hallowed bed! Joy of the aban-
doned boat-yards, the prey to the August evenings which quick-
ened these corruptions!

How she weeps, now, under the ramparts! the breath of the
poplars above is all there is for a breeze. Then it is the sheet of
water without reflections and without a spring, grey: an old man,
a dredger, in his motionless boat, labours.

V

Plaything of this eye of mournful water, I cannot reach – O boat
without motion! O too short arms! – either this flower or that
one: neither the yellow one which importunes me here; nor the
blue one, the beloved in the ashen water.

Ah! la poudre des saules qu'une aile secoue!
Les roses des roseaux dès longtemps dévorées!
Mon canot, toujours fixe; et sa chaîne tirée
Au fond de cet œil d'eau sans bords, – à quelle boue?

———————

Qu'est-ce pour nous, mon cœur, que les nappes de
    sang
Et de braise, et mille meurtres, et les longs cris
De rage, sanglots de tout enfer renversant
Tout ordre; et l'Aquilon encor sur les débris;

Et toute vengeance? Rien! ... – Mais si, toute encor,
Nous la voulons! Industriels, princes, sénats:
Périssez! Puissance, justice, histoire: à bas!
Ça nous est dû. Le sang! le sang! la flamme d'or!

Tout à la guerre, à la vengeance, à la terreur,
Mon esprit! Tournons dans la morsure: Ah! passez,
Républiques de ce monde! Des empereurs,
Des régiments, des colons, des peuples, assez!

———————

Ah! the pollen of willows which a wing shakes! The roses of the
reeds, long since eaten away! My boat still fast; and its anchor chain
taut to the bottom of this limitless eye of water, – in what slime?

———————

What does it matter to us, my heart, the sheets of blood and of
coals, and a thousand murders, and long howls of rage; sobbings
from every inferno destroying every [kind of] order; and still the
North wind across the wreckage;
    and all vengeance? Nothing! ... But still, yes: we desire it! In-
dustrialists, princes, senates: perish! Power, justice, history: down!
It is our due. Blood! blood! the golden flame!
    All to war, to vengeance, to terror, my soul! Let us turn in
the wound: Ah! away with you, republics of this world! Of Em-
perors, regiments, colonists, peoples – enough!

Qui remuerait les tourbillons de feu furieux,
Que nous et ceux que nous nous imaginons frères?
À nous, romanesques amis: ça va nous plaire.
Jamais nous ne travaillerons, ô flots de feux!

Europe, Asie, Amérique, disparaissez.
Notre marche vengeresse a tout occupé,
Cités et campagnes! – Nous serons écrasés!
Les volcans sauteront! Et l'Océan frappé …

Oh! mes amis! – Mon cœur, c'est sûr, ils sont des frères:
Noirs inconnus, si nous allions! Allons! allons!
Ô malheur! je me sens frémir, la vieille terre,
Sur moi de plus en plus à vous! la terre fond.

Ce n'est rien: j'y suis; j'y suis toujours.

MICHEL ET CHRISTINE

ZUT alors, si le soleil quitte ces bords!
Fuis, clair déluge! Voici l'ombre des routes.
Dans les saules, dans la vieille cour d'honneur,
L'orage d'abord jette ses larges gouttes.

Who should stir the vortices of furious flames but we and those
whom we imagine brothers? It's our turn, romantic friends: we are
going to enjoy it. Never shall we labour, O fiery waves!

Europe, Asia, America – vanish! Our march of vengeance has
occupied every place, cities and countrysides! – We shall be
smashed! The volcanoes will explode! And the Ocean, smitten …

Oh! my friends! – My heart, it is certain; they are brothers: dark
strangers, if we began! Come on! Come on! – O evil fortune! I
feel myself tremble, the old earth, on me who am more and more
yours! the earth melts.

It is nothing: I am here; I am still here.

Michel and Christine

DAMN it then, if the sun leaves these shores! Fly, bright flood!
Here is the shade of the roads. In the willows, in the old courtyard,
the storm at first sheds its great drops.

Ô cent agneaux, de l'idylle soldats blonds,
Des aqueducs, des bruyères amaigries,
Fuyez! plaine, déserts, prairie, horizons
Sont à la toilette rouge de l'orage!

Chien noir, brun pasteur dont le manteau s'engouffre,
Fuyez l'heure des éclairs supérieurs;
Blond troupeau, quand voici nager ombre et soufre,
Tâchez de descendre à des retraits meilleurs.

Mais moi, Seigneur! voici que mon esprit vole,
Après les cieux glacés de rouge, sous les
Nuages célestes qui courent et volent
Sur cent Solognes longues comme un railway.

Voilà mille loups, mille graines sauvages
Qu'emporte, non sans aimer les liserons,
Cette religieuse après-midi d'orage
Sur l'Europe ancienne où cent hordes iront!

O hundred lambs, blond soldiers of the idyll, fly from the aqueducts, from the thinned bracken! the plains, the wildernesses, the meadows, the horizons are washing themselves red in the storm!

Black dog, brown shepherd whose cloak is swallowed up, fly the hour of lightnings from above; fair flock, when darkness and brimstone shall hang here, take care to go down to safer retreats.

But I, Lord! see how my spirit flies in pursuit of the skies glazed with red, under the heavenly clouds which run flying across a hundred Solognes as long as a railway.

See the thousand wolves, the thousand wild seeds which this religious stormy afternoon carries away, not without loving the bindweeds, over old Europe where a hundred hordes will flow!

Après, le clair de lune! partout la lande,
Rougis et leurs fronts aux cieux noirs, les guerriers
Chevauchent lentement leurs pâles coursiers!
Les cailloux sonnent sous cette fière bande!

– Et verrai-je le bois jaune et le val clair,
L'Épouse aux yeux bleus, l'homme au front rouge, ô
    Gaule,
Et le blanc Agneau Pascal, à leurs pieds chers,
– Michel et Christine, – et Christ! – fin de l'Idylle.

LARME

Loin des oiseaux, des troupeaux, des villageoises,
Je buvais, accroupi dans quelque bruyère
Entourée de tendres bois de noisetiers,
Par un brouillard d'après-midi tiède et vert.

Afterwards, moonlight! All over the heath, reddened, and with
their faces turned to the black skies, the warriors slowly ride their
pale coursers! Pebbles ring under this proud troop!
    – And shall I see the yellow wood and the bright valley? the
blue-eyed Bride, the red-faced man, O Gaul, and the white Paschal
Lamb at their beloved feet – Michel and Christine – and Christ! –
end of the Idyll.

Tear

FAR away from birds and herds and village girls, I was drinking,
kneeling down in some heather surrounded by soft hazel copses, in
an afternoon mist, warm and green.

Que pouvais-je boire dans cette jeune Oise,
Ormeaux sans voix, gazon sans fleurs, ciel couvert.
Que tirais-je à la gourde de colocase?
Quelque liqueur d'or, fade et qui fait suer.

Tel, j'eusse été mauvaise enseigne d'auberge.
Puis l'orage changea le ciel, jusqu'au soir.
Ce furent des pays noirs, des lacs, des perches,
Des colonnades sous la nuit bleue, des gares.

L'eau des bois se perdait sur des sables vierges.
Le vent, du ciel, jetait des glaçons aux mares ...
Or! tel qu'un pêcheur d'or ou de coquillages,
Dire que je n'ai pas eu souci de boire!

Mai 1872

What can I have been drinking from this youthful Oise, voice-less elms, flowerless turf, cloudy sky. What did I draw from the gourd of the vine? Some golden liquor, pale, which causes sweating.

Such as I was, I should have been a bad inn-sign. Then the storm changed the sky, until the evening. It was black countries, lakes, [long] poles, colonnades under the blue night, railway stations.

The water from the woods trickled away into virgin sands. The wind, from the sky, threw sheets of ice across the ponds ... But! like a fisher for gold or shellfish, to think that I did not bother to drink!

May 1872

LA RIVIÈRE DE CASSIS

L A Rivière de Cassis roule ignorée
        En des vaux étranges:
La voix de cent corbeaux l'accompagne, vraie
        Et bonne voix d'anges:
Avec les grands mouvements des sapinaies
        Quand plusieurs vents plongent.

Tout roule avec des mystères révoltants
        De campagnes d'anciens temps;
De donjons visités, de parcs importants:
        C'est en ces bords qu'on entend
Les passions mortes de chevaliers errants:
        Mais que salubre est le vent!

Que le piéton regarde à ces claires-voies:
        Il ira plus courageux.
Soldats des forêts que le Seigneur envoie,
        Chers corbeaux délicieux!
Faites fuir d'ici le paysan matois
        Qui trinque d'un moignon vieux.

Mai 1872

Blackcurrant River

BLACKCURRANT River rolls unknown in strange valleys: the voices of a hundred rooks go with it, the true benevolent voice of angels: with the wide movements of the fir woods when several winds sweep down.

Everything flows with [the] horrible mysteries of ancient landscapes; of strongholds visited, of large estates: it is along these banks that you can hear the dead passions of errant knights: but how the wind is wholesome!

Let the traveller look through these clerestories: he will journey on more bravely. Forest soldiers whom the Lord sends, dear delightful rooks! Drive away from here the crafty peasant, clinking glasses with his old stump of an arm.

May 1872

COMÉDIE DE LA SOIF

1. *Les Parents*

N OUS sommes tes Grands-Parens,
    Les Grands!
Couverts des froides sueurs
De la lune et des verdures.
Nos vins secs avaient du cœur!
Au soleil sans imposture
Que faut-il à l'homme? boire.

M O I : Mourir aux fleuves barbares.

Nous sommes tes Grands-Parents
        Des champs.
L'eau est au fond des osiers:
Vois le courant du fossé
Autour du château mouillé.
Descendons en nos celliers;
Après, le cidre ou le lait.

M O I : Aller où boivent les vaches.

Comedy of Thirst

1. THE PARENTS

WE are your Grand-Parents, the Grown-Ups! covered with the
cold sweats of the moon and the greensward. Our dry wines had
heart in them! In the sunshine where there is no deception, what
does man need? to drink.

Myself: To die among barbarous rivers.

We are your Grand-Parents of the fields. The water lies at the
foot of the willows: see the flow of the moat round the damp castle.
Let us go down to our storerooms; afterwards, cider or milk.

Myself: To go where the cows drink.

Nous sommes tes Grands-Parents;
Tiens, prends
Les liqueurs dans nos armoires;
Le Thé, le Café, si rares,
Frémissent dans les bouilloires.
– Vois les images, les fleurs.
Nous rentrons du cimetière.

MOI: Ah! tarir toutes les urnes!

2. *L'Esprit*

Éternelles Ondines,
Divisez l'eau fine.
Vénus, sœur de l'azur,
Émeus le flot pur,

Juifs errants de Norwège,
Dites-moi la neige.
Anciens exilés chers,
Dites-moi la mer.

We are your Grand-Parents; here, take some of the liqueurs in our cupboards; Tea and Coffee, so rare, sing in our kettles. Look at the pictures, the flowers. We are back from the cemetery.

Myself: Ah! to drink all urns dry!

2. THE SOUL

Eternal Undines, split the pure water. Venus, sister of azure, stir up the clear wave.

Wandering Jews of Norway, tell me of snow; old beloved exiles tell me of the sea.

MOI: Non, plus ces boissons pures,
    Ces fleurs d'eau pour verres;
    Légendes ni figures
      Ne me désaltèrent;
    Chansonnier, ta filleule
      C'est ma soif si folle,
    Hydre intime sans gueules
      Qui mine et désole.

3. *Les Amis*

Viens, les Vins vont aux plages,
Et les flots par millions!
Vois le Bitter sauvage
Rouler du haut des monts!
Gagnons, pèlerins sages,
L'Absinthe aux verts piliers ...

MOI: Plus ces paysages.
    Qu'est-ce l'ivresse, Amis?

J'aime autant, mieux, même,
Pourrir dans l'étang,
Sous l'affreuse crème,
Près des bois flottants.

Myself: No, no more of these pure drinks, these water-flowers for glasses; neither legends nor faces quench my thirst; singer, your god-child is my thirst so mad, a mouthless intimate hydra which consumes and ravages.

3. FRIENDS

Come, the Wines are off to the seaside, and the waves by the million! Look at wild Bitter rolling from the mountain tops! Let us reach, like good pilgrims, green-pillared Absinthe ...

Myself: No more of these landscapes. What is drunkenness, friends?

I had as soon – rather, even – rot in the pond, beneath the horrible scum, near the floating driftwood.

4. *Le Pauvre Songe*

Peut-être un Soir m'attend
Où je boirai tranquille
En quelque vieille Ville,
Et mourrai plus content:
Puisque je suis patient!

Si mon mal se résigne,
Si j'ai jamais quelque or,
Choisirai-je le Nord
Ou le Pays des Vignes? ...
– Ah! songer est indigne

Puisque c'est pure perte!
Et si je redeviens
Le voyageur ancien,
Jamais l'auberge verte
Ne peut bien m'être ouverte.

4. THE POOR MAN DREAMS

Perhaps an Evening awaits me when I shall drink in peace in some old Town, and die the happier: since I am patient!

If my pain submits, if I ever have any gold, shall I choose the North or the Country of Vines? ... – Oh! it is shameful to dream – since it is pure loss! And if I become once more the old traveller, never can the green inn be open to me again.

5. *Conclusion*

Les pigeons qui tremblent dans la prairie,
Le gibier, qui court et qui voit la nuit,
Les bêtes des eaux, la bête asservie,
Les derniers papillons! ... ont soif aussi.

Mais fondre où fond ce nuage sans guide,
– Oh! favorisé de ce qui est frais!
Expirer en ces violettes humides
Dont les aurores chargent ces forêts?

Mai 1872

BONNE PENSÉE DU MATIN

À QUATRE heures du matin, l'été,
Le sommeil d'amour dure encore.
Sous les bosquets l'aube évapore
L'odeur du soir fêté.

5. CONCLUSION

The pigeons which flutter in the meadow, the game which runs and sees in the dark, the water animals, the animal enslaved, the last butterflies! ... also are thirsty.

But to dissolve where that wandering cloud is dissolving – Oh! favoured by what is fresh! to expire in those damp violets whose awakening fills these woods?

May 1872

Pleasant Thought for the Morning

AT four o'clock on a summer morning the sleep of love still lasts. Under the spinneys the dawn disperses scents of the festive night.

Mais là-bas dans l'immense chantier
Vers le soleil des Hespérides,
En bras de chemise, les charpentiers
    Déjà s'agitent.

Dans leur désert de mousse, tranquilles,
Ils préparent les lambris précieux
Où la richesse de la ville
    Rira sous de faux cieux.

Ah! pour ces Ouvriers charmants
Sujets d'un roi de Babylone,
Vénus! laisse un peu les Amants,
    Dont l'âme est en couronne.

    Ô Reine des Bergers!
Porte aux travailleurs l'eau-de-vie,
Pour que leurs forces soient en paix
En attendant le bain dans la mer, à midi.
               Mai 1872

But down there in the huge workshop near the Hesperidean sun, the carpenters in their shirtsleeves are already astir.

Peaceful in the midst of their wilderness of foam, they are preparing the costly canopies where the riches of the city will smile beneath painted skies.

Ah! for these charming Labourers' sakes, subjects of a king of Babylon, Venus! leave Lovers for a little while, whose souls are wearing crowns.

O Queen of the Shepherds! take strong liquor to the workers, so that their strength may be calmed until the sea-bathe at noon.
               May 1872

FÊTES DE LA PATIENCE

BANNIÈRES DE MAI

Aux branches claires des tilleuls
Meurt un maladif hallali.
Mais des chansons spirituelles
Voltigent parmi les groseilles.
Que notre sang rie en nos veines,
Voici s'enchevêtrer les vignes.
Le ciel est joli comme un ange.
L'azur et l'onde communient.
Je sors. Si un rayon me blesse
Je succomberai sur la mousse.

Qu'on patiente et qu'on s'ennuie
C'est trop simple. Fi de mes peines.
Je veux que l'été dramatique
Me lie à son char de fortune.
Que par toi beaucoup, ô Nature,
– Ah! moins seul et moins nul! – je meure.

FESTIVALS OF ENDURANCE

May Banners

In the bright lime-tree branches dies a fainting mort. But lively songs flutter among the currant bushes. So that our blood may laugh in our veins, see the vines tangling themselves. The sky is as pretty as an angel. The azure and the wave commune. I go out. If a sunbeam wounds me I shall succumb on the moss.

Being patient and being bored are too simple. To the devil with my cares. I want dramatic summer to bind me to its chariot of fortune. Let me most because of you, O Nature – Ah! less alone, and

Au lieu que les Bergers, c'est drôle,
Meurent à peu près par le monde.

Je veux bien que les saisons m'usent.
À toi, Nature, je me rends;
Et ma faim et toute ma soif.
Et, s'il te plaît, nourris, abreuve.
Rien de rien ne m'illusionne;
C'est rire aux parents, qu'au soleil,
Mais moi je ne veux rire à rien;
Et libre soit cette infortune.

Mai 1872

CHANSON DE LA PLUS HAUTE TOUR

OISIVE jeunesse
À tout asservie,
Par délicatesse
J'ai perdu ma vie.
Ah! Que le temps vienne
Où les cœurs s'éprennent.

less useless! – die. There where the Shepherds, it's strange, die
more or less because of the world.

I am willing that the seasons should wear me out. To you,
Nature, I surrender; with my hunger and all my thirst. And if it
please you, feed and water me. Nothing, nothing at all deceives me;
to laugh at the sun is to laugh at one's parents, but I do not wish
to laugh at anything; and may this misfortune go free.

May 1872

Song of the Highest Tower

IDLE youth enslaved to everything, by being too sensitive I have
wasted my life. Ah! Let the time come when hearts are enamoured.

Je me suis dit: laisse,
Et qu'on ne te voie:
Et sans la promesse
De plus hautes joies.
Que rien ne t'arrête,
Auguste retraite.

J'ai tant fait patience
Qu'à jamais j'oublie;
Craintes et souffrances
Aux cieux sont parties,
Et la soif malsaine
Obscurcit mes veines.

Ainsi la prairie
A l'oubli livrée,
Grandie, et fleurie
D'encens et d'ivraies
Au bourdon farouche
De cent sales mouches.

Ah! Mille veuvages
De la si pauvre âme
Qui n'a que l'image
De la Notre-Dame!
Est-ce que l'on prie
La Vierge Marie?

I said to myself: let be, and let no one see you: do without the promise of higher joys. Let nothing delay you, majestic retirement.

I have endured so long that I have forgotten everything; fear and suffering have flown to the skies, and morbid thirst darkens my veins.

Thus the meadow, given over to oblivion, grown up, and flowering with frankincense and tares, to the wild buzzing of a hundred filthy flies.

Oh! the thousand bereavements of the poor soul which possesses only the image of Our Lady! Can one pray to the Virgin Mary?

Oisive jeunesse
À tout asservie,
Par délicatesse
J'ai perdu ma vie.
Ah! Que le temps vienne
Où les cœurs s'éprennent!

Mai 1872

L'ÉTERNITÉ

Elle est retrouvée.
Quoi? – L'Éternité.
C'est la mer allée
Avec le soleil.

Âme sentinelle,
Murmurons l'aveu
De la nuit si nulle
Et du jour en feu.

Des humains suffrages,
Des communs élans
Là tu te dégages
Et voles selon.

Idle youth enslaved by everything, by being too sensitive I have wasted my life. Ah! let the time come when hearts are enamoured!

May 1872

Eternity

It has been found again. What? – Eternity. It is the sea fled away with the sun.

Sentinel soul, let us whisper the confession of the night full of nothingness and the day on fire.

From human approbation, from common urges, you diverge here and fly off as you may.

Puisque de vous seules,
Braises de satin,
Le Devoir s'exhale
Sans qu'on dise: enfin.

Là pas d'espérance,
Nul orietur.
Science avec patience,
Le supplice est sûr.

Elle est retrouvée.
Quoi? – l'Éternité.
C'est la mer allée
Avec le soleil.

Mai 1872

ÂGE D'OR

QUELQU'UNE des voix
Toujours angélique
– Il s'agit de moi, –
Vertement s'explique:

Since from you alone, satiny embers, Duty breathes without anyone saying: at last.

Here is no hope, no *orietur*. Knowledge and fortitude, no torture is certain.

It has been found again. What? – Eternity. It is the sea fled away with the sun.

May 1872

Golden Age

ONE of the voices, always angelic – it is about me – greenly expresses itself:

218

Ces mille questions
Qui se ramifient
N'amènent, au fond,
Qu'ivresse et folie;

Reconnais ce tour
Si gai, si facile:
Ce n'est qu'onde, flore,
Et c'est ta famille!

Puis elle chante. Ô
Si gai, si facile,
Et visible à l'œil nu …
– Je chante avec elle, –

Reconnais ce tour
Si gai, si facile,
Ce n'est qu'onde, flore,
Et c'est ta famille! … etc. …

Et puis une voix
– Est-elle angélique! –
Il s'agit de moi,
Vertement s'explique;

those thousand questions spreading their roots bring in the end only drunkenness and madness;

understand this trick [which is] so gay, so simple: it is only wave, only flower, and that is your family!

Then it sings. O so gay, so simple, and visible to the naked eye … – I sing with it –

understand this trick so gay and simple, it is only wave, only flower, and that is your family! … etc. …

And then a voice – how angelic it is! – talking of me, greenly utters;

Et chante à l'instant
En sœur des haleines:
D'un ton Allemand,
Mais ardente et pleine:

Le monde est vicieux;
Si cela t'étonne!
Vis et laisse au feu
L'obscure infortune.

Ô! joli château!
Que ta vie est claire!
De quel Âge es-tu,
Nature princière
De notre grand frère? etc. ...

Je chante aussi, moi:
Multiples sœurs! Voix
Pas du tout publiques!
Environnez-moi
De gloire pudique ... etc. ...

Juin 1872

And sings at this moment like a sister to breath: with a German
tone, but ardent and full:

The world is vicious – if that surprises you! Live, and leave to
the fire dark misfortune.

O! pretty country house! How bright your life is! What Age do
you belong to, princely nature of our elder brother? etc. ...

I also sing: Many sisters! Voices not at all public! Surround me
with chaste glory ... etc. ...

June 1872

JEUNE MÉNAGE

La chambre est ouverte au ciel bleu-turquin;
Pas de place: des coffrets et des huches!
Dehors le mur est plein d'aristoloches
Où vibrent les gencives des lutins.

Que ce sont bien intrigues de génies
Cette dépense et ces désordres vains!
C'est la fée africaine qui fournit
La mûre, et les résilles dans les coins.

Plusieurs entrent, marraines mécontentes,
En pans de lumière dans les buffets,
Puis y restent! le ménage s'absente
Peu sérieusement, et rien ne se fait.

Le marié a le vent qui le floue
Pendant son absence, ici, tout le temps.
Même des esprits des eaux, malfaisants
Entrent vaguer aux sphères de l'alcôve.

Young Couple

The room is open to the turquoise blue sky; no room here: boxes and bins! Outside the wall is overgrown with birthwort where the brownies' gums buzz.

How truly these are the plots of genii – this expense and this foolish untidiness! It is the African fairy who supplies the mulberry and the hairnets in the corners.

Several, cross godmothers [dressed] in skirts of light, go into the cupboards, and stay there! the people of the house are out, they are not serious, and nothing gets done.

The bridegroom has the wind which cheats him during his absence, here, all the time. Even some water sprites, mischievous, come in to wander about among the spheres under the bed.

La nuit, l'amie oh! la lune de miel
Cueillera leur sourire et remplira
De mille bandeaux de cuivre le ciel
Puis ils auront affaire au malin rat.

— S'il n'arrive pas un feu follet blême,
Comme un coup de fusil, après des vêpres,
— Ô Spectres saints et blancs de Bethléem,
Charmez plutôt le bleu de leur fenêtre!

27 juin 1872

BRUXELLES

Juillet   *Boulevard du Régent*

PLATES-BANDES d'amarantes jusqu'à
L'agréable palais de Jupiter.
— Je sais que c'est Toi qui, dans ces lieux,
Mêles ton Bleu presque de Sahara!

At night, beloved oh! the honeymoon will gather their smiles
and fill the sky with a thousand copper diadems. Then they will
have to deal with the crafty rat.

— As long as no ghastly will o' the wisp comes, like a gunshot,
after vespers, – O holy white Spirits of Bethlehem, charm, rather
than that, the blueness of their window!

27 June 1872

Brussels

July   *Boulevard du Régent*

FLOWERBEDS of amaranths right up to the pleasant palace of
Jupiter. – I know it is Thou who in this place minglest thine almost
Saharan Blue!

Puis, comme rose et sapin du soleil
Et liane ont ici leurs jeux enclos,
Cage de la petite veuve! ...

                                    Quelles

Troupes d'oiseaux, ô ia io, ia io! ...

– Calmes maisons, anciennes passions!
Kiosque de la Folle par affection.
Après les fesses des rosiers, balcon
Ombreux et très bas de la Juliette.

– La Juliette, ça rappelle l'Henriette,
Charmante station du chemin de fer,
Au cœur d'un mont, comme au fond d'un verger
Où mille diables bleus dansent dans l'air!

Banc vert où chante au paradis d'orage,
Sur la guitare, la blanche Irlandaise.
Puis, de la salle à manger guyanaise,
Bavardage des enfants et des cages.

Then, since rose and fir-tree of the sun and tropical creeper have their play enclosed here, the little widow's cage! ... What flocks of birds, o ia io, ia io! ...

Calm houses, old passions! Summerhouse of the Lady who ran mad for love. And, after the buttocks of the rosebushes, [here is] the balcony of Juliet, shadowy and very low.

– *La Juliette*, that reminds me of *l'Henriette*, a charming railway station at the heart of a mountain, as if at the bottom of an orchard where a thousand blue devils dance in the air!

Green bench where in stormy paradise the white Irish girl sings to the guitar. Then, from the Guianian dining-room, chatter of children and of cages.

Fenêtre du duc qui fais que je pense
Au poison des escargots et du buis
Qui dort ici-bas au soleil.
                    Et puis
C'est trop beau! trop! Gardons notre silence.

– Boulevard sans mouvement ni commerce,
Muet, tout drame et toute comédie,
Réunion des scènes infinie,
Je te connais et t'admire en silence.

————

Est-elle almée? ... aux premières heures bleues
Se détruira-t-elle comme les fleurs feues ...
Devant la splendide étendue où l'on sente
Souffler la ville énormément florissante!

C'est trop beau! c'est trop beau! mais c'est nécessaire
– Pour la Pêcheuse et la chanson du Corsaire,
Et aussi puisque les derniers masques crurent
Encore aux fêtes de nuit sur la mer pure!

Juillet 1872

The duke's window which makes me think of the poison of snails and of boxwood sleeping down here in the sun. And then it is too beautiful! too [beautiful]! Let us maintain our silence.

– Boulevard without movement or business, dumb, every drama and every comedy, unending concentration of scenes, I know you and I admire you in silence.

————

Is she an Almeh? ... will she destroy herself in the first blue hours like flowers of fire? In front of the splendid sweep where one may smell the enormous flowering city's breath!

It's too beautiful! it's too beautiful! but it is necessary – for the Woman of Sin and the Corsair's song, and also because the last masqueraders still believed in nocturnal festivities on the pure sea!

July 1872

FÊTES DE LA FAIM

MA faim, Anne, Anne,
Fuis sur ton âne.

Si j'ai du *goût*, ce n'est guères
Que pour la terre et les pierres.
Dinn! dinn! dinn! dinn! Mangeons l'air,
Le roc, les charbons, le fer.

Mes faims, tournez. Paissez, faims,
Le pré des sons!
Attirez le gai venin
Des liserons;

Mangez
Les cailloux qu'un pauvre brise,
Les vieilles pierres d'églises,
Les galets, fils des déluges,
Pains couchés aux vallées grises!

Mes faims, c'est les bouts d'air noir;
L'azur sonneur;
— C'est l'estomac qui me tire.
C'est le malheur.

Feasts of Hunger

MY hunger, Anne, Anne, flee on your donkey.
If I have any *taste*, it is for hardly anything but earth and stones.
Dinn! dinn! dinn! dinn! Let us eat air, rock, coal, iron.
Turn, my hungers. Feed, hungers, on the meadow of sounds!
Suck the gaudy poison of the convolvuli;
Eat
the stones a poor man breaks, the old masonry of churches,
boulders, children of floods, loaves lying in the grey valleys!
Hungers, it is bits of black air; the azure trumpeter; it is my
stomach that makes me suffer. It is unhappiness.

Sur terre ont paru les feuilles!
Je vais aux chairs de fruit blettes.
Au sein du sillon je cueille
La doucette et la violette.

Ma faim, Anne, Anne!
Fuis sur ton âne.

Aout 1872

LE loup criait sous les feuilles
En crachant les plus belles plumes
De son repas de volailles:
Comme lui je me consume.

Les salades, les fruits
N'attendent que la cueillette;
Mais l'araignée de la haie
Ne mange que des violettes.

Que je dorme! que je bouille
Aux autels de Salomon,
Le bouillon court sur la rouille,
Et se mêle au Cédron.

Leaves have appeared on earth! I go looking for the sleepy flesh
of fruit. At the heart of the furrow I pick Venus's looking-glass and
the violet.

My hunger, Anne, Anne, flee on your donkey.

August 1872

THE fox howled under the leaves, spitting out the brightest
feathers of his feast of fowl: like him, I consume myself.

Salads and fruit are only waiting to be picked: but the hedge
spider eats nothing but violets.

Let me sleep! let me simmer on the altars of Solomon, the scum
runs down over the rust and mingles with the Kedron.

Entends comme brame
près des acacias
en avril la rame
viride du pois!

Dans sa vapeur nette,
vers Phœbé! tu vois
s'agiter la tête
de saints d'autrefois …

Loin des claires meules
des caps, des beaux toits,
ces chers Anciens veulent
ce philtre sournois …

Or ni fériale
ni astrale! n'est
la brume qu'exhale
ce nocturne effet.

Néanmoins ils restent,
– Sicile, Allemagne,
dans ce brouillard triste
et blêmi, justement!

Listen to the way the green shoot of the pea bellows near the acacias in April!

In its clear haze, towards Phoebe! you see, moving, the heads of the old saints …

Far from the pale stacks of the headlands, from the fine roofs, these Ancient fellows desire this sly philtre …

Gold neither of haloes nor of stars! is the mist breathed out by this nocturnal effect.

Nevertheless they remain – Sicily, Germany, in this sad and ghastly pale fog – precisely!

Ô SAISONS, ô châteaux,
Quelle âme est sans défauts?

Ô saisons, ô châteaux,

J'ai fait la magique étude
Du bonheur, que nul n'élude.

Ô vive lui, chaque fois
Que chante le coq gaulois.

Mais je n'aurai plus d'envie,
Il s'est chargé de ma vie.

Ce charme! il prit âme et corps,
Et dispersa tous efforts.

Que comprendre à ma parole?
Il fait qu'elle fuie et vole!

Ô saisons, ô châteaux!

O SEASONS, O towers, what soul is blameless?
  O seasons, O towers,
  I pursued the magic lore of happiness which no one escapes.
  Oh long live that [happiness], every time that the Gallic cock crows.
  But I shall never want again, it has taken charge of my life.
  That charm! it took hold of soul and body, and dissipated every effort.
  What is to be understood from what I say? It makes [my words] disappear in the air!
  O seasons, O towers!

HONTE

TANT que la lame n'aura
Pas coupé cette cervelle,
Ce paquet blanc, vert et gras,
A vapeur jamais nouvelle,

(Ah! Lui, devrait couper son
Nez, sa lèvre, ses oreilles,
Son ventre! et faire abandon
De ses jambes! ô merveille!)

Mais, non; vrai, je crois que tant
Que pour sa tête la lame,
Que les cailloux pour son flanc,
Que pour ses boyaux la flamme,

N'auront pas agi, l'enfant
Gêneur, la si sotte bête,
Ne doit cesser un instant
De ruser et d'être traître,

Comme un chat des Monts-Rocheux,
D'empuantir toutes sphères!
Qu'à sa mort pourtant, ô mon Dieu!
S'élève quelque prière!

Shame

So long as the blade has not cut off that brain, that white, green, fatty parcel, whose steam is never fresh,

(Ah! *He* should cut off his nose, his lips, his ears, his belly! and abandon his legs! Oh what a marvel!)

But no; truly, I believe that so long as the blade to his head, and the stones to his side, and the flame to his guts,

have not done execution, the tiresome child, the so stupid animal, must never for an instant cease to cheat and betray,

and like a Rocky Mountain cat to make all places stink! But still, when he dies, O my God! may there rise up some prayer!

LES ILLUMINATIONS

I

APRÈS LE DÉLUGE

Aussitot que l'idée du Déluge se fut rassise, un lièvre s'arrêta dans les sainfoins et les clochettes mouvantes, et dit sa prière à l'arc-en-ciel à travers la toile de l'araignée.

Oh! les pierres précieuses qui se cachaient, – les fleurs qui regardaient déjà.

Dans la grande rue sale les étals se dressèrent, et l'on tira les barques vers la mer étagée là-haut comme sur les gravures.

Le sang coula, chez Barbe-Bleue, – aux abattoirs, – dans les cirques, où le sceau de Dieu blêmit les fenêtres. Le sang et le lait coulèrent.

Les castors bâtirent. Les «mazagrans» fumèrent dans les estaminets.

I

After the Flood

As soon as the idea of the Flood had subsided, a hare stopped among the clover and the swaying flower bells, and said his prayer to the rainbow through the spider's web.

Oh, the precious stones that began to hide! – the flowers already looking about them!

In the dirty main street, stalls were set up, and boats were hauled down to the sea which rose in steps, as in old prints.

Blood flowed: at Bluebeard's – in the slaughterhouses – in the circuses, where God's seal turned the windows pale. Blood flowed, and milk.

Beavers built. Coffee-cups[1] steamed in the little bars.

---

1. '*Mazagrans*' are cups without handles, like goblets, usually made of thick china.

Dans la grande maison de vitres encore ruisselante, les enfants en deuil regardèrent les merveilleuses images.

Une porte claqua, et, sur la place du hameau, l'enfant tourna ses bras, compris des girouettes et des coqs des clochers de partout, sous l'éclatante giboulée.

Madame *** établit un piano dans les Alpes. La messe et les premières communions se célébrèrent aux cent mille autels de la cathédrale.

Les caravanes partirent. Et le Splendide-Hôtel fut bâti dans le chaos de glaces et de nuit du pôle.

Depuis lors, la Lune entendit les chacals piaulant par les déserts de thym – et les églogues en sabots grognant dans le verger. Puis, dans la futaie violette, bourgeonnante, Eucharis me dit que c'était le printemps.

Sourds, étang; – Écume, roule sur le pont et pardessus les bois; – draps noirs et orgues, – éclairs et tonnerre, – montez et roulez; – Eaux et tristesses, montez et relevez les Déluges.

In the big greenhouse, which was still dripping, the children in mourning looked at the marvellous pictures.

A door banged, and on the village green the child waved his arms, and was understood by weathervanes and cocks on steeples everywhere under the bursting shower.

Madame So-and-so installed a piano in the Alps. Mass, and first communions, were celebrated at the hundred thousand altars of the cathedral.

Caravans set out. And the Hotel Splendide was built in the chaos of ice and of polar night.

Ever afterwards, the Moon heard jackals howling across the deserts of thyme – and eclogues in wooden shoes grumbling in the orchard. Then, in the violet-coloured and budding forest, Eucharis told me that it was spring.

Surge, pond – Foam, roll over the bridge and over the woods – black palls and organs – lightnings and thunder – rise and roll – Waters and sorrows, rise and unleash the Floods again.

Car depuis qu'ils se sont dissipés, – oh! les pierres précieuses s'enfouissant, et les fleurs ouvertes! – c'est un ennui! et la Reine, la Sorcière qui allume sa braise dans le pot de terre, ne voudra jamais nous raconter ce qu'elle sait, et que nous ignorons.

II

ENFANCE

I

CETTE idole, yeux noirs et crin jaune, sans parents ni cour, plus noble que la fable, mexicaine et flamande: son domaine, azur et verdure insolents, court sur des plages nommées par des vagues sans vaisseaux de noms férocement grecs, slaves, celtiques.

À la lisière de la forêt – les fleurs de rêve tintent, éclatent, éclairent, – la fille à lèvre d'orange, les genoux

Because since they rolled away – oh! the precious stones burying themselves, and the opened flowers! – it's unbearable! and the Queen, the Witch who lights her fire in an earthen pot, will never consent to tell us what she knows, and what we do not know.

II

Childhood

I

THAT idol, black eyes and yellow mop of hair, without ancestors or court, nobler than fable, Mexican and Flemish: his domain, insolent azure and green, runs along beaches which the shipless waves call by names ferociously Greek, Slav, Celtic.

At the edge of the forest – dream flowers tinkle, flash, flare – the girl with orange lips, her knees crossed in the clear flood surging

235

croisés dans le clair déluge qui sourd des prés, nudité qu'ombrent, traversent et habillent les arcs-en-ciel, la flore, la mer.

Dames qui tournoient sur les terrasses voisines de la mer; enfantes et géantes, superbes noires dans la mousse vert-de-gris, bijoux debout sur le sol gras des bosquets et des jardinets dégelés, — jeunes mères et grandes sœurs aux regards pleins de pèlerinages, sultanes, princesses de démarche et de costumes tyranniques, petites étrangères et personnes doucement malheureuses.

Quel ennui, l'heure du «cher corps» et «cher cœur»!

II

C'est elle, la petite morte, derrière les rosiers. — La jeune maman trépassée descend le perron. — La calèche du cousin crie sur le sable. — Le petit frère — (il est aux Indes!) là, devant le couchant, sur le pré d'œillets. — Les vieux qu'on a enterrés tout droits dans le rempart aux giroflées.

from the meadows, nakedness shaded, crossed, clothed by rainbows, flora, the sea.

Ladies strolling on terraces by the sea; little girls and giantesses, superb negresses in the verdigris moss, jewels standing on the rich soil of the groves and the little thawed gardens — young mothers and elder sisters with their eyes full of pilgrimages, Sultanas, princesses with tyrannical costumes and carriage, little foreign girls and gently unhappy people.

What a bore, the moment of the 'beloved body' and 'dear heart'!

II

It is she, the little dead girl, behind the rose-bushes — The young mamma, deceased, comes down the steps — The cousin's carriage squeaks on the sand — The little brother — (he is in India!) there, against the sunset, in the meadow of pinks — The old men who are buried upright in the rampart overgrown with wallflowers.

L'essaim des feuilles d'or entoure la maison du général. Ils sont dans le midi. – On suit la route rouge pour arriver à l'auberge vide. Le château est à vendre; les persiennes sont détachées. – Le curé aura emporté la clef de l'église. – Autour du parc, les loges des gardes sont inhabitées. Les palissades sont si hautes qu'on ne voit que les cimes bruissantes. D'ailleurs, il n'y a rien à voir là-dedans.

Les prés remontent aux hameaux sans coqs, sans enclumes. L'écluse est levée. Ô les calvaires et les moulins du désert, les îles et les meules.

Des fleurs magiques bourdonnaient. Les talus le berçaient. Des bêtes d'une élégance fabuleuse circulaient. Les nuées s'amassaient sur la haute mer faite d'une éternité de chaudes larmes.

III

Au bois, il y a un oiseau, son chant vous arrête et vous fait rougir.

Il y a une horloge qui ne sonne pas.

A swarm of golden leaves surrounds the general's house. They are in the South – You follow the red road and arrive at the empty inn. The country house is for sale; the shutters are hanging loose – The priest will have taken away the key of the church – Around the park, the keepers' cottages are uninhabited. The fences are so high that nothing can be seen but the rustling tops of trees. Besides, there is nothing to be seen in there.

The meadows climb up to hamlets without cockerels or anvils. The sluice gate is raised. O the Calvaries and windmills of the wilderness, the islands and the stacks!

Magic flowers were droning. The slopes cradled him. Fabulously elegant beasts wandered about. The clouds gathered over the open sea which was formed of an eternity of warm tears.

III

In the woods there is a bird, his song makes you stop and blush. There is a clock that never strikes.

Il y a une fondrière avec un nid de bêtes blanches.

Il y a une cathédrale qui descend et un lac qui monte.

Il y a une petite voiture abandonnée dans le taillis, ou qui descend le sentier en courant, enrubannée.

Il y a une troupe de petits comédiens en costumes, aperçus sur la route à travers la lisière du bois.

Il y a enfin, quand l'on a faim et soif, quelqu'un qui vous chasse.

IV

Je suis le saint, en prière sur la terrasse, – comme les bêtes pacifiques paissent jusqu'à la mer de Palestine.

Je suis le savant au fauteuil sombre. Les branches et la pluie se jettent à la croisée de la bibliothèque.

Je suis le piéton de la grand'route par les bois nains; la rumeur des écluses couvre mes pas. Je vois longtemps la mélancolique lessive d'or du couchant.

Je serais bien l'enfant abandonné sur la jetée partie à la haute mer, le petit valet suivant l'allée dont le front touche le ciel.

There is a hollow with a nest full of white animals.

There is a cathedral that goes down and a lake that goes up.

There is a little carriage left in the copse, or which runs down the lane with ribbons on it.

There is a troupe of little actors in costume, glimpsed on the road through the edge of the woods.

There is, finally, when you are hungry and thirsty, someone who drives you away.

IV

I am the saint, praying on the terrace – as the peaceful beasts graze down to the sea of Palestine.

I am the scholar in the dark armchair. Branches and rain hurl themselves at the library windows.

I am the traveller on the high road through the stunted woods; the roar of the sluices drowns [the sound of] my steps. I watch for a long time the melancholy golden wash of the sunset.

I might be the child left on the jetty washed out to sea, the little farm boy following the lane whose crest touches the sky.

Les sentiers sont âpres. Les monticules se couvrent de
genêts. L'air est immobile. Que les oiseaux et les sources
sont loin! Ce ne peut être que la fin du monde, en
avançant.

V

Qu'on me loue enfin ce tombeau, blanchi à la chaux avec
les lignes du ciment en relief, – très loin sous terre.

Je m'accoude à la table, la lampe éclaire très vivement
ces journaux que je suis idiot de relire, ces livres sans
intérêt.

À une distance énorme au-dessus de mon salon sou-
terrain, les maisons s'implantent, les brumes s'assemblent.
La boue est rouge ou noire. Ville monstrueuse, nuit sans
fin!

Moins haut, sont des égouts. Aux côtés, rien que
l'épaisseur du globe. Peut-être des gouffres d'azur, des
puits de feu. C'est peut-être sur ces plans que se rencon-
trent lunes et comètes, mers et fables.

The paths are rough. The hillocks are covered with broom. The
air is motionless. How far away the birds and the springs are! It
can only be the end of the world, ahead.

V

Let them rent me this tomb at the last, whitewashed and showing
the lines of the cement in relief – far down under the ground.

I lean my elbows on the table, the lamp lights up brightly these
newspapers which I am a fool to read again, these books devoid of
interest.

At an enormous distance above my underground living-room,
houses spread their roots, fogs gather. The mud is either red or
black. Monstrous city, night without end!

Not so high up, there are sewers. At each side, nothing but the
thickness of the globe. Perhaps chasms of azure, wells of fire. Per-
haps it is on these levels that moons and comets, seas and fables,
meet.

Aux heures d'amertume je m'imagine des boules de saphir, de métal. Je suis maître du silence. Pourquoi une apparence de soupirail blêmirait-elle au coin de la voûte?

III

CONTE

Un Prince était vexé de ne s'être employé jamais qu'à la perfection des générosités vulgaires. Il prévoyait d'étonnantes révolutions de l'amour, et soupçonnait ses femmes de pouvoir mieux que cette complaisance agrémentée de ciel et de luxe. Il voulait voir la vérité, l'heure du désir et de la satisfaction essentiels. Que ce fût ou non une aberration de piété, il voulut. Il possédait au moins un assez large pouvoir humain.

Toutes les femmes qui l'avaient connu furent assassinées. Quel saccage du jardin de la beauté! Sous le sabre, elles le bénirent. Il n'en commanda point de nouvelles. — Les femmes réapparurent.

In my hours of bitterness I imagine balls of sapphire, of metal. I am the master of silence. Why should something which resembles a skylight pale at the corner of the vault?

III

A Tale

A Prince was chagrined at only ever having devoted himself to the perfection of ordinary generosities. He foresaw amazing revolutions in love, and suspected his wives of being capable of something better than the complaisance which the sky and luxury enhanced. He wanted to see the truth, the moment of essential desire and gratification. Whether it was an aberration of piety or not, this was what he wanted. He possessed at least sufficient worldly power.

Every woman who had known him was killed. What havoc in the garden of beauty! Under the edge of the sword, they blessed him. He ordered no more women — Women reappeared.

Il tua tous ceux qui le suivaient, après la chasse ou les libations. – Tous le suivaient.

Il s'amusa à égorger les bêtes de luxe. Il fit flamber les palais. Il se ruait sur les gens et les taillait en pièces. – La foule, les toits d'or, les belles bêtes existaient encore.

Peut-on s'extasier dans la destruction, se rajeunir par la cruauté! Le peuple ne murmura pas. Personne n'offrit le concours de ses vues.

Un soir il galopait fièrement. Un Génie apparut, d'une beauté ineffable, inavouable même. De sa physionomie et de son maintien ressortait la promesse d'un amour multiple et complexe! d'un bonheur indicible, insupportable même! Le Prince et le Génie s'anéantirent probablement dans la santé essentielle. Comment n'auraient-ils pas pu en mourir? Ensemble donc ils moururent.

Mais ce Prince décéda, dans son palais, à un âge ordinaire. Le prince était le Génie. Le Génie était le Prince.

La musique savante manque à notre désir.

He killed all those who followed him, to the hunt or in drinking-bouts – All followed him.

He amused himself by cutting the throats of rare animals. He set the palaces on fire. He rushed on people and cut them to pieces – Crowds, golden roofs, beautiful animals continued to exist.

Is it possible to delight in destruction, to be rejuvenated by cruelty? The populace did not murmur. No one offered to assist him with his own views.

One evening he was galloping along proudly. A Genie appeared, ineffably beautiful, with a beauty impossible even to acknowledge. From his face and bearing shone out the promise of a multiple and complex love! of an unutterable, even unendurable, happiness! The Prince and the Genie annihilated each other probably in idiopathic health. How could they have helped dying of it? Together, then, they died.

But the Prince died, in his palace, at a normal age. The Prince was the Genie. The Genie was the Prince.

Great music falls short of our desire.

IV

PARADE

DES drôles très solides. Plusieurs ont exploité vos mondes. Sans besoins, et peu pressés de metttre en œuvre leurs brillantes facultés et leur expérience de vos consciences. Quels hommes mûrs! Des yeux hébétés à la façon de la nuit d'été, rouges et noirs, tricolores, d'acier piqué d'étoiles d'or; des facies déformés, plombés, blêmis, incendiés; des enrouements folâtres! La démarche cruelle des oripeaux! – Il y a quelques jeunes, – comment regarderaient-ils Chérubin? – pourvus de voix effrayantes et de quelques ressources dangereuses. On les envoie prendre du dos en ville, affublés d'un *luxe* dégoûtant.

Ô le plus violent Paradis de la grimace enragée! Pas de comparaison avec vos Fakirs et les autres bouffonneries scéniques. Dans des costumes improvisés avec le goût du mauvais rêve ils jouent des complaintes, des tragédies de malandrins et de demi-dieux spirituels comme l'histoire ou les religions ne l'ont jamais été. Chinois, Hottentots,

IV

Sideshow

VERY sturdy rascals. Several have exploited your worlds. Without needs, and in no hurry to bring into play their brilliant faculties and their familiarity with your consciences. What mature men! Eyes bewildered like the summer night, red and black, tricoloured, steel pricked out with golden stars; features deformed, leaden, whitened, aflame; burlesque hoarsenesses! The cruel, flashy swagger! – There are some young people – what would they think of Cherubino? – endowed with frightening voices and with some dangerous tricks up their sleeves. They are sent out to solicit as catamites in the town, rigged out in revolting *luxury*.

O most violent Paradise of the maddened grimace! No comparison with your Fakirs or other theatrical buffooneries. Wearing improvised costumes in nightmarish taste they play romances and tragedies of brigands and demigods which are spirited as history and religions never were. Chinamen, Hottentots, gipsies, simple-

bohémiens, niais, hyènes, Molochs, vieilles démences, démons sinistres, ils mêlent les tours populaires, maternels, avec les poses et les tendresses bestiales. Ils interpréteraient des pièces nouvelles et des chansons «bonnes filles». Maîtres jongleurs, ils transforment le lieu et les personnes et usent de la comédie magnétique. Les yeux flambent, le sang chante, les os s'élargissent, les larmes et des filets rouges ruissellent. Leur raillerie ou leur terreur dure une minute, ou des mois entiers.

J'ai seul la clef de cette parade sauvage.

V

ANTIQUE

GRACIEUX fils de Pan! Autour de ton front couronné de fleurettes et de baies tes yeux, des boules précieuses, remuent. Tachées de lies brunes, tes joues se creusent. Tes crocs luisent. Ta poitrine ressemble à une cithare, des tintements circulent dans tes bras blonds. Ton cœur bat

tons, hyenas, Molochs, old insanities, sinister demons, they mingle popular, homespun turns with bestial poses and caresses. They would [willingly] render new plays and sentimental songs. Master jugglers, they transmogrify place and person and have recourse to magnetic stagecraft. Eyes flame, blood sings, bones thicken, tears and red trickles run down. Their banter and their terror last a minute, or whole months.

I am alone in possessing the key to this barbarous sideshow.

V

Antique

GRACEFUL son of Pan! About your head crowned with flowerets and berries your eyes, precious spheres, move. Stained with brown lees, your cheeks are hollow. Your eye-teeth gleam. Your breast is like a cithara, plucked notes run in your pale arms. Your blood

dans ce ventre où dort le double sexe. Promène-toi, la nuit, en mouvant doucement cette cuisse, cette seconde cuisse et cette jambe de gauche.

VI

BEING BEAUTEOUS

Devant une neige un Être de Beauté de haute taille. Des sifflements de mort et des cercles de musique sourde font monter, s'élargir et trembler comme un spectre ce corps adoré; des blessures écarlates et noires éclatent dans les chairs superbes. Les couleurs propres de la vie se foncent, dansent, et se dégagent autour de la Vision, sur le chantier. Et les frissons s'élèvent et grondent, et la saveur forcenée de ces effets se chargeant avec les sifflements mortels et les rauques musiques que le monde, loin derrière nous, lance sur notre mère de beauté, – elle recule, elle se dresse. Oh! nos os sont revêtus d'un nouveau corps amoureux.

*

pulses in that belly where sleeps the double sex. Walk, in the night, gently moving that thigh, that second thigh, and that left leg.

VI

Being Beauteous

Against the snow a high-statured Being of Beauty. Whistlings of death and circles of faint music cause this adored body to rise, expand, and quiver like a ghost; scarlet and black wounds burst in the fine flesh. The colours proper to life deepen, dance, and detach themselves round the Vision in the making. And shudders rise and rumble, and the frenetic flavour of these effects is filled with the mortal whistlings and the raucous music which the world, far behind us, hurls at our mother of beauty – she recedes, she rears herself up. Oh! our bones are clothed with a new and amorous body.

*

Ô la face cendrée, l'écusson de crin, les bras de cristal! le canon sur lequel je dois m'abattre à travers la mêlée des arbres et de l'air léger!

VII

VIES

I

Ô LES énormes avenues du pays saint, les terrasses du temple! Qu'a-t-on fait du brahmane qui m'expliqua les Proverbes? D'alors, de là-bas, je vois encore même les vieilles! Je me souviens des heures d'argent et de soleil vers les fleuves, la main de la compagne sur mon épaule, et de nos caresses debout dans les plaines poivrées. — Un envol de pigeons écarlates tonne autour de ma pensée. — Exilé ici, j'ai eu une scène où jouer les chefs-d'œuvre dramatiques de toutes les littératures. Je vous indiquerais

O the ashen face, the escutcheon of horsehair, the crystal arms! the cannon at which I must charge across the skirmish of the trees and the light air!

VII

Lives

I

O THE vast avenues of the holy land, the terraces of the temple! What became of the Brahmin who explained the Proverbs to me? Of that time, of that place, I can still see even the old women! I remember hours of silver and of sunlight near the rivers, the hand of my companion on my shoulder, and our caresses as we stood on the spicy plains — A flock of scarlet pigeons thunders about my thought — Exiled here, I had a stage on which to play the theatrical masterpieces of every literature. I could show you unheard-of

les richesses inouïes. J'observe l'histoire des trésors que vous trouvâtes. Je vois la suite! Ma sagesse est aussi dédaignée que le chaos. Qu'est mon néant, auprès de la stupeur qui vous attend?

II

Je suis un inventeur bien autrement méritant que tous ceux qui m'ont précédé; un musicien même, qui ai trouvé quelque chose comme la clef de l'amour. À présent, gentilhomme d'une campagne aigre au ciel sobre, j'essaye de m'émouvoir au souvenir de l'enfance mendiante, de l'apprentissage ou de l'arrivée en sabots, des polémiques, des cinq ou six veuvages, et quelques noces où ma forte tête m'empêcha de monter au diapason des camarades. Je ne regrette pas ma vieille part de gaieté divine: l'air sobre de cette aigre campagne alimente fort activement mon atroce scepticisme. Mais comme ce scepticisme ne peut désormais être mis en œuvre, et que d'ailleurs je suis dévoué à un trouble nouveau, – j'attends de devenir un très méchant fou.

riches. I note the history of the treasures you discovered. I see the outcome! My wisdom is as much despised as chaos. What is my nothingness compared with the stupor which awaits you?

II

I am an inventor more deserving by far than all who have gone before me; a musician, moreover, who has discovered something like the key-signature of love. At present, a country gentleman of a harsh countryside under a sober sky, I try to be affected by the memory of my beggar's childhood, of my apprenticeship or my arrival in clogs, of my controversial discussions, of five or six widowhoods, and of a few convivialities at which my strong head prevented me from rising to the same pitch as my comrades did. I do not look back with regret on my old part in divine gaiety: the sober air of this harsh countryside feeds my atrocious scepticism very actively. But because this scepticism can never, henceforth, be put to any use, and since, besides, I am dedicated to a new uneasiness – I expect to become a very spiteful madman.

III

Dans un grenier où je fus enfermé à douze ans j'ai connu le monde, j'ai illustré la comédie humaine. Dans un cellier j'ai appris l'histoire. À quelque fête de nuit dans une cité du Nord j'ai rencontré toutes les femmes des anciens peintres. Dans un vieux passage à Paris on m'a enseigné les sciences classiques. Dans une magnifique demeure cernée par l'Orient entier j'ai accompli mon immense œuvre et passé mon illustre retraite. J'ai brassé mon sang. Mon devoir m'est remis. Il ne faut même plus songer à cela. Je suis réellement d'outre-tombe, et pas de commissions.

VIII

DÉPART

Assez vu. La vision s'est rencontrée à tous les airs.

Assez eu. Rumeurs des villes, le soir, et au soleil, et toujours.

III

In a loft in which I was shut up when I was twelve, I came to know the world; I illustrated the human comedy. In a storeroom I learned history. At some nocturnal festival in a northern city I met all the wives of the old painters. In an old alley in Paris, I was taught the classical sciences. In a magnificent dwelling surrounded by the whole East, I completed my vast work and spent my illustrious retirement. I stirred up my blood. My duty has been remitted. It need not even be thought of any more. I really am from beyond the grave, and no commissions.

VIII

Departure

Enough seen. The vision was encountered under all skies.

Enough had. Noises of cities, in the evening, and in the sunshine, and always.

Assez connu. Les arrêts de la vie. – Ô Rumeurs et Visions!

Départ dans l'affection et le bruit neufs!

IX

ROYAUTÉ

Un beau matin, chez un peuple fort doux, un homme et une femme superbes criaient sur la place publique: «Mes amis, je veux qu'elle soit reine!» «Je veux être reine!» Elle riait et tremblait. Il parlait aux amis de révélation, d'épreuve terminée. Ils se pâmaient l'un contre l'autre.

En effet, ils furent rois toute une matinée, où les tentures carminées se relevèrent sur les maisons, et toute l'après-midi, où ils s'avancèrent du côté des jardins de palmes.

Enough known. The pauses of life – O Sounds and Visions!
Departure into new affection and new noise!

IX
Royalty

One fine morning, in a country of very gentle people, a magnificent man and woman were shouting in the public square: 'Friends, I want her to be queen!' 'I want to be queen!' She laughed, trembling. He spoke to his friends about revelation, about trials undergone. They swooned against each other.

Indeed, they were kings for a whole morning, during which carmine-coloured hangings festooned the houses, and for the whole afternoon, as they made their way towards the gardens of palm-trees.

X

À UNE RAISON

Un coup de ton doigt sur le tambour décharge tous les sons et commence la nouvelle harmonie.

Un pas de toi, c'est la levée des nouveaux hommes et leur en-marche.

Ta tête se détourne: le nouvel amour! Ta tête se retourne, – le nouvel amour!

«Change nos lots, crible les fléaux, à commencer par le temps», te chantent ces enfants. «Élève n'importe où la substance de nos fortunes et de nos vœux», on t'en prie.

Arivée de toujours, qui t'en iras partout.

XI

MATINÉE D'IVRESSE

Ô mon Bien! Ô mon Beau! Fanfare atroce où je ne trébuche point! Chevalet féerique! Hourra pour l'œuvre

X

To a Reason

A blow of your finger on the drum unleashes all sounds and be-gins the new harmony.

One step of yours is the arising of new men and their marching forward.

Your head turns away: the new love! Your head turns back – O the new love!

'Change our lots, annihilate the plagues, starting with time,' sing these children to you. 'Breed, no matter where, the substance of our fortunes and of our wishes,' people beg you.

Arrival from forever, you will go away everywhere.

XI

Morning of Drunkenness

O my Good! O my Beautiful! Appalling fanfare in which I do not falter! Enchanted rack! Hurrah for the undreamed-of work and for

inouïe et pour le corps merveilleux, pour la première fois!
Cela commença sous les rires des enfants, cela finira par
eux. Ce poison va rester dans toutes nos veines même
quand, la fanfare tournant, nous serons rendu à l'ancienne
inharmonie. Ô maintenant nous si digne de ces tortures!
rassemblons fervemment cette promesse surhumaine faite
à notre corps et à notre âme créés: cette promesse, cette
démence! L'élégance, la science, la violence! On nous a
promis d'enterrer dans l'ombre l'arbre du bien et du mal,
de déporter les honnêtetés tyranniques, afin que nous
amenions notre très pur amour. Cela commença par quel-
ques dégoûts et cela finit, – ne pouvant nous saisir sur-le-
champ de cette éternité, – cela finit par une débandade de
parfums.

Rire des enfants, discrétion des esclaves, austérité des
vierges, horreur des figures et des objets d'ici, sacrés
soyez-vous par le souvenir de cette veille. Cela commen-
çait par toute la rustrerie, voici que cela finit par des anges
de flamme et de glace.

the marvellous substance, for the first time! It began in the laughter
of children, it will finish with it. This poison will remain in all our
veins, even when, by a turn of the fanfare, we are brought back to
the old disharmony. Oh let us now, so deserving of these tortures,
ardently gather this superhuman promise made to our created
bodies and souls: this promise, this madness! Elegance, knowledge,
violence! We have been promised that the tree of good and evil
shall be buried in darkness, that tyrannical respectabilities shall be
exiled, so that we can bring here our very pure love. It began with
a certain amount of disgust and it ends – being unable to seize at
once this eternity – it ends with a riot of perfumes.

Children's laughter, discretion of slaves, austerity of virgins,
horror of the faces and objects of this place, hallowed be you by the
memory of this vigil. It began with all boorishness, behold it ends
with angels of flame and ice.

Petite veille d'ivresse, sainte! quand ce ne serait que pour le masque dont tu nous as gratifié. Nous t'affirmons, méthode! Nous n'oublions pas que tu as glorifié hier chacun de nos âges. Nous avons foi au poison. Nous savons donner notre vie tout entière tous les jours.

Voici le temps des ASSASSINS.

XII

PHRASES

QUAND le monde sera réduit en un seul bois noir pour nos quatre yeux étonnés, – en une plage pour deux enfants fidèles, – en une maison musicale pour notre claire sympathie, – je vous trouverai.

Qu'il n'y ait ici-bas qu'un vieillard seul, calme et beau, entouré d'un «luxe inouï», – et je suis à vos genoux.

Little drunken vigil, holy! even if only on account of the mask you have granted us. We assert you, method! We do not forget that yesterday you glorified our every age. We have faith in poison. We know how to give our whole life each day.

Now is the time of the ASSASSINS.[1]

XII

Sentences

WHEN the world has been reduced to a single dark wood for our four astonished eyes – to a beach for two faithful children – to a musical house for our unclouded sympathy – I shall find you.

Let there be here below but a single old man, calm and beautiful, surrounded by 'unparalleled luxury' – and I shall be at your feet.

---

1. 'Assassins' comes from the Arabic hashshashīn, lit. 'hashish-eaters'. As Enid Starkie says, the 'marvellous substance [made] for the first time' is probably alchemical gold.

Que j'aie réalisé tous vos souvenirs, – que je sois celle
qui sait vous garrotter, – je vous étoufferai.

*

Quand nous sommes très-forts, – qui recule? très-gais, –
qui tombe de ridicule? Quand nous sommes très-
méchants, – que ferait-on de nous?

Parez-vous, dansez, riez. – Je ne pourrai jamais envoyer
l'Amour par la fenêtre.

*

Ma camarade, mendiante, enfant monstre! comme ça t'est
égal, ces malheureuses et ces manœuvres, et mes em-
barras. Attache-toi à nous avec ta voix impossible, ta
voix! unique flatteur de ce vil désespoir.

*

Une matinée couverte, en juillet. Un goût de cendres vole
dans l'air; – une odeur de bois suant dans l'âtre, – les

Let me have brought into being all your memories – let me be
she who can bind you hand and foot – I shall suffocate you.

*

When we are very strong – who draws back? very gay – who
crumbles with ridicule? When we are very spiteful – what would
they make of us? Deck yourself, dance, laugh – I shall never be
able to send Love out at the window.

*

My comrade, beggar-girl, monstrous child! how little you care
about these unhappy women and these manoeuvrings, or my diffi-
culties. Tie yourself to us with your impossible voice, your voice!
the only hope of this vile despair.

*

An overcast morning, in July. A taste of ashes floats in the air – a
smell of wood sweating on the hearth – soaked flowers – havoc of

fleurs rouies, – le saccage des promenades, – la bruine des canaux par les champs, – pourquoi pas déjà les joujoux et l'encens?

*

J'ai tendu des cordes de clocher à clocher; des guirlandes de fenêtre à fenêtre; des chaînes d'or d'étoile à étoile, et je danse.

*

Le haut étang fume continuellement. Quelle sorcière va se dresser sur le couchant blanc? Quelles violettes frondaisons vont descendre!

*

Pendant que les fonds publics s'écoulent en fêtes de fraternité, il sonne une cloche de feu rose dans les nuages.

*

avenues – the mist from the canals in the fields – why not indeed toys and incense?

*

I have stretched ropes from belfry to belfry; garlands from window to window; golden chains from star to star, and I am dancing.

*

The highland pond steams continually. What witch is going to rise against the pale sunset? What violet foliage is going to fall!

*

While the public funds are poured out in feasts of brotherhood, a bell of rose-coloured fire tolls in the clouds.

*

Avivant un agréable goût d'encre de Chine, une poudre
noire pleut doucement sur ma veillée. – Je baisse les feux
du lustre, je me jette sur le lit, et, tourné du côté de
l'ombre, je vous vois, mes filles! mes reines!

XIII

OUVRIERS

Ô CETTE chaude matinée de février! Le Sud inopportun
vint relever nos souvenirs d'indigents absurdes, notre
jeune misère.

Henrika avait une jupe de coton à carreau blanc et
brun, qui a dû être portée au siècle dernier, un bonnet à
rubans et un foulard de soie. C'était bien plus triste qu'un
deuil. Nous faisions un tour dans la banlieue. Le temps
était couvert, et ce vent du Sud excitait toutes les vilaines
odeurs des jardins ravagés et des prés desséchés.

Releasing a pleasant flavour of Indian ink, a black powder falls
softly on my vigil. – I lower the gas jets, throw myself on the bed,
and turning towards the shadows, I see you, my daughters! my
queens!

XIII

Workmen

O THAT warm February morning! The untimely South wind came
and awakened our absurd paupers' memories, our young destitu-
tion.

Henrika was wearing a cotton skirt in brown and white check,
which must have been fashionable in the last century, a bonnet
with ribbons and a silk scarf. It was far sadder than mourning. We
were taking a stroll in the suburbs. The sky was overcast, and that
South wind stirred up all the nasty smells of the ravaged gardens
and the dried-up meadows.

Cela ne devait pas fatiguer ma femme au même point que moi. Dans une flache laissée par l'inondation du mois précédent à un sentier assez haut, elle me fit remarquer de très-petits poissons.

La ville, avec sa fumée et ses bruits de métiers, nous suivait très loin dans les chemins. Ô l'autre monde, l'habitation bénie par le ciel, et les ombrages! Le Sud me rappelait les misérables incidents de mon enfance, mes désespoirs d'été, l'horrible quantité de force et de science que le sort a toujours éloignée de moi. Non! nous ne passerons pas l'été dans cet avare pays où nous ne serons jamais que des orphelins fiancés. Je veux que ce bras durci ne traîne plus une *chère image*.

XIV

LES PONTS

DES ciels gris de cristal. Un bizarre dessin de ponts, ceux-ci droits, ceux-là bombés, d'autres descendant en

---

It can't have wearied my wife as much as it did me. In a sheet of water left by the floods of the previous month near a fairly high path, she drew my attention to some tiny fishes.

The town, with its smoke and its noise of factories, followed us for a long way down the roads. O other world, dwelling-place blessed by the sky, and the shadows! The South wind reminded me of the unhappy incidents of my childhood, my summer despairs, the hideous quantity of strength and knowledge which fate has always kept far from me. No! we shall not spend the summer in this miserly country where we shall never be anything but betrothed orphans. I do not wish this hardened arm to drag, any longer, a *dear image*.

XIV

The Bridges

GREY crystal skies. A strange design of bridges, some straight, others curved, others again coming down at oblique angles to the

obliquant en angles sur les premiers, et ces figures se renouvelant dans les autres circuits éclairés du canal, mais tous tellement longs et légers que les rives, chargées de dômes, s'abaissent et s'amoindrissent. Quelques-uns de ces ponts sont encore chargés de masures. D'autres soutiennent des mâts, des signaux, de frêles parapets. Des accords mineurs se croisent, et filent; des cordes montent des berges. On distingue une veste rouge, peut-être d'autres costumes et des instruments de musique. Sont-ce des airs populaires, des bouts de concerts seigneuriaux, des restants d'hymnes publics? L'eau est grise et bleue, large comme un bras de mer.

Un rayon blanc, tombant du haut du ciel, anéantit cette comédie.

XV

VILLE

JE suis un éphémère et point trop mécontent citoyen d'une métropole crue moderne parce que tout goût connu

first, and all these patterns repeating themselves in the other windings of the canal that are lit up, but all of them so long and light that the banks, laden with domes, sink and shrink. Some of these bridges are still covered with hovels. Others bear masts, signals, fragile parapets. Minor chords cross each other and fade; ropes go up from the embankments. You can make out a red coat, possibly other clothes and musical instruments. Are these popular tunes, snatches from manorial concerts, left-overs of public anthems? The water is grey and blue, wide as an arm of the sea.

A ray of white light, falling from high in the sky, annihilates this make-believe.

XV
City

I AM an ephemeral and not at all too discontented citizen of a metropolis which is believed to be modern because every known

a été éludé dans les ameublements et l'extérieur des maisons aussi bien que dans le plan de la ville. Ici vous ne signaleriez les traces d'aucun monument de superstition. La morale et la langue sont réduites à leur plus simple expression, enfin! Ces millions de gens qui n'ont pas besoin de se connaître amènent si pareillement l'éducation, le métier et la vieillesse, que ce cours de vie doit être plusieurs fois moins long que ce qu'une statistique folle trouve pour les peuples du continent. Aussi comme, de ma fenêtre, je vois des spectres nouveaux roulant à travers l'épaisse et éternelle fumée de charbon — notre ombre des bois, notre nuit d'été! — des Erinnyes nouvelles, devant mon cottage qui est ma patrie et tout mon cœur puisque tout ici ressemble à ceci, — la Mort sans pleurs, notre active fille et servante, un Amour désespéré et un joli Crime piaulant dans la boue de la rue.

taste has been avoided in the furnishing and the exteriors of the houses as well as in the layout of the city. Here you cannot point out the trace of a single monument to the past. Morals and language have been reduced to their simplest expression, in short! These millions of people who have no need to know each other carry on their education, their work, and their old age so similarly that the course of their lives must be several times shorter than the findings of absurd statistics allow the peoples of the continent. Thus, from my window, I see new apparitions roaming through the thick and endless coal-smoke — our woodland shade, our summer's night! — new Erinnyes, in front of my cottage which is my country and my whole heart since everything here is like this: Death without tears, our active daughter and servant, a desperate Love and a pretty Crime whimpering in the mud of the street.

XVI

ORNIÈRES

À DROITE l'aube d'été éveille les feuilles et les vapeurs et les bruits de ce coin du parc, et les talus de gauche tiennent dans leur ombre violette les mille rapides ornières de la route humide. Défilé de féeries. En effet: des chars chargés d'animaux de bois doré, de mâts et de toiles bariolées, au grand galop de vingt chevaux de cirque tachetés, et les enfants et les hommes sur leurs bêtes les plus étonnantes; – vingt véhicules, bossés, pavoisés et fleuris comme des carrosses anciens ou de contes, pleins d'enfants attifés pour une pastorale suburbaine; – même des cercueils sous leur dais de nuit dressant les panaches d'ébène, filant au trot des grandes juments bleues et noires.

XVI
Ruts

To the right the summer dawn awakens the leaves and the mists and the sounds of this corner of the park, and the banks on the left hold in the grasp of their violet shadow the thousand rapid ruts of the wet road. A procession of enchantments. It is true: wagons loaded with animals of gilded wood, poles, and variegated bunting, drawn by twenty furiously galloping dappled circus horses; and the children and the men on their most astonishing animals – twenty vehicles, carved, decked, and covered with flowers like the carriages of olden times, or of fairy tales, filled with children dressed up for a suburban pastoral – even coffins under their canopies of night rearing their ebony plumes, moving past to the trot of the great blue-black mares.

XVII

VILLES

Ce sont des villes! C'est un peuple pour qui se sont montés ces Alleghanys et ces Libans de rêve! Des chalets de cristal et de bois qui se meuvent sur des rails et des poulies invisibles. Les vieux cratères ceints de colosses et de palmiers de cuivre rugissent mélodieusement dans les feux. Des fêtes amoureuses sonnent sur les canaux pendus derrière les chalets. La chasse des carillons crie dans les gorges. Des corporations de chanteurs géants accourent dans des vêtements et des oriflammes éclatants comme la lumière des cimes. Sur les plates-formes au milieu des gouffres les Rolands sonnent leur bravoure. Sur les passerelles de l'abîme et les toits des auberges l'ardeur du ciel pavoise les mâts. L'écroulement des apothéoses rejoint les champs des hauteurs où les centauresses séraphiques évoluent parmi les avalanches. Au-dessus du niveau des plus hautes crêtes, une mer troublée par la naissance éternelle de Vénus, chargée de flottes orphéoniques et de la

XVII

Cities

What cities! This is a people for whom these dream Alleghanies and dream Lebanons were staged! Chalets of crystal and of wood which move on invisible rails and pulleys. The old craters surrounded with colossi and copper palm-trees roar melodiously in the flames. Feasts of love sound across the canals hanging behind the chalets. The hunting of the chimes halloos in the passes. Guilds of gigantic singers come flocking with robes and oriflammes as dazzling as the light of the mountain-tops. On platforms in the midst of the gulfs, Rolands trumpet their valour. On the footbridges across the abyss, and on the roofs of the inns, the sky's heat decks the masts with flags. The crumbling of apotheoses overtakes the higher fields where angelic centauresses move about among the avalanches. Above the level of the highest crests, a sea stirred up by the continual birth of Venus, bearing choral fleets and the murmur

rumeur des perles et des conques précieuses; – la mer
s'assombrit parfois avec des éclats mortels. Sur les ver-
sants, des moissons de fleurs, grandes comme nos armes et
nos coupes, mugissent. Des cortèges de Mabs en robes
rousses, opalines, montent des ravines. Là-haut, les pieds
dans la cascade et les ronces, les cerfs tettent Diane. Les
Bacchantes de banlieues sanglotent et la lune brûle et
hurle. Vénus entre dans les cavernes des forgerons et des
ermites. Des groupes de beffrois chantent les idées des
peuples. Des châteaux bâtis en os sort la musique in-
connue. Toutes les légendes évoluent et les élans se ruent
dans les bourgs. Le paradis des orages s'effondre. Les
sauvages dansent sans cesse la fête de la nuit. Et, une
heure, je suis descendu dans le mouvement d'un boule-
vard de Bagdad où des compagnies ont chanté la joie du
travail nouveau, sous une brise épaisse, circulant sans
pouvoir éluder les fabuleux fantômes des monts où l'on a
dû se retrouver.

Quels bons bras, quelle belle heure me rendront cette
région d'où viennent mes sommeils et mes moindres
mouvements?

---

of the precious pearls and conchs – the sea darkens at times with
deadly flashes. On the slopes, harvests of flowers, huge as our wea-
pons and goblets, bellow. Processions of Mabs in russet and opaline
robes climb from the ravines. Up there, their feet in the waterfall
and the brambles, the deer suckle at Diana's breast. The Bacchantes
of the suburbs sob, and the moon burns and howls. Venus enters
the caves of blacksmiths and hermits. Groups of belfries sing out
the ideas of peoples. From castles built of bones comes unknown
music. All the legends develop and the elks rush into the towns.
The paradise of storms subsides. The savages dance without ceas-
ing at the nocturnal festival. And, at one time, I went down into the
bustle of a Baghdad street where gatherings of people sang of the
joy of new labours, in a heavy breeze, moving about without being
able to escape the incredible phantoms of the mountains where they
must have met.

What kind arms, what lovely hour will bring me back that re-
gion from which my slumbers and my slightest movements come?

XVIII

VAGABONDS

Pɪᴛᴏʏᴀʙʟᴇ frère! Que d'atroces veillées je lui dus! «Je ne me saisissais pas fervemment de cette entreprise. Je m'étais joué de son infirmité. Par ma faute nous retournerions en exil, en esclavage.» Il me supposait un guignon et une innocence très bizarres, et il ajoutait des raisons inquiétantes.

Je répondais en ricanant à ce satanique docteur, et finissais par gagner la fenêtre. Je créais, par delà la campagne traversée par des bandes de musique rare, les fantômes du futur luxe nocturne.

Après cette distraction vaguement hygiénique, je m'étendais sur une paillasse. Et, presque chaque nuit, aussitôt endormi, le pauvre frère se levait, la bouche pourrie, les yeux arrachés, – tel qu'il se rêvait! – et me tirait dans la salle en hurlant son songe de chagrin idiot.

XVIII
Tramps

Pɪᴛɪꜰᴜʟ brother! What hideous vigils I owed to him!

'I did not seize ardently on this venture. I made game of his weakness. It would be my fault if we went back into exile, into slavery.' He credited me with a strange ill-luck and innocence, and would add disquieting reasons.

I would reply by jeering at this satanic scholar, and would end by going to the window. I would create, beyond the countryside crossed by stretches of unusual music, mirages of the nocturnal luxury to come.

After this vaguely hygienic diversion, I would stretch out on a straw mattress. And, almost every night, as soon as I was asleep, the poor brother would get up, his mouth rotted away, his eyes torn out – as he had dreamed of himself! – and would drag me into the hall, howling his dream of idiot sorrow.

J'avais an effet, en toute sincérité d'esprit, pris l'engagement de le rendre à son état primitif de fils du soleil, — et nous errions, nourris du vin des cavernes et du biscuit de la route, moi pressé de trouver le lieu et la formule.

XIX

VILLES

L'ACROPOLE officielle outre les conceptions de la barbarie moderne les plus colossales. Impossible d'exprimer le jour mat produit par le ciel immuablement gris, l'éclat impérial des bâtisses, et la neige éternelle du sol. On a reproduit dans un goût d'énormité singulier toutes les merveilles classiques de l'architecture. J'assiste à des expositions de peinture dans des locaux vingt fois plus vastes qu'Hampton-Court. Quelle peinture! Un Nabuchodonosor norwégien a fait construire les escaliers des ministères; les subalternes que j'ai pu voir sont déjà plus

In fact, I had, in all sincerity, pledged myself to restore him to his original state as child of the sun – and we wandered, nourished on the wine of the caverns and the biscuit of the road, myself impatient to find the place and the formula.

XIX

Cities

THE official acropolis outdoes the most colossal conceptions of modern barbarity. It is impossible to describe the dull light produced by the unchanging grey sky, the imperial brightness of the masonry, and the eternal snow on the ground. They have reproduced, in singularly outrageous taste, all the classical marvels of architecture. I go to exhibitions of painting in places twenty times vaster than Hampton Court. What painting! A Norwegian Nebuchadnezzar designed the staircases of the ministries; the minor offi-

fiers que des brahmanes, et j'ai tremblé à l'aspect des gardiens de colosses et officiers de constructions. Par le groupement des bâtiments, en squares, cours et terrasses fermées, on a évincé les clochers. Les parcs représentent la nature primitive travaillée par un art superbe. Le haut quartier a des parties inexplicables: un bras de mer, sans bateaux, roule sa nappe de grésil bleu entre des quais chargés de candélabres géants. Un pont court conduit à une poterne immédiatement sous le dôme de la Sainte-Chapelle. Ce dôme est une armature d'acier artistique de quinze mille pieds de diamètre environ.

Sur quelques points des passerelles de cuivre, des plates-formes, des escaliers qui contournent les halles et les piliers, j'ai cru pouvoir juger la profondeur de la ville! C'est le prodige dont je n'ai pu me rendre compte: quels sont les niveaux des autres quartiers sur ou sous l'acropole? Pour l'étranger de notre temps la reconnaissance est impossible. Le quartier commerçant est un circus d'un seul style, avec galeries à arcades. On ne voit pas de

cials I did see are prouder than Brahmins as it is, and the looks of the guardians of colossi and of the building foremen made me tremble. By their grouping of the buildings, in closed squares, terraces, and courtyards, they have squeezed out the bell-towers. The parks present primeval nature cultivated with marvellous art. There are parts of the better district which are inexplicable: an arm of the sea, without boats, rolls its sheet of blue ground glass between quays covered with giant candelabra. A short bridge leads to a postern immediately below the dome of the Holy Chapel. This dome is an artistic framework of steel about fifteen thousand feet in diameter.

From certain [vantage-]points on the copper foot-bridges, the platforms, the stairways which wind round the covered markets and the pillars, I thought I could judge the depth of the city. This was the marvel I was unable to verify: what are the levels of the other districts above or below the acropolis? For the foreigner in our times exploration is impossible. The commercial district is a circus all in the same style, with galleries of arcades. One can see no

boutiques, mais la neige de la chaussée est écrasée; quelques nababs, aussi rares que les promeneurs d'un matin de dimanche à Londres, se dirigent vers une diligence de diamants. Quelques divans de velours rouge: on sert des boissons polaires dont le prix varie de huit cents à huit mille roupies. À l'idée de chercher des théâtres sur ce circus, je me réponds que les boutiques doivent contenir des drames assez sombres? Je pense qu'il y a une police; mais la loi doit être tellement étrange, que je renonce à me faire une idée des aventuriers d'ici.

Le faubourg, aussi élégant qu'une belle rue de Paris, est favorisé d'un air de lumière; l'élément démocratique compte quelques cents âmes. Là encore, les maisons ne se suivent pas; le faubourg se perd bizarrement dans la campagne, le «Comté» qui remplit l'occident éternel des forêts et des plantations prodigieuses où les gentilshommes sauvages chassent leurs chroniques sous la lumière qu'on a créée.

shops, but the snow on the roadway is trampled; a few nabobs, as rare as walkers on a Sunday morning in London, move towards a stage-coach made of diamonds. There are a few red velvet divans: polar drinks are served, whose prices range from eight hundred to eight thousand rupees. To my idea of looking for theatres in this circus, I reply that the shops must contain some pretty gloomy dramas? I think there is a police force; but the laws must be so strange that I give up trying to imagine what the adventurers of this place are like.

The outlying part, as elegant as a fine street in Paris, is favoured with the appearance of light; the democratic element numbers a few hundred souls. Here again, the houses are not in rows; the suburb loses itself oddly in the country, the 'County' which fills the endless west of forests and huge plantations where misanthropic gentlemen hunt for news in the light which is their own creation.

XX

VEILLÉES

I

C'est le repos éclairé, ni fièvre ni langueur, sur le lit ou sur le pré.

C'est l'ami ni ardent ni faible. L'ami.

C'est l'aimée ni tourmentante ni tourmentée. L'aimée.

L'air et le monde point cherchés. La vie.

— Était-ce donc ceci?

— Et le rêve fraîchit.

II

L'éclairage revient à l'arbre de bâtisse. Des deux extrémités de la salle, décors quelconques, des élévations harmoniques se joignent. La muraille en face du veilleur est une succession psychologique de coupes de frises, de

XX

Vigils

I

It is rest in the light, neither fever nor languor, on the bed or on the meadow.

It is the friend neither ardent nor weak. The friend.

It is the beloved neither tormenting nor tormented. The beloved.

The air and the world one has not sought. Life.

— Was it this, then?

— And the dream is growing cold.

II

The lighting comes back to the king-post. From the two ends of the room, scenes of some sort, harmonic risers join. The wall facing the person watching is a psychological succession of cross-sections

bandes atmosphériques et d'accidences géologiques. –
Rêve intense et rapide de groupes sentimentaux avec des
êtres de tous les caractères parmi toutes les apparences.

III

Les lampes et les tapis de la veillée font le bruit des vagues,
la nuit, le long de la coque et autour du steerage.
La mer de la veillée, telle que les seins d'Amélie.
Les tapisseries, jusqu'à mi-hauteur, des taillis de den-
telle teinte d'émeraude, où se jettent les tourterelles de la
veillée.

. . . .

La plaque du foyer noir, de réels soleils des grèves: ah!
puits des magies; seule vue d'aurore, cette fois.

of friezes, of atmospheric layers, and of geological strata – Intense
and rapid dream of sentimental groups involving all kinds of beings
in all atmospheres.

III

The lamps and the rugs of the vigil make the sound of waves, at
night, along the hull and round the steering gear.
The sea of the vigil, like Amélie's breasts.
The hangings, up to half-way, copses of lace dyed emerald, into
which the doves of the vigil dart.

. . . .

The slab of the black hearth, real suns of the beaches: ah! wells
of magic; the only sight of dawn, this time.

XXI

MYSTIQUE

Sur la pente du talus, les anges tournent leurs robes de laine dans les herbages d'acier et d'émeraude.

Des prés de flammes bondissent jusqu'au sommet du mamelon. À gauche le terreau de l'arête est piétiné par tous les homicides et toutes les batailles, et tous les bruits désastreux filent leur courbe. Derrière l'arête de droite la ligne des orients, des progrès.

Et, tandis que la bande en haut du tableau est formée de la rumeur tournante et bondissante des conques des mers et des nuits humaines,

La douceur fleurie des étoiles et du ciel et du reste descend en face du talus, comme un panier, – contre notre face, et fait l'abîme fleurant et bleu là-dessous.

XXI

Mystique

On the slope of the bank, angels swirl their robes of wool in pastures of steel and emerald.

Meadows of flames leap up to the top of the round hill. To the left, the mould of the ridge is stamped down by all homicides and all battles, and all calamitous noises describe their curve. Behind the right-hand ridge, the line of risings, of progress.

And, whereas the strip at the top of the picture is formed of the turning and leaping sound of the conchs of human seas and nights,

The flowery sweetness of the stars and the sky and the rest comes down, opposite the embankment, like a basket – against our face, and creates the flowering blue abyss below.

XXII

AUBE

J'ai embrassé l'aube d'été.

Rien ne bougeait encore au front des palais. L'eau était morte. Les camps d'ombres ne quittaient pas la route du bois. J'ai marché, réveillant les haleines vives et tièdes, et les pierreries regardèrent, et les ailes se levèrent sans bruit.

La première entreprise fut, dans le sentier déjà empli de frais et blêmes éclats, une fleur qui me dit son nom.

Je ris au wasserfall blond qui s'échevela à travers les sapins: à la cime argentée je reconnus la déesse.

Alors je levai un à un les voiles. Dans l'allée, en agitant les bras. Par la plaine, où je l'ai dénoncée au coq. À la grand'ville, elle fuyait parmi les clochers et les dômes, et, courant comme un mendiant sur les quais de marbre, je la chassais.

XXII
Dawn

I embraced the summer dawn.

Nothing was stirring yet on the façades of the palaces. The water was dead. The camps of shadows in the woodland road had not been struck. I walked, awakening vivid warm breaths, and the precious stones looked up, and wings rose without a sound.

The first adventure was, in the path already filled with cool, pale gleams, a flower which told me its name.

I laughed at the blond waterfall, dishevelled between the fir trees: in the silvery peak I recognized the goddess.

Then I lifted the veils, one by one. In the avenue, waving my arms. On the plain, where I declared her to the cock. In the city, she fled among the belfries and domes, and I, running like a beggar across the marble quays, chased after her.

En haut de la route, près d'un bois de lauriers, je l'ai entourée avec ses voiles amassés, et j'ai senti un peu son immense corps. L'aube et l'enfant tombèrent au bas du bois.

Au réveil il était midi.

XXIII

FLEURS

D'un gradin d'or, – parmi les cordons de soie, les gazes grises, les velours verts et les disques de cristal qui noircissent comme du bronze au soleil, – je vois la digitale s'ouvrir sur un tapis de filigranes d'argent, d'yeux et de chevelures.

Des pièces d'or jaune semées sur l'agate, des piliers d'acajou supportant un dôme d'émeraudes, des bouquets de satin blanc et de fines verges de rubis entourent la rose d'eau.

At the top of the road, near a laurel wood, I surrounded her with her heaped-up veils, and I felt, a little, her immense body. Dawn and the child fell down at the bottom of the wood.

When I woke up it was noon.

XXIII

Flowers

From a golden step – among cords of silk, grey gauzes, green velvets, and discs of crystal which darken like bronze in the sun – I see the foxgloves opening on a carpet of silver filigree, of eyes, and of hair.

Coins of yellow gold sown on agate, columns of mahogany supporting a dome of emeralds, bunches of white satin and of fine sprays of rubies surround the water-rose.

Tels qu'un dieu aux énormes yeux bleus et aux formes de neige, la mer et le ciel attirent aux terrasses de marbre la foule des jeunes et fortes roses.

XXIV

NOCTURNE VULGAIRE

Un souffle ouvre des brèches opéradiques dans les cloisons, – brouille le pivotement des toits rongés – disperse les limites des foyers, – éclipse les croisées.

Le long de la vigne, m'étant appuyé du pied à une gargouille, – je suis descendu dans ce carrosse dont l'époque est assez indiquée par les glaces convexes, les panneaux bombés et les sophas contournés. Corbillard de mon sommeil, isolé, maison de berger de ma niaiserie, le véhicule vire sur le gazon de la grande route effacée: et dans un défaut en haut de la glace de droite tournoient les blêmes figures lunaires, feuilles, seins.

Like a god with huge blue eyes and shapes of snow, the sea and the sky draw to the marble terraces the throng of young vigorous roses.

XXIV
Common Nocturne

A breath opens operatic breaches in the walls – smudges the pivoting of the crumbling roofs – disperses the boundaries of the hearths – eclipses the windows.

Down the length of the vine, having rested my foot on a gargoyle – I climbed into this coach whose period is sufficiently indicated by the convex panes of glass, the bulging panels, and the elaborately shaped seats. Hearse of my slumber, alone, crofter's cottage of my silliness, the vehicle turns on the turf of the obliterated highway: and, in a flaw at the top of the right-hand windowpane, pale lunar figures revolve, leaves, breasts.

– Un vert et un bleu très foncés envahissent l'image.
Dételage aux environs d'une tache de gravier.

– Ici va-t-on siffler pour l'orage, et les Sodomes et les
Solymes, et les bêtes féroces et les armées,

(– Postillon et bêtes de songe reprendront-ils sous les
plus suffocantes futaies, pour m'enfoncer jusqu'aux yeux
dans la source de soie.)

– Et nous envoyer, fouettés à travers les eaux clapo-
tantes et les boissons répandues, rouler sur l'aboi des
dogues ...

– Un souffle disperse les limites du foyer.

XXV

MARINE

LES chars d'argent et de cuivre –
Les proues d'acier et d'argent –
Battent l'écume, –
Soulèvent les souches des ronces.

– A green and a blue, both very deep, invade the picture. Un-
harnessing in the vicinity of a patch of gravel.

– Here one will whistle for the storm, and the Sodoms and the
Solymas, and the wild beasts and the armies,

(Coachman and animals of dreams, will they start again into
the most stifling thickets, in order to sink me up to the eyes in the
silken spring.)

– And send us, lashed on, across splashing waters and spilt
drinks, rolling over the barking of the bulldogs ...

– A breath disperses the boundaries of the hearth.

XXV

Seascape

CHARIOTS of silver and of copper –
Prows of steel and of silver –
Scour the foam –
Tear up the stumps of the thorns.

Les courants de la lande,
Et les ornières immenses du reflux,
Filent circulairement vers l'est,
Vers les piliers de la forêt,
Vers le fûts de la jetée,
Dont l'angle est heurté par des tourbillons de lumière.

XXVI

FÊTE D'HIVER

LA cascade sonne derrière les huttes d'opéra-comique.
Des girandoles se prolongent, dans les vergers et les allées
voisins du méandre, – les verts et les rouges du couchant.
Nymphes d'Horace coiffées au Premier Empire. – Rondes
Sibériennes, Chinoises de Boucher.

The currents of the heath,
And the huge ruts of the ebb-tide,
Flow away in a circle towards the East,
Towards the pillars of the forest,
Towards the posts of the jetty,
Whose corner is battered by whirlwinds of light.

XXVI

Winter Festival

THE waterfall murmers behind the comic-opera shanties. Catherine
wheels extend, in the orchards and avenues near the meandering
river, the greens and reds of the sunset. Nymphs out of Horace
with Empire hair styles. – Round Siberian women, Chinese girls
like Bouchers.

XXVII

ANGOISSE

SE peut-il qu'Elle me fasse pardonner les ambitions continuellement écrasées, – qu'une fin aisée répare les âges d'indigence, – qu'un jour de succès nous endorme sur la honte de notre inhabileté fatale?

(Ô palmes! diamant! – Amour! force! – plus haut que toutes joies et gloires! – de toutes façons, partout, – Démon, dieu, – jeunesse de cet être-ci: moi!)

Que les accidents de féerie scientifique et des mouvements de fraternité sociale soient chéris comme restitution progressive de la franchise première? ...

Mais la Vampire qui nous rend gentils commande que nous nous amusions avec ce qu'elle nous laisse, ou qu'autrement nous soyons plus drôles.

Rouler aux blessures, par l'air lassant et la mer; aux supplices, par le silence des eaux et de l'air meurtriers; aux tortures qui rient, dans leur silence atrocement houleux.

XXVII

Anguish

Is it possible that She will obtain pardon for my continually crushed ambitions – that a wealthy end will make up for ages of poverty – that a day of success will lull us asleep on the shame of our fatal clumsiness?

(O palms! diamond! – Love! strength! – higher than all joys and glories! – of all kinds, everywhere – Demon, god, – youth of this being: myself!)

[Is it possible] that the accidents of scientific magic and the movements of social brotherhood will be cherished as the progressive restitution of primal freedom? ...

But the Vampire who makes us well-behaved commands us to amuse ourselves with what she leaves us, or else to be more amusing.

Rolling on wounds through the tiring air and the sea; in torment, through the silence of the murderous waters and air; in the grip of tortures which laugh, in their hideously tumultuous silence.

XXVIII

MÉTROPOLITAIN

Du détroit d'indigo aux mers d'Ossian, sur le sable rose et orange qu'a lavé la ciel vineux viennent de monter et de se croiser des boulevards de cristal habités incontinent par de jeunes familles pauvres qui s'alimentent chez les fruitiers. Rien de riche. – La ville!

Du désert de bitume fuient droit en déroute avec les nappes de brumes échelonnées en bandes affreuses au ciel qui se recourbe, se recule et descend formé de la plus sinistre fumée noire que puisse faire l'Océan en deuil, les casques, les roues, les barques, les croupes. – La bataille!

Lève la tête: ce pont de bois, arqué; les derniers pota- gers de Samarie; ces masques enluminés sous la lanterne fouettée par la nuit froide; l'ondine niaise à la robe bru- yante, au bas de la rivière; les crânes lumineux dans les plants de pois, – et les autres fantasmagories, – la cam- pagne.

XXVIII
Metropolitan

From the indigo strait to the seas of Ossian, on the pink and orange sand which the vinous sky has washed, crystal boulevards have just risen and crossed, at once occupied by young poor families who get their food at the greengrocers' shops. Nothing rich – The city!

From the desert of bitumen flee in headlong flight under sheets of fog spread out in frightful layers in the sky which curves back, recedes, and descends, formed of the most sinister black smoke that the Ocean in mourning can produce, helmets, wheels, ships, crup- pers – The battle!

Raise your head: that arched wooden bridge; the last kitchen gardens of Samaria; those masks lit by the lantern whipped by the cold night; the silly undine with the noisy dress, at the bottom of the river; luminous skulls among the pea seedlings – and the other phantasmagoria – the country.

Des routes bordées de grilles et de murs, contenant à peine leurs bosquets, et les atroces fleurs qu'on appellerait cœurs et sœurs, Damas damnant de longueur, — possessions de féeriques aristocraties ultra-Rhénanes, Japonaises, Guaranies, propres encore à recevoir la musique des anciens, — et il y a des auberges qui pour toujours n'ouvrent déjà plus; — il y a des princesses, et, si tu n'es pas trop accablé, l'étude des astres, — le ciel.

Le matin où, avec Elle, vous vous débattîtes parmi les éclats de neige, les lèvres vertes, les glaces, les drapeaux noirs et les rayons bleus, et les parfums pourpres du soleil des pôles — ta force.

XXIX

BARBARE

Bien après les jours et les saisons, et les êtres et les pays,

Le pavillon en viande saignante sur la soie des mers et des fleurs arctiques; (elles n'existent pas.)

Roads bordered by railings and walls, hardly containing their spinneys, and the frightful flowers you would call souls and sisters, Damask damning with tedium — the property of fairy-tale nobilities from beyond the Rhine, Japanese, Guarani, still fit to receive the music of the ancients — and there are inns which are never open any more — there are princesses, and, if you are not too overwhelmed, the study of the stars — the sky.

The morning when, with Her, you wrestled among the gleams of snow, the green lips, the ice, the black flags and the blue beams of light, and the purple odours of the Polar sun — your strength.

XXIX
Barbarian

Long after the days and the seasons, and the creatures and the countries,

The banner of bloody meat over the silk of the seas and the arctic flowers; (they do not exist.)

Remis des vieilles fanfares d'héroïsme – qui nous atta-
quent encore le cœur et la tête – loin des anciens assas-
sins.

– Oh! le pavillon en viande saignante sur la soie des
mers et des fleurs arctiques; (elles n'existent pas.)

Douceurs!

Les brasiers, pleuvant aux rafales de givre, – Douceurs!
– les feux à la pluie du vent de diamants jetée par le cœur
terrestre éternellement carbonisé pour nous. – Ô monde! –

(Loin des vieilles retraites et des vieilles flammes, qu'on
entend, qu'on sent,)

Les brasiers et les écumes. La musique, virement des
gouffres et choc des glaçons aux astres.

Ô Douceurs, ô monde, ô musique! Et là, les formes, les
sueurs, les chevelures et les yeux, flottant. Et les larmes
blanches, bouillantes, – ô douceurs! – et la voix féminine
arrivée au fond des volcans et des grottes arctiques.

Le pavillon ...

Recovered from the old fanfares of heroism – which still attack
our heart and head – far from the old assassins.

– Oh! the banner of bloody meat over the silk of the seas and the
arctic flowers; (they do not exist.)

Ecstasy!

The fires of coals, raining in squalls of frost – Ecstasy! – fires
in the rain of the wind of diamonds thrown out by the heart of the
earth eternally carbonized for us – O world! –

(Far from the old retreats and the old fires, which can be heard,
felt)

Braziers and foam. Music, veerings of gulfs and impact of icicles
on the stars.

O Ecstasy, O world, O music! And here, shapes, sweats, heads
of hair and eyes, floating. And white tears, boiling – O ecstasy! –
and the female voice reaching to the bottom of the volcanoes and
the arctic caverns.

The banner ...

XXX

PROMONTOIRE

L'AUBE d'or et la soirée frissonnante trouvent notre brick en large en face de cette villa et de ses dépendances, qui forment un promontoire aussi étendu que l'Épire et le Péloponnèse ou que la grande île du Japon, ou que l'Arabie! Des fanums qu'éclaire la rentrée des théories; d'immenses vues de la défense des côtes modernes; des dunes illustrées de chaudes fleurs et de bacchanales; de grands canaux de Carthage et des embankments d'une Venise louche; de molles éruptions d'Etnas et des crevasses de fleurs et d'eaux des glaciers; des lavoirs entourés de peupliers d'Allemagne; des talus de parcs singuliers penchant des têtes d'Arbres du Japon; et les façades circulaires des «Royal» ou des «Grand» de Scarborough ou de Brooklyn; et leurs railways flanquent, creusent, surplombent les dispositions de cet hôtel, choisies dans l'histoire des plus élégantes et des plus colossales constructions

XXX

Promontory

THE golden dawn and the shivering evening find our brig in the offing opposite this villa and its grounds, which form a promontory as extensive as Epirus and the Peloponnese, or the great island of Japan, or Arabia! Temples lit up by the return of the processions; immense views of the defences of modern coasts; dunes illustrated with hot flowers and bacchanals; great canals of Carthage and embankments of a sleazy Venice; faint eruptions of Etnas and glacier crevasses of flowers and waters; wash-houses surrounded by German poplars; slopes of strange parks leaning with the heads of Trees of Japan; and the curved fronts of Scarborough or Brooklyn 'Royals' or 'Grands'; and their railways flank, undermine, and overhang the elevations of this hotel, chosen from the history of the most elegant and the most colossal buildings of Italy, of

de l'Italie, de l'Amérique et de l'Asie, dont les fenêtres et les terrasses, à présent pleines d'éclairages, de boissons et de brises riches, sont ouvertes à l'esprit des voyageurs et des nobles, – qui permettent, aux heures du jour, à toutes les tarentelles des côtes, – et même aux ritournelles des vallées illustres de l'art, de décorer merveilleusement les façades du Palais-Promontoire.

XXXI

SCÈNES

L'ANCIENNE Comédie poursuit ses accords et divise ses idylles:

Des boulevards de tréteaux.

Un long pier en bois d'un bout à l'autre d'un champ rocailleux où la foule barbare évolue sous les arbres dépouillés.

America, and of Asia, and whose windows and terraces, now full of costly illuminations and drinks and wafts of air, are open to the influence of travellers and of the nobility – who allow, during the hours of daylight, all the tarantellas of the coasts, and even the ritornellos of the illustrious valleys of art, to decorate marvellously the façades of the Promontory Palace.

XXXI

Stages

THE ancient Theatre pursues its harmonies and apportions its idylls:

Boulevards of raised platforms.

A long wooden pier from one end to the other of a rocky field where the barbarous multitude moves about under the bare trees.

Dans des corridors de gaze noire, suivant le pas des promeneurs aux lanternes et aux feuilles,

Des oiseaux comédiens s'abattent sur un ponton de maçonnerie mû par l'archipel couvert des embarcations des spectateurs.

Des scènes lyriques, accompagnées de flûte et de tambour, s'inclinent dans des réduits ménagés sur les plafonds autour des salons de clubs modernes ou des salles de l'Orient ancien.

La féerie manœuvre au sommet d'un amphithéâtre couronné de taillis, – ou s'agite et module pour· les Béotiens, dans l'ombre des futaies mouvants, sur l'arête des cultures.

L'opéra-comique se divise sur notre scène à l'arête d'intersection de dix cloisons dressées de la galerie aux feux.

In corridors of black gauze, following the walkers with their lanterns and leaves,

Birds who are actors swoop down on to a landing-stage of masonry which is moved by the archipelago covered with boat-loads of spectators.

Lyrical scenes, with flute and drum accompaniment, slope down into recesses arranged at ceiling height round the public rooms of modern clubs or ancient Oriental halls.

The enchanted spectacle operates at the top of an amphitheatre crowned with thickets – or stirs and modulates for the Boeotians, in the shadow of waving forest trees, on the headland of the fields.

The comic opera is divided on our stage at the ridge of inter-section of ten upright partitions stretching from the gallery to the footlights.

XXXII

SOIR HISTORIQUE

En quelque soir, par exemple, que se trouve le touriste naïf, retiré de nos horreurs économiques, la main d'un maître anime le clavecin des prés; on joue aux cartes au fond de l'étang, miroir évocateur des reines et des mignonnes; on a les saintes, les voiles, et les fils d'harmonie, et les chromatismes légendaires, sur le couchant.

Il frissonne au passage des chasses et des hordes. La comédie goutte sur les tréteaux de gazon. Et l'embarras des pauvres et des faibles sur ces plans stupides!

À sa vision esclave, l'Allemagne s'échafaude vers des lunes; les déserts tartares s'éclairent; les révoltes anciennes grouillent dans le centre du Céleste Empire; par les escaliers et les fauteuils de rocs un petit monde blême et plat, Afrique et Occidents, va s'édifier. Puis un ballet de mers et de nuits connues, une chimie sans valeur, et des mélodies impossibles.

XXXII

Historic Evening

In whatever evening, for instance, the simple tourist, retiring from our economic horrors, finds himself, the hand of a master awakens the harpsichord of the meadows; they are playing cards at the bottom of the pond, the mirror which evokes queens and favourites; there are the saints, the sails, and the threads of harmony, and legendary iridescences, on the sunset.

He shivers at the passing of the hunts and the hordes. Drama drips on the stages of turf. And the superfluity of poor people and weak people on these stupid levels!

To his slave's eye, Germany scaffolds upward towards moons; Tartar deserts light up; ancient revolts ferment in the heart of the Celestial Empire; across the stairways and armchairs of rocks, a little world, pale and flat, Africa and Occidents, is to be built. Then a ballet of known seas and nights, chemistry without virtue, and impossible melodies.

La même magie bourgeoise à tous les points où la malle nous déposera! Le plus élémentaire physicien sent qu'il n'est plus possible de se soumettre à cette atmosphère personnelle, brume de remords physiques, dont la constatation est déjà une affliction.

Non! Le moment de l'étuve, des mers enlevées, des embrasements souterrains, de la planète emportée, et des exterminations conséquentes, certitudes si peu malignement indiquées dans la Bible et par les Nornes et qu'il sera donné à l'être sérieux de surveiller. – Cependant ce ne sera point un effet de légende!

XXXIII

MOUVEMENT

LE mouvement de lacet sur la berge des chutes du fleuve,
Le gouffre à l'étambot,
La célérité de la rampe,

The same bourgeois magic wherever the mailboat takes us! The most elementary physicist feels that it is no longer possible to submit oneself to this personal atmosphere, this fog of physical remorse, which to observe is already an affliction.

No! The moment of the drying cupboard, of the evaporation of seas, of underground conflagrations, of the planet carried away, and of the consequent exterminations, certainties indicated with so little malice by the Bible and by the Norns, and which it will fall to the serious being to witness – Nevertheless it will be nothing like a legend!

XXXIII

Movement

THE rocking movement against the embankment at the river falls,
The whirlpool at the sternpost,
The swiftness of the slope,

L'énorme passade du courant
Mènent par les lumières inouïes
Et la nouveauté chimique
Le voyageurs entourés des trombes du val
Et du strom.

Ce sont les conquérants du monde
Cherchant la fortune chimique personnelle;
Le sport et le confort voyagent avec eux;
Ils emmènent l'éducation
Des races, des classes et des bêtes, sur ce vaisseau
Repos et vertige
À la lumière diluvienne,
Aux terribles soirs d'étude.

Car de la causerie parmi les appareils, le sang, les fleurs, le
    feu, les bijoux,
Des comptes agités à ce bord fuyard,

The vast to and fro of the current
Bring through unheard-of lights
And chemical change
The travellers surrounded by the waterspouts of the valley
And of the strom.

These are the conquerors of the world
Seeking their personal chemical fortunes;
Amusement and comfort travel with them;
They carry away with them the education
Of races, of classes, and of animals, on this vessel
Repose and vertigo
In the diluvian light,
And the terrible nights of study.

For from the talk among the equipment, the blood, the flowers
the fire, the gems,
From the anxious calculations on board this fugitive ship,

– On voit, roulant comme une digue au delà de la route
    hydraulique motrice,
Monstrueux, s'éclairant sans fin, – leur stock d'études;
Eux chassés dans l'extase harmonique,
Et l'héroïsme de la découverte.

Aux accidents atmosphériques les plus surprenants,
Un couple de jeunesse s'isole sur l'arche,
   – Est-ce ancienne sauvagerie qu'on pardonne? –
Et chante et se poste.

XXXIV

BOTTOM

LA réalité étant trop épineuse pour mon grand carac-
tère, – je me trouvai néanmoins chez ma dame, en gros
oiseau gris-bleu s'essorant vers les moulures du plafond
et traînant l'aile dans les ombres de la soirée.

– You can see, rolling past like a dyke beyond the hydraulic pro-
pulsive road,
Monstrous, lighting up without end – their store of studies;
Themselves driven into harmonic ecstasy.
And the heroism of discovery.

And among the most extraordinary meteorological events,
A young couple holds aloof on the ark,
– Is it a pardonable primitive shyness? –
And sings and mounts guard.

XXXIV

Bottom

REALITY being too thorny for my great personality – I never-
theless found myself at my lady's house, in the form of a big grey-
blue bird soaring towards the mouldings of the ceiling and drag-
ging my wing in the shadows of the evening.

Je fus, au pied du baldaquin supportant ses bijoux
adorés et ses chefs-d'œuvre physiques, un gros ours aux
gencives violettes et au poil chenu de chagrin, les yeux
aux cristaux et aux argent des consoles.

Tout se fit ombre et aquarium ardent.

Au matin, – aube de juin batailleuse, – je courus aux
champs, âne, claironnant et brandissant mon grief, jus-
qu'à ce que les Sabines de la banlieue vinrent se jeter à
mon poitrail.

XXXV

H

TOUTES les monstruosités violent les gestes atroces
d'Hortense. Sa solitude est la mécanique érotique; sa lassi-
tude, la dynamique amoureuse. Sous la surveillance d'une
enfance, elle a été, à des époques nombreuses, l'ardente

I became, at the foot of the bed-head which supported her adored
jewels and her physical masterpieces, a big bear with violet gums
and fur grizzled with sorrow, my eyes on the crystal and silver of
the console-tables.

All became shadow and burning aquarium.

In the morning – bellicose June dawn – I ran towards the fields,
a donkey, braying and brandishing my grievance, until the Sabine
women of the suburbs came and threw themselves on my neck.

XXXV

H

ALL things unnatural fly in the face of Hortense's atrocious ges-
tures. Her solitude is the mechanism of love; her lassitude, its
dynamic. Under the supervision of children, she has been, in many

hygiène des races. Sa porte est ouverte à la misère. Là, la moralité des êtres actuels se décorpore en sa passion ou en son action. – Ô terrible frisson des amours novices sur le sol sanglant et par l'hydrogène clarteux! trouvez Hortense.

XXXVI

DÉVOTION

À MA sœur Louise Vanaen de Voringhem: – Sa cornette bleue tournée à la mer du Nord. – Pour les naufragés.

À ma sœur Léonie Aubois d'Ashby. Baou! – l'herbe d'été bourdonnante et puante. – Pour la fièvre des mères et des enfants.

À Lulu, – démon – qui a conservé un goût pour les oratoires du temps des Amies et de son éducation incomplète. Pour les hommes. – À madame***.

ages, the burning hygiene of all races. Her door is open to destitution. There, the morality of beings of the present is disembodied in her passion or her actions – O terrible shudder of unpractised loves on the bleeding ground and in transparent hydrogen! find Hortense.

XXXVI

Prayer

To Sister Louise Vanaen de Voringhem – her blue coif turned towards the North Sea – For the shipwrecked.

To Sister Léonie Aubois d'Ashby. Baow! – the buzzing, stinking summer grass. – For the fevers of mothers and children.

To Lulu – demon – who has, still, a taste for the oratories of the period of *Les Amies* and of her incomplete education. For men – To Madame ***.

À l'adolescent que je fus. À ce saint vieillard, ermitage ou mission.

À l'esprit des pauvres. Et à un très haut clergé.

Aussi bien à tout culte en telle place de culte mémoriale et parmi tels événements qu'il faille se rendre, suivant les aspirations du moment ou bien notre propre vice sérieux.

Ce soir, à Circeto des hautes glaces, grasse comme le poisson, et enluminée comme les dix mois de la nuit rouge – (son cœur ambre et spunk), – pour ma seule prière muette comme ces régions de nuit et précédant des bravoures plus violentes que ce chaos polaire.

À tout prix et avec tous les airs, même dans des voyages métaphysiques. – Mais plus *alors*.

To the adolescent that I was. To this holy old man, hermitage or mission.

To the spirit of the poor. And to a very high clergy.

Also to every cult in such a place of memorial cult and among such events that one must surrender, according either to the aspirations of the moment or to our own serious vice.

This evening, to Circeto of the icy heights, fat as a fish and illuminated like the ten months of the red light – (her heart amber and spunk) – as my only prayer which shall be as silent as those regions of night, and shall go before feats of daring more violent than this polar chaos.

At any price, under any semblance, even in metaphysical journeys – But *then* no more.

XXXVII

DÉMOCRATIE

«Le drapeau va au paysage immonde, et notre patois étouffe le tambour.

«Aux centres nous alimenterons la plus cynique prostitution. Nous massacrerons les révoltes logiques.

«Aux pays poivrés et détrempés! – au service des plus monstrueuses exploitations industrielles ou militaires.

«Au revoir ici, n'importe où. Conscrits du bon vouloir, nous aurons la philosophie féroce; ignorants pour la science, roués pour le confort; la crevaison pour le monde qui va. C'est la vraie marche. En avant, route!»

XXXVII

Democracy

'The flag suits the filthy landscape, and our dialect drowns the sound of the drum.

'In the interior we shall nourish the most cynical prostitution. We shall massacre all logical revolts.

'To the spicy, softened countries! – at the service of the most monstrous industrial or military exploitations.

'Until we meet again: here, no matter where. Conscripts of our own accord, we shall have a ferocious philosophy; ignorant of science, cunning for comfort; let the rest of the world kick the bucket. That's the real way. Forward – march!'

XXXVIII

FAIRY

Pour Hélène se conjurèrent les sèves ornementales dans les ombres vierges et les clartés impassibles dans le silence astral. L'ardeur de l'été fut confiée à des oiseaux muets et l'indolence requise à une barque de deuils sans prix par des anses d'amours morts et de parfums affaissés.

Après le moment de l'air des bûcheronnes à la rumeur du torrent sous la ruine des bois, de la sonnerie des bestiaux à l'écho des vals, et des cris des steppes.

Pour l'enfance d'Hélène frissonnèrent les fourrés et les ombres, et le sein des pauvres, et les légendes du ciel.

Et ses yeux et sa danse supérieurs encore aux éclats précieux, aux influences froides, au plaisir du décor et de l'heure uniques.

XXXVIII

Fairy

For Helen, embellishing saps conspired together in astral silence, in the virgin shadows and the unmoved radiance. The heat of the summer was entrusted to dumb birds, and the necessary indolence to a mourning barge beyond price [sailing] over bays of dead loves and sunken perfumes.

After the time of the tune of the woodcutters' wives to the sound of the torrent below the ruin of the woods, of the bells of the cattle to the echoing of the valleys, and of the cries of the steppes.

For Helen's childhood thickets and shadows trembled, and the breast of the poor, and the legends of heaven.

And her eyes and her dancing, superior even to the precious gleams, to the cold influences, and to the pleasure of the unique scenery and time.

XXXIX

GUERRE

Enfant, certains ciels ont affiné mon optique: tous les caractères nuancèrent ma physionomie. Les phénomènes s'émurent. À présent, l'inflexion éternelle des moments et l'infini des mathématiques me chassent par ce monde où je subis tous les succès civils, respecté de l'enfance étrange et des affections énormes. Je songe à une guerre, de droit ou de force, de logique bien imprévue.

C'est aussi simple qu'une phrase musicale.

XL

GÉNIE

Il est l'affection et le présent puisqu'il a fait la maison ouverte à l'hiver écumeux et à la rumeur de l'été, lui qui a

XXXIX

War

As a child, certain skies refined my perspective: all characters shaded my features. Phenomena were in a commotion. Now, the eternal inflexion of the moments and the infinity of mathematics drive me through this world where I undergo every civil honour, respected by strange children and by huge affection. I dream of a war, of right or of might, of quite unexpected logic.

It is as simple as a phrase of music.

XL

Genie

He is affection and the present because he has made the house which is open to the frothy winter and to the murmur of summer, he who

purifié les boissons et les aliments, lui qui est le charme des lieux fuyants et le délice surhumain des stations. Il est l'affection et l'avenir, la force et l'amour que nous, debout dans les rages et les ennuis, nous voyons passer dans le ciel de tempête et les drapeaux d'extase.

Il est l'amour, mesure parfaite et réinventée, raison merveilleuse et imprévue, et l'éternité: machine aimée des qualités fatales. Nous avons tous eu l'épouvante de sa concession et de la nôtre: ô jouissance de notre santé, élan de nos facultés, affection égoïste et passion pour lui, lui qui nous aime pour sa vie infinie ...

Et nous nous le rappelons et il voyage ... Et si l'Adoration s'en va, sonne, sa promesse sonne: «Arrière ces superstitions, ces anciens corps, ces ménages et ces âges. C'est cette époque-ci qui a sombré!»

Il ne s'en ira pas, il ne redescendra pas d'un ciel, il n'accomplira pas la rédemption des colères de femmes et des gaietés des hommes et de tout ce péché: car c'est fait, lui étant, et étant aimé.

has purified drink and food, he who is the charm of fugitive places and the superhuman delight of halts. He is affection and the future, the strength and the love which we, standing in rage and boredom, see passing in the stormy sky among banners of ecstasy.

He is love, the measure perfect and reinvented, marvellous and unexpected reason, and eternity: beloved machine of the fatal powers. We have all known the terror of his yielding and of our own: O delight in our health, impetus of our faculties, selfish affection and passion for him, him who loves us for his eternal life ...

And we call him back to us and he travels on ... And if Adoration goes away, ring, his promise rings: 'Away with these superstitions, these old bodies, these couples and these ages. It is this epoch that has sunk!'

He will not go away, he will not descend from any heaven again, he will not achieve the redemption of women's anger and men's gaieties and all that sin: because it is done, because he exists and is loved.

Ô ses souffles, ses têtes, ses courses: la terrible célérité de la perfection des formes et de l'action!

Ô fécondité de l'esprit et immensité de l'univers!

Son corps! le dégagement rêvé, le brisement de la grâce croisée de violence nouvelle!

Sa vue, sa vue! tous les agenouillages anciens et les peines *relevés* à sa suite.

Son jour! l'abolition de toutes souffrances sonores et mouvantes dans la musique plus intense.

Son pas! les migrations plus énormes que les anciennes invasions.

Ô Lui et nous! l'orgueil plus bienveillant que les charités perdues.

Ô monde! et le chant clair des malheurs nouveaux!

Il nous a connus tous et nous a tous aimés. Sachons, cette nuit d'hiver, de cap en cap, du pôle tumultueux au château, de la foule à la plage, de regards en regards, forces et sentiments las, le héler et le voir, et le renvoyer, et, sous les marées et au haut des déserts de neige, suivre ses vues, ses souffles, son corps, son jour.

O his breaths, his heads, his runnings: the terrible swiftness of the perfection of forms and of action.

O fruitfulness of the mind and immensity of the universe!

His body! the dreamed-of redemption, the shattering of grace meeting with new violence!

The sight of him, the sight of him! all the old kneelings and pains *lifted* at his passing.

His light! the abolition of all audible and moving suffering in more intense music.

His step! migrations more enormous than the old invasions.

O He and we! pride more benign than wasted charities.

O world! and the clear song of new misfortunes!

He has known us all and has loved us all. May we know, this winter night, from promontory to promontory, from the tumultuous pole to the country house, from the multitude to the beach, from looks to looks, strength and feelings wearied, how to hail him and see him, and to send him away, and, beneath the tides and at the top of the deserts of snow, to follow his vision, his breath, his body, his light.

XLI

JEUNESSE

I

DIMANCHE

LES calculs de côté, l'inévitable descente du ciel et la visite des souvenirs et la séance des rhythmes occupent la demeure, la tête et le monde de l'esprit.

– Un cheval détale sur le turf suburbain et le long des cultures et des boisements, percé par la peste carbonique. Une misérable femme de drame, quelque part dans le monde, soupire après des abandons improbables. Les desperadoes languissent après l'orage, l'ivresse et les blessures. De petits enfants étouffent des malédictions le long des rivières.

Reprenons l'étude au bruit de l'œuvre dévorante qui se rassemble et remonte dans les masses.

XLI

Youth

I

SUNDAY

PROBLEMS laid aside, the inevitable descent from the sky and the visit of memories and the gathering of rhythms occupy the dwelling, the head, and the world of the mind.

– A horse canters off on the suburban race-course past the fields and woodlands, riddled with the carbonic plague. A miserable woman out of a play, somewhere in the world, sighs for improbable abandonments. Desperadoes long for storm, drunkenness, and wounds. Little children smother curses along the rivers.

Let us resume our studies to the sound of the consuming work which gathers and rises among the masses.

II

SONNET

Homme de constitution ordinaire, le chair n'était-elle pas un fruit pendu dans le verger, ô journées enfantes! le corps un trésor à prodiguer; ô aimer, le péril ou la force de Psyché? La terre avait des versants fertiles en princes et en artistes, et la descendance et la race nous poussaient aux crimes et aux deuils: le monde, votre fortune et votre péril. Mais à présent, ce labeur comblé, toi, tes calculs, toi, tes impatiences, ne sont plus que votre danse et votre voix, non fixées et point forcées, quoique d'un double événement d'invention et de succès une raison, en l'humanité fraternelle et discrète par l'univers sans images; – la force et le droit réfléchissent la danse et la voix à présent seulement appréciées ...

II

SONNET

Man of normal constitution, was not the flesh a fruit hanging in the orchard – oh childish days! – the body a treasure to squander; oh loving, the peril or the strength of Psyche? The earth had slopes fertile with princes and artists, and progeny and the race drove us to crime and mourning: the world, your fortune and your danger. But now, with that ploughing rewarded, you and your calculations, you and your impatience, are no more than your dancing and your voice, neither fixed nor forced, although they are for the double consequence of invention and success a reason, among brotherly and discrete humanity in the imageless universe – might and right reflect the dance and the voice which are only now appreciated ...

III

VINGT ANS

Les voix instructives exilées ... L'ingénuité physique amèrement rassise ... Adagio. Ah! l'égoïsme infini de l'adolescence, l'optimisme studieux: que le monde était plein de fleurs cet été! Les airs et les formes mourant ... Un chœur, pour calmer l'impuissance et l'absence! Un chœur de verres de mélodies nocturnes ... En effet les nerfs vont vite chasser.

IV

Tu en es encore à la tentation d'Antoine. L'ébat du zèle écourté, les tics d'orgueil puéril, l'affaiblissement et l'effroi. Mais tu te mettras à ce travail: toutes les possibilités harmoniques et architecturales s'émouvront autour de ton siège. Des êtres parfaits, imprévus, s'offriront à tes expériences. Dans tes environs affluera rêveusement la curiosité d'anciennes foules et de luxes oisifs. Ta mémoire et tes

III

TWENTY

Instructive voices exiled ... Physical ingenuousness bitterly calmed ... Adagio. Ah! the infinite selfishness of adolescence, studious optimism: how full the world was of flowers that summer! Airs and forms dying ... A choir, to calm impotence and absence! A choir of glasses of nocturnal melodies ... Indeed the nerves will soon go hunting.

IV

You are still at the temptation of Anthony. The antics of docked zeal, the grimaces of puerile pride, collapse, and terror. But you will set yourself to this work: all harmonic and architectural possibilities will be in commotion at your feet. Perfect, unforeseen beings will offer themselves for your experiments. About you will gather dreamily the curiosity of old multitudes and of idle wealth. Your

sens ne seront que la nourriture de ton impulsion créa-
trice. Quant au monde, quand tu sortiras, que sera-t-il
devenu? En tout cas, rien des apparences actuelles.

XLII

SOLDE

À vendre ce que les Juifs n'ont pas vendu, ce que
noblesse ni crime n'ont goûté, ce qu'ignore l'amour
maudit et la probité infernale des masses; ce que le temps
ni la science n'ont pas à reconnaître:

Les Voix reconstituées; l'éveil fraternel de toutes les
énergies chorales et orchestrales et leurs applications in-
stantanées; l'occasion, unique, de dégager nos sens!

À vendre les corps sans prix, hors de toute race, de
tout monde, de tout sexe, de toute descendance! Les
richesses jaillissant à chaque démarche! Solde de diamants
sans contrôle!

memory and your senses will be only the food of your creative im-
pulse. As for the world, when you emerge, what will have be-
come of it? In any case, nothing that it seems to be now.

XLII

Clearance Sale

For sale what the Jews have not sold, what neither noble birth nor
crime have tasted, what accursed love and the infernal integrity of
the masses know nothing of; what neither time nor learning need
recognize:

The Voices reconstituted; the fraternal awakening of all choral
and orchestral energies and their immediate application; the oppor-
tunity, unique, of freeing our senses!

For sale bodies above price, not to be found in any race, world,
sex, or line of descent! Riches spurting at every step! Unrationed
sale of diamonds!

À vendre l'anarchie pour les masses; la satisfaction irrépressible pour les amateurs supérieurs; la mort atroce pour les fidèles et les amants!

À vendre les habitations et les migrations, sports, féeries et conforts parfaits, et le bruit, le mouvement et l'avenir qu'ils font!

À vendre les applications de calcul et les sauts d'harmonie inouïs. Les trouvailles et les termes non soupçonnés, possession immédiate.

Élan insensé et infini aux splendeurs invisibles, aux délices insensibles, et ses secrets affolants pour chaque vice et sa gaîté effrayante pour la foule.

À vendre les corps, les voix, l'immense opulence inquestionable, ce qu'on ne vendra jamais. Les vendeurs ne sont pas à bout de solde! Les voyageurs n'ont pas à rendre leur commission de sitôt!

For sale anarchy for the masses; irrepressible satisfaction for connoisseurs; frightful death for the faithful and for lovers!

For sale dwelling-places and migrations, sports, perfect magic and perfect comfort, and the noise, the movement, and the future they create!

For sale unheard-of applications of reckoning and leaps of harmony. Lucky finds and terms unsuspected, with immediate possession.

Wild and infinite impulse towards invisible splendours, intangible delights, with its maddening secrets for every vice and its frightful gaiety for the crowd.

For sale bodies, voices, the immense unquestionable opulence, that which will never be sold. The firm is not at the end of its clearance stock! Our travellers won't have to turn in their accounts for a long time yet!

UNE SAISON EN ENFER

Jadis, si je me souviens bien, ma vie était un festin où s'ouvraient tous les cœurs, où tous les vins coulaient.

Un soir, j'ai assis la Beauté sur mes genoux. – Et je l'ai trouvée amère. – Et je l'ai injuriée.

Je me suis armé contre la justice.

Je me suis enfui. Ô sorcières, ô misère, ô haine, c'est à vous que mon trésor a été confié!

Je parvins à faire s'évanouir dans mon esprit toute l'espérance humaine. Sur toute joie pour l'étrangler j'ai fait le bond sourd de la bête féroce.

J'ai appelé les bourreaux pour, en périssant, mordre la crosse de leurs fusils. J'ai appelé les fléaux, pour m'étouffer avec le sable, le sang. Le malheur a été mon dieu. Je me suis allongé dans la boue. Je me suis séché à l'air du crime. Et j'ai joué de bons tours à la folie.

Et le printemps m'a apporté l'affreux rire de l'idiot.

Once, if I remember correctly, my life was a feast at which all hearts opened and all wines flowed.

One evening I sat Beauty on my knees – And I found her bitter – And I reviled her.

I armed myself against justice.

I fled. O witches, O misery, O hatred, it was to you that my treasure was entrusted!

I managed to erase in my mind all human hope. Upon every joy, in order to strangle it, I made the muffled bound of the wild beast.

I called up executioners in order to bite their gun-butts as I died. I called up plagues, in order to suffocate myself with sand and blood. Bad luck was my god. I stretched myself out in the mud. I dried myself in the air of crime. And I played some fine tricks on madness.

And spring brought me the hideous laugh of the idiot.

Or, tout dernièrement m'étant trouvé sur le point de faire le dernier *couac*! j'ai songé à rechercher la clef du festin ancien, où je reprendrais peut-être appétit.

La charité est cette clef. – Cette inspiration prouve que j'ai rêvé!

«Tu resteras hyène, etc. ...», se récrie le démon qui me couronna de si aimables pavots. «Gagne la mort avec tous tes appétits, et ton égoïsme et tous les péchés capitaux.»

Ah! j'en ai trop pris: – Mais, cher Satan, je vous en conjure, une prunelle moins irritée! et en attendant les quelques petites lâchetés en retard, vous qui aimez dans l'écrivain l'absence des facultés descriptives ou instructives, je vous détache ces quelques hideux feuillets de mon carnet de damné.

But just lately, finding myself on the point of uttering the last croak, I thought of looking for the key to the old feast, where perhaps I might find my appetite again.

Charity is this key – This inspiration proves that I have been dreaming!

'You'll go on being a hyena, etc. ...' cries indignantly the demon who crowned me with such pleasing poppies. 'Reach death with all your appetites, your selfishness, and all the deadly sins.'

Ah! I have brought too many – But my dear Satan, I beg you, an eye a little less inflamed! And while we are waiting for the few little overdue dirty deeds, you, who like in a writer the absence of descriptive or instructive talent, for you I tear off these few hideous pages from my notebook of a damned soul.

MAUVAIS SANG

J'AI de mes ancêtres gaulois l'œil bleu blanc, la cervelle étroite, et la maladresse dans la lutte. Je trouve mon habillement aussi barbare que le leur. Mais je ne beurre pas ma chevelure.

Les Gaulois étaient les écorcheurs de bêtes, les brûleurs d'herbes les plus ineptes de leur temps.

D'eux, j'ai: l'idolâtrie et l'amour du sacrilège; – oh! tous les vices, colère, luxure, – magnifique, la luxure; – surtout mensonge et paresse.

J'ai horreur de tous les métiers. Maîtres et ouvriers, tous paysans, ignobles. La main à plume vaut la main à charrue. – Quel siècle à mains! – Je n'aurai jamais ma main. Après, la domesticité mène trop loin. L'honnêteté de la mendicité me navre. Les criminels dégoûtent comme des châtrés: moi, je suis intact, et ça m'est égal.

Mais! qui a fait ma langue perfide tellement, qu'elle ait guidé et sauvegardé jusqu'ici ma paresse? Sans me servir pour vivre même de mon corps, et plus oisif que le

---

Bad Blood

I INHERIT from my Gaulish ancestors my whitish-blue eye, my narrow skull, and my lack of skill in fighting. My attire seems to me as barbarous as theirs. But I don't butter my hair.

The Gauls were the clumsiest flayers of cattle and burners of grass of their epoch.

From them I have: idolatry and love of sacrilege – oh! every vice, anger, luxury – magnificent, luxury – above all, mendacity and sloth.

I loathe all trades. Masters and servants, all peasants, base. The hand with the pen is no better than the hand on the plough – What an age of hands! – I shall never get my hand in. And then servitude leads too far. The honesty of beggary breaks my heart. Criminals disgust me like eunuchs: as for me, I am entire, and I don't care.

But! who made my tongue so perfidious that it has been able until now to guide and protect my laziness? Without using even my body to make a living, and idler than a toad, I have lived

crapaud, j'ai vécu partout. Pas une famille d'Europe que je ne connaisse. – J'entends des familles comme la mienne, qui tiennent tout de la déclaration des Droits de l'Homme. – J'ai connu chaque fils de famille!

*

Si j'avais des antécédents à un point quelconque de l'histoire de France!

Mais non, rien.

Il m'est bien évident que j'ai toujours été race inférieure. Je ne puis comprendre la révolte. Ma race ne se souleva jamais que pour piller: tels les loups à la bête qu'ils n'ont pas tuée.

Je me rappelle l'histoire de la France fille aînée de l'Eglise. J'aurais fait, manant, le voyage de terre sainte; j'ai dans la tête des routes dans les plaines souabes, des vues de Byzance, des remparts de Solyme; le culte de Marie, l'attendrissement sur le crucifié s'éveillent en moi parmi mille féeries profanes. – Je suis assis, lépreux, sur les pots cassés et les orties, au pied d'un mur rongé par le

everywhere. Not a family in Europe that I don't know – I mean families like mine, who owe everything to the declaration of the Rights of Man – I've known every young man of good family!

*

If only I had antecedents at some point or other in the history of France!

But no; nothing.

It is perfectly evident to me that I have always belonged to an inferior race. I don't understand rebellion. My race never rebelled except to loot: as hyenas [devour] an animal they have not killed.

I remember the history of France, eldest daughter of the Church. I would have made, as a villein, the journey to the Holy Land; I have in my head all the roads in the Swabian plains, and views of Byzantium, and of the ramparts of Suleiman. The cult of the Virgin Mary, and compassion for the crucified one, awaken in me among a thousand profane enchantments – I sit, stricken with leprosy, on pot-sherds and nettles, at the foot of a wall ravaged by the sun –

soleil. – Plus tard, reître, j'aurais bivaqué sous les nuits d'Allemagne.

Ah! encore: je danse le sabbat dans une rouge clairière, avec des vieilles et des enfants.

Je ne me souviens pas plus loin que cette terre-ci et le christianisme. Je n'en finirais pas de me revoir dans ce passé. Mais toujours seul; sans famille; même, quelle langue parlais-je? Je ne me vois jamais dans les conseils du Christ; ni dans les conseils des Seigneurs, – représentants du Christ.

Qu'étais-je au siècle dernier: je ne me retrouve qu'aujourd'hui. Plus de vagabonds, plus de guerres vagues. La race inférieure a tout couvert – le peuple, comme on dit, la raison; la nation et la science.

Oh! la science! On a tout repris. Pour le corps et pour l'âme, – le viatique, – on a la médecine et la philosophie, – les remèdes de bonnes femmes et les chansons populaires arrangées. Et les divertissements des princes et les jeux qu'ils interdisaient! Géographie, cosmographie, mécanique, chimie! ...

Later, as a mercenary, I should have bivouacked under the nights of Germany.

Ah! again: I am dancing the witches' sabbath in a red glade, with old women and children.

I do not remember anything more distant than this country and Christianity. I should never have enough of seeing myself in this past. But always alone; without family; what language, even, did I speak? I never see myself in Christ's counsels; nor in the counsels of the Lords – Christ's representatives.

What was I in the last century? I only find myself today. No more wanderers, no more vague wars. The inferior race has spread everywhere – the people, as they say; reason, nationality, science.

Oh! science! Everything has been revised. For the body and for the soul – the viaticum – we have medicine and philosophy – old wives' remedies and arrangements of popular songs. As well as the amusements of princes and the games which they forbade! Geography, cosmography, mechanics, chemistry! ...

La science, la nouvelle noblesse! Le progrès. Le monde marche! Pourquoi ne tournerait-il pas?

C'est la vision des nombres. Nous allons à l'*Esprit*. C'est très-certain, c'est oracle, ce que je dis. Je comprends, et ne sachant m'expliquer sans paroles païennes, je voudrais me taire.

*

Le sang païen revient! L'Esprit est proche, pourquoi Christ ne m'aide-t-il pas, en donnant à mon âme noblesse et liberté. Hélas! l'Évangile a passé! l'Évangile! l'Évangile.

J'attends Dieu avec gourmandise. Je suis de race inférieure de toute éternité.

Me voici sur la plage armoricaine. Que les villes s'allument dans le soir. Ma journée est faite; je quitte l'Europe. L'air marin brûlera mes poumons; les climats perdus me tanneront. Nager, broyer l'herbe, chasser,

Science, the new nobility! Progress. The world is on the march! Why shouldn't it turn, too?

It is the vision of numbers. We are moving towards the *Spirit*. It is absolutely certain, it is the voice of the oracle, what I say. I understand, and, not knowing how to express myself without pagan words, I would rather be silent.

*

Pagan blood returns! The Spirit is near. Why does Christ not help me by giving my soul nobility and freedom? Alas! the Gospel has passed by! the Gospel! the Gospel.

I await God greedily. I have been of inferior race from all eternity.

Here I am on the Breton shore. How the towns light up in the evening. My day is done; I am leaving Europe. The sea air will scorch my lungs; lost climates will tan my skin. I shall swim, stamp down the grass, hunt, above all smoke; I shall drink liquors

fumer surtout; boire des liqueurs fortes comme du métal bouillant, — comme faisaient ces chers ançêtres autour des feux.

Je reviendrai, avec des membres de fer, la peau sombre, l'œil furieux: sur mon masque, on me jugera d'une race forte. J'aurai de l'or: je serai oisif et brutal. Les femmes soignent ces féroces infirmes retour des pays chauds. Je serai mêlé aux affaires politiques. Sauvé.

Maintenant je suis maudit, j'ai horreur de la patrie. Le meilleur, c'est un sommeil bien ivre, sur la grève.

*

On ne part pas. — Reprenons les chemins d'ici, chargé de mon vice, le vice qui a poussé ses racines de souffrance à mon côté, dès l'âge de raison — qui monte au ciel, me bat, me renverse, me traîne.

La dernière innocence et la dernière timidité. C'est dit. Ne pas porter au monde mes dégoûts et mes trahisons.

Allons! La marche, le fardeau, le désert, l'ennui et la colère.

as strong as boiling metal — as my dear ancestors did, round their fires.

I shall return with limbs of iron, dark skin, a furious eye: from my mask, I shall be judged as belonging to a mighty race. I shall have gold: I shall be idle and brutal. Women take care of these ferocious invalids returned from hot countries. I shall be involved in politics. Saved.

At present I am damned, I loathe the fatherland. The best thing of all is a good drunken sleep on the beach.

*

One does not escape — Let us take to the roads of this country again, full of my vice, the vice which has thrust its roots of suffering into my side, ever since the age of reason — and which rises to the sky, beats me, knocks me down, drags me along.

The last bit of innocence and the last trace of shyness. I have said it. Not to carry my disgusts and my betrayals through the world.

Forward! Marching, burden, desert, boredom, anger.

À qui me louer? Quelle bête faut-il adorer? Quelle sainte image attaque-t-on? Quels cœurs briserai-je? Quel mensonge dois-je tenir? – Dans quel sang marcher?

Plutôt, se garder de la justice. – La vie dure, l'abrutissement simple, – soulever, le poing desséché, le couvercle du cercueil, s'asseoir, s'étouffer. Ainsi point de vieillesse, ni de dangers: la terreur n'est pas française.

– Ah! je suis tellement délaissé que j'offre à n'importe quelle divine image des élans vers la perfection.

Ô mon abnégation, ô ma charité merveilleuse! ici-bas, pourtant!

De profundis Domine, suis-je bête!

*

Encore tout enfant, j'admirais le forçat intraitable sur qui se referme toujours le bagne; je visitais les auberges et les garnis qu'il aurait sacrés par son séjour; je voyais *avec son idée* le ciel bleu et le travail fleuri de la campagne; je

To whom shall I hire myself? Which beast must be worshipped? What holy image attacked? Whose hearts shall I break? What lie must I uphold? – In what blood shall I wade?

Rather, one should guard onself against justice. – A hard life, pure brutalization – to open, with a withered hand, the coffin lid, to sit inside it, to stop one's breath. And so, no old age, and no danger: fear is not a French emotion.

– Ah! I am so forsaken that I could dedicate to any divine image that came along all my urges towards perfection.

O my self-denial, O my marvellous charity! even down here!

De profundis Domine, what a fool I am!

*

When I was still quite a child, I used to admire the stubborn convict on whom the prison gates always close again; I used to visit inns and lodgings which he might have sanctified with his presence; I saw *with his mind* the blue sky and the flowering labour of the

flairais sa fatalité dans les villes. Il avait plus de force qu'un saint, plus de bon sens qu'un voyageur – et lui, lui seul! pour témoin de sa gloire et de sa raison.

Sur les routes, par des nuits d'hiver, sans gîte, sans habits, sans pain, une voix étreignait mon cœur gelé: «Faiblesse ou force: te voilà, c'est la force. Tu ne sais ni où tu vas ni pourquoi tu vas, entre partout, réponds à tout. On ne te tuera pas plus que si tu étais cadavre» Au matin j'avais le regard si perdu et la contenance si morte, que ceux que j'ai rencontrés *ne m'ont peut-être pas vu.*

Dans les villes la boue m'apparaissait soudainement rouge et noire, comme une glace quand la lampe circule dans la chambre voisine, comme un trésor dans la forêt! Bonne chance, criais-je, et je voyais une mer de flammes et de fumée au ciel; et, à gauche, à droite, toutes les richesses flambant comme un milliard de tonnerres.

Mais l'orgie et la camaraderie des femmes m'étaient interdites. Pas même un compagnon. Je me voyais devant une foule exaspérée, en face du peloton d'exé-

---

countryside; I sniffed out his fate in the towns. He had more strength than a saint, and more common sense than a traveller – and himself, himself alone! as witness to his glory and his rightness.

On the roads, on winter nights, without shelter, without clothing, without bread, a voice would clutch my frozen heart: 'Weakness or strength: look at you, it's strength. You know neither where you are going nor why you are going: go everywhere, respond to everything. They won't kill you any more than if you were a corpse.' In the morning, I would have such a lost look and such a dead face, that those I met *perhaps did not see me at all.*

In the towns the mud would suddenly seem to me to be red and black, like a mirror when the lamp is being carried about in the next room, like a treasure in the forest! Good luck, I would cry, and I would see a sea of flames and smoke in the sky; and to right and left of me all riches flaming like a thousand million thunderflashes.

But orgy and the comradeship of women were forbidden me. Not even a companion. I could see myself in front of an angry

cution, pleurant du malheur qu'ils n'aient pu comprendre, et pardonnant! – Comme Jeanne d'Arc! – «Prêtres, professeurs, maîtres, vous vous trompez en me livrant à la justice. Je n'ai jamais été de ce peuple-ci; je n'ai jamais été chrétien; je suis de la race qui chantait dans le supplice; je ne comprends pas les lois; je n'ai pas le sens moral, je suis une brute: vous vous trompez ...»

Oui, j'ai les yeux fermés à votre lumière. Je suis une bête, un nègre. Mais je puis être sauvé. Vous êtes de faux nègres, vous maniaques, féroces, avares. Marchand, tu es nègre; magistrat, tu es nègre; général, tu es nègre; empereur, vieille démangeaison, tu es nègre: tu as bu d'une liqueur non taxée, de la fabrique de Satan. – Ce peuple est inspiré par la fièvre et le cancer. Infirmes et vieillards sont tellement respectables qu'ils demandent à être bouillis. – Le plus malin est de quitter ce continent, où la folie rôde pour pourvoir d'ôtages ces misérables. J'entre au vrai royaume des enfants de Cham.

Connais-je encore la nature? me connais-je? – *Plus de*

crowd, facing the firing-squad, weeping with the unhappiness which they would not have been able to understand, and forgiving them! – Like Joan of Arc! – 'Priests, doctors, masters, you are mistaken in handing me over to justice. I have never belonged to this people; I have never been a Christian; I belong to the race which used to sing under torture; I do not understand the laws; I have no moral sense, I am an animal: you are making a mistake ...'

Yes, my eyes are closed to your light. I am an animal, a negro. But I am capable of being saved. You, maniacs, wild beasts, misers, are negroes in disguise. Merchant, you're a negro; magistrate, you're a negro; general, you're a negro; emperor, you old scabby itch, you're a negro: you have drunk untaxed liquor, Satan's moonshine – This people is inspired by fever and cancer. Invalids and old people are so respectable that they *ask* to be boiled – The cunningest thing to do is to leave this continent, where madness prowls searching for hostages for these wretches. I am going into the real kingdom of the children of Ham.

Do I know nature yet? do I know myself? – *No more words.* I

mots. J'ensevelis les morts dans mon ventre. Cris, tambour, danse, danse, danse, danse! Je ne vois même pas l'heure où, les blancs débarquant, je tomberai au néant.

Faim, soif, cris, danse, danse, danse, danse!

*

Les blancs débarquent. Le canon! Il faut se soumettre au baptême, s'habiller, travailler.

J'ai reçu au cœur le coup de grâce. Ah! je ne l'avais pas prévu!

Je n'ai point fait le mal. Les jours vont m'être légers, le repentir me sera épargné. Je n'aurai pas eu les tourments de l'âme presque morte au bien, où remonte la lumière sévère comme les cierges funéraires. Le sort du fils de famille, cercueil prématuré couvert de limpides larmes. Sans doute la débauche est bête, le vice est bête; il faut jeter la pourriture à l'écart. Mais l'horloge ne sera pas arrivée à ne plus sonner que l'heure de la pure douleur! Vais-je être enlevé comme un enfant, pour jouer au paradis dans l'oubli le tout le malheur!

bury the dead in my belly. Shouts, drums, dance, dance, dance, dance! I cannot even see the time when the whites will land and I shall collapse into nothing.

Hunger, thirst, shouts, dance, dance, dance, dance!

*

The whites are landing. The cannon! We shall have to submit to baptism, dress, and work.

I have received in my heart the stroke of mercy. Ah! I had not foreseen it!

I have done no evil. I shall have easy days, repentance will be spared me. I shall not have had the torments of the soul that is almost dead to goodness, in which the light rises severe as funeral tapers. The fate of the son of good family, a premature coffin sprinkled with limpid tears. Without a doubt, debauchery is stupid, vice is stupid, all rottenness must be thrown out. But the clock has not yet begun to strike *only* the hour of pure sorrow! Shall I be carried off like a child, to play in paradise, forgetful of all unhappiness?

Vite! est-il d'autres vies? – Le sommeil dans la richesse est impossible. La richesse a toujours été bien public. L'amour divin seul octroie les clefs de la science. Je vois que la nature n'est qu'un spectacle de bonté. Adieu chimères, idéals, erreurs.

Le chant raisonnable des anges s'élève du navire sauveur: c'est l'amour divin. – Deux amours! je puis mourir de l'amour terrestre, mourir de dévouement. J'ai laissé des âmes dont la peine s'accroîtra de mon départ! Vous me choisissez parmi les naufragés; ceux qui restent sont-ils pas mes amis?

Sauvez-les!

La raison m'est née. Le monde est bon. Je bénirai la vie. J'aimerai mes frères. Ce ne sont plus des promesses d'enfance. Ni l'espoir d'échapper à la vieillesse et à la mort. Dieu fait ma force, et je loue Dieu.

*

L'ennui n'est plus mon amour. Les rages, les débauches, la folie, dont je sais tous les élans et les désastres, – tout

Quick! are there other lives? – Slumber in wealth is impossible. Wealth has always been so public. Only divine love bestows the keys of knowledge. I see that nature is only a display of kindness. Farewell, chimeras, ideals, errors.

The reasoned song of the angels rises from the rescue ship: it is divine love – Two loves! I can die of earthly love or die of devotion. I have left souls whose pain will grow for my departure! You have chosen me from among the shipwrecked; are those who are left behind not my friends?

Save them!

Reason is born in me. The world is good. I will bless life. I will love my brothers. These are no longer childhood vows. Nor are they the hope of escaping old age and death. God is my strength, and I praise God.

*

I am no longer in love with boredom. Frenzies, debaucheries, madness, whose joys and disasters I know – my whole burden is

mon fardeau est déposé. Apprécions sans vertige l'étendue de mon innocence.

Je ne serais plus capable de demander le réconfort d'une bastonnade. Je ne me crois pas embarqué pour une noce avec Jésus-Christ pour beau-père.

Je ne suis pas prisonnier de ma raison. J'ai dit: Dieu. Je veux la liberté dans le salut: comment la poursuivre? Les goûts frivoles m'ont quitté. Plus besoin de dévouement ni d'amour divin. Je ne regrette pas le siècle des cœurs sensibles. Chacun a sa raison, mépris et charité: je retiens ma place au sommet de cette angélique échelle de bon sens.

Quant au bonheur établi, domestique ou non ... non, je ne peux pas. Je suis trop dissipé, trop faible. La vie fleurit par le travail, vieille vérité: moi, ma vie n'est pas assez pesante, elle s'envole et flotte loin au-dessus de l'action, ce cher point du monde.

Comme je deviens vieille fille, à manquer du courage d'aimer la mort!

laid down. Let us contemplate without vertigo the extent of my innocence.

I should no longer be capable of asking for the comfort of a bastinado. I do not think that I have embarked for a wedding celebration with Jesus Christ for a father-in-law.

I am not a prisoner of my reason. I have said: God. I desire freedom in salvation: how is it to be pursued? Frivolous tastes have left me. No more need for self-sacrifice, nor for divine love. I do not look back with longing to the age of sensitive hearts. Everyone has his own rightness, contempt, charity: I keep my place at the top of this angelic ladder of good sense.

As for established happiness, domestic or not ... no, I cannot. I am too dissipated, too weak. Life flowers in work, is an old truth: but my own life is not substantial enough, it flies away and drifts far above action, that focal point so dear to the world.

What an old maid I am becoming, to lack the courage to love death!

Si Dieu m'accordait le calme céleste, aérien, la prière, – comme les anciens saints. – les saints! des forts! les anachorètes, des artistes comme il n'en faut plus!

Farce continuelle! Mon innocence me ferait pleurer. La vie est la farce à mener par tous.

*

Assez! Voici la punition. – *En marche!*

Ah! les poumons brûlent, les tempes grondent! la nuit roule dans mes yeux, par ce soleil! le cœur ... les membres ...

Où va-t-on? au combat? Je suis faible! les autres avancent. Les outils, les armes ... le temps! ...

Feu! feu sur moi! Là! ou je me rends. – Lâches! – Je me tue! Je me jette aux pieds des chevaux!

Ah! ...

– Je m'y habituerai.

Ce serait la vie française, le sentier de l'honneur!

If God would grant me celestial, aerial calm, and prayer, – like the old saints – the saints! strong men! the anchorites, artists whose like is no longer needed!

A continual farce! My innocence would make me weep. Life is the farce which everyone has to perform.

*

Enough! Here is the punishment – *March!*

Ah! my lungs are burning, my temples are throbbing! night revolves in my eyes, under this sun! my heart ... my limbs ...

Where are we going? to battle? I am so weak! the others are advancing. Equipment, weapons ... the weather! ...

Fire! fire at me! Here! or I'll give myself up – Cowards! – I shall kill myself! I'll throw myself under the horses' feet!

Ah! ...

– I shall get used to it.

That would be the French way to live, the path of honour!

*

NUIT DE L'ENFER

J'AI avalé une fameuse gorgée de poison. – Trois fois béni soit le conseil qui m'est arrivé! – Les entrailles me brûlent. La violence du venin tord mes membres, me rend difforme, me terrasse. Je meurs de soif, j'étouffe, je ne puis crier. C'est l'enfer, l'éternelle peine! Voyez comme le feu se relève! Je brûle comme il faut. Va, démon!

J'avais entrevu la conversion au bien at au bonheur, le salut. Puis-je décrire la vision, l'air de l'enfer ne souffre pas les hymnes! C'était des millions de créatures charmantes, un suave concert spirituel, la force et la paix, les nobles ambitions, que sais-je?

Les nobles ambitions!

Et c'est encore la vie! – Si la damnation est éternelle! Un homme qui veut se mutiler est bien damné, n'est-ce pas? Je me crois en enfer, donc j'y suis. C'est l'exécution de catéchisme. Je suis esclave de mon baptême. Parents, vous avez fait mon malheur et vous avez fait le vôtre. Pauvre innocent! – L'enfer ne peut attaquer les païens. –

Night in Hell

I HAVE swallowed a famous gulp of poison – Thrice blessed be the idea which came to me! – My entrails are burning. The violence of the poison racks my limbs, twists me out of shape, throws me to the ground. I am dying of thirst, I am choking, I cannot cry out. This is hell, the everlasting torment! Look, how the fire rises higher! I am burning in the proper manner. There then, demon!

I had just glimpsed a conversion to goodness and happiness, salvation. Let me describe the vision; the air of hell suffers no hymns! It was of millions of enchanting creatures, a suave spiritual harmony, strength, and peace, noble ambitions, I don't know what.

Noble ambitions!

And this is still life! – What if damnation is eternal! A man who wishes to mutilate himself is truly damned, is he not? I believe that I am in hell, therefore I am there. It is the ratification of the catechism. I am the slave of my baptism. Parents, you have caused my misfortune, and you have caused your own. Poor innocent! –

C'est la vie encore! Plus tard, les délices de la damnation seront plus profondes. Un crime, vite, que je tombe au néant, de par la loi humaine.

Tais-toi, mais tais-toi! ... C'est la honte, le reproche, ici: Satan qui dit que le feu est ignoble, que ma colère est affreusement sotte. – Assez! ... Des erreurs qu'on me souffle, magies, parfums faux, musiques puériles. – Et dire que je tiens la vérité, que je vois la justice: j'ai un jugement sain et arrêté, je suis prêt pour la perfection ... Orgueil. – La peau de ma tête se dessèche. Pitié! Seigneur, j'ai peur. J'ai soif, si soif! Ah! l'enfance, l'herbe, la pluie, le lac sur les pierres, *le clair de lune quand le clocher sonnait douze* ... le diable est au clocher, à cette heure. Marie! Saint Vierge! ... – Horreur de ma bêtise.

Là-bas, ne sont-ce pas des âmes honnêtes, qui me veulent du bien? ... Venez ... J'ai un oreiller sur la bouche, elles ne m'entendent pas, ce sont des fantômes. Puis, jamais personne ne pense à autrui. Qu'on n'approche pas. Je sens le roussi, c'est certain.

Hell cannot touch pagans – I am still alive! Later on, the delights of damnation will deepen. A crime, quickly, so that I may fall into the void, in the name of human law.

Be quiet, be quiet then! ... Here is shame, and reproach: Satan himself says that the fire is ignoble, that my anger is fearfully stupid – Enough! ... of the errors whispered to me, of magic, false perfumes, puerile music – And to think that I grasp the truth, that I witness justice: my judgement is sane and sound, I am ready for perfection ... Pride – The skin of my head is drying up. Pity! Lord, I am afraid. I am thirsty, so thirsty! Ah! childhood, the grass, the rain, the lake over the stones, *the moonlight as the church clock was striking twelve* ... the devil is in the belfry, at this time. Mary! Holy Virgin! ... – O the horror of my stupidity.

Over there, are they not honest souls, who wish me well? ... Come ... There is a pillow over my mouth, they cannot hear me, they are ghosts. Besides, no one ever thinks of others. Let no one come near. I smell of scorching, that's certain.

Les hallucinations sont innombrables. C'est bien ce que j'ai toujours eu: plus de foi en l'histoire, l'oubli des principes. Je m'en tairai: poëtes et visionnaires seraient jaloux. Je suis mille fois le plus riche, soyons avare comme la mer.

Ah çà! l'horloge de la vie s'est arrêtée tout à l'heure. Je ne suis plus au monde. – La théologie est sérieuse, l'enfer est certainement *en bas* – et le ciel en haut. – Extase, cauchemar, sommeil dans un nid de flammes.

Que de malices dans l'attention dans la campagne ... Satan, Ferdinand, court avec les graines sauvages ... Jésus marche sur les ronces purpurines, sans les courber ...Jésus marchait sur les eaux irritées. La lanterne nous le montra debout, blanc et des tresses brunes, au flanc d'une vague d'émeraude ...

Je vais dévoiler tous les mystères: mystères religieux ou naturels, mort, naissance, avenir, passé, cosmogonie, néant. Je suis maître en fantasmagories.

Écoutez! ...

The hallucinations are innumerable. That's what has always been the matter with me, in fact: no belief in history, obliviousness of principles. I shall say no more about this: poets and visionaries would be jealous. I am a thousand times the richest; let's be as miserly as the sea.

Will you look at that! the clock of life has just stopped. I am no longer in the world – Theology is no joke; hell is certainly *down below* – and heaven above – Ecstasy, nightmare, sleep in a nest of flames.

What tricks during this waiting in the countryside ... Satan, Ferdinand, runs rife with the wild seeds ... Jesus walks on the purplish brambles, without bending them ... Jesus used to walk on the troubled waters. The lantern showed him to us standing, pale, with brown tresses, on the flank of a wave of emerald ...

I shall now unveil all the mysteries: mysteries religious or natural, death, birth, future, past, cosmogony, void. I am a master of phantasmagoria.

Listen! ...

J'ai tous les talents! – Il n'y a personne ici et il y a quelqu'un: je ne voudrais pas répandre mon trésor. – Veut-on des chants nègres, des danses de houris? Veut-on que je disparaisse, que je plonge à la recherche de l'*anneau*? Veut-on? Je ferai de l'or, des remèdes.

Fiez-vous donc à moi, la foi soulage, guide, guérit. Tous, venez, – même les petits enfants, – que je vous console, qu'on répande pour vous son cœur, – le cœur merveilleux! – Pauvres hommes, travailleurs! Je ne demande pas de prières; avec votre confiance seulement, je serai heureux.

– Et pensons à moi. Ceci me fait peu regretter le monde. J'ai de la chance de ne pas souffrir plus. Ma vie ne fut que folies douces, c'est regrettable.

Bah! faisons toutes les grimaces imaginables.

Décidément, nous sommes hors du monde. Plus aucun son. Mon tact a disparu. Ah! mon château, ma Saxe, mon bois de saules. Les soirs, les matins, les nuits, les jours … Suis-je las!

I possess all the talents! – There is no one here, and there is someone: I do not wish to spill my treasure – Shall it be negro songs, houri dances? Shall I disappear, shall I dive in search of the *ring*? Shall I? I shall manufacture gold, cures.

Have faith in me, then; faith soothes, guides, cures. Come, all of you – even the little children – let me console you, let a heart go out to you – the marvellous heart! – Poor men, workers! I do not ask for prayers; with your trust alone, I shall be happy.

– And let us consider myself. This makes me regret very little having left the world. I am lucky not to suffer more. My life was nothing but sweet follies, it's a great pity.

Pooh! let us make every possible grimace.

Decidedly, we have left the world behind. Not a single sound, any more. My sense of touch has disappeared. Ah! my castle, my Saxony, my willow wood. Evenings, mornings, nights, days … How tired I am!

Je devrais avoir mon enfer pour la colère, mon enfer pour l'orgueil, – et l'enfer de la caresse; un concert d'enfers.

Je meurs de lassitude. C'est le tombeau, je m'en vais aux vers, horreur de l'horreur! Satan, farceur, tu veux me dissoudre, avec tes charmes. Je réclame. Je réclame! un coup de fourche, une goutte de feu.

Ah! remonter à la vie! Jeter les yeux sur nos difformités. Et ce poison, ce baiser mille fois maudit! Ma faiblesse, la cruauté du monde! Mon Dieu, pitié, cachez-moi, je me tiens trop mal! – Je suis caché et je ne le suis pas.

C'est le feu qui se relève avec son damné.

I ought to have a hell for my anger, a hell for my pride – and a hell for caresses; a whole concert of hells.

I am dying of lassitude. This is the tomb, I am going to the worms, horror of horrors! Satan, cheat, you intend to destroy me with your enchantments. I appeal. I appeal! for one prick of the fork, one drop of fire.

Ah! to rise again to life! To set eyes upon our deformities. And that poison, that kiss a thousand times damned! My weakness, the world's cruelty! My God, have pity, hide me, I cannot defend myself! – I am hidden and I am not hidden.

The flame rises again with its damned soul.

DÉLIRES I

VIERGE FOLLE

L'ÉPOUX INFERNAL

ÉCOUTONS la confession d'un compagnon d'enfer:

«Ô divin Époux, mon Seigneur, ne refusez pas la confession de la plus triste de vos servantes. Je suis perdue. Je suis soûle. Je suis impure. Quelle vie!

«Pardon, divin Seigneur, pardon! Ah! pardon! Que de larmes! Et que de larmes encore plus tard, j'espère!

«Plus tard, je connaîtrai le divin Époux! Je suis née soumise à Lui. – L'autre peut me battre maintenant!

«À présent, je suis au fond du monde! Ô mes amies! ... non, pas mes amies ... Jamais délires ni tortures semblables ... Est-ce bête!

«Ah! je souffre, je crie. Je souffre vraiment. Tout pour-

Ravings I

FOOLISH VIRGIN

THE INFERNAL BRIDEGROOM

LET us hear the confession of a companion in hell:

'O divine Bridegroom, my Lord, do not refuse the confession of the most unhappy of your handmaids. I am lost. I am drunk. I am impure. What a life!

'Forgiveness, divine Lord, forgiveness! Ah! forgiveness! How many tears! And how many more tears later on, I hope!

'Later, I shall come to know the divine Bridegroom! I was born His slave – The other one can beat me for the present!

'But now I am at the bottom of the world! O my friends! ... no, not my friends ... Never were such ravings or torments ... How silly it is!

'Ah! I am suffering, I am crying out. I suffer in earnest. And yet

tant m'est permis, chargée du mépris des plus méprisables cœurs.

«Enfin, faisons cette confidence, quitte à la répéter vingt autres fois, – aussi morne, aussi insignifiante!

«Je suis esclave de l'Époux infernal, celui qui a perdu les vierges folles. C'est bien ce démon-là. Ce n'est pas un spectre, ce n'est pas un fantôme. Mais moi qui ai perdu la sagesse, qui suis damnée et morte au monde, – on ne me tuera pas! – Comment vous le décrire! Je ne sais même plus parler. Je suis en deuil, je pleure, j'ai peur. Un peu de fraîcheur, Seigneur, si vous voulez, si vous voulez bien!

«Je suis veuve ... – J'étais veuve ... – mais oui, j'ai été bien sérieuse jadis, et je ne suis pas née pour devenir squelette! ... – Lui était presque un enfant ... Ses déli-catesses mystérieuses m'avaient séduite. J'ai oublié tout mon devoir humain pour le suivre. Quelle vie! La vraie vie est absente. Nous ne sommes pas au monde. Je vais où il va, il le faut. Et souvent il s'emporte contre moi, *moi, la pauvre âme*. Le Démon! – C'est un Démon, vous savez, *ce n'est pas un homme*.

all is permitted to me, who am weighed down with the contempt of the most contemptible hearts.

'Well then, let us confide this thing, though we repeat it twenty times more – just as dreary, just as insignificant!

'I am the slave of the infernal Bridegroom, he who ruined the foolish virgins. It is certainly that same demon. It is no ghost, and no phantom. But I who have lost my virtue, who am damned and dead to the world, – they won't kill me! – How can I describe him to you! I cannot even speak any more. I am in mourning, I am weeping, I am frightened. A little coolness, Lord, if you please, if you graciously please!

'I am a widow ... – I was a widow ... – oh yes, I was very re-spectable once, and I was not born to become a skeleton! ... – He was almost a child ... His mysterious tendernesses had seduced me. I forgot all my duties as a human being to follow him. What a life! True life is elsewhere. We are not in the world. I go where he goes, I have to. And often he flies into a rage with me – *me, poor soul*. The Demon! – He *is* a Demon, you know: *he is not a man*.

«Il dit: «Je n'aime pas les femmes. L'amour est à réinventer, on le sait. Elles ne peuvent plus que vouloir une position assurée. La position gagnée, cœur et beauté sont mis de côté: il ne reste que froid dédain, l'aliment du mariage, aujourd'hui. Ou bien je vois des femmes, avec les signes du bonheur, dont, moi, j'aurai pu faire de bonnes camarades, dévorées tout d'abord par des brutes sensibles comme des bûchers …»

«Je l'écoute faisant de l'infamie une gloire, de la cruauté un charme. «Je suis de race lointaine: mes pères étaient Scandinaves: ils se perçaient les côtes, buvaient leur sang. – Je me ferai des entailles par tout le corps, je me tatouerai, je veux devenir hideux comme un Mongol: tu verras, je hurlerai dans les rues. Je veux devenir bien fou de rage. Ne me montre jamais de bijoux, je ramperais et me tordrais sur le tapis. Ma richesse, je la voudrais tachée de sang partout. Jamais je ne travaillerai …» Plusieurs nuits, son démon me saisissant, nous nous roulions, je luttais avec lui! – Les nuits, souvent, ivre, il

'He says: "I don't like women. Love must be invented afresh, that is sure. All *they* can do is wish for a secure position. Once they have gained it, their hearts and their beauty are put aside: nothing remains but cold disdain, the food of marriage, nowadays. Or else I see women who bear the signs of happiness, and whom *I* could have turned into good comrades, devoured from the start by brutes who are about as sensitive as piles of faggots …"

'I listen to him glorying in infamy, and turning cruelty into his charm. "I am of a far-off race: my forefathers were Scandinavian: they pierced their sides and drank their own blood – I am going to make gashes all over my body, I am going to tattoo myself, I want to become as hideous as a Mongol: you'll see, I shall yell in the streets. I want to become quite mad with rage. Never show me jewels, I should crawl and writhe on the carpet. My treasure I should like to be spotted with blood all over. I shall never work …" On several nights his demon seized me and we rolled about together, I wrestled with him! – Often, at night, drunk, he

se poste dans des rues ou dans des maisons, pour m'épouvanter mortellement. – «On me coupera vraiment le cou; ce sera «dégoûtant.» Oh! ces jours où il veut marcher avec l'air du crime!

«Parfois il parle, en une façon de patois attendri, de la mort qui fait repentir, des malheureux qui existent certainement, des travaux pénibles, des départs qui déchirent les cœurs. Dans les bouges où nous nous enivrions, il pleurait en considérant ceux qui nous entouraient, bétail de la misère. Il relevait les ivrognes dans les rues noires. Il avait la pitié d'une mère méchante pour les petits enfants. – Il s'en allait avec des gentillesses de petite fille au catéchisme. – Il feignait d'être éclairé sur tout, commerce, art, médecine. – Je le suivais, il le faut!

«Je voyais tout le décor dont, en esprit, il s'entourait: vêtements, draps, meubles; je lui prêtais des armes, une autre figure. Je voyais tout ce qui le touchait, comme il aurait voulu le créer pour lui. Quand il me semblait avoir l'esprit inerte, je le suivais, moi, dans des actions étranges

lies in wait in the streets or in houses, in order to frighten me to death – "They really will cut my throat; it'll be 'disgusting'." Oh! those days when he insists on walking about with an air of crime!

'Sometimes he speaks, in a kind of tender dialect, about death which brings repentance, about the unfortunate people there must be in the world, about painful toil, and partings which rend hearts. In the hovels where we used to get drunk, he would weep to see the people who surrounded us, cattle of poverty. He would help up drunkards in dark streets. He had the pity of a wicked mother for little children – He would go about with the pretty airs of a little girl on her way to catechism – He pretended to be an expert on everything, business, art, medicine – I followed him, I have to!

'I could see the whole setting with which he surrounded himself in his imagination: clothes, materials, furniture; I lent him insignia, another face. I saw everything which touched him as he would have wished to create it for himself. When he seemed listless, I would follow him, myself, in strange and complicated actions,

et compliquées, loin, bonnes ou mauvaises: j'étais sûre de ne jamais entrer dans son monde. À côté de son cher corps endormi, que d'heures des nuits j'ai veillé, cherchant pourquoi il voulait tant s'évader de la réalité. Jamais homme n'eut pareil vœu. Je reconnaissais, – sans craindre pour lui, – qu'il pouvait être un sérieux danger dans la société. – Il a peut-être des secrets pour *changer la vie?* Non, il ne fait qu'en chercher, me répliquais-je. Enfin sa charité est ensorcelée, et j'en suis la prisonnière. Aucune autre âme n'aurait assez de force, – force de désespoir! – pour la supporter, – pour être protégée et aimée par lui. D'ailleurs, je ne me le figurais pas avec une autre âme: on voit son Ange, jamais l'Ange d'un autre, – je crois. J'étais dans son âme comme dans un palais qu'on a vidé pour ne pas voir une personne si peu noble que vous: voilà tout. Hélas! je dépendais bien de lui. Mais que voulait-il avec mon existence terne et lâche? Il ne me rendait pas meilleure, s'il ne me faisait pas mourir! Tristement dépitée, je lui dis quelquefois: «Je te comprends.» Il haussait les épaules.

a long way, whether it was good or evil: I was sure I should never enter his world. Beside his dear sleeping body, how many hours I have sat up at night, trying to discover why he wished so hard to escape from reality. No man ever had a wish like it. I realized – without fearing on his account – that he might be a serious danger to society. – Perhaps he possesses secrets for *transforming life?* No, he is only looking for them, I would answer myself. Then his charity is bewitched, and I am its prisoner. No other soul would have had the strength – strength of despair! – to bear it – to be protected and loved by him. Besides, I never imagined it happening with another soul: one sees one's own Angel, never someone else's Angel – I think. I was, in his soul, like someone in a palace which has been emptied so that no one so base as yourself shall be seen: that's all. Alas! I depended on him sorely. But what did he want with my dull and cowardly existence? He was making me no better, although he was not killing me! Sadly upset, I said to him sometimes: "I understand you." He would shrug his shoulders.

«Ainsi, mon chagrin se renouvelant sans cesse, et me trouvant plus égarée à mes yeux, – comme à tous les yeux qui auraient voulu me fixer, si je n'eusse été condamnée pour jamais à l'oubli de tous! – j'avais de plus en plus faim de sa bonté. Avec ses baisers et ses étreintes amies, c'était bien un ciel, un sombre ciel, où j'entrais, et où j'aurais voulu être laissée, pauvre, sourde, muette, aveugle. Déjà j'en prenais l'habitude. Je nous voyais comme deux bons enfants, libres de se promener dans le Paradis de tristesse. Nous nous accordions. Bien émus, nous travaillions ensemble. Mais, après une pénétrante caresse, il disait: «Comme ça te paraîtra drôle, quand je n'y serai plus, ce par quoi tu as passé. Quand tu n'auras plus mes bras sous ton cou, ni mon cœur pour t'y reposer, ni cette bouche sur tes yeux. Parce qu'il faudra que je m'en aille, très loin, un jour. Puis il faut que j'en aide d'autres: c'est mon devoir. Quoique ce ne soit guère ragoûtant ..., chère âme ...» Tout de suite je me pressentais, lui parti, en proie au vertige, précipitée dans l'ombre la plus affreuse: la mort. Je lui faisais promettre qu'il ne me lâcherait pas. Il

'Thus, as my grief was continually renewed, and I saw myself even more bewildered – as others would have seen me who had wished to stare at me, had I not been condemned forever to be forgotten by everyone! – I became hungrier and hungrier for his kindness. With his kisses and loving embraces, it was truly a heaven, a dark heaven, into which I came, and where I would gladly have been left, poor, deaf, dumb, blind. I was already getting the habit of it. I saw us as two good children, free to wander in the Paradise of sorrow. We were suited to each other. Deeply moved, we toiled together. But, after a piercing caress, he would say: "How strange it will seem to you, when I am no longer here, all this you have been through. When you no longer have my arms under your neck, nor my heart to rest on, nor this mouth on your eyes. Because I shall have to go away, very far, one day. And then I must help others: it is my duty. Though I shall hardly enjoy it ... dear soul ..." At once I could see myself, after he had gone, in the grip of vertigo, hurled into the most frightful darkness: death. I made him promise

l'a faite vingt fois, cette promesse d'amant. C'était aussi frivole que moi lui disant: «Je te comprends.»

«Ah! je n'ai jamais été jalouse de lui. Il ne me quittera pas, je crois. Que devenir? Il n'a pas une connaissance; il ne travaillera jamais. Il veut vivre somnambule. Seules, sa bonté et sa charité lui donneraient-elles droit dans le monde réel? Par instants, j'oublie la pitié où je suis tombée: lui me rendra forte, nous voyagerons, nous chasserons dans les déserts, nous dormirons sur les pavés des villes inconnues, sans soins, sans peines. Ou je me réveillerai, et les lois et les mœurs auront changé, – grâce à son pouvoir magique, – le monde, en restant le même, me laissera à mes désirs, joies, nonchalances. Oh! la vie d'aventures qui existe dans les livres des enfants, pour me récompenser, j'ai tant souffert, me la donneras-tu? Il ne peut pas. J'ignore son idéal. Il m'a dit avoir des regrets, des espoirs: cela ne doit pas me regarder. Parle-t-il à Dieu? Peut-être devrais-je m'adresser à Dieu. Je suis au plus profond de l'abîme, et je ne sais plus prier.

not to leave me. He gave it twenty times, this lover's promise. It was as meaningless as my saying to him: "I understand you."

'Ah! I have never been jealous of him. He won't leave me. I don't think so. What would he do? He knows no one; he will never work. He wants to live as a sleepwalker. Would his goodness and kindness alone give him any rights in the world of reality? Sometimes I forget the pitiful condition into which I have fallen: he will make me strong, we shall travel, we shall hunt in the deserts, we shall sleep on the stones of unknown towns, without cares, without troubles. Or I shall wake up, and laws and customs will have changed – thanks to his magic powers – the world, remaining the same, will leave me to my desires, my joys, and my carelessness. Oh! a life of adventures like they have in children's books, to make up for everything, I have suffered so much, will you give it me? *He* cannot. I don't know what his ideal is. He told me he had regrets, hopes: but they can't be about me. Does he speak to God? Perhaps I ought to appeal to God. I am at the bottom of the abyss, and I no longer know how to pray.

«S'il m'expliquait ses tristesses, les comprendrais-je plus que ses railleries? Il m'attaque, il passe des heures à me faire honte de tout ce qui m'a pu toucher au monde, et s'indigne si je pleure.

« – Tu vois cet élégant jeune homme, entrant dans la belle et calme maison: il s'appelle Duval, Dufour, Armand, Maurice, que sais-je? Une femme s'est dévouée à aimer ce méchant idiot: elle est morte, c'est certes une sainte au ciel, à présent. Tu me feras mourir comme il a fait mourir cette femme. C'est notre sort, à nous, cœurs charitables ...» Hélas! il avait des jours où tous les hommes agissant lui paraissaient les jouets de délires grotesques; il riait affreusement, longtemps. – Puis, il reprenait ses manières de jeune mère, de sœur aimée. S'il était moins sauvage, nous serions sauvés! Mais sa douceur aussi est mortelle. Je lui suis soumise. – Ah! je suis folle!

«Un jour peut-être il disparaîtra merveilleusement; mais il faut que je sache, s'il doit remonter à un ciel, que je voie un peu l'assomption de mon petit ami!»

Drôle de ménage!

'If he explained his sadnesses to me, would I understand them any better than I do his teasing? He attacks me, he spends hours making me feel ashamed of everything in the world that has ever had power to touch me, and becomes indignant if I weep.

' "You see that elegant young man going into that fine, peaceful house: his name is Duval, Dufour, Armand, Maurice, or something. A woman dedicated herself to loving this spiteful fool: she is dead, she is certainly a saint in heaven, now. You will kill me as he killed that woman. That is the fate of us charitable hearts ..." Alas! he had days when all men in their activities seemed to him the play-things of grotesque deliriums; he would laugh horribly, for a long time – Then he would resume his manner of a young mother, of a beloved sister. If only he were less wild, we should be saved! But his sweetness, too, is deadly. I am in his power – Ah! I am mad!

'Perhaps one day he will magically disappear; but I must know, if he is to go to some heaven, so that I may catch a glimpse of my little friend's assumption!'

A queer couple!

DÉLIRES II

ALCHIMIE DU VERBE

À moi. L'histoire d'une de mes folies.

Depuis longtemps je me vantais de posséder tous les paysages possibles, et trouvais dérisoires les célébrités de la peinture et de la poésie moderne.

J'aimais les peintures idiotes, dessus de portes, décors, toiles de saltimbanques, enseignes, enluminures populaires; la littérature démodée, latin d'église, livres érotiques sans orthographe, romans de nos aïeules, contes de fées, petits livres de l'enfance, opéras vieux, refrains niais, rhythmes naïfs.

Je rêvais croisades, voyages de découvertes dont on n'a pas de relations, républiques sans histoires, guerres de religion étouffées, révolutions de mœurs, déplacements de races et de continents: je croyais à tous les enchantements.

Ravings II

ALCHEMY OF THE WORD

My turn. The history of one of my follies.

For a long time I boasted of possessing all possible landscapes, and found the celebrities of modern painting and poetry ridiculous.

I loved absurd pictures, fanlights, stage scenery, mountebanks' backcloths, inn-signs, cheap coloured prints; unfashionable literature, church Latin, pornographic books badly spelt, grandmothers' novels, fairy stories, little books for children, old operas, empty refrains, simple rhythms.

I dreamed of crusades, voyages of discovery never reported, unrecorded republics, suppressed religious wars, revolutions in manners, movements of races and of continents: I believed in all enchantments.

J'inventai la couleur des voyelles! – *A* noir, *E* blanc,
I rouge, *O* bleu, *U* vert. – Je réglai la forme et le mouve-
ment de chaque consonne, et, avec des rhythmes instinc-
tifs, je me flattai d'inventer un verbe poétique accessible,
un jour ou l'autre, à tous les sens. Je réservais la traduc-
tion.

Ce fut d'abord une étude. J'écrivais des silences, des
nuits, je notais l'inexprimable. Je fixais des vertiges.

*

Loin des oiseaux, des troupeaux, des villageoises,
Que buvais-je, à genoux dans cette bruyère
Entourée de tendres bois de noisetiers,
Dans un brouillard d'après-midi tiède et vert?

Que pouvais-je boire dans cette jeune Oise,
– Ormeaux sans voix, gazon sans fleurs, ciel couvert! –
Boire à ces gourdes jaunes, loin de ma case
Chérie? Quelque liqueur d'or qui fait suer.

I invented the colours of the vowels! – *A* black, *E* white, *I* red,
O blue, *U* green – I made rules for the form and movement of each
consonant, and, with instinctive rhythms, I flattered myself that I
had created a poetic language accessible, some day, to all the senses.
I reserved translation rights.

At first this was an academic study. I wrote of silences and of
nights, I expressed the inexpressible. I defined vertigos.

*

Far away from birds and herds and village girls, what was I drink-
ing, on my knees in that heather surrounded by soft hazel copses in
a warm green afternoon mist?

What could I be drinking in that young Oise – voiceless elms,
flowerless turf, overcast sky! – drinking from those yellow gourds,
far from my beloved cabin? Some golden liquor which causes
sweating.

Je faisais une louche enseigne d'auberge.
– Un orage vint chasser le ciel. Au soir
L'eau des bois se perdait sur les sables vierges,
Le vent de Dieu jetait des glaçons aux mares;

Pleurant, je voyais de l'or – et ne pus boire.

*

À quatre heures du matin, l'été,
Le sommeil d'amour dure encore.
Sous les bocages s'évapore
    L'odeur du soir fêté.

Là-bas, dans leur vaste chantier
Au soleil des Hespérides,
Déjà s'agitent – en bras de chemise –
    Les Charpentiers.

Dans leurs Déserts de mousse, tranquilles,
Ils préparent les lambris précieux
    Où la ville
    Peindra de faux cieux.

I made a cross-eyed inn-sign – A storm came and chased the sky away. In the evening the water in the woods trickled away into virgin sands, the wind of God threw sheets of ice across the ponds;
    Weeping, I saw gold – and could not drink.

*

At four o'clock on a summer morning, the sleep of love still lasts. Under the spinneys evaporate scents of the festive night.
    Down there, in their huge workshop in the Hesperidean sun, already stir – in shirtsleeves – the Carpenters.
    In their Wilderness of foam, peacefully, they prepare costly canopies, on which the town will paint false skies.

Ô, pour ces Ouvriers, charmants
Sujets d'un roi de Babylone,
Vénus! quitte un instant les Amants
Dont l'âme est en couronne.

Ô Reine de Bergers,
Porte aux travailleurs l'eau-de-vie,
Que leurs forces soient en paix
En attendant le bain dans la mer à midi.

*

La vieillerie poétique avait une bonne part dans mon alchimie du verbe.

Je m'habituai à l'hallucination simple: je voyais très franchement une mosquée à la place d'une usine, une école de tambours faite par des anges, des calèches sur les routes du ciel, un salon au fond d'un lac; les monstres, les mystères; un titre de vaudeville dressait des épouvantes devant moi.

Puis j'expliquai mes sophismes magiques avec l'hallucination des mots!

O, for these Workmen, charming subjects of a king of Babylon, Venus! leave for a moment the lovers, whose souls are wearing crowns.

O Queen of the Shepherds, take the workers spirits, so that their strength may be at peace until the sea-bathe at noon.

*

Poetical archaism played an important part in my alchemy of the word.

I accustomed myself to pure hallucination: I saw very clearly a mosque instead of a factory, a drummers' school consisting of angels, coaches on the roads of the sky, a drawing-room at the bottom of a lake; monsters, mysteries; a music-hall title could raise up terrors in front of me.

Then I explained my magic sophisms by means of the hallucination of words!

Je finis par trouver sacré le désordre de mon esprit. J'étais oisif, en proie à une lourde fièvre: j'enviais la félicité des bêtes, – les chenilles, qui représentent l'innocence des limbes, les taupes, le sommeil de la virginité!

Mon caractère s'aigrissait. Je disais adieu au monde dans d'espèces de romances:

CHANSON DE LA PLUS HAUTE TOUR

Qu'il vienne, qu'il vienne,
Le temps dont on s'éprenne.

J'ai tant fait patience
Qu'à jamais j'oublie.
Craintes et souffrances
Aux cieux sont parties.
Et la soif malsaine
Obscurcit mes veines.

Qu'il vienne, qu'il vienne,
Le temps dont on s'éprenne.

I ended up by regarding my mental disorder as sacred. I was idle, the prey of a heavy fever: I envied the happiness of beasts – caterpillars, who represent the innocence of limbo, and moles, the sleep of virginity.

My character became bitter. I took leave of the world in some sort of ballads:

SONG OF THE HIGHEST TOWER

Let it come, let it come, the age of our desire.

I have endured so long that I have forgotten everything. Fear and suffering have flown to the skies. And morbid thirst darkens my veins.

Let it come, let it come, the age of our desire.

Telle la prairie
A l'oubli livrée,
Grandie, et fleurie
D'encens et d'ivraies,
Au bourdon farouche
Des sales mouches.

Qu'il vienne, qu'il vienne,
Le temps dont on s'éprenne.

J'aimai le désert, les vergers brûlés, les boutiques fanées, les boissons tiédies. Je me traînais dans les ruelles puantes et, les yeux fermés, je m'offrais au soleil, dieu de feu.

«Général, s'il reste un vieux canon sur tes remparts en ruine, bombarde-nous avec des blocs de terre sèche. Aux glaces des magasins splendides! dans les salons! Fais manger sa poussière à la ville. Oxyde les gargouilles. Emplis les boudoirs de poudre de rubis brûlante …»

Oh! le moucheron enivré à la pissotière de l'auberge, amoureux de la bourrache, et que dissout un rayon!

Thus the meadow, given over to oblivion, grown up, and flowering with frankincense and tares, amid the wild buzzing of filthy flies.

Let it come, let it come, the age of our desire.

I loved the wilderness, dried-up orchards, faded shops, luke-warm drinks. I would drag myself through stinking alleys, and, with closed eyes, I would offer myself to the sun, god of fire.

'General, if there remains one old cannon on your ruined ramparts, bombard us with blocks of dried earth. Fire on the windows of magnificent shops! Into the drawing-rooms! Make the town eat its own dust. Oxidize the waterpipes. Fill the boudoirs with burning powder of rubies …'

Oh! the drunken gnat in the pub urinal, in love with borage, and dissolved by a ray of sunlight!

FAIM

Si j'ai du goût, ce n'est guère
Que pour la terre et les pierres.
Je déjeune toujours d'air,
De roc, de charbons, de fer.

Mes faims, tournez. Paissez, faims,
    Le pré des sons.
Attirez le gai venin
    Des liserons.

Mangez les cailloux qu'on brise,
Les vieilles pierres d'églises;
Les galets des vieux déluges,
Pains semés dans les vallées grises.

*

Le loup criait sous les feuilles
En crachant les belles plumes
De son repas de volailles:
Comme lui je me consume.

Les salades, les fruits
N'attendent que la cueillette;
Mais l'araignée de la haie
Ne mange que des violettes.

HUNGER

If I have any taste, it is for hardly anything but earth and stones. I breakfast always on air, on rock, on coal, on iron.

Turn, my hungers. Feed, hungers, on the meadow of sounds. Suck the gaudy poison from the convolvuli.

Eat the broken stone; the old masonry of churches; boulders from old floods, loaves sown in the grey valleys.

*

The fox howled under the leaves, spitting out the bright feathers of his feast of fowl: like him, I consume myself.

Salads and fruits are only waiting to be picked; but the hedge spider eats nothing but violets.

Que je dorme! que je bouille
Aux autels de Salomon.
Le bouillon court sur la rouille,
Et se mêle au Cédron.

Enfin, ô bonheur, ô raison, j'écartais du ciel l'azur, qui est du noir, et je vécus, étincelle d'or de la lumière *nature*. De joie, je prenais une expression bouffonne et égarée au possible:

Elle est retrouvée!
Quoi? l'éternité.
C'est la mer mêlée
  Au soleil.

Mon âme éternelle,
Observe ton vœu
Malgré la nuit seule
Et le jour en feu.

Donc tu te dégages
Des humains suffrages,
Des communs élans!
Tu voles selon ...

Let me sleep! let me simmer on Solomon's altars. The scum runs down over the rust, and mingles with the Kedron.

At last, O happiness, O reason, I removed from the sky the azure, which is a blackness, and I lived, a spark of gold of the *natural* light. Out of joy, I took on the most clownish and exaggerated mode of expression possible:

It has been found again! What? eternity. It is the sea mingled with the sun.

My immortal soul, keep your vow despite the lonely night and the day on fire.

Thus you detach yourself from human approval, from common impulses! You fly off as you may ...

– Jamais l'espérance,
Pas d'*orietur*.
Science et patience,
Le supplice est sûr.

Plus de lendemain,
Braises de satin,
Votre ardeur
Est le devoir.

Elle est retrouvée!
– Quoi? – l'Eternité.
C'est la mer mêlée
Au soleil.

*

Je devins un opéra fabuleux: je vis que tous les êtres ont une fatalité de bonheur: l'action n'est pas la vie, mais une façon de gâcher quelque force, un énervement. La morale est la faiblesse de la cervelle.

A chaque être, plusieurs *autres* vies me semblaient dues. Ce monsieur ne sait ce qu'il fait: il est un ange. Cette famille est une nichée de chiens. Devant plusieurs

– No hope, never; and no *orietur*. Knowledge and fortitude, torture is certain.

No more tomorrow, satiny embers, your own heat is the [only] duty.

It has been found again! – What? – Eternity. It is the sea mingled with the sun.

*

I became a fabulous opera: I saw that all beings are fated to happiness: action is not life, but a way of wasting some force, an enervation. Morality is the weakness of the brain.

To every being, several *other* lives seemed to me to be due. This gentleman does not know what he is doing: he is an angel. This family is a pack of dogs. In front of several men, I conversed aloud

hommes, je causai tout haut avec un moment d'une de leurs autres vies. – Ainsi, j'ai aimé un porc.

Aucun des sophismes de la folie, – la folie qu'on enferme, – n'a été oublié par moi: je pourrais les redire tous, je tiens le système.

Ma santé fut menacée. La terreur venait. Je tombais dans des sommeils de plusieurs jours, et, levé, je continuais les rêves les plus tristes. J'étais mûr pour le trépas, et par une route de dangers ma faiblesse me menait aux confins du monde et de la Cimmérie, patrie de l'ombre et des tourbillons.

Je dus voyager, distraire les enchantements assemblés sur mon cerveau. Sur la mer, que j'aimais comme si elle eût dû me laver d'une souillure, je voyais se lever la croix consolatrice. J'avais été damné par l'arc-en-ciel. Le Bonheur était ma fatalité, mon remords, mon ver: ma vie serait toujours trop immense pour être dévouée à la force et à la beauté.

Le Bonheur! Sa dent, douce à la mort, m'avertissait au chant du coq, – *ad matutinum*, au *Christus venit*, – dans les plus sombres villes:

with a moment out of one of their other lives – Thus, I have loved a pig.

None of the sophistries of madness – the sort of madness that gets shut up – was forgotten by me: I could recite them all, I have the system.

My health was threatened. Terror came upon me. I fell into sleeps which lasted several days, and, when I awoke, continued in the saddest dreams. I was ripe for death, and by a road of perils my weakness led me to the confines of the world and of Cimmeria, the home of shadows and whirlwinds.

I was forced to travel, to distract the enchantments crowding in my brain. On the sea, which I loved as if it was sure to cleanse me of a defilement, I saw rising the cross of comfort. I had been damned by the rainbow. Happiness was my fatality, my remorse, my worm: my life would always be too vast to be devoted to strength and beauty.

Happiness! Its tooth, sweet unto death, warned me at cockcrow – *ad matutiunm*, at the *Christus venit* – in the darkest cities:

Ô saisons, ô châteaux!
Quelle âme est sans défauts?

J'ai fait la magique étude
Du bonheur, qu'aucun n'élude.

Salut à lui, chaque fois
Que chante le coq gaulois.

Ah! je n'aurai plus d'envie:
Il s'est chargé de ma vie.

Ce charme a pris âme et corps
Et dispersé les efforts.

Ô saisons, ô châteaux!

L'heure de sa fuite, hélas!
Sera l'heure du trépas.

Ô saisons, ô châteaux!

*

Cela s'est passé. Je sais aujourd'hui saluer la beauté.

O seasons, O towers! What soul is blameless?
I pursued the magic lore of happiness, which no one escapes.
Long live it, every time that the Gallic cock crows.
Ah! I shall never want again: it has taken charge of my life.
That charm has taken body and soul and dissipated my efforts.
O seasons, O towers!
The hour of its flight, alas! will be the hour of death.
O seasons, O towers!

*

That is all past. Today I know how to greet beauty.

L'IMPOSSIBLE

Aн! cette vie de mon enfance, la grande route par tous les temps, sobre surnaturellement, plus désintéressé que le meilleur des mendiants, fier de n'avoir ni pays, ni amis, quelle sottise c'était. – Et je m'en aperçois seulement!

– J'ai eu raison de mépriser ces bonshommes qui ne perdraient pas l'occasion d'une caresse, parasites de la propreté et de la santé de nos femmes, aujourd'hui qu'elles sont si peu d'accord avec nous.

J'ai eu raison dans tous mes dédains: puisque je m'évade!

Je m'évade!

Je m'explique.

Hier encore, je soupirais: «Ciel! sommes-nous assez de damnés ici-bas! Moi, j'ai tant de temps déjà dans leur troupe! Je les connais tous. Nous nous reconnaissons toujours; nous nous dégoûtons. La charité nous est inconnue. Mais nous sommes polis; nos relations avec le monde sont très-convenables.» Est-ce étonnant? Le monde! les marchands, les naïfs! – Nous ne sommes pas

The Impossible

Aн! that life of my childhood, the highway in all weathers, supernaturally sober, more disinterested than the best of beggars, proud of having neither country nor friends, how foolish it was – And I only realize it now!

– I was right to despise those jolly chaps who never miss an opportunity of a caress, parasites on the cleanliness and health of our women, today when they are so little in agreement with us.

I was right in all my contempts: because I am running away!

I am running away!

I shall explain.

Yesterday, still, I was sighing: 'Heavens! there are enough of us damned souls down here! I have spent so long myself among that crew! I know them all. We always recognize each other; we find each other disgusting. Charity is unknown to us. But we are polite; our relations with people are perfectly correct.' Is that surprising? People! merchants, simpletons! – We are not dishonoured – But

337

déshonorés. – Mais les élus, comment nous recevraient-
ils? Or il y a des gens hargneux et joyeux, de faux élus,
puisqu'il nous faut de l'audace ou de l'humilité pour les
aborder. Ce sont les seuls élus. Ce ne sont pas des bénis-
seurs!

M'étant retrouvé deux sous de raison – ça passe vite! –
je vois que les malaises viennent de ne m'être pas figuré
assez tôt que nous sommes à l'Occident. Les marais occi-
dentaux! Non que je croie la lumière altérée, la forme
exténuée, le mouvement égaré ... Bon! voici que mon
esprit veut absolument se charger de tous les développe-
ments cruels qu'a subis l'esprit depuis la fin de l'Orient ...
Il en veut, mon esprit!

... Mes deux sous de raisons sont finis! – L'esprit est
autorité, il veut que je sois en Occident. Il faudrait le
faire taire pour conclure comme je voulais.

J'envoyais au diable les palmes des martyrs, les rayons
de l'art, l'orgueil des inventeurs, l'ardeur des pillards; je
retournais à l'Orient et à la sagesse première et éternelle. –
Il paraît que c'est un rêve de paresse grossière!

the elect, how would they receive us? For there are cross-grained
and joyous folk, a false elect, since we need neither audacity or
humility in order to accost them. These are the only elect. They do
not bless others!

Having found two pennyworth of sense again – it's soon spent! –
I see that my discomfort comes of not realizing soon enough that
we are in the West. The western swamps! Not that I believe that
the light is impaired, the form extenuated, the movement mis-
directed ... Well then! my mind wishes absolutely to load itself
with all the cruel developments which mind has suffered since the
end of the East ... It bears a grudge, my mind!

... My two pennyworth of sense are spent! – The mind is
authority, it wishes me to be in the West. It would be necessary to
silence it, if I am to conclude in the way I wished.

I consigned to the devil the palms of martyrs, the glories of art,
the pride of inventors, the frenzy of looters; I returned to the East
and to original and eternal wisdom – It seems to be a dream of
gross laziness!

Pourtant, je ne songeais guère au plaisir d'échapper aux souffrances modernes. Je n'avais pas en vue la sagesse bâtarde du Coran. – Mais n'y a-t-il pas un supplice réel en ce que, depuis cette déclaration de la science, le christianisme, l'homme *se joue*, se prouve les évidences, se gonfle du plaisir de répéter ces preuves, et ne vit que comme cela! Torture subtile, niaise; source de mes divagations spirituelles. La nature pourrait s'ennuyer, peut-être! M. Prudhomme est né avec le Christ.

N'est-ce pas parce que nous cultivons la brume! Nous mangeons la fièvre avec nos légumes aqueux. Et l'ivrognerie! et le tabac! et l'ignorance! et les dévouements! – Tout cela est-il assez loin de la pensée, de la sagesse de l'Orient, la patrie primitive? Pourquoi un monde moderne, si de pareils poisons s'inventent!

Les gens d'Église diront: C'est compris. Mais vous voulez parler de l'Éden. Rien pour vous dans l'histoire des peuples orientaux. – C'est vrai; c'est à l'Éden que je songeais! Qu'est-ce que c'est pour mon rêve, cette pureté des races antiques!

Still, I was hardly thinking about the pleasure of escaping from modern sufferings. I did not have the bastard wisdom of the Koran in mind – But is there not real torture in the fact that, ever since that declaration of knowledge, Christianity, man has *cheated himself*, proving the obvious to himself, puffing himself up with the pleasure of repeating these proofs, and living in no other way than that! Subtle, silly torture; the root of my spiritual divagations. Nature might get bored, perhaps! M. Prudhomme was born at the same time as the Messiah.

It is not because we cultivate fogs! We eat fever along with our watery vegetables. And drunkenness! and tobacco! and ignorance! and devoutness! – Is all that far enough away from the thought, from the wisdom of the East, the primeval motherland? Why a modern world, if poisons like this are invented!

Men of the Church will say: Understood. But you really mean Eden. Nothing to do with you, the history of Oriental peoples. – And it's true; it was of Eden that I was dreaming! What does that purity of ancient races have to do with my dream!

Les philosophes: Le monde n'a pas d'âge. L'humanité se déplace, simplement. Vous êtes en Occident, mais libre d'habiter dans votre Orient, quelque ancien qu'il vous le faille, – et d'y habiter bien. Ne soyez pas un vaincu. Philosophes, vous êtes de votre Occident.

Mon esprit, prends garde. Pas de partis de salut violents. Exerce-toi! – Ah! la science ne va pas assez vite pour nous!

– Mais je m'aperçois que mon esprit dort.

S'il était bien éveillé toujours à partir de ce moment, nous serions bientôt à la vérité, qui peut-être nous entoure avec ses anges pleurant! ... – S'il avait été éveillé jusqu'à ce moment-ci, c'est que je n'aurais pas cédé aux instincts délétères, à une époque immémoriale! ... – S'il avait toujours été bien éveillé, je voguerais en pleine sagesse! ...

Ô pureté! pureté!

C'est cette minute d'éveil qui m'a donné la vision de la pureté! – Par l'esprit on va à Dieu!

Déchirante infortune!

Philosophers: The world has no age. Humanity, quite simply, moves about. You are in the West, but free to live in your East, as old as you wish it – and to live there well. Do not be one of the defeated. Philosophers, you belong to your West.

My mind, take care. No violent decisions on salvation. Stir yourself! – Ah! science does not travel fast enough for us!

– But I see that my mind is asleep.

If it were always wide awake from now on, we should soon arrive at the truth, which perhaps surrounds us [even now] with its angels weeping! ... – If it had been awake up to this moment, then I should not have surrendered to pernicious instincts, in an immemorial epoch! ... – If it had always been wide awake, I should be sailing in full wisdom! ...

O purity! purity!

This is the moment of wakefulness which has given me the vision of purity! – By intelligence one goes to God!

Heart-rending misfortune!

L'ÉCLAIR

Le travail humain! c'est l'explosion qui éclaire mon abîme de temps en temps.

«Rien n'est vanité; à la science, et en avant!» crie l'Ecclésiaste modern, c'est-à-dire *Tout le monde*. Et pourtant les cadavres des méchants et des fainéants tombent sur le cœur des autres ...Ah! vite, vite un peu; là-bas, par delà la nuit, ces récompenses futures, éternelles ... les échappons-nous? ...

– Qu'y puis-je? Je connais le travail; et la science est trop lente. Que la prière galope et que la lumière gronde ... je le vois bien. C'est trop simple, et il fait trop chaud; on se passera de moi. J'ai mon devoir, j'en serai fier à la façon de plusieurs, en le mettant de côté.

Ma vie est usée. Allons! feignons, fainéantons, ô pitié! Et nous existerons en nous amusant, en rêvant amours monstres et univers fantastiques, en nous plaignant et en querellant les apparences du monde, saltimbanque,

Flash of Lightning

Human labour! this is the explosion which lights up my abyss from time to time.

'Nothing is vanity; to knowledge, forward!' cries the modern Ecclesiastes, which is to say, *Everybody*. And yet the corpses of the wicked and of the idle still fall upon the hearts of others ... Ah! quick, *quick!* over there, beyond the night, those future, everlasting rewards ... shall we escape them? ...

– What can I do about it? I know what work is; and science is too slow. That prayer gallops and that light grumbles ... I see it clearly. It is too simple, and the weather is too warm; they will do without me. I have my duty, and I shall be proud of it in the way that several others are, putting it aside.

My life is worn out. Come! let us deceive, let us do nothing, O the pity of it! And we shall exist by amusing ourselves, by dreaming of our monstrous loves and our fantastic universes, complaining and quarrelling with the world's outward shows, a mountebank,

mendiant, artiste, bandit, – prêtre! Sur mon lit d'hôpital, l'odeur de l'encens m'est revenue si puissante; gardien des aromates sacrés, confesseur, martyr ...

Je reconnais là ma sale éducation d'enfance. Puis quoi! ... Aller mes vingt ans, si les autres vont vingt ans ...

Non! non! à présent je me révolte contre la mort! Le travail paraît trop léger à mon orgueil: ma trahison au monde serait un supplice trop court. Au dernier moment, j'attaquerais à droite, à gauche ...

Alors, – oh! – chère pauvre âme, l'éternité serait-elle pas perdue pour nous!

MATIN

N'eus-je pas *une fois* une jeunesse aimable, héroïque, fabuleuse, à écrire sur des feuilles d'or, – trop de chance! Par quel crime, par quelle erreur, ai-je mérité ma faiblesse actuelle? Vous qui prétendez que des bêtes poussent des sanglots de chagrin, que des malades désespèrent, que des

a beggar, an artist, a ruffian – a priest! On my hospital bed, the smell of incense came back to me so strong; keeper of the holy aromatics, confessor, martyr ...

Here I recognize my rotten upbringing. What of it! ... I'll be twenty, if the others are going to be twenty ...

No! no! at this moment I rebel against death! Work seems too slight to my pride: my betrayal of myself to the world would be too brief a torment. At the last moment I should strike out, right and left ...

And then – oh! – poor dear soul, eternity would not be lost to us!

Morning

Did I not have *once upon a time* a pleasant childhood, heroic, fabulous, to be written on pages of gold – too lucky! Through what crime, through what error, have I deserved my present weakness? You who claim that animals sob with grief, that sick people despair,

morts rêvent mal, tâchez de raconter ma chute et mon sommeil. Moi, je ne puis pas plus m'expliquer que le mendiant avec ses continuels *Pater* et *Ave Maria*. *Je ne sais plus parler!*

Pourtant, aujourd'hui, je crois avoir fini la relation de mon enfer. C'était bien l'enfer; l'ancien, celui dont le fils de l'homme ouvrit les portes.

Du même désert, à la même nuit, toujours mes yeux las se réveillent à l'étoile d'argent, toujours, sans que s'émeuvent les Rois de la vie, les trois mages, le cœur, l'âme, l'esprit. Quand irons-nous, par delà les grèves et les monts, saluer la naissance du travail nouveau, la sagesse nouvelle, la fuite des tyrans et des démons, la fin de la superstition, adorer – les premiers! – Noël sur la terre!

Le chant des cieux, la marche des peuples! Esclaves, ne maudissons pas la vie.

that the dead have bad dreams, try to give an account of my fall and my slumbers. *I* can explain myself no better than the beggar with his incessant Our Father's and Hail Mary's. *I don't know how to speak any more!*

And yet today I think I have finished the account of my hell. It certainly was hell; the old one, whose gates were opened by the son of man.

From the same desert, in the same night, always my weary eyes awaken to the silver star, always, without disturbing the Kings of life, the three magi, the heart, the soul, the mind. When shall we journey, beyond the beaches and the mountains, to hail the birth of the new labour, the new wisdom, the rout of tyrants and demons, the end of superstition; to adore – as the first comers! – Christmas on earth!

The song of the heavens, the march of nations! Slaves, let us not curse life.

ADIEU

L'automne déjà! – Mais pourquoi regretter un éternel soleil, si nous sommes engagés à la découverte de la clarté divine, – loin des gens qui meurent sur les saisons.

L'automne. Notre barque élevée dans les brumes immobiles tourne vers le port de la misère, la cité énorme au ciel taché de feu et de boue. Ah! les haillons pourris, le pain trempé de pluie, l'ivresse, les mille amours qui m'ont crucifié! Elle ne finira donc point cette goule reine de millions d'âmes et de corps morts *et qui seront jugés*! Je me revois la peau rongée par la boue et la peste, des vers plein les cheveux et les aisselles et encore de plus gros vers dans le cœur, étendu parmi les inconnus sans âge, sans sentiment ... J'aurais pu y mourir ... L'affreuse évocation! J'exècre la misère.

Et je redoute l'hiver parce que c'est la saison du confort!

– Quelquefois je vois au ciel des plages sans fin couvertes de blanches nations en joie. Un grand vaisseau

Farewell

Autumn already! – But why look back with longing at an eternal sun, if we are pledged to the discovery of divine light – far from the people who die according to the seasons.

Autumn. Our ship towering in the motionless mists turns towards the port of poverty, the enormous city whose sky is flecked with fire and mud. Ah! the rotting rags, the bread soaked with rain, the drunkenness, the thousand loves which have crucified me! She will never then have done, this ghoul queen of millions of souls and dead bodies – *and they will be judged*! I see again my skin ravaged with mud and pestilence, my hair and my armpits full of worms, and still bigger worms in my heart, lying stretched out among unknown people with no age and no feelings ... I might have died there ... Horrible evocation! I detest poverty.

And I fear winter because it is the season of comfort!

– Sometimes I see in the sky beaches without end covered with white nations full of joy. A great golden vessel above me waves its

d'or, au-dessus de moi, agite ses pavillons multicolores sous les brises du matin. J'ai créé toutes les fêtes, tous les triomphes, tous les drames. J'ai essayé d'inventer de nouvelles fleurs, de nouveaux astres, de nouvelles chairs, de nouvelles langues. J'ai cru acquérir des pouvoirs surnaturels. Eh bien! je dois enterrer mon imagination et mes souvenirs! Une belle gloire d'artiste et de conteur emportée!

Moi! moi qui me suis dit mage ou ange, dispensé de toute morale, je suis rendu au sol, avec un devoir à chercher, et la réalité rugueuse à étreindre! Paysan!

Suis-je trompé? la charité serait-elle sœur de la mort, pour moi?

Enfin, je demanderai pardon pour m'être nourri de mensonge. Et allons.

Mais pas une main amie! et où puiser le secours?

*

Oui, l'heure nouvelle est au moins très-sévère.

Car je puis dire que la victoire m'est acquise: les grincements de dents, les sifflements de feu, les soupirs

many-coloured standards in the morning breezes. I have created all feasts, all triumphs, all dramas. I have tried to invent new flowers, new stars, new flesh, new tongues. I believed I had acquired supernatural powers. Well! I must bury my imagination and my memories! A fine fame as an artist and story-teller swept away!

I! I who called myself magus or angel, exempt from all morality, I am given back to the earth, with a task to pursue, and wrinkled reality to embrace! A peasant!

Am I mistaken? is charity, for me, the sister of death?

Well, now I shall ask forgiveness for having fed on lies. And let us go.

But no friendly hand! and whence shall I draw succour?

*

Yes; the latest hour is, to say the least, very severe.

For I can say that I have won the victory: the gnashing of teeth, the hissing of flames, and the pestilent sighings are dying

empestés se modèrent. Tous les souvenirs immondes s'effacent. Mes derniers regrets détalent, – des jalousies pour les mendiants, les brigands, les amis de la mort, les arriérés de toutes sortes. – Damnés, si je me vengeais!

Il faut être absolument moderne.

Point de cantiques: tenir le pas gagné. Dure nuit! le sang séché fume sur ma face, et je n'ai rien derrière moi, que cet horrible arbrisseau! ... Le combat spirituel est aussi brutal que la bataille d'hommes; mais la vision de la justice est le plaisir de Dieu seul.

Cependant c'est la veille. Recevons tous les influx de vigueur et de tendresse réelle. Et à l'aurore, armés d'une ardente patience, nous entrerons aux splendides villes.

Que parlais-je de main amie! Un bel avantage, c'est que je puis rire des vieilles amours mensongères, et frapper de honte ces couples menteurs, – j'ai vu l'enfer des femmes là-bas; – et il me sera loisible de *posséder la vérité dans une âme et un corps.*

Avril–août, 1873

down. All the filthy memories are disappearing. My last regrets take to their heels – jealousies of beggars, brigands, friends of death, all kinds of backward creatures – Damned, too, if I took vengeance!

One must be absolutely modern.

No hymns: hold on to the yard one has gained. Severe night! the dried blood smokes on my face, and I have nothing at my back but that horrible stunted tree! ... Spiritual combat is as brutal as the battle of men; but the vision of justice is God's pleasure alone.

Still, now is the eve. Let us receive all influxes of strength and of real tenderness. And at dawn, armed with a burning patience, we shall enter into the splendid cities.

What was I saying about a friendly hand! One fine advantage: I can laugh at the old false loves, and strike shame into those lying couples – I have seen the hell of women down there – and it will now be permitted to me *to possess truth in a soul and a body.*

April–August 1873

INDEX OF FIRST LINES

INDEX OF TITLES